PSYCHIC'S SPELL

LEGION OF ANGELS: BOOK 6

ELLA SUMMERS

PSYCHIC'S SPELL
Legion of Angels: Book 6

www.ellasummers.com/psychics-spell

ISBN 978-1-9875-6796-0

CHAPTERS

PROLOGUE

*H*ave you ever had a moment of perfect clarity? You're wandering in darkness, confused, unfocused—and then, snap! A light penetrates the fog of uncertainty. All the pieces of the world fall into place, and your life finally makes sense.

I've never encountered this elusive 'light bulb moment' myself. Not in my journeys across the plains of monsters. Not in the great cities of Earth, nor the Frontier towns that sit at the sunset of civilization.

Honestly, I think light bulb moments are pretty much reserved for normal people. When you're a soldier in the gods' army, when you dance with angels and battle the forces of hell in an immortal war—you live in a different world. It's a world where the normal rules simply don't apply.

I'd love to proclaim that unearthing my past was the answer, that it filled a hole inside of me and made everything all right. But as you can probably guess by now, my past was just the beginning. And unlocking it was opening the biggest can of worms the universe has ever known.

1

After all, I'm Pandora, and chaos is my middle name.

CHAPTER 1

NEXT STOP: PURGATORY

"Next stop: Purgatory," the intercom roared over the rumbling of the train.

The announcement elicited a chorus of chortles from my fellow passengers. Looking up from the book I was reading, I glanced across the aisle. The proud owners of that merry laughter were six twenty-somethings—college guys, their matching fraternity rings told me. They looked like the sort of guys you'd expect to find flexing their muscles in some posh gym. Their shoulders were wide, their faces clean-shaven, and their haircuts straight out of an expensive New York City salon. A bunch of rich kids living their lives on trust funds and no-limit credit cards, toeing the line between doing stupid things for the sheer fun of it and keeping in daddy's good graces.

"Purgatory," one of them snickered. He was distinguished by the tangerine-orange cowboy boots on his feet.

"They have got to work on their marketing campaign," said his companion with the tan suede jacket. It had a hundred tassels dangling from it, which at least a hundred too many. "Paradise." He mulled that over. "Yes, I like the sound of that."

"People don't come out here to experience paradise," said their friend in the black-and-white cow pattern pants. All that was missing was an enormous cow bell around his neck. "They come here to experience the wild Frontier life."

"And the brothels," commented Orange Boots, which elicited cat-calls from the others.

An angel had once told me that rolling my eyes wasn't becoming of a soldier in the gods' army, so I kept the eye-rolling to myself.

My hometown of Purgatory didn't usually get many tourists. Soldiers, yes, but not tourists. That was the consequence of lying at the far end of the civilized world.

But this was a special time, the one week each year when tourists left the comfort of their cities and flocked to the edge of the Frontier for the Party at the Wall festival. Tourists and townies alike partied at the base of the towering wall that separated civilization from the plains of monsters.

"I can see it," declared Suede Jacket.

They all gathered in front of the large, wood-framed window, each one trying to catch their first glimpse of Purgatory. The window was like a looking glass that took you back in time, back to a rougher era. It was a world of rugged charm and frontier justice, a world of cowboy boots and big belt buckles—or so the tourists thought.

In reality, no one out here dressed like that.

One of the college guys had peeled away from the others. He was standing in the aisle, a concentrated squint to his eyes as he swung his gun between his fingers. The gun was glossy silver, so shiny that it reflected off the swaying iron lanterns that hung from the ceiling.

Cow Pants glanced over and commented, "Hey, you're pretty good at that."

"I've been practicing in front of the television," Gunslinger told him.

While watching old cowboy movies, no doubt. That was how they saw the Frontier, like one big cowboy movie marathon.

Gunslinger's grip slipped, and his gun let out an impressive, thunderous boom.

"That hurt!" Suede Jacket yelped, clutching the back of his jeans as he hopped around.

Luckily for him, his friend's gun didn't shoot real bullets. It just shot cartridges filled with potions that dissolved upon impact, leaving the unlucky victim with a mild burning feeling.

Suede Jacket's friends were laughing at all the fuss he was making, but there was nothing funny about shooting people, not even with fake bullets. Guns were designed with a single purpose in mind: killing. They weren't toys for boys playing at being men. Right now, I didn't have to resist rolling my eyes. This time, I was resisting the urge to grab these jokers by the collars and clunk their heads together, to knock some sense into them, to show them that pain was no joke. They were naive—irresponsible even. They'd never seen the world outside their mansions and penthouses, and it was high time someone taught them a lesson.

I stopped myself at that thought. Gods, I was thinking more and more like an angel every day.

So I didn't grab them and clunk their heads together, nor did I pull out the gun in my backpack or the knife tucked inside my boot. I couldn't say I wasn't tempted, though, especially as they continued in their foolish games.

They were now pretending to shoot one another in their vision of a Frontier shootout, the kind you'd see in an old cowboy movie. And this time when one of them shot another, it wasn't an accident. It was a game. They'd come to the Frontier to play out their fantasy, hitting all the stereotypes, then they would return to their normal lives of comfort, none the wiser.

The Party at the Wall was just a moment in time for these city folk, a brief escape into another world, the wild Frontier of civilization. They'd romanticized the rugged look, the cowboy justice. But they had no idea what it was really like out here, where magical resources were spread thin, most of them going to powering the big Magitech wall that separated humanity from the plains of monsters.

I stretched out my legs, which were eager for a walk. Thank goodness we'd be arriving in Purgatory soon. You wouldn't know it from the nostalgic wood benches and soft red velvet of the carriage interiors, but this train was as modern as you could get, crossing the five-hundred-mile distance between New York City and Purgatory in only an hour.

The bundle of bells over the door jingled as three women with identical high ponytails entered the carriage. They were wearing what I could only describe as cheer-leader-cowgirl outfits, leotard tops with short denim skirts and tasseled suede boots. More role-players taking part in the Frontier fantasy.

The college guys immediately stopped shooting one another with magic pellets. Frozen, mesmerized, they watched the cheerleaders walk down the red velvet runway. As the women passed by, one of the guys, a fellow clad solely in a tan leather vest and matching pants stepped into their path.

"Hey there," Leather Vest said in a slow, lazy drawl.

The head cheerleader looked him up and down and coolly declared, "Not interested."

Leather Vest's friends chuckled and slapped him on the back.

"Not any of you either," said the cheerleader in the red leotard.

"Oh, that's *cold*," Cow Pants said, trying to keep a smile on his face.

"Yeah," agreed Gunslinger. "What's wrong with us?"

The cheerleader in blue glanced at his play gun and declared, "You're not real cowboys."

Then the three ladies continued down the aisle toward the exit doors. The train was slowing. We'd be stopping at the Purgatory station soon.

The college guys watched the cowgirl-cheerleader squad go. They too had come here to live out some fantasy, to meet rugged, rogue cowboys. The sort who wore ass-hugging jeans, thumping boots, big hats, and nothing else. The sort who went around shirtless in the scorching Frontier sun.

They would be sorely disappointed. Purgatory was not the home of sexy, single cowboys just waiting to give their hearts away to some special lady. It was the home of bartenders and grocers. Of mechanics and tailors. And some more bartenders. We had a lot of bartenders. Purgatory was a little more fun with a side order of hard liquor.

I got up and made my way toward the exit. The college guys perked up as they noticed me for the first time. During the journey, I'd used magic to mask my presence, to make myself a little less noticeable. It was the best way to get some peace and quiet while I finished my book.

The one wearing the enormous yellow hat glanced at the book, then met my eyes. "Good book?" he asked in a practiced, polished voice.

"Very."

"The Secret World of Angels," Cow Pants read aloud the title, amusement sparkling in his eyes.

"You're interested in angels?" Yellow Hat asked me.

They were all trying hard not to snicker now. As though my fantasy was worse than theirs.

"Isn't everyone interested in angels?" I countered.

He nodded. "I know a fellow who can get people into Heaven," he said, moving in closer. "You know the place?"

"The Legion of Angels club in New York."

"*Exclusive* club," he said. "It's the favorite watering hole of top members of the Legion. Including angels."

Watering hole? He sure was getting into his cowboy character. I wondered what the angels I knew would think of their exclusive club being referred to as a 'watering hole'. I swallowed a chuckle.

Yellow Hat must have mistaken my amusement for a purr of glee because he was moving in even closer. "This guy I know could get us in. I could take you there. What do you say?" He went in for the kill, wrapping his arm around my shoulder.

I flashed him a grin. "I would love to pay Heaven another visit."

He froze at the realization that I'd been there before, his play ruined. He must have been wondering how I'd gotten into Heaven because his offer was completely bogus, a cheap pickup line. He might not know it, but the bouncers at Heaven wouldn't let in any Legion soldier under level five, not without an invitation from a higher level soldier. They wouldn't let in a human *period*, not even if an angel invited them.

I patted his arm. "But right now, I'm looking to meet some authentic cowboys." Winking, I shrugged off his hand. "See you around."

Then I pushed past them and took the exit. As I walked away, I could feel the guys' eyes glued on me.

"Shot down again, cowboy," Suede Jacket snickered.

"Oh, shut up," grumbled Yellow Hat.

As they tried to get back into character by shooting one another again, I went to go chat with the conductor. He was standing on the platform, watching the passengers disembark the train.

"Hey, Jon."

"Leda, good to see you again," he said, his wrinkled face drawing up into a warm smile. Dressed in a navy sweater vest over a dress shirt and a pair of heather-grey wool pants, he looked like everyone's favorite grandfather. A golden pocket watch even dangled from his vest.

Unlike the collegiate cowboys and cheerleaders, I wasn't a tourist. Though I lived in New York now, this town, for better or for worse, was home. It had been a year since I gave up my life to join the Legion, but I could never really give up my family and those I loved.

I smiled back at him. "Good to see you too."

He glanced down at my big bag, tensing. "Is trouble brewing here?"

"Not this time. I'm just here to visit."

His shoulders relaxed. "Good to hear it. You don't come back home often enough."

Though the trip from New York to Purgatory was only an hour with the high-speed train, I hadn't been back for an actual visit since I'd left. I'd only passed through a few times when my work for the Legion of Angels brought me to the nearby Black Plains.

But I needed a little down time from the constant training and endless battles, from fighting monsters and chasing supernatural conspiracies. And there was no place like home to kick up your feet and breathe in the Frontier air.

"You're too busy saving the world to pay us a visit, I suppose?" Jon asked me.

"It's a dirty job, but someone has to do it," I replied with a smirk.

His lips spread into a smile, drawing up the wrinkles around his eyes. "You're a good girl, Leda."

"Well, when I want to be anyway."

Then I walked off to the sound of his chuckles.

The tourists poured out of the train, flooding the station's single platform. I could smell the slick city on them; I could see the innocence in the twinkle in their eyes as they stepped out into a whole new world. Purgatory was the end of the line. Literally. It was a small town that sat on the doorstep of the Black Plains, where monsters ruled and civilization ended. The Earth had been overrun by monsters centuries ago, and humanity had been caught in the crossfire of the war between gods and demons ever since.

I followed the swarms of tourists out of the station, watching them stare around in starry-eyed wonder. The citizens of Purgatory had gone all out for the festival. They'd decorated the town to appeal to the tourists' wild Frontier fantasies, the tick box for every stereotype nicely checked. It looked so different than it usually did.

There were old wooden signs, carved and painted, that

hung outside the doors of each and every business in town. The signs were one of the things the tourists wanted to see —*expected* to see—but they were not a part of everyday life here.

In reality, the extreme, constantly-shifting weather out here, so close to the Black Plains, would have ruined the lovely, handmade signs in no time. We often had summer and winter in one day—a mismatch of hard rain and snow, of storms and sunny skies, of scorching heat and extreme humidity. That was the consequence of the monsters, their close proximity throwing all magic and nature out of whack.

The people of Purgatory were a practical bunch. Once a year, they brought out the signs and donned the costumes for tourists who came for the Party at the Wall— and the money they brought with them.

And it worked. Mesmerized by the cowboy spice, enamored of the rugged charm, the tourists saw only the signs, the Frontier charm, the cowboy outfits. Some of the braver souls even sampled the local moonshine. Sadly, the homemade alcohol wasn't a stereotype. It was a fact of life here, a staple of the Frontier existence.

The tourists didn't see beyond the pretty facade. They didn't see the monsters lurking on the Black Plains beyond, nor did they hear the soft, persistent grumble of white noise, the hum of the monsters beyond.

The monsters on the plains were restless. I could feel it. The influx of people was drawing them closer. In anticipation, the golden Magitech barrier had been turned on. It was so bright that you could see the magical glow from every part of town. The tourists certainly appreciated that glow. If they'd all been a little less drunk, they'd have appreciated it for something much more than as a light show.

They would have realized that barrier was all that stood between them and being eaten by monsters.

"Leda!"

I turned to find Carmen Wilder, the daughter of Purgatory's sheriff, running toward me. Dressed in a green tank top and very tiny denim shorts, cowgirl boots and a cowgirl hat with sparkles, she was all dolled up for the festival. Slim, tall, and sweet, Carmen was always popular with the tourists.

She squeezed me into a tight hug. Her caramel hair, braided in two pigtails, smelled like strawberries. I knew that shampoo; there weren't many hair product choices in Purgatory. Strawberry was one and the other was vanilla. And then there was a neutral, noncommittal scent that just smelled like plain old soap.

"What you're doing for Zane is so brave, Leda," Carmen said.

She was referring to last year. She'd been out on a date with my brother Zane when they were attacked and Zane was abducted. He disappeared without a trace. So I joined the Legion of Angels to gain the rare magic of telepathy, to link to his mind and find him. But telepathy, the power known as Ghost's Whisper, was high level magic. Before I could gain that power, I would need to become an angel. I still had a long way to go.

We later discovered that Zane had been taken by the Guardians, who were supposed to be the peacekeepers of the original immortals and all-around good people. But only fools believed everything they heard. There was always more to the stories. I wanted to see Zane for myself, especially since the Guardians would not allow him to leave their realm. That bothered me. This time-out from Earth was supposedly a cleansing to balance his magic, but just because he couldn't leave, that didn't mean I couldn't go see him.

"The sacrifice you made to find Zane—" Carmen said.

"He'll be all right," I cut her off.

You never knew who was listening. There were a lot of people trying to find Zane for his magic, gods and demons among them.

I started walking toward the festival again, and Carmen matched pace beside me.

"Gods, I missed that smell," I teased, looking around.

She laughed. "It's not so bad right now. It rained last night."

Purgatory was rough around the edges. It smelled like wilderness and metal and magic, courtesy of the glowing Magitech wall. And thanks to last night's rain, the smell was almost pleasant, like a forest after a storm, which covered up the inevitable sweaty stench of so many people in such a small space.

But the rain had done nothing to cool down the town. Though the day was closing in on evening, it was hot. No, make that *scorching*. The weather reminded me of last summer, of how I'd started the night with a mark to catch and a bounty to collect. Then it had all gone downhill from there. My brother was abducted and then before I knew it, I was joining the Legion of Angels.

"I'm glad you survived, Leda," Carmen told me, squeezing my hand.

I smiled at her. "Thanks."

Half of my initiation group hadn't survived the first sip of Nectar. Six more had died when we'd drunk the Nectar again, their wills crushed, unable to absorb the magic that tore through our bodies like a firestorm. The survival rates had gotten a little better after that. A certain sadistic angel excepted, the Legion tried not to push its soldiers up for promotion before we were ready. It did no one any good if we died.

The Legion's soldiers were the gods' army on Earth, and we were therefore bestowed with supernatural powers, the gods' gifts of magic. We trained long and hard for each and every level. It was literally a matter of life or death. Each gift of magic—each promotion ceremony in the Legion—was marked by an increase in power, or you failed and died from the Nectar. The strongest soldiers, the most powerful of us, became angels. They commanded territories on the continents and led soldiers to protect the Earth from threats, mortal and immortal alike.

"What does it feel like? The Nectar?" Carmen added shyly.

"Why? Thinking of joining the Legion yourself?"

"I've always wanted to have magic," she admitted, chewing on her lower lip. "But I don't think I'd survive. I would be one of the bodies on the floor at the end."

"Don't underestimate yourself. You're strong."

I could see it in her, a strong-willed resolve. She had a decent chance of surviving the initiation ceremony.

"You think I should join?" Her voice was quiet, full of reverence, as though I'd just told her she was everything she ever wanted to be.

I turned to face her, setting my hands on her shoulders. "No, I think you should live your life, staying far away from the world of angels."

"Is it so bad?"

"Sometimes. The training, the pressure to perform, to succeed. The battles, the beasts. The Legion breaks you, Carmen. And then they leave it to you to put yourself back together again."

"And the angels?" she asked, her voice hardly above a whisper.

"The angels might just be the scariest part of all," I said honestly. I took her arm. "Come on."

Then I led her toward the music in the distance. With every step that we took, it grew louder, its rhythm intertwined with the chorus of cheering people and the pop and beep of carnival games.

As always, the paranormal soldiers walked the streets of Purgatory, though there were more of them in town than usual. No doubt they'd been brought in for the Party at the Wall, a festival that drew tourists from all over the Eastern Territory.

The paranormal soldiers didn't react to me at all. Fear didn't crinkle their brows when they saw me.

Which was just as it should be. Before getting on that train, I'd made a conscious decision to dress in a casual halter top and a skirt rather than wear my Legion uniform. That was why the paranormal soldiers on patrol didn't salute, bow, or cower before me. Even they feared our reputation—and our absolute authority over them and every other citizen of Earth.

The paranormal soldiers were never stationed here for more than a few months. Purgatory was just a means to an end, a gateway to more prestigious assignments. They came and left and never looked back.

So none of them had been here the last time I was in town. Otherwise, they'd probably have recognized me, uniform or not. Soldiers who'd encountered me remembered me well. Nero said it was because I created an impact crater wherever I went. A shock wave, he liked to call it. That's why he'd given me the nickname Pandora, the Bringer of Chaos.

I, on the other hand, liked to think people remembered me for my smile. Nero hadn't been convinced by my stellar argument. In fact, his response had been a not-so-gentle reminder to never argue with an angel.

"Hey, Carmen, introduce us to your new friend?" a paranormal soldier called out. He obviously thought I was a soft city girl, a tourist who'd come to gawk at the cowboys and dance on the wall. He had no idea.

The soldier was standing with two other bulky male soldiers. There wasn't much to do in Purgatory, so the paranormal soldiers spent a lot of time pumping iron at their private gym.

"I don't know if you can handle her," Carmen called back. "She's a sophisticated city girl, here on visit from New York City."

Sophisticated? I contained a snort, which was apparently as unseemly for a soldier in the gods' army as rolling your eyes.

"I'm sophisticated," the soldier declared.

"Your favorite food is macaroni and cheese," his comrade pointed out.

"And?" he shot back. "Yours is pizza."

Mmm, they were making me hungry. I'd missed lunch and it was already dinnertime.

"You're *both* savages," a third soldier told them.

They all laughed.

"Hey, Brokers? How about you?" the second soldier called out. "You've joined us from New York City. You're fancy. You even eat with a knife *and* a fork."

A fourth soldier joined us, Brokers presumably. "Whereabouts in New York do you live?" he asked me, a pleasant smile on his face.

"Close to the Promenade."

The Promenade was a street of high skyscrapers, each one the home of an important global organization. Among them was the black building that housed the League, a worldwide bounty hunting company. Another was the paranormal soldiers' blue glass skyscraper. And the crown jewel of the Promenade, the focal point of the block, was a sparkling white obelisk, the east coast headquarters of the Legion of Angels. The building shone so brightly, it looked as though diamonds had been crushed into the facade. I wouldn't have been the least bit surprised if that were actually the case. The angels at the top of the Legion didn't spare any expense when it came to showing off how superior they were.

Brokers's eyebrows drew up at the mention of the Promenade. "How close?"

"Pretty close," I said evasively. Ok, *pretty* close was a bit of an understatement. "And you?" I added quickly, trying to take the focus off of me.

"I live on the Promenade," he replied. "I have a pretty good view of the city from my window."

I lived dead center on the Promenade, at the top of the highest tower. I could look over the whole city from my living room window. I didn't say that, though. I hadn't come here to be the center of attention. I'd come here to blend into the crowd—and then find my family and live a few normal days before I had to go back to work.

"After the festival, I'm heading back to New York," he continued. But he was looking at Carmen now. She was obviously more his type. You know, cuter. Sweeter. More innocent. Less likely to break both his kneecaps if he got cheeky.

As we walked toward the heart of the festival, he kept talking, telling Carmen about where he lived and praising the beauty of New York, filling her head with silly notions about clean streets and orderly garbage removal.

Ok, yes, you could literally eat off the streets of the Promenade. Some people actually did that, believing that brought them closer to the gods. But they were the same sort who scoured the sidewalks and city parks for angel feathers.

When we reached the wall, Brokers parted ways with us, giving Carmen a gentlemanly bow before climbing up the ladder to one of the watchtowers. From there, the paranormal soldiers could stare across the Black Plains, looking for signs of gathering monsters. But they didn't go out onto the plains themselves. When danger brewed beyond the wall, the Legion of Angels was brought in.

It was only fitting, I suppose, for the gods' army to clean up this mess. Long ago, the monsters had been the battle beasts of the gods and demons, but the deities had lost control over them, and so the monsters had overrun the Earth.

Humans didn't know this. They thought the demons, at the eve of their defeat, had unleashed the monsters on Earth. The truth was both gods and demons lost control over the monsters when the beasts began to interbreed, the new monsters of mixed light and dark magic being immune to the deities' control. The gods had won the war, and the people of Earth were still paying the price. Humanity was protected in our cities past the walls, but we were not safe. Not as long as monsters still lurked past the wall. Not as long as we were caught in the epic war between gods and demons, between light and dark, a war that spanned worlds and stretched back millennia.

"The tourists look happy," Carmen commented,

watching them laugh as they played carnival games and ate deep-fried snacks.

The deliciously unhealthy smell of it made my stomach growl in hunger.

"The locals look happy too," I said.

"This morning, an extra hundred paranormal soldiers arrived in town. Of course we're happy. For a few days, we're all safe."

That was the point of the extra paranormal soldiers: to keep things safe for the wealthy tourists. It was easy to let the flashing disco balls, the colorful carousels, and the bubblegum music fool you, but at its core the Frontier was a dangerous, uncivilized place to be. A place where the monsters on this side of the wall were as dangerous as the ones out on the plains.

"How bad has it gotten?" I asked Carmen.

"Bad." Her voice was solemn. "The district lords rule this town now. My father hardly has any power left."

The sheriff didn't have the resources to keep the city criminals from flooding to our town and using it as a convenient hiding place. The district lords *did* have those resources and then some. People here looked to them for help, even as they knew they were trading one devil for another.

"You have to do something, Leda," Carmen pleaded with me. "The Legion could end this."

Except the Legion of Angels answered to the gods. And the gods didn't give a damn about earthly matters. As long as the district lords paid tribute to the gods, as long as they did not impede the Pilgrims, the voice of the gods' teachings, from doing their work, the Legion of Angels would do nothing. And it was that indifference that the district lords had been thriving on for years.

"We're not allowed to interfere in local affairs," I told Carmen.

She frowned at me. "Now that's just bullshit."

I couldn't have said it better myself. We at the Legion of Angels, the hand of the gods, dealt only with threats to the Earth, to the gods. We were not supposed to interfere in mortal affairs. We were told that such things were beneath us, that we were not to sully our hands with squabbles between mortals and so-called 'lesser' supernaturals. Those were to be left to the local sheriffs and other law enforcement.

Except the local law enforcement didn't get the resources they needed to keep the people safe. So the district lords had stepped in, and now they ruled like kings. That's how they saw themselves: as cowboy royalty.

It was disgusting, I thought as I watched one of the district lords walk down the street in his expensive royal-blue cowboy boots and hat, surrounded by an entourage of bodyguards. He was acting like a king, like he owned this town. *My* town. And he was just one of many district lords in Purgatory.

The royal blue lord crossed paths with a cowboy lord from another district. They took a moment to stop and glare at each other. Tension brewed between them, heavy and thick, approaching a boiling point.

But then, just like that, they each moved along. It hadn't come to a fight—at least not today. Who knew what tomorrow held? Each of the district lords was a different strain of the same disease, and that disease was consuming Purgatory from the inside. It made me sick.

"I know, Carmen." I unclenched my fists. "I don't like it any more than you do." I had to get a hold on my anger.

The Legion told us it was wrong to get caught up in

earthly matters. We needed to be separate, above humanity, not mixing with it. Connections with humans were discouraged. They were seen as a weakness.

Except I saw them as a strength. My friends and my family were part of who I was. My connection to them helped me stay human, even as I grew closer to becoming an angel. My humanity was my anchor. You see, sometimes, it was not only about being 'right' or 'just'; it was about being kind. About caring for others. Compassion—that's what was too often missing when you tried so hard to do things in a perfectly orderly manner.

"I couldn't join the Legion," Carmen said, her voice trembling with anger. "And not just because I'm scared. I think it would be even worse to have all that power and yet be completely powerless to use it, to stand by as everything crumbles to ash. I don't know how you do it, Leda."

Well, the truth was I didn't always follow the rules. I was the black sheep of the Legion. Soldiers in the gods' army were trained to fight with proper technique, with dignity. With finesse.

I, on the other hand, was a dirty fighter. I had no qualms about using anything around me, fighting not only with swords or guns. I was not above fighting with a water bottle, a clothesline, or a car antenna. Or even the dirt beneath my feet. Many Legion soldiers—especially the angels—saw that as abhorrent behavior. But it did give me an advantage. Fighting with dignity was too predictable and not always practical. I'd learned to fight out here on the streets of the Frontier, in the dark alleys of Purgatory, where survival was more important than how polished your steel was and more relevant than how shiny you kept your leather.

"Adjusting to the Legion's ways has been challenging," I

told Carmen. Honestly, adapting to the code of conduct had been harder than the training or the poisonous Nectar I had to survive to gain new magic.

I waved at Dale and Cindy as they passed us, their hands inside the back pockets of each other's jeans. Dale, my sixty-year-old former neighbor, was a kind man, though he enjoyed the moonshine a little too much. The curvy, buxom Cindy with her long legs, full lips, and bouncy locks, looked like a retired model who spared no expense when it came to looking fabulous. Her crimson lipstick was a perfect match to her hair, and her dark eyeshadow really made her green eyes pop. I'd been present in the Witch's Watering Hole, Purgatory's favorite bar, at the dawn of Dale and Cindy's relationship. It had been that same fateful night Zane went missing.

"Your secret admirer is stalking us," Carmen whispered to me.

I turned around and waved at Jak, the shy nerdy kid who'd had a crush on me since third grade. "Hi, how's it going?"

"F-fine," he stuttered, looking even more nervous than usual. No, forget nervous; he was downright intimidated. "You j-joined the Legion."

"Yep."

"I've h-heard scary things about the L-Legion."

"Those stories are exaggerations," I said, which was only partially true.

I'd heard all the stories too. At least half of them were pretty close to reality. In the case of the other half, reality was much worse than the rumors. Still, there was no reason to scare Jak any more than he already was. He was actually a nice guy.

"Is it true angels' wings glow?" someone asked.

The townies were gathering around me.

"Is it true that you drink poison for breakfast every morning?"

"Do you really set each other on fire?"

"She'll set you on fire, Mick, if you don't give her some space."

They all laughed. If I'd been any other Legion soldier, they'd never have dared bombard me with their questions, but they'd known me for years. And they knew Calli had raised me not to set my neighbors on fire.

"Are your uniforms made of dragon leather?"

"Are your swords made of angel tears?"

"Show us some magic tricks, Leda," Mick said.

"Yeah, show us, Leda."

I folded my arms across my chest.

"Show us! Show us!" chanted the crowd, over and over again.

"I'm not a stage magician," I said drily.

I glanced at the magician performing nearby. Though he was dressed in a very nice silk robe, he wasn't using any actual magic. His fire-breathing display was just a trick. Not that there weren't real fire elementals out there. It's just this guy wasn't one of them. In fact, he was as human as they came. What he lacked in magic, however, he made up for in showmanship. He was a natural performer, possessing an innate ability to captivate an audience. When the townies realized I wasn't nearly as entertaining as they'd thought, they peeled away from me and went to watch the magician's show.

Over the roar of the fire and the clink of fake magic, I picked up a soft scratching noise. It was a few blocks away but coming in fast. Running footsteps. Four pairs. I looked past the houses and blinking carnival lights. I saw three women in the distance running after a man. They were bounty hunters, their outfits of shorts and tank tops complemented by light-colored scarves and goggles to protect their eyes from the sand in the air. From the looks of them, they were Magitech goggles with information readouts, high-end tech that allowed you to lock on to a target and track them through thick crowds and behind blind spots.

That ability was coming in handy for them as the man they were chasing darted behind the carousel and cut through the sea of people. He was running fast, but they were gaining on him. Realizing he was cornered, the man grabbed a child from beside the balloon booth.

"Don't take a single step!" he shouted at the bounty hunters.

They stopped. The crowd fell quiet. Everything was silent, all except the mechanical tune of the turning carousel and the little girl's howl of despair as her airship balloon floated up, lost to the wind.

"No one move!" the man snapped, holding the little girl in front of himself as a shield.

Now that just made me mad. No matter how desperate he was—which was *very* desperate from the manic twitch in his eyes and the stain of sweat on his silk suit—you didn't take children hostage. But if the man had ever possessed any moral boundaries, they'd dissolved under the weight of his desperation. He looked like he would do anything to not be captured. He would cross any line.

From the looks of him, he wasn't a hardcore criminal. His crimes were probably really minor. But that was then, and this was now. Taking a child hostage was worse than whatever he had done to get a bounty on his head. And it wiped away any sympathy I might have had for him. My foster mother Calli used to say that most people only showed their true colors when put under enormous stress, and he'd done that surely enough. By taking a child hostage, he'd shown the world that he was a piece of shit.

"How can you just stand there?" Carmen demanded of me as the man began backing up with the little girl. "You have to do something!"

Despite my feelings, my humanity screaming at me, I wasn't allowed to interfere. Those were the Legion's rules. I could only fight monsters and threats to the gods' order. These lesser matters were not relevant to the gods. They were handled by local law enforcement and bounty hunters.

The gods didn't get that these small things—how we acted in everyday life—all added up to one big picture. It determined what kind of people we strived to be. We had to fight for what was right. We couldn't just battle the monsters beyond the wall. We had to tackle the monsters within head-on.

I was considering interfering anyway, Legion rules be damned, but before I could act, the bounty hunter in the blue outfit pressed a button on her arm band. A tiny flying robot, roughly the shape of a ship and the size of an alley cat, flew through the crowd and shot straight at the man. It stopped mere inches from his face, a cannon pointed right between his eyes.

"Put your hands in the air, or I'll blow out your brains," the robot's mechanical voice declared cheerfully.

He raised his hands. The bounty hunter in the stylish outfit of dusk pink and light beige ran forward, whisking the little girl away. The bounty hunter in black tackled the man. She pulled his arms behind his back, slamming him to the ground when he struggled against her hold. And she wasn't too gentle about it either. I didn't blame her.

Her knee pressed to his back, she cuffed him. Then she slid up her goggles and pushed the scarf away from her face, revealing my foster mother Calli.

"Hi, Leda," she said, glancing over her shoulder at me. "You're late. You missed all the fun."

Fun was tackling criminals to the ground. What could I say? That was my family.

CHAPTER 2

JINX

*C*alli grinned at me. "So the Legion of Angels hotshot finally came back down to Earth for a visit."

It was a joke, but Calli's prisoner wasn't laughing. He paled at the mention of the Legion.

"What did he do?" I asked Calli.

"Magitech Leech," she said darkly.

Magitech Leech was the term for people who snuck into Magitech plants and bottled a little extra power off the top, hoping no one would ever notice. They'd then peddle the magic on the black market. They'd get rich, and the rest of the world would have a little less magic to power important things like the walls that kept the monsters out. These kind of selfish people just pissed me off.

The machine-wielding bounty hunter joined us, her robot hovering behind her. She pulled off her blue scarf and goggles to reveal my sister Gin.

"When did you get in?"

My sister Tessa, the pink and beige bounty hunter, was right behind her. "You didn't tell us you were coming!"

"Just now. And it was supposed to be a surprise," I answered my sisters in turn.

Tessa sighed. "How are we supposed to throw you a proper homecoming party with zero notice?"

"You don't have to throw me a party."

"Leda, please don't talk about things you don't understand," Tessa said with agitated patience.

"Then I suppose I shouldn't mention that Bella is coming too."

Bella was my third sister, and my best friend. She'd just completed the first of two years at the New York University of Witchcraft.

Delight sparkled in Tessa's eyes, even as she threw her hands up in the air. "Honestly, it almost feels like you two don't want parades and parties in your honor."

I would have told her we didn't need any of that, but it wouldn't have changed a thing. Tessa already knew it. The party was more for her than for us, a way for her to show how much she'd missed us. I was torn between being glad I wouldn't have to be the center of attention for once, and feeling guilty for unwittingly thwarting my little sister's plans.

As I stood there, watching Calli pull the prisoner off the ground, Gin do a check of her robot, and Tessa try to recruit them both into helping her pull off an impromptu celebration, my heart clenched up. Yes, I'd missed my family, but it wasn't until this moment that I realized just how homesick I was.

Gin gave her robot a final pat. "How's your life of dancing with angels?"

"Busy." I sighed. "Exhausting."

Gin's grin lit up her whole face. "And you love it."

"I must be crazy," I admitted.

"But we all already knew that, Leda," Gin chuckled.

Tessa's finger slid at top speed across her phone. "Flowers, a cake…two dozen doves," she muttered.

"Whose wedding are you planning?" I teased her.

Tessa glanced up from her screen, meeting my eyes. "Yours, smart ass." Then she returned her attention to her list. "…silk runners, acrobats…"

"She's not serious, is she?" I asked Gin.

"About the acrobats? I wouldn't put it past her. She's always wanted to plan an angel wedding with acrobats." Mischief twinkled in her eyes.

"Haha, very funny."

They were just messing with me. I hoped. A change of subject was desperately in order.

As though on cue, Calli said, "When's Bella arriving?"

Thank you, Calli.

"She's arriving on the next train," I told her.

To keep up with all the festival traffic, for the next few days, the trains were running every hour between here and New York. I was really looking forward to seeing Bella again. We both lived in the city, but I hadn't seen her in such a long time. We were both too busy—I working day and night to be ready for the upcoming Crystal Falls training, she taking her end-of-year exams at the New York University of Witchcraft. We hadn't had lunch together in ages.

"Bella says she has some news," I told my family.

Tessa perked up from her list-making. "What is it?"

I shook my head. "I don't know."

"But you and Bella tell each other *everything*," Tessa pressed me.

I shrugged. "She's been acting strangely lately. Distant."

29

"Whatever she's hiding, it must be big," Tessa said, her gaze drifting up in thought.

A loud crash and a series of booms roared over the constant churn of the carnival tunes. A putrid green smoke filled the air. My lungs burning, my eyes watering, I coughed. I waved my hand, air magic crackling off my fingers. A breeze formed around us, carrying the smoke away.

The prisoner was on the move and running fast.

"He's got magic?" I asked Calli.

"He's not supposed to."

She was already running after him, and she was gaining on him fast. If the man was an elemental, he wasn't any stronger or faster than a human. Elementals fought with the magic of nature, not with their fists. Calli was almost upon him, getting ready for the tackle.

Then the man just froze and let out a startled breath. A second later, he shot backwards like some spell had just sucked him in.

At second glance, I realized it wasn't magic. A transparent rope was looped around his waist like a lasso. And at the end of that lasso was a very smug face framed by a dark goatee. Jinx, another bounty hunter. The bastard always used to trail me on my jobs. He'd make me do all the work, then he'd steal my mark out from under me. And now he was leeching off my family's hard work, stealing food out of their mouths.

Tessa and Gin burst forward, looping off into side alleys as Calli sprinted after Jinx. The slippery bastard hopped on a motorcycle, tossed the prisoner in the side car, and then zoomed away, his laughter ringing over the roar of the engine. He was getting away.

As he threw a smirk back at Calli and my sisters, my

knuckles cracked under the pressure of my clenched fists. Securing my backpack into place, I lowered into my knees for the sprint. I didn't care if he was in a motorcycle. I had the magic of the gods' gifts burning in my blood. I could outrun him. I *would* outrun him. He'd stolen my mark for the last time.

I paused, reminding myself that the Leech wasn't my mark—and that I wasn't a bounty hunter anymore. I was a soldier in the Legion of Angels. Funny how easy it was to forget that when coming home. And how easily I fell into my old patterns.

I wasn't supposed to interfere. But there were always ways around the rules while still following them to the letter. I'd learned that well in my time at the Legion.

I ran up the brick wall of the nearest building and swung onto the roof. Dashing over the rooftops, leaping between buildings, I tracked the motorcycle down on the ground. I passed it, then continued for a block before jumping down to the street. I tucked myself right behind the next curve he'd have to take.

Just three seconds to go.

The motorcycle roared closer. I flipped up the hood of my sporty halter top, covering my face.

One second.

I stepped onto the road as the motorcycle came around the corner. Jinx's eyes flickering in alarm, he swerved to avoid me. I gave the motorcycle a little extra nudge with my wind magic, and it tipped over. It slid across the street, skidded through a pile of garbage cans, and slammed against a brick wall.

Jinx jumped up from his ruined motorcycle, a string of curses pouring out of his mouth. "You stupid girl!" he screamed at me.

He grabbed the prisoner and threw him over his back. Calli, Tessa, and Gin were closing in now from three sides. They'd caught up to him. Jinx ran straight toward me. I was blocking the only way out now, and I didn't move.

"Get out of the way!" he shouted.

Calli and my sisters were almost upon him.

Jinx ran faster, shouting louder at me this time. "Move it!"

I just stood there and waited.

"What's the matter with you?! Are you deaf?!" He shoved me out of the way.

I took the hit, but I didn't budge. He crashed into me and fell, the prisoner tumbling off his back. Jinx looked up at me as my hood fell back, revealing my face. Surprise flashed across his face as he recognized me. He froze.

"That was a mistake," I told him.

Jinx tried to duck, but I knocked him to the ground with a solid strike to the head. Disoriented, he stumbled, narrowly catching himself before he fell. I pivoted around him and kicked the back of his knees. His legs collapsed, and his knees hit the brick road.

"I'd heard you'd joined the Legion." He spat out blood. "You're interfering. This isn't your jurisdiction. You're making a big mistake."

"No, you're the one who made a mistake by striking a soldier in the Legion of Angels," I told him.

Defeat and anger swirled inside his eyes. "You might be a soldier of heaven now, but you still fight dirty."

I stomped my boot against his back, pinning him in place. "Always," I said with a smile.

I had no handcuffs, but it didn't matter. I yanked a strand of wire off a nearby clothesline and used it to bind his hands together. As he struggled, the wire cut into his skin. A few drops of blood pooled up. He stopped moving, shooting a dirty look over his shoulder.

"Brokers," I called out to the paranormal soldier I'd met before.

He'd come back down to the ground to check out the commotion, and he wasn't the only one. Every paranormal soldier in the area was staring at me now that they'd all realized I was a member of the Legion of Angels.

And they weren't the only ones staring. The festival had paused, and everyone was gawking at us. From the sidelines, Yellow Hat, the tourist who'd hit on me earlier, now looked as pale as a sheet. He was probably wondering if I'd toss him to the Interrogators so they could investigate his boasts of sneaking into Legion clubs. As though the Interrogators didn't have better things to do.

The paranormal soldiers didn't speak, waiting for me to tell them what to do. They looked ready to piss themselves. Legion soldiers might kill the monsters hunting humanity, but we also brought in people who threatened the gods' order. And no one wanted to be declared a threat. You really had to walk on eggshells around many of my fellow Legion soldiers, especially the angels. All they had to do was declare you suspicious, and then the Legion Interrogators swooped in and tossed you into an interrogation cell. You might be released—eventually—but the Interrogators would be very, *very* thorough in their interviews.

Except I had no intention of throwing people to the Interrogators on a whim, just because they'd annoyed me. Even so, I had to maintain the Legion's image.

"Put this bounty hunter in jail for the night," I told Brokers, my tone sharp, commanding. I even put a little siren magic behind my words, just enough to give them kick. "That will teach him not to strike a member of the Legion of Angels."

I didn't allow emotion to show on my face. I was professional, cold. Dispassionate. Nero would have been so proud.

Truth be told, it was a lenient sentence, but I had no interest in torturing people. I just wanted Jinx out of the way so my family could do their job without him stealing their mark. And besides, I *had* tricked him into attacking me.

Brokers and another paranormal soldier each took hold of one of Jinx's arms.

"He is a slippery one," I told them. "If he so much as twitches, you have my permission to knock him upside the head with your guns."

They nodded solemnly and headed off toward the sheriff's office, looking relieved that the bounty hunter was the one being punished instead of them. The show over, everyone returned to their festivities. Music boomed, conversations sprouted up, and the high-pitched beeps of the carnival games filled the festival grounds once more. It was as though the whole thing had never happened.

I looked down at the Magitech Leech at my feet. He shuddered and averted my eyes, fear freezing him. He didn't try to escape. He didn't even move. His body was slouched over in defeat, no fight left in him.

"Why didn't you use cuffs to restrain Jinx?" Gin asked me as she checked the prisoner's restraints.

"I came here for some family time. For a vacation. I didn't expect to be dispensing Legion justice, so I didn't bring any handcuffs. I don't carry them around for fun."

Grinning from ear to ear, Tessa whispered something

to Gin. I picked up the words 'handcuffs' and 'playing with angels'. They both laughed.

I glared at them, but they didn't cower before my stare. They were used to it. And I didn't think it would have been fair to put the full force of my magic behind that glare. Though watching their snickering at my expense, I had to admit I was tempted.

"Let's go, you comedians. We need to get Leechy over to the sheriff's station," Calli told them, prodding their prisoner forward.

"But we'll be right back, so no running off," Tessa added, wiggling her finger at me.

I could almost see the thoughts of grand parades and color-coordinated parties swirling in her eyes.

After they'd left, I turned my attention to the festival—and, more specifically, to the delectable scents wafting from the food stands. My tummy rumbled. If I'd been hungry before my little rooftop sprint, I was now positively famished. I looked around for some really unhealthy carnival food, my first choices being onion rings and deep-fried candy bars. They were so delectably, deliciously disgusting. I had to have them.

But I never made it to the cluster of food stands. Something cast a dark shadow over the festival, rolling in like a storm cloud. Every single person on the ground stopped and stared, a chorus of oohs and aahs rising from the crowd. The shadow shifted, diving.

An angel landed, his boots kissing the ground in a soft whisper, his wings extended in a perfect heavenly blend of black, blue, and green. Everyone stared at him in awe, mesmerized, completely caught in his spell.

CHAPTER 3

ARCHANGEL'S SPELL

The angel was not just any angel. He was General Nero Windstriker, an archangel and my lover.

Unlike me, Nero was wearing the black leather uniform of the Legion of Angels. Trained from birth to fulfill his destiny of becoming an angel, he didn't really have a casual and relaxed mode. He was rarely out of uniform. I regularly teased him about that, but right now, as I watched him walk, the admiring crowd parting before him, I couldn't help but appreciate the sight of him in that uniform.

The black armor shone—no, *glowed*—in the light of the setting sun, the smooth leather accentuating every muscle. The soft, deliciously-subtle creak of leather against his hard, unyielding body as he moved was a wicked tease —and a sweet temptation.

Framed in a halo of sunshine and floodlights, his caramel hair was lit up, sparkling like liquid gold. A ceiling of clouds hung over the carnival—all but a single open patch of sunlight directly over Nero. It looked like a skylight from heaven. He was obviously manipulating the elements to create that effect, to make himself shine. Angels did that when they wanted to inspire awe, respect, or fear.

And it worked. Every human at the festival was one hundred percent fixated on Nero. They were so enthralled by him that they didn't realize how unnatural it was for the skylight to move with him, like a spotlight framing an actor on stage.

A few overly enthusiastic young women were moving toward him. Their eyes wide with appreciation, they took in the sight of his immortal beauty, of his larger-than-life body and his dark, glossy wings. In a few more seconds, they'd throw their panties at him.

A low snarl tugged back my lips. I felt a rush of heat, of adrenaline-pumping jealousy. All for no reason, I told myself. Nero was mine. I couldn't tear these women to pieces for looking at him, and I certainly couldn't blame them. Nero was a sight to behold, as gorgeous as he was deadly.

But my rational brain was having a hard time reconciling with the dark, deeply possessive instincts of my primal brain. I didn't like the way they were undressing my angel with their eyes. I could smell the hormonal shift in the air, the thick musk of lust wafting off them.

"Pandora," Nero said. My nickname flowed off his lips like a little drop of heaven.

His eyes met mine, lit up by magic, shining like a forest after a rainfall.

And then I saw nothing else. No one else. His admirers faded away. Everything faded away except Nero. I moved toward him, as though there an invisible string between us, an irresistible force drawing me in.

I stopped in front of him. He lifted his hand and

brushed it softly down my face, his touch like a million tiny fireworks going off under my skin. It had been entirely too long since I'd seen him. He'd been away on a mission for weeks.

Nero didn't kiss me. He hardly touched me; his hand was as soft as a feather on my cheek. As it dipped lower to trace my neck, my pulse quickened, pounding beneath his fingertips. His eyes dropped to my throat, to my throbbing vein. From the subtle flicker of silver in his eyes, I knew he wanted to drink from my well, to merge our blood and magic. I wanted him too. My blood burning, I wet my lips. I felt myself turning, presenting my neck to him. The silver in his eyes glowed stronger.

He was close, so close that I could feel his pulse tearing through me, rocking me. The rhythm of my heart synched with his. His hand caught on the strap of my halter top, lingering there for a moment. I arched toward him, an invitation. And a demand.

But he stepped back. "I saw what happened with that bounty hunter."

There was no reprimand in his voice. There was only amusement, as well as a little pride. After all, he'd been the one to teach me how to make the Legion's rules work to my advantage.

The thought of Jinx was enough to snap me out of my daze. I was suddenly very self-conscious about the scene we were making—and even more so, about all the eyes trained on us. No, on Nero. The whole crowd was frozen, bewitched by the angel in their midst. And I'd been bewitched right along with them. I gave myself a mental slap for getting so caught up in Nero's aura. It's just that he was such a beautiful diversion.

"You are beautiful," he told me, his hand tracing down

my throat. He caught the end of my braid between his fingers. He spoke the next bit, low, intimate, the words only for me. "And your hair is glowing."

Damn it. My hair had always been somewhat of a nuisance. Back before I'd had magic, it used to glow just a little, enough to mesmerize vampires. I'd never figured out why it did that. To be honest, it wasn't a great superpower. It meant I couldn't stay around a vampire for too long before he inevitably tried to open up my throat and drain me dead.

But since I'd joined the Legion, since I'd drunk the gods' Nectar and gained their gifts of magic, things were changing. *I* was changing. And my hair was changing right along with me. It glowed brighter now, the pale blonde changing pink, blue, and any number of other colors. It did that when I used too much magic or my emotions were running hot. It wasn't hard to guess which one was the culprit this time.

In the last year, I'd learned to control my thoughts better, to hide them. Angels were telepathic, after all. But my hair didn't hide anything. It changed to show exactly how I was feeling, like a mood ring, a window into my soul. Nero liked it. He'd learned to read the colors and glow, to gauge what I was feeling from the tone of my hair.

"Your hair is beautiful, Leda," he told me. "But you need to calm it. You need to make it go back to normal."

I swallowed hard, even as my face flushed hot with embarrassment. He was right. I was making a complete fool of myself.

"You're not making a fool of yourself," he said. "You're mesmerizing everyone. And if you don't dim your halo, I will have to kill those men."

I followed his hard glare to a group of men gawking at

me, their eyes dilated wide. They were entranced. That was my siren magic at work. Humans had no resistance to it. I hadn't even realized that I was projecting my mood, that I'd dipped into my magic.

"You can't kill people for how they're looking at me," I told Nero.

Nero gave me a pitiless look that said he could and would do just that.

"There are rules," I said. "You can't attack humans who aren't a threat to the gods' order."

Nero was unrelenting. "As you just demonstrated, I can attack them if they attack me first."

"You fight dirty, General Windstriker."

"You're rubbing off on me," he replied, his words loaded with wicked intentions.

My thighs clenched at the rush of heat that crashed over me. Cruel, hard reality hit me like a train: there was too much space between us, too much clothing. Even though every fiber of my being, every cell in me, every instinct, was screaming at me in desperation to do something about that, I stayed perfectly still. I held my hands at my sides as what precious little remained of my rational brain tried to put the reins on the impatient, insatiable nymphomaniac who'd taken hold of me.

Nero leaned in closer. "Pandora, if you don't tone down your magic, I can't be held responsible for the consequences."

His voice was deep and dangerous, teetering on the edge of civilization, between man and beast. I was sorely tempted to not tone down my magic, to not get it under control. Just to see how long he would hold out—and what would happen when the dam of his self-control finally broke.

But that would be irresponsible with all these humans here, not to mention unprofessional. So I concentrated and reeled in my siren magic, retracting the invisible tendrils of enchantment that had wound around the crowd. Of course, Nero wasn't making it easy, not with the way he was looking at me. Putting away my magic felt wrong, unnatural, like the rub of sandpaper on raw flesh, but I clenched my teeth and bore it. I took several long, deep breaths, and the light in my hair went out.

"Now come with me," Nero said.

I followed him away from the crowds, behind a row of buildings to a quiet street. There wasn't another soul in sight. By the time we'd walked a few blocks, the carnival music started up again, conversations resumed, and the clinks and clanks of the games were more numerous than ever. It was as though Nero's arrival had never happened. Had he wiped the memory from everyone's mind?

We reached the end of the street. He turned to face me and just waited.

I folded my arms across my chest. "I am not having sex with you in a dark alley."

"Your thoughts say otherwise," he said in a silky voice.

"I do have some shame."

"Do you?"

"Yes," I said defiantly.

His hand darted out, and my breath caught in anticipation. An easy, arrogant smile twisted his lips as he plucked a leaf out of my hair.

"You didn't feel that way back in New York," he said. His hand was on my back now, stroking it gently.

My face went hot at the memory of us having sex in a dark alley. "Ok," I admitted. "You've got me. I have no shame."

At least not when it came to Nero. The moment he'd landed at the festival, I realized how desperately I'd missed him.

Responding to my thoughts, he told me, "I missed you too." He dipped his mouth to my neck, kissing me softly. "I could see only you in the crowd of hundreds." His mouth paused before mine. "You are a light that blinded me to all else, that outshone everything, making it all fall away and disappear into the shadows."

I smiled, basking in the light of his words, lapping up every seductive syllable.

"I've been dreaming of you," he told me.

"I've been dreaming of you too." Heat blossomed in my core at the memory of what we'd done in those dreams.

"We're connected," he said. "Our magic, our minds, our bodies are drawn together, wishing to be one. Always. In sleep, my mind reached out to you, calling you to me."

And I'd come. Again and again, night after night, my mind had found him. In our dreams, we'd been free. Free from the Legion, free from the gods, free from humanity.

"Without borders or boundaries, no propriety, no rules," he added to my thoughts. "Connected by love, driven by passion."

His words were intoxicating. It was too easy to get caught up in them.

I cleared my throat. "What's brought you to Purgatory, General? Chasing down rogues and thieves for the First Angel?"

Nero was Nyx's second, the number two in the Legion of Angels. There were other archangels, but she trusted him the most. His work for her, all those trips all over the world, kept him busy. It felt like he was away more than he was home.

42

"No, I didn't come here for Nyx. I came here for you." He didn't sound amused by my joke. "I came home to find you weren't there."

Nero and I lived together in an apartment in New York's Legion of Angels office, where I worked.

"I left you a note," I said.

"I didn't want a note." His voice was almost a growl. "I wanted you."

If I hadn't known better, I would have called the expression on his face a pout.

"What's the matter? Was there no one to torture in training?" I teased him.

Training with Nero was torture. You gave it your all, and if you somehow managed to be on your feet at the end, he made you go again, declaring if you could still stand, you hadn't trained hard enough. Of course, if you weren't still standing, you also hadn't tried hard enough, and he made you keep going anyway. That was Nero Windstriker in a nutshell. Nero loved me and was only trying to make me stronger, so I could level up my magic. I tried to remember that when I was cursing his name in training.

Nero leaned in and growled against my lips, "Are you mocking me, Pandora?"

"Maybe a little."

"Didn't anyone ever tell you how dangerous it is to incite an angel?"

My heart skipped as his hands closed around my shoulders. Smirking through my racing pulse, I said, "I seem to remember a certain self-serving angel lecturing me about that."

"Self-serving?" he repeated.

I nodded. "Very."

"Sometimes, Pandora, I don't think you know what's good for you."

"*You* are good for me," I said, looping my arms over his shoulders.

"No one in their right mind would fall in love with an angel."

"Being in your right mind is completely overrated." I took his hand in mine, giving it a squeeze. Then I met his eyes and said seriously, "Being right in the heart is much more important."

I leaned in and gave him a quick kiss on the cheek. Tempting as seven minutes in heaven with Nero was, I needed to go find Calli and my sisters. They would be back from dropping off the Leech soon. And frankly, I didn't think seven minutes was nearly enough time. Sex with Nero was not a quick once-off. It was a long, savoring affair.

I started walking back to the carnival, giving my hips a good sway. I threw a glance over my shoulder at Nero. "You coming?"

Nero didn't follow me. He was just suddenly right beside me, as though he'd materialized there. Man, he moved fast.

As we walked, Nero didn't hold my hand—that wasn't very Legion-like—but he did glare at any man who dared to glance my way. I knew I should have felt bad for the poor guys, but I didn't. I liked that I belonged to Nero and that he belonged to me. Besides, I might have given the panty-throwing women a glare or two of my own.

I scanned the crowd for my family, but they were nowhere in sight. They must have still been processing the Leech at the sheriff's station.

A cloud of pink fluff attracted my attention. I cut over to a nearby food booth and bought the biggest bundle of cotton candy that they had. Then I handed it to Nero with a smile.

He looked down at the big fluffy bundle of pink cotton candy in his hands, completely perplexed. And so adorable.

"It's cotton candy," I said helpfully.

"I know what it is. The question is, Pandora, what is it doing in my possession?"

"Even angels have to eat. And what's better than something light, fluffy, and sweet? Just like an angel."

The look he gave me promised his revenge would be far sweeter. I almost shuddered thinking about our next training session. And yet it was *so* worth it. Nero was a very elegant, very proper guy. He'd been groomed to be an angel since he was born. Seeing him hold a bundle of pink cotton candy was priceless. I took out my phone and snapped a photo for posterity.

"I've killed people for less than this," he grumbled, low. I wasn't sure I was supposed to hear it.

I tore a piece off the cotton candy and ate it. "Oh, come on. You'll want something to show your kids someday to prove you're a fun, approachable kind of guy."

He said nothing. The annoyance in his eyes went out. His face was completely blank.

I guess I'd hit a nerve, pushing him too far. You never knew with angels. One moment you were handing them cotton candy and the next they were chaining you to an interrogation chair. Time to move on.

"Let's check out the games," I said quickly. "Maybe my family is there."

We walked in silence toward the flashing epicenter of

the carnival, its highlight the gigantic, flashing, multi-deck carrousel. His silence was even more pronounced by its contrast to the cheesy, upbeat music.

Finally, as we passed the dunk tank, he broke that silence. "Angels don't typically endeavor to be fun and approachable."

I smiled. "Of course not. Quite the opposite, actually. The Legion puts angels on a pedestal, above everyone else. You are supposed to be unattainable, perfect, professional. And mercilessly lethal. Let's not forget that one."

I wasn't being facetious. Not this time. I was dead serious. Nero was all those things. But he was also more. Much more.

"We angels can't afford to show weakness. Not even to our children. For those of us who have them," he added. His voice was clinical, detached.

Something compelled me to ask, "Do you want children?"

He met my eyes. "Yes."

I blinked, turning away from the intensity of that emerald stare. Yet I could still feel him watching me, the weight of his eyes burning into me, as I scanned the game booths.

"Want to give it a try?" I indicated a tower of tin cans you had to topple by throwing a ball at them.

"No."

Angels didn't get to choose the person they married, the person with whom they had children. That was all arranged by the Legion and their tests—tests that predicted which pairings were most likely to produce offspring with the greatest potential to later become angels. I'd never really thought about what would happen when the Legion found Nero a magically-compatible soldier.

Ok, let's cut the bullshit for a moment. I had not *wanted* to think about it. And nothing had changed. I still didn't want to think about it.

I pointed at another game that involved hitting blinking lights with a toy foam sword. "How about that one?"

He looked offended at the suggestion.

"How else will you impress me with your manly prowess?" I teased him.

"I have better ways of doing that." The look in his eyes was dangerous.

I was saved by the bell. Or, more accurately, saved by the Bella.

"Leda," she said, giving me a very ladylike wave. It was the wave of a queen.

As always, my sister's hair and makeup were flawless. Her blue silk summer dress was perfectly ironed. Her silver sandals were spotless. Considering the dusty state of the streets, that was a feat only explainable by magic. But despite her put-together appearance, she was obviously completely unraveled. She had a rattled, nervous look in her eyes.

"What's wrong?" I asked, embracing her.

I hadn't seen Bella since our lunch date in the city a few weeks ago, but she'd seemed fine then.

"I need to speak to you. *Alone*," she added.

"I know what happened," Nero said.

Surprise flashed across her face—surprise and betrayal. "Harker told you?"

"No, your thoughts did," he replied. "They are screaming it out. You are fortunate there are no other telepaths in town right now."

Bella paled.

"What's going on, Bella? Did you and Harker…" A smirk curling my lips, I allowed the unspoken implication to hang in the air between us.

"Oh, gods, Leda, no! Nothing like that."

The color returned to her face with a vengeance. That was one impressive blush. So she must have really liked Harker. Interesting. I made a mental note to tease her more about that later.

"Bella!" Gin called out with glee, running through the crowd. She gave our sister a big hug.

Calli and Tessa weren't far behind.

"Why is Bella blushing?" Tessa asked.

Which, of course, only made Bella blush more.

Nero looked at her, then at me. "Come with me." He started walking.

Bella, Calli, and I walked behind him. Gin and Tessa moved into line behind us.

"Do you think he means *all* of us?" Gin whispered to Tessa as we followed Nero past the festival grounds.

"Gods, I hope so."

"Tessa, stop staring at my boyfriend's ass," I warned her.

"What makes you think I'm staring at his ass? You can't even see me," she said, her voice defiant.

"I know you. And I have eyes in the back of my head."

"That's not one of the gods' gifts."

"What can I say? I'm special."

"You sure are *special*."

I glanced back at her "Watch it, missy. If you're not nice, I'll curse you with pimples."

"Mom! Leda's threatening me with mortal harm!" Tessa cried out.

"Since when are pimples considered mortal harm?" I asked Calli.

"When you're eighteen, *everything* is a matter of life and death," she replied wisely.

We'd reached the Legion office in Purgatory. A towering, sparkling skyscraper housed our New York City office, but out here we had only a single room tucked inside the Pilgrims' temple of worship.

The Pilgrims were our counterpart. The Legion of Angels was the hand of the gods' justice. The Pilgrims were the other part of the equation: the voice of the gods, of their teachings, their gospel. Their job was to spread the stories of the gods, of their great deeds and immortal triumphs.

Two Pilgrims stood outside the entrance, dressed in plain brown cotton robes. The moment they saw Nero, they both immediately swept into a low bow.

"General Windstriker, we're honored by your visit," said the Pilgrim on the left. "What can we do for you?"

"We require use of our room." Nero didn't slow down. He kept walking, right past them.

The Pilgrim who had spoken hurried to match pace beside him. The other stayed at his post.

"We are completely at your service of course."

Though they served a divine purpose, the Pilgrims were not considered equal to the angels. The angels were as close to gods as you got on Earth. As we walked down the hall, Pilgrims were bowing left and right, over and over again, at Nero. They didn't pay me or my family any mind—except for the chatty Pilgrim.

"Do you require use of the bigger jail cells downstairs, General?" he asked Nero, his gaze flickering briefly to me.

He seemed to remember me—and my 'subversive'

nature—from my days living here, egging on the Pilgrims in the streets when they tried to sell me their religion. It was the clothes. Right now I was dressed like a civilian. When I was in uniform, the Pioneers didn't see past the Legion paraphernalia. They didn't see me. They saw only a soldier in the Legion of Angels.

Nero gave me a look that was cool and emotionless, but I'd learned to read the feelings beyond the chilled facade. He was laughing inside.

"Not just yet, but I will let you know if I need you to bring out the chains. Or the gag," he told the Pilgrim, his face still completely blank.

He was getting me back for the cotton candy snapshot. I was sure of it.

Nero went over to a silent Pilgrim standing in the hall and handed him the fluffy pink bundle. The Pilgrim looked just as perplexed as Nero had when I'd given it to him.

The chatty Pilgrim bowed and left, stars in his eyes, so happy that an angel would ask anything of him. He was acting as though Nero had just done him the biggest favor in the world. I rolled my eyes.

Nero closed the door. As he turned around to face us, he caught the tail end of my eye-roll. He didn't comment, and he didn't have to. I knew that look. It was the look that said eye-rolling was not becoming of a soldier in the gods' army.

But now was not the time to debate propriety. I had to know what was bothering Bella—and whether there was anything I could do to help her. Now that the door was closed, at least we had some privacy.

I turned to her and asked, "What's going on? Why all the secrecy?"

Bella took in a deep breath, and then it all spilled out at once. "I found out where I come from. I am the daughter of the former first dark angel and granddaughter of Valerian, the Dark Lord of Witchcraft, one of the ruling demons of hell."

CHAPTER 4

SILVER PLATTER

*B*ella's revelation surprised me so much that it was a moment before I could speak. "The granddaughter of the Dark Lord of Witchcraft? That certainly explains your magic. I've never met a more natural witch."

When the gods had come to Earth, they'd not only given us the gift of monsters. They'd also given us magic. The seven ruling gods created the seven groups of supernaturals: shifters, elementals, telekinetics, vampires, sirens, witches, and fairies. Each god had a specialty, a magical strength that they bestowed upon humanity. For example, the God of Nature made elementals, and the God of Faith made vampires.

Each supernatural group prayed to their patron gods and gave them offerings in thanks for their magic, but the gods never responded. It was not a conversation; it was a monologue, a poem of praise to the deities of heaven. The gods existed on a whole other level, high above humanity. There weren't even many Legion soldiers who'd met a god.

The demons were the flip side. On worlds where they

reigned, the seven ruling demons had created their own seven groups of supernaturals, the dark magic equivalents to the shifters, elementals, telekinetics, vampires, sirens, witches, and fairies.

And then there were the super soldiers, the gods' and demons' armies: the Legion of Angels and its equivalent, the Dark Force of Hell. A Legion or Dark Force soldier drank directly from the source of magic, the food of gods or demons.

As the granddaughter of a demon, Bella was also close to the source. That meant her magic was much more potent than that of a normal dark witch.

"How did you find out about this?" I asked Bella.

"There was an incident of dark magic at the university," she said. "The Legion suspected there was a demon-worshipper there. Harker came to investigate, and he asked for my help in identifying the culprit. I didn't know the investigation would lead back to me, that the source of my magic is the demon blood inside of me. When we discovered it, Harker covered it up."

Good for him.

"Lately, the Legion has been cracking down hard on dark magic," I commented.

"It's the gods," Nero said. "After recent events, they've grown concerned that the demons are looking for a way back to Earth. They believe exterminating dark magic would wipe out all the demons' followers and therefore their influence on Earth."

"That's like killing a fly with a flame thrower. You kill a lot of innocents too," I protested. "Bella didn't even know about her origin. And she is the last person on Earth who would ever try to take over the world."

"That's the problem with these sorts of policies," Nero

said. "But the gods consider those acceptable losses. They don't like dark magic. They never have. Every few decades, they push the Legion to conduct a dark magic purge."

Nero's father Damiel had been the victim of one of those purges. And he was an archangel, the highest order of angel too. No one was safe. No one was above extermination.

No, we're really not, Nero spoke in my mind.

Well, they wouldn't be getting my sister. She wasn't going to be a casualty of their latest purge. No way, no how.

"We're here for you," I told Bella, setting my hand on hers. "No matter what."

Gin set her hand over mine. "Always."

"And forever," Tessa said, adding her hand to the stack.

Calli was the practical one, less romantic than the rest of us. She said to Bella, straight to the point, "I'll put a bullet in anyone who tries to hurt my girl." Then she set her hand on top.

"I love you all," Tearing up, Bella pulled us all into a big family hug.

"You're going to have to hide your dark magic," I said to Bella when we all finally stepped back.

"I'm not sure how." Her voice was uncertain, frightened.

"How is dark magic identified? Through blood tests?" I asked Nero.

The Legion took regular blood samples from its soldiers. They were primarily used for tracking our magical development and for making matches, for marrying angels to other soldiers. But I wouldn't have been surprised if the Legion was using them to track us in other ways.

"We haven't figured out how to identify light and dark

magic through blood tests," Nero told me. "Some powerful dark or light spells leave an imprint, though. An echo. Those can be tracked to a location, but they are not so easily linked to a person."

"That's what happened at the university," said Bella. "While studying for my exams, I cast a powerful spell, and since my magic is apparently dark, it was detected."

"Only use spells that don't leave an imprint," Nero said to her. "And if at all possible, do not use your magic around angels or gods. Light and dark magic can sometimes be felt by powerful magic users. It's just a feeling, very hard to quantify and almost impossible to track. You need to be especially wary of angels."

"Well, being wary of angels is just good common sense anyway," I said, smirking.

"Of which you possess none," he retorted.

I winked at him. "Don't flirt with me in public, honey. It's unbecoming of a Legion soldier."

He froze, the look on his face absolutely priceless. But it was gone almost instantly, and a dangerous, predatory smile slowly curled back his lips. Oh, I was really in for it now. Our next training session was going to be hell on Earth.

I looked at Bella. "What does Harker know about your origin?"

"Everything," she sighed.

"I'm hurt. How is it your boyfriend knows before we do?" I teased her.

She frowned. "Firstly, Harker is not my boyfriend."

I nodded. "Which is why you blush every time someone says his name."

Her cheeks went red.

"Yep, just like that," I told her.

Bella cleared her throat. "Secondly, there was no way around Harker finding out. He was right there when Valerian put me into some kind of trance. Harker drank my blood to link us together, to see what I saw so he could pull me out of the trance. And he healed me with his blood."

"You exchanged blood?"

"Yes."

"There will be consequences of exchanging blood with an angel," I warned her.

"I am not an angel or a Legion soldier, so there should be no lasting effects. I researched the topic thoroughly afterwards."

Of course she had. Bella researched everything. It was one of the reasons she was so smart. But books didn't know everything, and now I had to break the bad news.

"When your books promised no lasting effects, they were referring to mortals or typical supernaturals who'd exchanged blood with an angel," I said. "But you are neither mortal, nor are you a normal witch. You are the daughter of a dark angel and the granddaughter of a demon. Your well of magic is deep, your potential power enormous. Take, for example, the Legion brats, the children of angels. The laws of magic work somewhat differently in them. You have immortal blood, Bella. This blood exchange will have consequences."

She mulled that over for a moment. "You have a point." She didn't look happy about it.

"You'd better get used to Harker hanging around," I teased. "He might even show up in your dreams."

Bella stiffened. "He wouldn't dare."

"Of course he would. He's an angel."

"Leda is right," Nero said.

"Three words I always love to hear," I told him with a grin. No, I hadn't teased him enough for one day. After all, once you were damned anyway, you might as well have fun and really deserve it.

Gold and silver sparks lit up his eyes. "I've heard more humility from angels," he said seriously.

"I…um…crap!" I hissed. Seriously, nothing came to me. No snappy comebacks, no snark, no sass, nothing.

"I'll give you some time to work on that," Nero told me without a shred of sympathy. Then he looked at Bella. "For better or for worse, you and Harker have a connection now. This isn't something you can just wash away."

"I'll cross that bridge when I come to it," she declared.

She tried to appear strong and logical, but she was obviously concerned about the consequences of the blood exchange. I completely understood. I'd been surprised by the effects of my blood exchange with Nero, but I'd come to appreciate its benefits. If we'd exchanged blood recently, we could track each other easily, even over great distances. And it allowed us to link our magic powers. And, well, our connection made for some pretty awesome sex too.

"Is there a way to mask my dark magic so angels and gods don't sense it?" Bella asked Nero.

"Yes, but it will take practice." Nero also possessed a bit of dark magic mixed in with all his light magic. He hid it well.

"Harker can teach you," Nero told Bella. "He is a very good magic Tracker. If you can hide your magic from him, you can hide it from almost anyone."

Calli looked at me, concern crinkling her brow. "Do the gods know about your mixed magic?"

She was referring to my balance of light and dark magic, both existing in complete harmony inside of me.

According to the gods, such a thing was impossible, not to mention sacrilege. It was a threat to their 'pure' magic. I was pretty sure they considered mixed magic even worse than plain old dark magic.

I exchanged glances with Nero. "We think at least one of the gods might know about me," I told Calli. "And that this god might have been the one to lace my Nectar with Venom once."

"Your magic has grown too powerful to go undetected," Nero told me. "Like your sister, you should practice masking your dark magic when any angel or god we don't trust is around."

"To be honest, I'm not sure that I trust any of the gods."

Nero nodded in approval. "Good."

"Do you think Harker has any time in his busy schedule to train me?" I asked him, an expression of perfect innocence on my face.

"*I* will train you, Pandora."

It was just too fun to tease him.

Calli sighed. "My special kids sure don't make it easy to keep them safe."

"Hey, how is it hard to keep *me* safe?" Tessa protested.

"Well, for one, you're always chasing after paranormal soldiers," said Calli.

"They're harmless," Tessa replied with a dismissive flick of her hand.

"Until the day you chase them out of town."

"The paranormal soldiers are all good and fun, but I'm saving my heart for an angel." Tessa gave Nero a demure look.

I rolled my eyes.

"Know any single angels?" Tessa asked him.

"None you want to give your heart to. They would serve it back to you on a silver platter."

Tessa giggled.

"I was not joking."

But Tessa looked unconvinced.

"Speaking of silver platters, who's in the mood for dinner?" I asked, my tummy rumbling for only the hundredth time this evening.

Gin's hand shot in the air. "Famished."

"Working always makes me hungry," Tessa agreed.

"Good," I told them. "Because today we're all going to dinner at the fanciest restaurant in town."

———

THE FANCIEST RESTAURANT in town was literally called the Silver Platter. I wasn't sure if the name was genuinely pretentious or was instead meant as a halfhearted jab at pretentious people everywhere.

The restaurant was actually pretty nice, especially for one in a rugged Frontier town. As we entered through the massive double doors, the high vaulted ceiling looming above us, Tessa and Gin let out a collective sigh of delight.

We'd never been past these gilded doors before. The closest we'd gotten was the Mermaid's Lagoon next door, the town's second fanciest restaurant. And we'd only gone there when we had a very special occasion to celebrate—or when we had a very big payday to spend.

But there was no comparison. The Mermaid's Lagoon was a nice, cozy place with comfort food like fried chicken and mashed potatoes. It was delicious comfort food, but it was comfort food nonetheless. The Silver Platter was in a whole other league. The menu was dominated by dishes I couldn't pronounce, and I was sure there were at least a few too many digits on the end of all the prices.

The tables were made of massive, thick rustic wood —*expensive* rustic, not dirty and run-down rustic. The benches were made from the same wood. Magic fires burned in the hearths, created by mixtures of expensive designer potions. Overhead, the candlelight consisted of thousands of tiny magic baubles. Out here where Magitech was scarce and expensive, that was an enormous splurge. It was no wonder the prices were so high.

The Silver Platter was where the VIP visitors of Purgatory went, people like the upper echelon of the paranormal soldiers' organization. This place was designed for people to whom money was not an issue.

As we were led to our table, my senses were bombarded with the smell of wood fires and a gentle earthy and sweet scent that made me desperate to eat now. I was so hungry that I was half-tempted to storm the kitchen and steal the steaks right off the grill.

"This place is awesome," Gin whispered.

"Did you see the silverware?" Tessa gasped as we sat down. "It's real, actual silver."

Tessa had an eye for design, for fashion, for anything pretty and fancy basically. She had an appreciation of finer things, and the ability to tell the difference between them and cheap knockoffs. She could see where corners had been cut, or where no expense had been spared. Her love of pretty things and pampering made her a true princess at heart. Calli had often said that Tessa would have to find herself a prince to marry because we certainly couldn't afford her fine taste.

Gin gently tapped the wall behind our table. "The walls are made of actual stone. It's not just a veneer."

Building with stone out here on the Frontier was exorbitantly expensive, so only people with money to burn did it. I wasn't surprised the Silver Platter was a member of that elite club.

Like Tessa, Gin appreciated nice things, but her taste was more down-to-earth, more practical. She wouldn't wear something pretty if it wasn't also practical. She wanted both. And she wasn't afraid to get her hands dirty. It wasn't uncommon to find her covered in motor oil in our garage, fixing up the vehicles or trying to figure out some gadget by taking it apart. She would keep disassembling something until she figured out how to rebuild it in the perfect way.

"Even the menus look expensive," Tessa commented.

I looked down at my menu, a piece of delicate art canvas set over a wooden board. The Silver Platter's decorator sure had an eye for detail; the board was made of the same wood as the furniture.

"The text moves!" Gin exclaimed.

Her squeal of delight drew a few reproving stares from the high brow clientele.

I glanced down at my menu. The dishes were handwritten onto the paper in graceful, calligraphic strokes. I tapped my finger against the edge of the canvas, and the text scrolled to the next page of the menu. It was like a phone screen. The menu must have been penned in magic ink—movable, dynamic ink.

But my wonder was cut short by the sight of the guest a few tables down from ours. It was the district lord in the royal blue cowboy boots I'd seen earlier this evening. Well, he'd changed outfits since then.

The blue-booted district lord was now dressed in a very expensive, very shiny white silk suit. Despite the color and the dusty state of the streets outside, his suit was spotless. He was showing off that he could walk around this rugged Frontier town, and yet his clothes remained immaculate.

But the district lord wasn't the source of my sudden lack of appetite. It was the man sitting at his feet, chained to an ivory column. Dressed in a simple cotton tunic, he wore no shoes. His eyes were hungry, his cheeks concave, as though he hadn't eaten in days. And yet the district lord's dog was devouring a steak from a crystal dish.

The man was eyeing the dog's dinner with hunger, watching in perfect silence, obviously too afraid to move, to try to snatch even the tiny pieces of meat that sprinkled the floor as the dog messily consumed its dinner.

Frontier towns were full of these poor souls, indentured servants who'd come here for a new life, a fresh start, all paid by a generous district lord. The price of this generosity: their life was not their own for ten whole years. They were handled like animals. No, worse than animals. The district lords' beloved dogs received better treatment.

Seeing that poor man chained to the column didn't just turn my stomach. It boiled my blood. I was so furious. I had to do something to end his inhumane treatment— something like set that smug district lord's spotless suit on fire. Then it wouldn't be so spotless anymore.

Nero caught my hand under the table. "Don't kill him."

"I wasn't going to kill him. I was just going to set him on fire a little."

"We cannot interfere unless we are threatened or the gods' order is disrupted," he reminded me.

"How can that *atrocity* not be a disruption of the gods' order?" I hissed under my breath. "It is an affront to all that is still good and decent in this world."

"Setting the district lord's suit on fire won't solve the problem. And it certainly won't help his servant."

Nero was right. If anything, the district lord would use his spontaneous combustion as an excuse to punish the starving man further.

I took calming breaths, trying to slow my racing pulse.

"He will get what's coming to him," Nero told me.

"When?" I demanded. "And how many lives will he ruin before that day comes?"

"You can't right every wrong."

Maybe not. But I damn sure well was going to try.

"Maybe you could save this one man by killing his master. You might even get away with it without the Legion finding out. But then what?" Nero asked. "The contract he signed is legally binding. It would be transferred to the next of kin. The man would still not be free."

I frowned. This system was so broken.

"Patience," Nero said calmly.

I frowned. "Your favorite immortal virtue."

"It will all turn out in the end."

"How do you know?"

"I just do."

His magic wrapped around me like a blanket, warm and comforting. I didn't resist. I allowed his magic to calm me. No, I couldn't walk up to the district lord and punch him in the face. It would just land me in trouble. He would call in his thugs, and my family would rise to defend me. That would land them in trouble too. But someday, one way or another, I would put an end to this.

I tried to distract myself with the menu—and the exquisite smells wafting out from the kitchen.

Tessa was looking through the menu with delight,

completely oblivious to the atrocity playing out behind her.

"Leda, these prices are outrageous," Gin whispered to me.

"Not when you take into account how much it costs them to run this place." Tessa glanced at the magic lights, the fire, the menu.

Gin wasn't convinced. "Still, our last job paid well, but not *this* well."

The way she looked around the room was analytical. Her delight at the posh surroundings faded to concern. Calli had been teaching Gin to do our bookkeeping. She always looked at how much something cost and then weighed whether or not it was worth it, whether or not the family could afford it. Tessa, on the other hand, appreciated things for the sheer luxury. She was not unaware that they were expensive. In fact, she was acutely aware of it, and she appreciated them even more for the fine details that added cost allowed. She just didn't tend to dwell so much on how to pay for them.

"Don't worry about it," I told Gin as the district lord and his entourage left. "I'm paying, remember?"

"Leda, do you know how much—"

"I said not to worry about it. We haven't all gone out together in a long time."

And it wasn't like I needed the money. The Legion paid well, a consequence of me putting my life on the line nearly every day.

I'd offered to set up my family somewhere safe and nice where they wouldn't have to work, but Calli was too proud to take it. She had agreed to let me pay off Bella's pricey tuition at the New York University of Witchcraft, but she hadn't taken a single cent more from me. She'd said the girls had to learn to work for their own money.

Also, Calli and my little sisters refused to leave Purgatory at the mercy of the district lords. If they didn't take the jobs of catching criminals, the district lords would sweep in and take care of it like knights in shining armor.

Except evil lay behind that armor. Every time the people of Purgatory took their help, the town became even more dependent on them. Soon, the district lords would reign supreme over all justice—which meant there would be no justice left to speak of.

Calli's cause was a noble one for sure. So I didn't tell her that I sometimes funded the bounties on the jobs she and my sisters took. I'd talked to the sheriff of Purgatory to arrange my secret donations. The sheriff's office was seriously underfunded, so there wasn't much money in the bounty kettle.

Tessa's eager gaze scanned the menu. "Leda, you are my favorite sister." She literally had stars in her eyes.

"For the next five minutes."

Tessa beamed at me. "Five minutes? No, I figure your favorite sister status will last at least until the end of the meal."

I snorted. At least Tessa was always honest.

The waiter came, and we ordered. Later, when our food arrived, Nero looked approvingly at his steak. He was clearly much more content with his fancy food than with the cotton candy I'd given him earlier.

"More to your liking?" I asked.

"Yes." He added in my mind, *You are to my liking.*

The smirk on my lips died, a vision flashing through my head. Dessert. Two pieces of chocolate cake lay abandoned on the table. Nero's fangs teased my neck. As they broke the surface of my skin, my breath stalled. Wildfire flashed through my veins, awakening my body. Every nerve ending tingling, I grabbed him and—

I shook my head, clearing the visions from it. Beside me, Nero gave me a knowing, self-satisfied smile. He'd projected those images into my head, and his ego was now basking in the consequences.

"Whoa, Leda, what is going on with your hair?" Tessa gasped.

Checking out my reflection in the windows, I saw that my hair was glowing. Again. Damn it. I patted it down with my hands, like I was trying to put out a fire. I really needed to gain some control over my hair. It was like a big flashing billboard advertising everything I was feeling to anyone who cared to watch.

"It's just something it does sometimes," I said, as the last of the glow faded.

"Around angels?" Tessa asked eagerly.

I looked at Nero. "Only when they're aggravating me."

He looked completely confident in his knowledge that he was at the top of the food chain.

"Angels," Tessa sighed with doe eyes. "You should have invited more angels to dinner."

She didn't seem to realize that you didn't invite angels. They came when they wanted to, whether they were invited or not. And they didn't come when summoned.

Like most eighteen-year-olds, Tessa had stars in her eyes when it came to angels. She loved them. She read fan fiction about them. She religiously followed the angel sightings and gossip columns in the tabloids.

"Don't go chasing angels, Tessa. They're dangerous," I told her.

"You're one to talk." Her gaze flickered to Nero, then back to me.

"That's different," I countered. "And I didn't chase Nero."

"You stole Calli's motorcycle to chase off after him across the Black Plains," Gin pointed out.

"To rescue him."

"I fail to see how that's relevant," Tessa said. "Did you or did you not cross a monster-infested prairie and break into a rogue vampire stronghold to get to him?"

"I—"

"Did," Gin finished for me. "And you disobeyed orders to go after him too."

"How could you two possibly know about that?" I demanded.

Gin shrugged. "Calli told us the Legion would never send a newly-initiated soldier all alone to rescue an angel."

I looked at Calli.

"Well, they wouldn't," she said. "It's not privileged information. Everyone knows that, Leda."

"Just as everyone knows the Legion disciplines their misbehaving soldiers." Tessa turned her eager eyes on Nero. "Did you punish her for her transgression?"

"For which transgression? You're going to have to be more specific. She transgresses every day."

I glowered at him. "Haha. Very funny."

"There's nothing funny about disobeying orders, Pandora. Especially, when they're *my* orders."

Tessa fanned herself. Oh, good grief.

"But to answer your question, yes, I did discipline her for going across the Black Plains," Nero told her.

"That's kind of backwards, right?" Gin said. "She

67

rescued you, and you punished her. You should have rewarded her."

"That's what Leda said."

"So what was her punishment?" Tessa asked him. "Like running laps or something?"

"Among other things."

"I heard he pinned her down," Bella volunteered.

"Hey, not you too!" I protested, the bitter taste of betrayal thick on my tongue.

Bella was usually more reserved, less into teasing than the rest of us, but maybe engaging in the banter was just what she needed to counter the stress she was under. And it had been so long since we'd all been together.

Tessa and Gin looked at Nero with wide, adoring eyes, eager to hear more. When he did not oblige, they turned their gazes on me.

"He pinned you?" Gin asked me.

"To the ground?" Tessa added.

"Before you say more, wipe those smirks off your faces," I said, blushing. "Nero sat on me, counting out my pushups as I performed them. Lots and lots of pushups. And if you two want to experience the specifics of that unpleasant exercise for yourself, I will sit on you while *you* do pushups. We'll start with an easy five hundred and go from there."

"You can't make us do pushups," Tessa protested, pouting out her lower lip.

"I wouldn't bet on that."

Tessa paled, if only a little. Gin was silent. They'd been subdued. Finally. But Calli was not. She was laughing so hard that people from the other tables were staring at us like we were a mobile circus.

"Sorry," I said to Nero, sighing. "That's my family,

always the center of attention. People gawk at us wherever we go."

"I'm used to people gawking at me."

Of course he was. He was an angel. People stopped and stared whenever he entered the area. When he walked amongst mortals, he was always the center of attention.

"So you could say you two are a match made in heaven," Tessa said. "In fact, I've never seen such a perfect couple."

I didn't like where this was going. She was plotting something.

"Remember what we were discussing earlier, Leda? About the acrobats?"

She wouldn't dare.

Tessa looked at us and said seriously, "So, when's the wedding?"

I nearly choked on my wine.

Nero remained silent, watching with perfect calmness as I suffocated on my own embarrassment. Even as I coughed, I sent him a mental apology for my family's improper behavior.

No need. They are not my soldiers. Nor are they yours.

"Tessa, that's enough. This is neither the time nor the place for this," Calli chastised her.

"So when *is* the time and place for this?" Tessa countered.

"I don't know, but I suppose you'll corner Leda as soon as we get home."

Tessa gave me a devilish look that promised she'd do just that.

"I don't think you're helping," Bella told Calli.

"Who said I was trying? Leda doesn't need my help. She never did. She can take care of herself."

Calli believed in tough love, in making you stand up for yourself. She gave me a proud look, a look that made me forget all my embarrassment. My heart swelled with happiness at her approval. She respected me. For that, I could put up with a little teasing.

A heavy crash, the sound of metal hitting the marble floor, echoed up the stairwell from below. The clamor was immediately followed by complete silence, even as the note of the clinging metal slowly faded out. Something wrong downstairs.

I couldn't see what was going on from up here. I'd have to get closer. On instinct, I reached for the knife hidden inside my boot.

Nero looked relaxed on the outside, but beneath the shield of his body, he was alert, ready to move. He could knock everyone in the restaurant to the ground in under a second, using only his psychic magic. His telekinesis was that powerful. I should know. I'd only been on the receiving end of it for months now as he tried to build up my resistance to that branch of magic. That was how you trained a new magic power: by building up your resistance to it. The other component of preparing for the gods' next gift was building up your willpower. Altogether, that equaled training—lots and lots of training.

Footsteps padded softly up the stairs. My concern faded away when I saw Harker. The restaurants' guests gawked openly at him, their elegance and refinement fading away at the sight of an angel in their presence. Their propriety was a poor defense against an angel's aura.

Harker sure was putting on a show. His magnificent wings were out, glossy black with bright blue accents. He was dressed like Nero, in the black leather armor uniform of the Legion of Angels. A small metallic insignia, in the shape of angel wings, was pinned to his chest. It broadcast his rank as a Legion soldier of the eighth level, and an angel of the first level.

Harker stopped in front of our table.

"Are you planning on standing there all day showing off your wings, or are you joining us for dinner?" I asked him.

He smiled pleasantly. "I'd love to."

"Put away those wings," Nero told him, his voice so low that no one but the people at our table could hear him. "You're always pulling them out and making a scene."

"You're one to talk," Harker retorted.

I swallowed a snort. At least this time there was no wine in my mouth.

Harker put away his wings. They vanished in a flash of magic, like a swarm of black butterflies dissolving out of sight, fading into the air. Impressive. He'd been practicing hard. Harker was a new angel; he'd become one only a few months ago. It took a lot of practice to make magic look easy, to have that much finesse. That was especially true when it came to our more recently acquired skills. Brute force was easy once you had the necessary magic. It was the finesse that took time—time and a whole lot of patience. That's what set the angels apart from everyone else: they made everything look simply effortless.

Harker took the seat next to Bella. He'd been watching her closely, judging her reaction to his magic. He'd clearly been showing off mainly for her benefit. Bella said nothing. In fact, she was avoiding looking at him at all.

Yep, she really liked him.

Harker lifted his hand, summoning our waiter, who practically ran to him. Harker ordered a steak and some fries.

"Dinner with angels," Tessa sighed, braiding her fingers together. She looked positively ecstatic about being sandwiched between the two of them. Glancing at Gin, she said, "Maybe we should join the Legion of Angels too."

"I don't know if you'd like it, Tessa. At the Legion, you have to wake up really early," I said.

Tessa would sleep until noon if she could.

"Do they have coffee at the Legion?" Gin asked.

"Yes, but you're not supposed to drink it," I told her. "Dependencies of any kind, including caffeine, are considered mortal weaknesses. You're supposed to survive solely on the strength of your own willpower."

"If you're not supposed to drink coffee, then why do they have it at all?" Gin said practically.

I shrugged. "To torture you mostly. It's there but you know you can't have it."

Tessa frowned at me. "Leda, are you bullshitting us?"

"Tessa, language," Calli reminded her.

"You swear like a sailor," Tessa retorted.

"But not while dining at a fancy restaurant."

"No, just when picking us up from school," Gin said.

"That was only once, many years ago, when Amanda Farthing put her hands on my stun gun. I told her it was dangerous, but she just had to touch it."

Harker's food arrived. Being jumped to the top of the queue was just one benefit of being an angel.

"Why did you bring a stun gun to a school?" Harker asked Calli casually as he began to cut his steak.

"I was on my way back from dropping off my mark at the sheriff's station, and I didn't have time to go home first."

"She came to school covered in blood," Tessa said melodramatically, her eyes wide.

"It wasn't that much blood," Bella said.

"It was enough. All the parents and teachers were staring at her." I chuckled at the memory. "She completely freaked them out."

Calli rolled her eyes at the show we were putting on. "I obviously didn't freak them out enough if Amanda Farthing tried to fiddle with my gun."

"Did you shoot her?" Harker asked.

"Of course not. There were young children present."

"But later that night, Calli shot an arrow through her front door," I added. "Then she shouted out, 'the next one will go through your leg if you ever touch any of my weapons again!' It was awesome."

Harker laughed.

"Threats were the only thing that got through to her. The woman was an idiot, playing with my gun at a school, not knowing what she was doing. My stun gun only knocks out adults, but it could put a kid in the hospital." Calli gave me a harsh look. "And you weren't supposed to see that."

I'd been twelve at the time. Calli had never sugarcoated the world for us, but she didn't like us to stand by and watch when she got her hands dirty, even if it was all for the greater good.

"I followed you when you went out that night," I told her.

"Of course you did." Resignation—and a bit of pride —shone in her eyes. "You always were a rebel. Maybe *I* should have made you do some pushups while I sat on you."

Tessa smirked at me. "Since you're not a hot angel, Calli, I don't think she would have enjoyed that very much."

73

"Undoubtably."

"We have to move to New York. It's apparently full of hot single angels," Tessa said to Gin.

I hated to burst her bubble, but… "There are only two angels who currently live in New York, and right now they're both sitting at this table."

"And neither of them are single," Tessa lamented.

"That's not exactly true," I told her.

She blinked.

"I asked out your sister Bella, and she turned me down," Harker said. He didn't sound the least bit embarrassed.

Tessa looked at Bella like she'd lost her mind. "Why would you do an idiotic thing like that? *Why*?" Her voice shook with emotion. "You're supposed to be the smart one in the family."

"I'm not giving up." Harker looked at us. "What sort of gestures of affection would Bella appreciate?"

"Fairy's Breath," Tessa said immediately.

Fairy's Breath was a fragrant, lacy flower that came in all kinds of colors.

"Also, hard-to-get potion supplies like liquid silver and crushed diamonds," Gin added. "Horned Ravager hooves. And other beastie parts."

"She apparently likes angels too," I commented.

Harker chuckled. "It runs in the family."

"It's hard to say no to all those muscles and magic." I even managed to say it with a straight face.

Gin was laughing her head off, but Bella looked positively mortified. It was only fair, especially after how Bella had teased me earlier. And, besides, this was just how our family rolled, passing the hot potato of mortification.

Harker finished his last bite of steak, drank a sip of

wine, then he set his napkin on the table. "Unfortunately, this is not a social call, ladies. I came here to get Nero. We have a mission from the First Angel."

"What kind of mission?" I asked.

"The secret kind." Harker looked at Nero and added, "And the urgent kind. We have to go now."

Nero gave me a quick kiss. "Try to stay out of trouble, Pandora," he whispered against my mouth.

I could feel the warmth of his kiss lingering on my lips like magic, even as he rose and left the restaurant with Harker.

"That sure was one powerful kiss." Tessa shivered. "It's giving me goosebumps, and they're not even my lips he kissed. Angels don't really do anything halfway, do they?"

I was still touching my lips, feeling the mark he'd left. It was a small one, but it was an angel's mark nonetheless. He'd left a part of him behind with me.

"No, they really don't," I agreed.

Gin and Tessa sighed in unison. Bella was quiet, probably still fighting with herself over whether she should go out with Harker. Angels were intense in everything they did. And, as Tessa had figured out, they did everything at a minimum of two hundred percent. Anything worth doing must be done perfectly. That was their motto. Bella looked like she wasn't sure if she wanted to jump into that world.

I paid the bill, then my family and I went back to the festival. It was so different out here, so bright. The scene was not magically darkened to create an atmosphere, then spot-lit with magic lanterns and magic fire. No, out here on the streets, it was noisy, alive. Vibrant. Corny carnival tunes repeated again and again as brightly-colored flags and banners rustled in the wind.

As we made our way through the festival, we picked up

packages of cookies, apple treats, onion rings, and all sorts of unhealthy things for dessert. The food was the exact opposite of the upscale meal we'd just had at the Silver Platter.

Tessa's gaze flickered around rapidly, scanning the crowd.

"Do you want me to check for monsters hiding behind the buildings?" I asked her.

Tessa's face lit up, and she grabbed Gin's hand. "We're meeting some friends. See you later."

Then they ran off without waiting for a response. I watched them join the growing crowd that had surrounded Brokers and a few other paranormal soldiers. They sure had a lot of fans from Purgatory's young lady population. Tessa had managed to squeeze through the wall of bodies to the front of the line. She was already talking to the soldiers.

"I guess we don't rank as high as the latest batch of paranormal soldiers to arrive in Purgatory," I said to Bella.

Calli wrapped an arm around each of us. "Let them have their fun. They're young and foolish. Sooner or later, they'll learn to stop chasing after boys and let the boys chase after them."

I watched Tessa flirt with three soldiers at once. "Unlikely."

"It's just the three of us for a bit," said Calli. "I've missed you both."

"And we've missed you," Bella told her. "Terribly."

Uncertainty trembled in her eyes, the lingering shock of discovering the truth of her origin. She must have felt really alone right now.

Calli saw it too because she squeezed us closer. "I know that must have been really tough for you, Bella, but I want you to forget all about it and just have fun with your family."

"Your *real* family," I added.

"I will." Bella looked fortified by our words.

"Don't you worry about anything," Calli said as we passed blinking game stalls. "I'm going to win you an egregiously large stuffed animal."

She stopped in front of a game that involved shooting a tin can. She slapped her one dollar bill down on the counter.

The gamekeeper, a teenage boy who looked like he'd been hit with the pimple curse I'd threatened Tessa with earlier, glanced from the money to Calli. He shook his head. "You can't play."

"Why not?" Calli demanded.

"The game's out of order."

"Don't bullshit me, kid. Two minutes ago, you were happy to take that boy's money for twenty rounds of the game as he tried in vain to win his girlfriend a unicorn. Yep, you took his money, even though he never had a chance because you've rigged the game."

Looking indignant, he huffed. "I can assure you that Shoot 'em Down is perfectly fair and—"

"I'll be the judge of that." Calli slid her dollar toward him.

He slid it back. It wasn't surprising that he didn't want to let Calli play. She was an excellent shot. She didn't miss, and the whole town knew it.

"Look," Calli said, her tone softening. "I promised my Bella a gigantic fluffy cat. If it will make you feel better, I'll play the game blindfolded."

He waved over his colleague. The two of them turned their backs to us and whispered for a while.

Finally, Pimples said, "All right, but *I* am tying the blindfold."

"I can't believe she convinced him to let her play," I commented as Bella and I watched him tie the blindfold securely over Calli's eyes.

Bella ate a piece of popcorn. "This will be good."

Calli shot and missed the target.

"I wonder how long she'll pretend to fool around," Bella said.

Calli could shoot blindfolded or not. It didn't matter.

"She's of course waiting until she has only one shot left before she aims at the target. To create drama," I said as Calli missed again.

Pimples was smiling in triumph. The fool was celebrating his victory too early.

"How many shots does she have left now?" Bella asked me.

"Three."

Calli was taking her time, pretending to be disoriented. She aimed far off the target. Pimples and his colleague ducked, afraid she was going to shoot them by mistake.

"So, now that we're alone, are we going to talk about the elephant in the room?" I asked Bella.

She blinked. "What elephant?"

"Don't be coy, Bella," I said, wiggling my eyebrows. "You know I'm referring to you and Harker."

"Honestly, there is no Harker and I. It's a very bad idea."

"You know, that's what I told myself about Nero. I had myself perfectly convinced that it was a bad idea to get involved with an angel."

"And I see logic won out as usual."

"Love isn't logical. And throwing caution to the wind

didn't turn out so badly for me."

"I'm not you, Leda. I'm not brave enough."

"Nonsense. You're one of the bravest people I know."

"Not this time. When I found out who I am—*what* I am—it toppled everything. My plans for the future, my dreams, all of it. The gods will hunt me to the ends of the Earth. And they will threaten everyone I care about. I shouldn't be making connections. I should be severing them. I should leave to protect you all."

I caught her by the shoulders. "Bella, stop. No. You're not leaving. They won't find out."

"And if they do?"

"Then I will protect you. We will *all* protect you."

Tears pooled in her eyes. "Leda—"

I wiped them away. "Promise me you won't leave."

Bella met my eyes. "I promise."

"Good," I said, nodding. "Now I won't have to tie you up."

Bella laughed. It was nice to see the wall of her fear and frustration burst.

"I'm glad you're my sister," she told me.

"Of course you are," I said, smirking. "I'm awesome."

She laughed again.

"I'm glad you're my sister too," I told her.

We turned to watch Calli take aim again.

"She's on her last shot," I said.

"She's still facing away from the target."

"She'll make it."

Calli lifted the gun. Then she quickly pivoted around and fired at the target board.

As her shot hit the bullseye, all the game stands around us blew up, the force of the explosion throwing me and Bella in opposite directions.

CHAPTER 5

A DUBIOUS SUPERPOWER

I opened my eyes, pushing the burning debris off my body. The festival was in ruins. The stands were broken, the wooden beams split, cracked, or on fire. Broken wood chips covered everything. People lay on the ground, moaning.

As I rose to my feet, pain blossomed all across my body. The hard fall of the explosion throwing me backwards had left me bruised. My top was stained with blood. A sharp piece of wood protruded from my side like a stake. I gritted my teeth, grabbed on to the piece of wood, and yanked it out. Dizzy, I swayed to the side but managed to stay on my feet. Thanks to the gods' gifts of magic, my body could take a rough beating before it gave out—not to mention, I was no stranger to pain. I'd had much worse in my time at the Legion.

I looked for my family and anyone else I could help. As far as I could see, no one appeared dead. But they needed healing. I reached for the tiny emergency potion vials I kept in my belt.

As I was leaning over the first victim, I picked up the

hint of a sound. And it was growing louder. I could hear them walking, the scrape of their thick boot soles against the cobbled road, the rough rasp of their breathing. There were six of them. And they were sneaking up on me.

The wind changed direction, and I smelled metal and gunpowder, the kind used for fireworks. The explosion had been caused by these new arrivals; I was sure of it.

There was something more, the scent of sweat, thick and harsh. Werewolves. I rose in my knees, facing them. There were six men, and they looked just how they smelled —wild, rugged, and untamed. A combination of denim and leather, of a cowboy posse and a motorcycle gang, they looked like the type of Frontier outlaws the festival visitors came here to gawk at.

The six bulky guys weren't part of the entertainment, however; they were mercenaries. There was no missing that distinctive hired-gun look in their eyes, in the way that they moved. They were trouble, plain and simple. Add in their werewolf magic, and that meant double trouble.

They hadn't shifted into beasts. They didn't have to. They were very strong in human form, and I was horribly outnumbered.

But I had the element of surprise on my side. When they looked at me, their gazes were dismissive. They didn't see me as a threat. I wasn't in uniform, so they didn't know I was a soldier in the Legion of Angels. They didn't know I'd wrestled their kind before.

The werewolves walked under a canopy of decorative lights. The explosion had left the strands of flickering bulbs in a twist. The lights hissed and zapped over the chime and jingle of the carousel music. The festival site was in ruins, but that eerie carnival melody continued to play, as though possessed by a dark spirit.

81

"What are you?" gasped the werewolf with the big belt, his voice distant. His eyes were wide, locked on my hair.

My hair had only ever mesmerized humans and vampires before. Now here it was bewitching a werewolf.

My hair was not mundane, and it never had been, even when I'd had no real magic. And the stronger my magic grew, the more it enthralled people. I had no idea why it did that. I'd never heard of anyone with glowing hair. The ability to make vampires—and now werewolves —want to bite me was apparently my special superpower. Lucky me.

"She's a woman," another mercenary told Big Belt, giving him a hard slap on the back. "Haven't you seen one of those before?"

Big Belt blinked, snapping out of the trance. His cheeks flushed red with embarrassment.

"Stop fooling around," said the biggest of the bunch, the flickering overhead lights dancing across his perfectly bald scalp. "She's just the right type." His eyes scanned me, dissecting my features one by one. "A bit old, but other- wise the right type. Bag her."

The right type? For what?

Slap Happy didn't give me much time to contemplate those questions. He was already closing in, his tree-trunk arms ready to grab me. The rest stood back and watched with cool detachment. Honestly, I'd have preferred at least two or three of the mercenaries to come at me. That would have allowed me to play them off one another, but I'd make do with what I had.

"What are you doing?" I asked, infusing my voice with panic. I backed up slowly.

Slap Happy's response was to lunge at me with a pair of handcuffs. I stepped aside and he stumbled past me.

"She's fast," he commented, glancing at the other mercenaries.

"You're just slow," I said, evading him again.

He tottered past me, and his hands bumped into a building. He turned away from the house, addressing me this time, "You're more trouble than you're worth."

"If I'm more trouble than I'm worth, then why don't you just leave me be?"

"No can do, darling. I've got orders."

"What orders?"

He grabbed at me, moving fast. But I was faster.

"Stop moving, you annoying girl," he grumbled.

"If you're annoyed now, just wait and see how annoying I'll be if you capture me," I said proudly to him. "Hours and hours of me talking. *Nonstop.*" I flashed him a grin.

He paused, looking like he was contemplating that. And he didn't like the thought of it at all.

"Just bag her already," Big and Bald told him.

Slap Happy didn't respond. He didn't move. I'd compelled him, locking him inside my siren magic.

Big and Bald pushed past his frozen comrade, moving to subdue me. Slap Happy swiveled around and jumped in front of me, shielding me with his body.

"What the hell are you doing?! Get out of the way!" Big and Bald shouted, shoving him aside.

Slap Happy caught his hands, heaved him over his head, and launched him across the street.

"He's been bewitched!" Big and Bald told the others, jumping off the pile of overturned trash cans. He pointed an accusatory finger at me. "*She* bewitched him."

"Not bewitched, but compelled. Not a witch but a siren," said the werewolf with the icy blue eyes.

The mercenaries were holding back, keeping their distance from me now. Sirens had an unsavory reputation of putting people under their spell by shattering their willpower. Werewolves didn't like the idea of weakness. In fact, most of them refused to acknowledge that they had any.

Big and Bald waved them forward. Slow and cautious, they surrounded me from all sides at once.

"Don't look at her," he told them. "That's how she put Gavin under her spell."

"Sirens don't just take control of your mind," Icy Blue said. "If you make eye contact with them, they can turn you to stone."

I laughed. "Those are just stupid stories. And, fyi, I don't need to look at you to take control of your minds."

The jaws of my magic clamped down on Icy Blue's mind, locking it in my will. He turned around and joined Slap Happy in defending me. I'd planted one simple thought in their heads: that the fate of the Earth depended on their protecting me. It was an easy sell to their werewolf brains, feeding their innate desire to be heroes. I could take over all the other mercenaries' minds without shedding a drop of blood.

The werewolves had other ideas. The four of them shifted all at once. I felt my two defenders slipping away as the magic of the pack worked on them, as they connected minds and combined willpower to resist my compulsion. My spell popped, ripping like a satin sash torn to shreds. My two werewolves changed into beasts, no longer mine.

They charged at me from all sides. I cast a fire barrier around myself, cutting them off.

"What are you?" Icy Blue demanded as they all stalked

the border of my fire wall. "You can't have the powers of a siren and an elemental."

I'd never before heard a shifter talk in beast form. While I pondered that, one of the wolves jumped high. He was almost over my fire barrier, and then he would drop down right on top of me. I'd stolen their free will from them. They wouldn't bag me now; they'd tear me to shreds.

I extended the orange flames up into the air, swallowing the wolf. Then I froze the fire to ice. The wolf fell to the ground with a thump, encased inside an ice block.

The other five werewolves snarled, spittle flying everywhere as they bared their yellow fangs at me. They circled around in a tight formation, jumping at me from different sides, like five silver cannonballs. Unfortunately, my last spell had dissolved my fire shield, so nothing stood between me and them.

I dodged the wolves' lunges, grabbing a string of the downed festival lights. They were still sizzling with a residual jolt of Magitech. I poured my own magic down the translucent string. The lightning charge on the string grew stronger, crackling and snapping. Slashing it like a whip at the wolves, I zapped one of them unconscious. There was enough power hissing on that string to take down an elephant—or one of those dinosaurs that thrived on the Black Plains, for that matter.

I slashed and snapped, striking down more wolves, then tying them up in the sizzling string. Four down, two to go.

Only I couldn't see one of the wolves anywhere. His comrade knocked me down from behind. We wrestled and rolled across the dusty street. I was pretty strong, but unlike my opponent, I didn't have claws or fangs. Under normal circumstances, I could have shifted to even the odds, but I'd already expended a lot of magic fighting the mercenaries. The wolf had me pinned down, his snapping fangs mere inches from my face.

He yelped once, then collapsed in a heap on top of me. Pushing his unconscious body off of me felt like bench-pressing a brick house, but with a few grunts and a lot of swearing, I made it back on my feet. Bella stood a few paces away, glittery magic powder glowing on her hands.

"I'm so glad to see you," I told her. "Perfect timing."

"Don't celebrate yet. There's another one around here somewhere."

"He's on the roof of the grocery building," I muttered under my breath.

"How do you know?"

"I can hear him breathing."

"How do you want to do this?" she asked me.

"We go to—"

Above us, a gun fired off a single shot. A large, furry mass dropped to the ground and landed with a sickening thump on the cobbled road. I looked down at the dead werewolf—and the bullet hole in his head. How had he died from that? Like vampires, werewolves were pretty resilient. It took more than a single shot to the head to kill them.

"The wound looks wrong," Bella said beside me.

I inhaled deeply, picking up a harsh bitter scent. "Poison?"

"Likely."

Wires snapped and magic sizzled behind me. I looked back to find the three mercenaries I'd wrapped up so neatly in festival lighting had broken free. They were all in human form now, their magic expended. In unison, they drew their guns and aimed them at me. As gunfire echoed off the buildings, I grabbed Bella and jumped out of the way.

But the shots weren't for us. The five remaining werewolves lay on the ground, dead. I ran up to the rooftops, looking across the town to find the shooter who'd executed the mercenaries, but whoever it was, he was long gone. It was as though he'd vanished into thin air.

Frustration and anger twisted up inside my stomach. That shooter was linked to the bombing of my town, and he'd gotten away. I really wanted to punch something, but knocking holes into people's houses wouldn't help matters. So I hopped down and joined Bella in looking after the wounded.

"You were right, Leda," croaked the townie who'd asked me to do magic tricks just an hour ago. "Magic isn't a toy."

"No, it isn't," Calli said.

Relief flooded me. She was all right. There were a few noticeable scratches and bruises on her skin, but nothing Bella couldn't heal.

"Magic is a weapon," Calli continued, brushing slivers of wood off of her. "And it's dangerous."

I gave the townie a small vial of healing potion to drink. "Rest now. Give the potion time to work." I joined Calli.

"Have you seen Gin and Tessa?" she asked me.

"No. They were over by the dunking tank right before the explosion."

Bella walked up beside us, and we searched the debris pile that covered the spot where the dunking tank had once stood. We didn't find Tessa or Gin. We found a dozen dead paranormal soldiers instead.

"They were attacked," Calli stated.

Bella looked down on their mauled bodies. "Those wounds were made with knives, not claws."

A pained moan called out from beneath a wood board. I grabbed it and tossed it aside to reveal Brokers, the paranormal soldier I'd spoken to earlier. He was still alive.

"What happened?" I asked him as Bella grabbed her potion pack and tried to heal his injuries.

"Attacked," he croaked, wincing like it hurt to speak.

One of his ribs had broken through his chest. I glanced at Bella, who shook her head. His injuries were too severe. He didn't have long.

"Mercenaries?" I asked, even as Bella tried to save him. She refused to give up.

"Yes."

"Werewolves?"

"No, different mercenaries," he choked out weakly. "Not sure what they were." His hand gripped my shoulder and he met my eyes. "The mercenaries took them."

"Who?"

"All the young ladies between the ages of seventeen and nineteen."

I looked around, frantically searching for my sisters. "My sisters?" I said.

His chest shook, and he coughed up blood.

"Tessa and Gin?" I asked, my heart racing.

"Gone," he said, his voice like the drop of a coffin lid. "The mercenaries took them and fled across the Black Plains."

CHAPTER 6

SHIFTING REALITY

*A*s Bella healed the wounded, I brought Calli up to speed on our encounter with the werewolf mercenaries.

"Why did the shooter on the roof kill them?" I finished. "What was he afraid of?"

"He was afraid the werewolves would be interrogated and give away something. Some information," Calli said.

"Like where Gin, Tessa, and the other kidnapped people are being taken. And who is behind this kidnapping."

Calli nodded. "Right."

"One of the werewolves is still alive," Bella called to us.

We joined her beside the mercenary I'd frozen inside an ice block. He'd shifted back into human form, but that hadn't helped him break free. His limbs were still trapped. I glanced at the bullet frozen inside the block. It hadn't been able to penetrate the magic ice. As Bella excavated the bullet, Calli turned her eyes on the werewolf. Her jaw was set, her mouth hard. She'd put on her interrogation face.

"Your allies abandoned you," she said. "They turned on

you and your pack. They tried to kill you all. They mostly succeeded. You're the only one who survived."

His jaw clenched up.

"You are obviously hired guns. Why be loyal to your employer when they were going to kill you to clean up their mess?" Calli asked him.

The man said nothing. What would inspire such loyalty in a mercenary? Why protect someone who'd turned on them?

"He won't talk." I could see it in his eyes.

"He'll talk," Calli assured me. "With the right pressure."

"You're little girls playing at a man's game," the mercenary sneered at us. What a gentleman.

Calli glared at him.

"Run away now before you get hurt," he said, grinning.

"We don't leave family behind," I told him, snapping my magic around him.

His grin wilted and he croaked out a choking noise.

"What's your name?" I was done taking it easy. This was brute force magic.

"Gideon," he said between clenched teeth.

"And the name of your pack?"

"The Whitefire Wolves."

Cute name.

"You're with the Legion." As he said the words, his eyes widened, terror taking hold of him.

I smiled. "That's right."

So he'd recognized the technique I was using, the Legion way. Maybe he'd been questioned by Legion Interrogators before. They weren't the nicest people, but they sure knew how to break people. And they liked their siren magic hard and cold.

"Why did the Whitefire Wolves abduct people from Purgatory?" I asked.

His shoulders shook under the strain of his resistance.

"Why did the Whitefire Wolves abduct people from Purgatory?" I repeated, tightening the screws on his mind. I had to do it; I had to be tough, to be vicious and cold. It was the only chance I had of saving my sisters and all those other young ladies.

He was biting down so hard on his lower lip that it was dripping blood.

"Why, Gideon?" I pushed harder. I could feel his will breaking under the hammer of my magic.

"We were hired to capture them," he ground out, still fighting.

Obviously.

"Who hired you?" I asked.

He shook his head.

I hit him with my magic again. His defenses shattered, and his body went limp.

"They want lots of young people," he said. "They hired us and another mercenary group to come here to Purgatory and get them."

Now we were getting somewhere.

"Why do they want these young people?" I asked him.

"I don't know. We were hired to capture them, not ask questions."

"So you came here and took these young people from their families, not caring what happened to them. You're a horrible person," I told him in disgust.

"I know." It was honesty, not an apology. I could feel it inside of him—he didn't feel the least bit guilty.

"Where are you bringing your victims?" I asked.

"To a meeting point on the Black Plains. The Doorway to Dusk."

Talk about far off. The Doorway to Dusk was halfway across the Black Plains. No one in their right mind ever went beyond the wall, let alone ventured so far out on the plains of monsters. What nefarious scheme were the mercenaries' employers hatching? And who the hell were these people?

"Who hired you?" I asked him.

"I don't know."

"Who hired you?" I repeated, putting more steel into my voice, and more power behind my magic.

"I don't know."

"I don't believe you." I pushed hard, my adrenaline pumping as my blood burned through my veins. His will was no match for mine. "Who hired you?"

"I don't know," he said, coughing.

No, he knew. He was holding it back, fearing for himself, for his pack. Fearing for what would happen if their client found out he'd confessed everything to the Legion of Angels. Well, he should have feared me more. I would not allow my sisters and those other young people to be sold off like they were things.

I clamped down harder with my magic. One way or another, I was going to force the answers out of him.

"Leda," Bella said gently.

I snapped out of my rage to see that the werewolf was spasming. And then he was dead. Just like that. I froze, my high crashing, my magic falling. Shock—shock at what I had done—washed away the fire inside of me, leaving me chilled.

Calli set her hand on my arm. "He was dead anyway,

Leda. His wounds were too severe. Bella couldn't save him."

But I had sped along his demise. The horror of that was eating away at me.

"You were just trying to save the mercenaries' prisoners," Calli said.

This wasn't the first time I'd crossed the line for the greater good, to save the innocents from this world of monsters. Did my actions make me the real monster in this story?

I could justify my actions all I wanted, and eventually maybe I'd even be able to convince myself that I'd had the best intentions at heart. But I couldn't justify the magic high, the rush of adrenaline, of absolute power that I'd felt burning inside of me as I'd cracked his mind and forced him to spill his secrets to me. And I couldn't shake the feeling that I was made just for this, like it was my destiny. My birthright. The feeling that this was as things should be, that I was right at home in these cruel acts—that scared me even more than the acts of interrogation I'd committed.

But now was not the time to be lost. I had to hold myself together if we had any chance of finding Tessa and Gin. Man, it felt like I was always running from one catastrophe to the other, always justifying that I would worry about the implications of my actions later.

Except later never came. I was just thrown into the next disaster, and those concerns—those debates of morality, of what was right and wrong, of what was justified or not—just fell to the wayside. They were pushed further and further into the future until they were completely forgotten, until I'd crossed the line so long ago that when I looked back, I couldn't even see it anymore. And I could no longer remember what I was so torn up about.

I didn't want to be that person.

"Why would someone hire a band of mercenaries to kidnap teenagers from Purgatory?" Bella wondered.

"There have been similar kidnappings recently," Calli said. "The common culprit is vampires. Some of them are addicted to the sweet taste of young blood. They have large appetites and very little self control. Within a few weeks, they drain their victims dry."

"That's horrible," Bella said.

"It's not only horrible. It's highly illegal," I told her. "The gods' laws always trump any other rules. That gives me all the authority I need to interfere and get Gin and Tessa back. We're going after them."

There was some old, obscure Legion rule that allowed me to recruit civilians in times of emergency. A few dozen abducted humans was a pretty big emergency as far as I was concerned. And I didn't have time to wait for the Legion to send a team. The mercenaries were getting away with the prisoners *now*. I had to stop the transfer before it happened and the buyers disappeared.

The old Legion rule was probably back from the days shortly after the Scourge, when the Legion was new and small, but I didn't care. If they couldn't be bothered to remove the rule, I was going to use it.

"We'll get them back," Calli said.

I looked at Bella. "You don't have to come."

Bella had never been a fighter. She wasn't someone who chased after trouble. She didn't try to grab danger by the tail and run with it.

"They are my sisters too. I'm coming," she told me, her voice ringing with conviction.

"Leda!"

I turned, watching Sheriff Wilder push through the

crowd that had gathered around us. "Carmen was one of the girls taken." His voice shook. "I'm coming with you."

Distressed and desperate, Carmen's father had the sort of look in his eyes that screamed he had nothing to lose. If I let him come with us, he would take crazy risks that might just get us all killed.

"You need to stay here and keep order in town," I said gently.

"I—"

"We'll get Carmen back," I promised him.

The commotion had drawn the Pilgrims out of their temple. They were staring at the horrible scene of destruction, solemn looks on their faces.

I marched up to the Pilgrim who'd showed us to the Legion room earlier. "I am Lieutenant Pierce of the Legion of Angels."

As soon as I said the words, it was like I was a completely different person to him. I wasn't a trouble-maker. I was a holy soldier touched by the gods' magic. A Legion soldier of my level wasn't all that common. Not many people survived so many doses of Nectar. After all, it was the strongest poison on Earth—a poison that literally killed you or made you stronger.

"What can I do for you, Lieutenant?" Not a hint of disgust tainted his tone. His words were professional and polite, even reverent.

"Bring the Legion truck around," I instructed him. "We're heading out to the Black Plains."

CHAPTER 7

THE HORDE

*W*e passed under the wall and drove out onto the Black Plains, rolling over scorched earth and blackened fields. The place looked like it had been hit by one enormous bolt of lightning. I let Calli drive. My mind was too preoccupied, too busy with thoughts of what had happened with the werewolf mercenary.

Back in my days living in Purgatory, life had been simpler. Back then, my biggest worry had been whether I would survive a dangerous job I'd taken so my family could eat. I hadn't dealt with these bigger issues of the soul, the fear that I had lost myself.

"Leda, you sure have learned to take charge," Calli commented, bringing me out of my thoughts. "When you talked to Sheriff Wilder back there, you were literally glow-ing. You looked so alive, so in your element. This is who you are. It is your destiny."

She sounded proud—but also sad. And her words reminded me once again of how much I was changing.

Calli glanced sidelong at me from the driver's seat. "You're worried."

"Yes. Who hires a team of mercenaries to abduct teenagers? The sort of people I don't want to have my little sisters, that's who."

"We'll get them back," Calli told me.

"Hopefully, before it's too late."

"Gin and Tessa are tough. Tessa is so resourceful that I have her do all our shopping. I can't believe the deals she gets."

An image flashed into my head—that of Tessa with pink shopping bags dangling from her arms, each one filled with medical supplies, ammunition, and machine parts.

"And Gin has a good, level head. She's been working in the garage, keeping the Magitech and vehicles for Pandora's Box in good order."

Pandora's Box was the bounty hunter company Calli had started long ago. Last year, I'd been preparing to take over from her, but then Zane was taken, and all our plans went to hell.

"I'm sorry about the burden I put on you by leaving," I told Calli. "I wish I could help more. If you would just take some money—"

"That's your money, Leda," Calli said, her jaw hard.

"I don't need it. But if you take it, you can improve your lives. You don't need to work in these conditions. You don't need to live in constant danger out here. Take the money. It's the least I can do for you after all that you've done for me."

"I never wanted you to take the burden of the whole world on your shoulders," said Calli.

I didn't tell her about the bounties I funded for them.

"Believe me, neither do I. The whole world just keeps falling apart whenever I'm around, and so I sort of feel obligated to put it back together."

"You certainly have a knack for attracting trouble," Calli chuckled.

"Once we get the girls back, you all can come to New York and get an apartment," I pushed on. "At least there I can look out for you. At least there you'll be safe."

"Your heart is in the right place, Leda, but no one is safe. Not as long as monsters walk the Earth." Her expression softened. "And the monsters aren't confined to the wild lands."

She was referring to the recent threat in New York, when Stash's army of supernaturals had tried to take over the world. And she had a point. Nowhere on Earth was completely safe, at least not as long as humanity was caught in the middle of this war of gods and demons.

"Besides, I can't abandon the people of Purgatory, not as long as the district lords rule," she told me.

"I know."

"Don't feel bad about leaving, Leda. You made the ultimate sacrifice. You left your whole life to join the Legion, not knowing if you would survive the gods' gifts of magic that kill so many. And you did all of it to save Zane."

"Lately, I've been wondering… well, is it really so much of a sacrifice? My life is nice. Sure, there's danger, but I actually like what I do. I like solving big problems. I like making a difference. I like my friends."

"And your angel," Bella said.

"Yes." I sighed. "I'm so selfish."

"You're not selfish for wanting to live a little," said Calli.

"I've been having trouble with telekinesis, the next ability. It isn't coming to me, no matter how much I train. It's like I'm blocked."

"You'll get through it," Calli said with confidence.

"See, that's not the point. Maybe I'll figure it out and maybe I won't, but the Legion won't put me through the next ceremony until I'm ready."

"So?"

"So there's no consequence to me for failure," I replied. "It's somehow too easy, too cushy of a life for me. I've become complacent."

"You're the first person I've ever heard refer to life at the Legion as 'cushy'."

"You've been working harder than anyone, pushing yourself, leveling up like no one else," Bella added.

Except Jace was leveling up faster. Even knowing that he was the son of an angel and had all those magic genes to help him, I couldn't help but feel guilty, like I could be doing more.

"What is blocking me from reaching the next level?" I wondered. "Can I *even* reach the next level? Most Legion soldiers never go this high. What if this is it? What if I've sped up the ranks only to hit a wall that I can't power through? What if this is the end of my potential? What if I fail Zane?"

"This isn't the end, Leda," said Calli. "It's just a challenge, something to overcome. Not everything comes easily. You just need to figure out what's wrong and how to solve it."

I wasn't sure I could figure it out, but I wasn't giving up. That's how Calli had raised us all. She hadn't taught us to be quitters.

A shrill shriek echoed across the plains, cutting through my thoughts like a bolt of lightning. Tiny dark dots danced across the barren field, and they were moving fast toward us. Like a stream, the dots took a wide loop around our truck. Now that they were closer, I got a better look at them. Each black dot was a small, raptor-like dinosaur with long claws and pointy teeth. Together, they made up a pack of a few dozen monsters. Swirling closer, moving as a perfect swarm, they watched us with vicious, hungry eyes, fully prepared to tear us apart.

One of the raptors leapt at the truck. It landed on the door, its claws scratching across the metal body. I hit it with a gust of air magic. The raptor went flying, bowling over a section of its own pack.

Agitated, the monsters let out a collective shriek that made my eardrums scream in pain. I took a closer look at them. The monsters' skin had an iridescent glow to it, like it wasn't completely opaque. A pulsing light shone from within, the light of their magic. What kind of magic was that?

I got my answer when one of the raptors opened up its mouth and spat a fireball at us. Calli jerked the steering wheel hard, swerving to avoid the flames.

"Since when can raptors spit fire?" I spun my sword around, slashing apart the next monster that launched itself at the truck.

"Lately, the monsters here are mutating, breeding with other monsters," Calli explained. "They are evolving faster than ever before."

I continued to slash at the dinosaurs. Charged with lightning magic, my blade cut right through them. "Evolving into what?"

"I don't think any of us want to find out," Calli said darkly.

The final raptor dropped dead to the ground, but we had little time to celebrate. Again, an ear-splitting shriek tore across the plains. Another pack of raptors was coming.

Except it wasn't just a single pack, I realized as I looked

across the plains. It was many packs. They covered the blackened fields before us, stretching out to the horizon. There were over a hundred of them, and they were charging straight at us. I wouldn't be able to take them out one by one. They'd tear us apart long before that.

I turned to Bella. "I have an idea. Do you have a flood potion?"

It would take too much of my magic to create a whole flood. There was no water nearby, so I had nothing to draw on but my own magic. It was much easier to redirect a river than it was to create one from scratch.

"I do. Well, it's more of a puddle than a flood. A big puddle," she added quickly.

"Big enough to cover all those monsters?"

"If they stand really close together. And don't move at all." She gave me an apologetic look.

I glanced at the monster horde. There sure were a lot of them.

"How long do you need them to stand still so the flood can cover them?" I asked Bella.

Bella looked at the field of monsters too. "Fifteen seconds." Her voice shook a little. "Twenty for maximum coverage."

I took a deep breath, then told Calli, "Keep driving at them. Right before we hit the horde, swerve off."

"Only you would try to play chicken with a horde of dinosaurs," she said in disbelief, but she kept driving straight at the monsters.

The raptors were getting close. I could smell the acidic tang of their breath. Closing my eyes, I reached for their minds. They popped up in my head like tons of tiny lights in a sea of blackness. Taking a long, slow breath, I snatched their minds, locking them inside my siren magic. One by one, I crushed their wills. My magic rippled across the horde, starting fast but then slowing as I met resistance. It hurt like a hammer to the head to hold so many monsters' minds at once, but I kept pushing on. The monsters were slowing down.

"How are you doing this?" Bella gasped in wonder.

I couldn't answer. I was putting all my power, all my concentration, into grabbing the monsters' minds and overriding their will to fight. Nero had once told me that it was easier to control someone or something if you moved with the flow, working with their nature and their instincts rather than fighting against them.

Well, there was no way around that with these raptors. This was an uphill battle, a fight against their very nature. They wanted to kill me and my family. They wanted to swarm us and rip the flesh from our bones. They didn't want to stop charging at us. Raptors were hyper, agitated monsters. They couldn't ever sit still. They were always moving, running, twitching, tearing. Making them stop in their tracks was as easy as making it snow in the scorching desert.

"Get ready to throw the potion," I said through clenched teeth. My head was pounding so hard I thought it would split open.

"Leda, your nose," Bella said.

I wiped away the blood dripping out of my nose. "No matter." I kept conquering the monsters' minds, winking out their willpower. Almost there.

And then, just like that, all the monsters suddenly stopped. They were frozen, suspended in time. The lands were silent, all but the roar of our truck. We were almost upon them, but they didn't move. They didn't even blink.

They looked like dozens of statues someone had placed on the plains.

But underneath their plaster-like facades, I could feel their minds pushing and clawing at me, trying to break free. If my plan didn't work, the beasts would explode out of my spell and tear us apart with all that bottled-up angry energy.

"Now!" I shouted.

Bella tossed the potion. The bottle landed in the center of the dinosaur army, shattering. A pool of clear water swelled up beneath the beasts' feet, slowly spreading outward even as it grew higher.

Calli swerved the truck away.

Turning, swirling, the whirlpool consumed the statuesque raptors. Soon, they were all caught in the whirlpool. I lifted my hand in the air, drawing on the lightning magic in the dark storm clouds above. The clouds swelled, growing heavier, darker, even as the pressure in the air grew thicker.

I unleashed all that magic at once, crashing down bolt after bolt into the whirlpool, electrocuting the raptors. The whirlpool stopped spinning a few seconds later and washed out across the plains.

Calli stopped the truck and we just all stared at the blast radius of my spell. The ground was burnt black and peppered with dead black raptors. Not a single monster had survived.

The crisis over, I slouched down into my seat, exhausted.

Calli drove us onto the old, broken road once more. The truck thumped and shook as the wheels rolled over the dinosaur graveyard.

"Where did you learn to control monsters?" Calli asked

me after a few minutes of silence. "That's not a Legion thing."

"No, it's pretty much a *me* thing."

"I didn't know such a thing was possible."

"According to the gods, it's not supposed to be possible. If they found out, they'd probably kill me. Or study me." I yawned. My head felt so heavy. Using all that magic had drained me down to the bone.

Calli glanced at me. "No one is killing you, kid. Not on my watch. You rest your eyes for a bit."

"Thanks," I muttered, closing my eyes, drifting into sleep.

In my dreams, the ground opened up beneath us and swallowed the truck. We fell into the fiery pits of hell, where a dark angel tried to convince us to part with our truck for five dollars. But Calli wouldn't take anything less than twenty dollars. They eventually settled on ten dollars, but the dark angel had to throw in a pack of Venom beer to sweeten the deal.

The dark angel and I were shaking hands on the deal. His grip was so tight I thought he'd pull my arm off.

I jumped awake. Torn out of the dream, I looked around wildly. My hand moved toward my sword.

I looked down at Calli's hand on my shoulder. I relaxed. She'd shaken me awake.

I rubbed the sleep from my eyes. "Status?"

Calli smirked, then she said in a very no-nonsense voice, "We've arrived at the edge of the Doorway to Dusk, Lieutenant. I've parked us out of sight so we can approach undetected on foot. With your permission, of course."

"Cute," I said, snickering.

Her eyes twinkled at me.

We all climbed out of the truck and began hiking up

the rocky path. When we reached the crest of the hill, we looked down, staying low to the ground. In the rocky valley below, a group of prisoners were chained to a cluster of boulders. Mercenaries surrounded them. They were everywhere. And every single one of them was armed to the teeth.

CHAPTER 8

DOORWAY TO DUSK

I counted six teams of mercenaries, each team identifiable by their distinct outfits.

With their long, pencil-straight hair, the vampires were certainly living up to their image. Some wore it in high ponytails, others in a whiplike braid; a few wore it down long. There were two teams of vampires, one group dressed in crimson leather bodysuits and one in maroon.

The group of elemental mercenaries wore boots over dark camouflage print pants, and crisscrossing, second-skin tank tops.

The witches were decked out in designer sportswear: tiny shorts and spaghetti straps for the ladies, muscle tanks and surfer shorts for the guys.

Like the shifters I'd fought in Purgatory, the ones here were wearing an even mix of leather and denim.

There was even a group of human mercenaries, all dressed in head-to-toe black.

This—whatever *this* was—had to be a huge operation, much bigger than a single isolated incident.

"They're late," the elemental leader complained.

"Why are you looking at me?" replied the crimson vampire leader. "We have nothing to do with the were-wolves." He turned up his proud vampire nose. It was the sort of nose you'd see on a magazine cover, or on the face of a prince. The vampire looked at the other shifters. "Where are your brethren?"

"Brethren?" the shifter leader said, offended. "We're not werewolves either."

"They're tigers," said a witch with a high-pitched voice. She plugged her nose. "You can tell from the smell."

The tiger shifter glared at the witch. "Watch yourself, little girl." He plucked the strap of her stretchy sport over-alls. "You wouldn't want to end up dangling from that tree over there."

A vampire rolled his eyes. "Oh, how original. A leather-bound meathead shifter making threats." He yawned loudly.

"You're sure one to point fingers, you walking stereo-type," a shifter retorted. "He indicated the vampire's outfit and hair. "All that's missing are the fangs."

The vampire flashed him a pearly-white smile. "You really want to see my fangs?"

"Please, no. I just ate," an elemental said.

The mercenaries all began talking at once, exchanging insults. This behavior was actually quite common between different supernatural groups. Even on a good day, they didn't play well together. On a bad day, they were one insult away from open warfare. The human mercenaries just watched them in silence.

"How much longer must we be kept waiting?" a female witch complained. "When will our mystery clients present themselves?"

A shifter put on a big smile. "What's the matter, pumpkin? Scared out here on the big, bad plains?"

The witch looked at him for a moment, disgust crinkling her brow. "No, *pumpkin*. I just want to get paid and move on to more profitable ventures." Her lips curled. "But if the howls of the wilds frighten you, curl up over here at my heels. I could use a pet kitty."

The shifter growled at her.

She clicked her tongue. "Temper, temper, pussycat."

Somewhere far out on the Black Plains, a monster howled. The mercenaries grew quiet, listening to see if there would be a followup—and if it was moving closer. When no other monster made itself heard, one of the elementals looked around, shivering.

"This place sits on unholy land," he said.

"I hate to break it to you, but *all* of the plains of monsters are unholy lands," said a vampire in crimson. "If the prospect of being eaten by a ten-foot hairy beast disturbs you, you'd best seek out a different line of work. A nice cushy desk job perhaps." He sneered. "I hear accountants are in high demand in the city."

"It's not just the monsters," the elemental told him. "The wilds are haunted by vengeful phantoms and spirits, the tormented souls of the people who died hundreds of years ago when monsters overran the Earth, when our world was torn apart by the war between heaven and hell."

"This place is particularly unholy," agreed another elemental. "Everything feels off. The elements are all out of whack here. They're all mixed and muddled, interfering with our spells."

"The sooner this business is settled, the sooner we can get out of here," the first elemental declared, sounding anxious.

"If this place bothers you so much, you go on ahead," a shifter told her. "We'll send your money along to you." He grinned.

She rolled her eyes. "Do I look like an idiot?"

"Is that a serious question?" a witch asked.

"What you and your elementals look like are superstitious, scared little girls," said a female vampire mercenary in maroon.

"Look at that manic twitch in her eye," a male elemental said to his teammates. "It looks like she's been sampling the local cuisine too much."

In other words, drinking the blood of monsters. It wasn't an advisable diet, even for vampires. Monster blood was unbalanced, unhinged—just like the monsters. It also tended to be incredibly poisonous.

"I'll open up your throat and sample *you* if you don't stop running your mouth," the female vampire shot back.

The elementals all snickered.

The vampire rushed toward them. She didn't make it far. The vampire maroon leader stepped into her path and punched her so hard that she flew twenty feet and crashed into the boulders. She got to her feet dizzily, her steps unbalanced.

"You're embarrassing yourself," the maroon vampire leader snapped. "And worse yet, you're embarrassing me. Talk to them again, and I'll feed *you* to the monsters."

The vampire nodded, silent and solemn.

"Charming folks," I commented to Bella and Calli.

"Indeed," Calli agreed. "So how about while they're waiting for their buyers to arrive, we steal their prisoners out from beneath their bickering noses?"

I smiled. "Nothing would please me more."

"How are we supposed to get to the prisoners?" Bella

asked. "The mercenaries aren't taking their eyes off of them."

"Don't worry," I told her. "I have a plan."

———

CREEPY SMOKE and fog floated across the rocky valley to a soundtrack of eerie howls and tortured moans. Dry leaves whistled over the low creak of aged wood.

Bella had really outdone herself this time. She'd created these visual and sound effects with a creative mixture of potions. She was setting the mood. Now it was our job to seal the deal.

A series of wet splats—raw flesh against water—clapped across the ground, and a grotesque zombie emerged from the fog. It was Calli. I'd cast a shifting spell on her to change her from human to monster. I'd taken a lot of creative liberty with her appearance, and the end result was positively disgusting. Loose, discolored skin melted off her face and arms like wax from a candle. Pus oozed from the lacerations that covered her torso. As she walked, she left behind a long line of bloody footprints. All in all, Calli looked like a moaning, oozing, slopping piece of melted and torn flesh.

As soon as they saw her, the superstitious elementals froze. Their fear was thick in the air. I drew on my siren magic to grow the elementals' panic, feeding it back on itself. Their anxiety spread, infecting the other mercenaries. They all looked at one another—then they ran for their lives.

But we couldn't let them get away. We needed answers. I split the earth beneath their feet. Half of the mercenaries managed to sidestep the pits, but the rest of them tumbled in, unable to catch themselves. Green vines shot out of the ground, coiling around their bodies.

As Bella continued the special effects to embellish the deception, Calli moved to block the remaining mercenaries. If her grotesque appearance didn't stop them, a bullet to the leg did.

While Calli and Bella dealt with the mercenaries, I made my way to the prisoners. A few brave mercenaries still guarded them. Unsurprisingly, it was the group of human mercenaries who'd been too professional to join in the insult tournament earlier. They were too shrewd to scare so easily.

Silent and unseen, I snuck up on them and knocked them out with my magic. Most humans had zero magic resistance, so I almost felt bad about doing it. But then I reminded myself that they were working for someone who kidnapped teenagers, and my guilt evaporated.

I hurried over to the prisoners and snapped their restraints. They watched me with wide eyes, completely terrified.

"Don't worry," Carmen told her fellow prisoners. "Leda is a soldier in the Legion of Angels, and she's here to save us all."

Relief washed across their faces, coupled with a touch of awe and a pinch of fear. But it was a good fear, as though they liked the taste of a little danger—as long as that danger was on their side. Legion soldiers had a fearsome reputation for upholding the gods' order with an iron fist. When we came to save you, though, you knew whoever had you, no matter how scary they were, would fall. The Legion of Angels gave your greatest nightmares some nightmares of their own.

I scanned the group of prisoners. There were about

twenty teenagers, but Carmen was the only one I knew by name. There were a few other girls I'd seen around in Purgatory—and there were a lot of girls and guys I'd never seen in my life. My little sisters, however, were nowhere to be found.

"Where are Tessa and Gin?" I asked Carmen.

"Another group of mercenaries took them away, along with some other prisoners," Carmen told me. "They were already bought by a slave trader." Her fear and outrage reverberated in her words.

There was no slavery allowed on Earth according to the gods' laws, but out here on the plains of monsters, beyond the borders of civilization, these things happened far too often.

I led the prisoners into the fog, to where Bella was brewing a potion pot.

"You have to help Calli," she told me. "A bunch of the mercenaries have cornered her."

I went to the edge of the fog, peering out. The mercenaries had Calli surrounded, their weapons and magic aimed at her head. They didn't realize she was a person. They only saw the monster. And they were going to decapitate her. That was the surest way to kill a monster.

I darted out of the fog, knocking out a mercenary with a quick punch to the head. I ran back into the fog and circled around to strike at the next. One by one, I took them down, unseen, like a phantom. The fog swelled and swallowed them. Plants shot out of the ground like lassos, capturing and dragging the others to me.

"Good job, Leda," Calli said as the last mercenary fell to the ground. "Now if you don't mind, I'd like my own face back."

"Why? I think this look is good for you," I teased, even

as I removed the shifting spell from her. The monstrous trimmings dissolved from her body.

Calli and I tied up the unconscious mercenaries, then headed back to Bella and the prisoners.

We didn't make it more than two steps before an arrow shot through the air and plunged into the earth at our feet. Lightning sizzled across its shaft, a telltale sign of magic.

I scanned the ridge. A man in black danced down the near vertical wall toward us, his long cloak rippling in the wind. Another elemental mercenary? I'd not seen him with the others. Where had he come from?

I ran out to meet him, dodging the telekinetic blast he shot at me. No, not an elemental. He swung his sword at me, moving with the speed of a vampire. As he cast a shifting spell on my hand, merging it with my own sword, I came to one unhappy conclusion: only a Legion soldier possessed all those abilities in combination. And Legion soldiers didn't work with mercenaries and slave traders. He was a deserter.

A band of new arrivals jumped down the ridge, a hodgepodge of five different supernaturals. The telekinetic softened her companions' fall, then shot them at Bella and Calli. My sister threw a potion bottle at her feet, and a protective barrier went up around her and Calli. As they fought off the two werewolves, the telekinetic, the fire elemental, and the vampire, I concentrated on the fallen Legion soldier.

"So a Legion deserter left and started his own mercenary band," I commented, shaking off his shifting spell to free my hand.

"You can't tell me that you haven't considered the same." The deserter's eyes twinkled with devilish delight, like someone who'd been caught doing something naughty

ELLA SUMMERS

and was proud of it. If he hadn't been trying to kill me, I might have even described him as charming.

"Deserting the Legion?" I said as our swords clashed. "Not really."

"The poison they call gifts. Never knowing if you will survive the next sip, or the next battle. Watching all of your friends die around you. Or watching them move up and leave you behind." He set his sword on fire.

I froze my sword, countering his flames. "You're over-simplifying."

His dark brows arched. "Am I? What about the control over who you can love, over who your friends are?"

He hit me in the stomach with a telekinetic punch. It went through me like an iron ball through a piece of tissue paper. I cringed, enduring the pain. He studied my face, calculation gleaming in his eyes. He knew he'd found my weakness.

For some reason, though, he didn't press his advantage. Either he was playing with me, or he really liked to hear himself speak.

"But the biggest problem with the Legion is the angels," he said. "Those cold, cruel, sadistic monsters are far worse than any you find out here beyond the vicious veil of civilization."

"Who are you working for? Why are you kidnapping people?"

"I'm afraid I can't tell you that. All I can tell you is that we will change the world."

It was the tired line of only every criminal mastermind ever. Even so, at least he knew what was going on, unlike the clueless werewolf I'd questioned in Purgatory. I just had to pull at the right end, and the whole plot would unravel at my feet.

"How will you change the world?" I asked him.

He flashed me a grin. "You can't compel me."

I wouldn't bet on it.

The iron gates of his mind slammed shut, and I was too busy fighting him to try to break through them.

He was very good. He could wield telekinetic magic, so he must have been at least a level six soldier before he'd deserted the Legion. And he was well-trained—faster, stronger, and far more experienced than I was.

But he didn't fight dirty like I did. Though he'd left the Legion, his Legion training hadn't left him. He fought like a proper and dignified soldier in the gods' army, not like a down and dirty mercenary.

He stood behind me, his arms locked around my body like a cage, pinning my arms to my sides. But I still had my feet. I shot my magic down my body, straight through my foot. An icy spike shot out of my heel, and I slammed that heel down on his foot. Like it was made of steel, the ice spike punctured his boot. He roared in pain. I slammed my icy heel down again, this time cutting through the other foot. A sheet of ice spread over the ground. His grip loosened.

I broke free and spun around, hammering my fists against the sides of his head. He stumbled back, disoriented. I ran at him, intending to finish the job and knock him out, but he darted away. His footsteps were so fast that they almost seemed to float over the ground.

"You're as good as they say, Leda Pierce," he told me. "Don't throw your life away fighting for the wrong team."

Then he snatched a potion bottle from his belt and threw it at his feet. Glass shattered, shrouding everything in a sparkling purple mist. When the smoky amethyst tendrils cleared, the deserter was gone. And so was his team. Damn it.

A tiny click echoed off the rocks, then our truck exploded. I gaped at the burning remains of our vehicle that would never run again. The deserter was getting away, and we had no way to chase after him because he'd seen fit to blow up our truck. I stormed over to a boulder and punched a hole in it, venting my frustration. The agonizing pain was almost worth it.

"We caught a few guys from the other mercenary bands," Calli said, watching me cradle my hand.

I didn't want the other mercenaries. They were clueless pawns. I wanted the deserter. He knew something, and now he was gone.

"A fire elemental was wounded in the last fight. He didn't escape with the others," Bella told me.

Hope sparked in me. The fire elemental worked for the deserter. Maybe I would get my answers after all.

"Let's go have a chat with him," I said, joining Bella beside the wounded mercenary.

"He was knocked out by your ice spell," she explained, indicating the patches of frost covering his skin in icy swirls.

Elementals were weak against the opposing element. In the case of a fire elemental, that meant ice and water. I grabbed a potion bottle from my pouch.

"What is that?" Bella asked.

"Winter's Kiss."

Drinking it felt like swallowing a blizzard. I'd taken the potion back when I'd trained my elemental magic at Storm Castle, and it hadn't been a fun experience. It would be worse for him.

I pulled out a syringe. I didn't have the time to force

him to swallow it. I was going to inject the ice straight into his bloodstream.

The elemental jolted awake. His pulse pounded fast in my ears, a deafening, racing drumbeat.

"Who hired you to kidnap the girls?" I asked him.

He spat at my feet. Nice.

Smiling at him, I grabbed his wrists. Ice crystals formed there, creeping higher up his arms. He shook, trying to break free, but I was stronger than he was—and I wasn't backing down. I couldn't shake the heavy, foreboding fear that my sisters were in great danger. I had to get to them.

"Let's try this again." My smile cut into my cheeks, even as my ice spell cut through him, mixing with the potion to chill his blood. "Who hired you to kidnap teenagers from the Frontier towns?"

His skin was turning blue. I brushed my siren magic against him, warm and inviting. It whispered soothing promises into his ear. He shook, resisting.

So I turned up the cold. I felt a tiny spark—a pop!—the moment his mind broke. His defenses folded and he let me into his mind. Wrapping my siren magic around him like a warm blanket, I repeated the question.

This time he answered. "Arius Hardwicke hired us to kidnap the teenagers. We sold them to him."

Arius Hardwicke? I had no idea who that was.

Calli supplied the answer. "Arius Hardwicke is a slave trader." Disgust and anger washed across her face as she added, "A prolific one. He has strongholds all over the world, each one hidden deep inside the plains of monsters."

What a swell guy.

"Where is Arius Hardwicke keeping the prisoners?" I demanded.

The fire elemental's face scrunched up. He was fighting me. I yanked the comforting blanket of my siren magic away, and the icy jaws chomped down on him once more.

"We brought them to Hardwicke's base at Crow's Crown," he said, shivering. "They are probably still there."

Crow's Crown. Those were some ruins further west, past the Black Plains, out on the vast, open, broken Field of Tears.

"And these two girls?" I pulled out a picture of Gin and Tessa and showed it to him. "What about them?"

His eyes widened. "They're special."

But he didn't mean 'special' in the same way Tessa and Gin were special to me.

"How are they special?" I asked him.

"Hardwicke asked for them especially."

"Why?"

"For their magic."

Magic? Aside from being a little faster and stronger than regular humans, Tessa and Gin had never shown any signs of magic. I looked at Calli for answers.

"Is he telling the truth?" she asked quietly.

"Yes."

Calli drew her gun and shot the mercenary right between the eyes. He dropped to the ground, dead. I blinked in shock.

There was a dark look on Calli's face, but before I could ask her what the hell was going on, blinding headlights rolled over us and a truck roared into the valley. It came to a stop right in front of us. I squinted, holding up my hand to see past the blinding glare. The truck was marked with the Legion's emblem.

The doors swung open, and Jace Fireswift stepped out. Tall and muscular, agile and fast, he was dressed in the uniform of a soldier in the Legion of Angels. Jace was my friend. He was also my biggest competition.

Jace stopped in front of me. "What are you doing here, Leda?"

"I'm on vacation."

His eyes scanned the bodies strewn across the ground, his brows lifting. "Vacation," he repeated drily.

"That's right."

His gaze flickered briefly to the dead man at my feet. What the hell had Calli been thinking?

"The others are still alive," I said quickly.

Jace sighed. "Here I am, finally the one on the important, world-changing mission, and I find you are at the center of it all. *Again*."

I glanced at the metallic pin with the emblem of a hand on his chest. It was the symbol of a captain in the Legion of Angels, a soldier of the sixth level. It meant he'd mastered the power of telekinesis, the ability that had completely stumped me.

Jace waved at his soldiers. They jumped out of the massive truck and began loading sleeping mercenaries into it.

"You're stealing my mercenaries," I complained.

"They're connected to my investigation."

"Which is?"

He looked at my family like they were as crazy as I was to be all the way out here. Then he began moving pointedly away from them. I walked beside him.

"We're tracking a Legion deserter and his team of mercenaries," he said in a low voice.

"I saw him."

"Of course you did. You're always at the center of everything."

"Believe me, Jace, I wish it weren't so. It's not as glamorous as it sounds. I can't even go on vacation without everything blowing up in my face."

He looked utterly unconvinced. I could tell from the wistful look on his face that he wished the trouble would find him, so he could sort it out and be a hero.

"What happened to the deserter?" he asked me.

"He and his band got away, except one."

"Let me guess. The one with the bullet in his brain."

"Unfortunately."

"Damn it, Leda. He might have known something. Something that would help me capture the deserter."

"I questioned him," I said.

"And?"

"I didn't get far."

Jace's soldiers had already loaded up the mercenaries. They were starting up the truck again.

"Where are you taking them?" I asked Jace.

"To the Legion Interrogators in Chicago."

"I'm coming along too," I insisted. "My mission is linked to yours. Somehow."

"Your *mission*?" He frowned. "I thought you were on vacation."

"I tried to go on vacation, but then mercenaries attacked my town, kidnapped people off the streets, and now here we are."

Jace looked at me for a moment, then said, "Very well. You might know something useful. Prepare your report."

I didn't tease him about how he was ordering me around, though I was tempted. Sure, he outranked me— right now—but that had never stopped me from teasing him before. After all, he was my friend. Ultimately, it was our friendship that compelled me to keep my mouth shut. I didn't want to make him look weak in front of his soldiers.

"You think you could give us a lift to Chicago?" I asked him.

His gaze fell over the remains of our truck. "You broke another one," he said, checking the disbelief in his voice.

"No, the deserter did that to cover his retreat. He didn't want anyone following him."

Jace shook his head. "Honestly, Leda, I don't know how you do it. I don't think there's been any soldier in the entire history of the Legion of Angels who's managed to destroy so much Legion property."

His soldiers weren't looking, so I figured it was safe to give his shoulder a friendly pat. "Don't worry, Fireswift. If you try really hard, you might just someday steal that honor from me."

Then I turned and walked to the truck, leaving him baffled.

CHAPTER 9

*T*he Doorway to Dusk was halfway between two Frontier towns, Purgatory and Infernal. The towns had such cheerful names out here. Calli, Bella, and I rode in Jace's truck all the way to Infernal—together with Jace's team, the captured mercenaries, and the rescued kidnap victims. The truck hadn't been designed to hold that many people, and Jace's soldiers didn't look pleased about all the elbows poking into their sides. I tried to cheer them up by singing a road song, but somehow that didn't help at all. Some people just wanted to be grumpy.

We weren't even attacked by monsters during the drive. They came close a few times, but all it took was a warning shot from the massive cannon on the top of the truck to convince the beasts that we weren't an easy meal.

At Infernal, we caught the train to Chicago. My family came along. They weren't allowed in the Legion train carriages. I was burning to ask Calli why she'd shot the fire elemental I'd been questioning, but I hadn't had the chance. During the drive, there had been Legion soldiers all around us, and now she and Bella were in a different part of the train, surrounded by civilians. This was something I had to do when we were alone.

I stepped inside the train carriage where Jace's men were guarding the prisoners. The soldiers watched me in stony silence as I passed through their carriage to the one behind it. There I found Jace alone, writing some reports.

I approached cautiously. I would have to be careful about what I said and how much I gave away. Jace was my friend, but he was also my superior now and very ambitious. I didn't completely trust him—and I definitely didn't trust his father.

Jace looked up. "Leda."

"You sure have a dour group of soldiers."

"Not everyone is as exciting as you are."

I wasn't sure whether he meant that as a compliment or a rebuke. From the look on his face, he wasn't so sure himself.

"What do you know about the kidnappings?" I asked him.

"What do *you* know?"

Nice trick. He wanted me to give up what I knew first. But two could play at that game.

"In other words, you know nothing," I said.

Jace stiffened. "You have to know that the details of my mission are classified."

"And you have to know that I could just ask Nero what you're up to." Nero had the highest clearance in the Legion, besides Nyx.

Annoyance flashed in Jace's eyes. I had him.

"There's no need to bother General Windstriker," Jace told me. "The deserter is named Balin Davenport, a former major in the Legion of Angels. He is trading in people, young ladies mostly. He sells them to vampires as slaves."

"Why young people?"

"People between the ages of seventeen and twenty are the most susceptible to being changed over into vampires, both physically and psychologically."

In other words, they were easily brainwashed. Children would be the easiest to brainwash, except children under sixteen didn't turn easily. Their bodies could not generally absorb vampiric magic.

"So the vampires aren't looking for dinner," I said. "They're looking for new recruits into their ranks."

"It would seem so."

"What do you know about Balin Davenport?" I asked him.

"Davenport was one of the first traitors the Legion of Angels had. He was a contemporary of my grandfather. Then one day he just disappeared without a trace. The Legion thought he was dead. It wasn't until they encountered his mercenary band years later that they realized he'd deserted. He's been running mercenary operations ever since."

"He's evaded capture for centuries?"

"Yes."

Jace didn't sound happy about it. Davenport was a black mark on the Legion name. He was out there, causing trouble, flaunting his disobedience of the gods' laws. He was a real hit to the Legion's pride. That was why Colonel Fireswift had sent his son to hunt him down. If Jace failed, everyone would blame his inexperience. If he succeeded, it would pave the way for him to become an angel. It was precisely the sort of plan Colonel Fireswift would come up with.

"Davenport isn't working alone," I said.

"No, he's working with a slave trader."

"Arius Hardwicke."

Jace's eyes narrowed. "You know a lot."

"I talked to one of Davenport's men. He told me."

"He told you all of this?"

"Of course. I'm a likable kind of gal." I smiled.

"Then how did the man you were questioning end up with a bullet in his head?"

My smile faded. "That wasn't supposed to happen."

I really needed to speak to Calli. What had gotten into her? I knew she'd killed people before, back in her days working for the League, but I'd never seen her shoot an unarmed man in the head.

Jace gave me a hard look. "What else did the mercenary tell you?"

"That they brought some of their kidnap victims to Hardwicke's base at Crow's Crown. We need to go there," I told him.

"We?"

"Yes, *we*. As we agreed."

"I never agreed to let you in on this mission. I said I would listen to your report. And give you a lift to Chicago because you managed to blow up your ride. Again."

I gave my hand a dismissive wave. "Technically, it was a rogue soldier who blew it up."

"If it hadn't been a rogue soldier, it would have been monsters or mercenaries or vampires."

"It's not my fault everyone's always trying to kill me," I said solemnly.

The corner of Jace's mouth twitched. "And just whose fault is it then?"

I didn't answer that.

"Tell me everything you know, and I promise I'll keep you up to date on the mission," he said.

"Not good enough. I'm coming with you. I'm going to see those kidnapped teenagers returned to their homes."

"That's not possible."

"Now that's just the excuse of a quitter," I told him. "Anything is possible if you just keep at it."

"Leda, you don't under—"

"Why don't you want me on this mission?" I demanded.

Was he so afraid that I'd try to steal his thunder? I didn't care about any of that. I just wanted to rescue my sisters and the other teenagers. He could have all the credit if he wanted.

"I don't want you on this mission because it's too personal for you," he said.

"What?"

"I spoke to the victims we rescued. One of them told me your little sisters were among the people still missing."

I planted my hands on my hips. "I don't see what that has to do with anything."

"Your priorities are wrong. Our goal is the capture of Balin Davenport. We have to stop him now. He isn't just a threat to the gods' order; he is a threat to our very way of life."

I couldn't believe what I was hearing. People were missing—young, scared, innocent people—and Jace was only concerned about bagging a deserter. He sounded just like his father.

"No, *your* priorities are wrong," I told him. "You should worry less about protecting the Legion's reputation and more about protecting the people of this Earth."

"This is about both. Before Davenport got involved, Hardwicke's hired guns weren't nearly as successful at kidnapping teenagers along the Frontier. Capturing the deserter means dealing the whole operation a mighty blow."

"I don't want to deal the operation a mighty blow. I want to blow it to smithereens. We're talking about human slavery here, Jace. That's not just against the gods' laws; it's *wrong*. On every level."

"And we'll take care of it," he said calmly. "First, we go after Davenport. Then we'll deal with Hardwicke. You need to have a little patience."

"Patience is for when you accidentally burn all your hair off and you have to wait for it to grow back. It's not for times like these," I shot back. "Davenport and Hardwicke are part of the same problem, and they're hiding in the same place. We go in together. You go after Davenport and his mercenaries, I go for Hardwicke and free his prisoners. Everyone gets what they want."

"The Legion of Angels isn't a store where you get to pick out the mission you want, Leda," he said gently. "But I'll see what I can do about putting you on the mission."

"That's all I ask."

"We'll have to talk to my father," he warned me.

"Whatever it takes."

Jace's father Colonel Fireswift was an angel, and pretty much my least favorite person on Earth. I wasn't looking forward to that meeting. Encounters with that angel never ended well. He'd done a lot of abhorrent things, including putting up soldiers for promotion that he knew full well would not survive the ceremony. That was his way of weeding out the weak in the Legion of Angels.

But if talking to Colonel Fireswift was my ticket to saving my sisters, then I'd do it a thousand times over. Sure, I could have gone off on my own, but if I really wanted to rescue all the kidnapped teenagers from a slave lord's fortress, I needed the Legion's resources.

CHAPTER 10

When the train pulled into Chicago, Calli and Bella hurried off to buy supplies in the city. They'd certainly need them if we were going to get Tessa and Gin back. This thing was big. Really big. It didn't feel as simple as some rogue vampires trying to grow their armies. The fire elemental I'd interrogated had mentioned my sisters' magic, how they'd been set apart because of it. There was something there. Calli had been tight-lipped so far, but sooner or later I was going to figure out what she was hiding.

Jace's team drove ahead with their mercenary prisoners, but he chose to walk to the Legion office. And I joined him. I'd been sitting still for too long.

"Why didn't you go with them?" I asked Jace.

"I like to walk the Promenade of the Gods when I come here," he told me. "It's a reminder of the gods' generosity, of their gifts of magic to us. And it's a reminder of their power. It's humbling to feel so small in front of the gods and their temples."

"Perhaps your father should visit this place to humble himself."

"He does." Jace's eyes twinkled. "But it doesn't help."

Chuckling, we entered the Promenade, a lakeshore path that led past seven sparkling skyscrapers, each one a monument to one of the ruling gods.

The first was the Temple of Valora, the Queen Goddess. Diffused light reflected off the stone walls. As the clouds rolled past, revealing the sun, the building seemed to change color completely, adjusting to the new light and weather conditions. The building was very regal, an example of tasteful opulence at its best.

The second temple we passed along the Promenade had been constructed in honor of Ronan, Lord of the Legion of Angels, God of War, God of Earth's Army. Between its high towers, thick castle walls, and retractable drawbridge, it looked like a military fortress. The building had a life to it, a vibrance. That life buzzed against my skin, a constant hum.

"Parts of the castle can be rearranged for different purposes," Jace explained, looking up at the skyscraper temple. "But Lord Ronan tends to prefer the battle-ready look."

The third temple was that of Faris, the God of Heaven's Army. Beautiful, bright, and white, it looked like a little slice of heaven on Earth. In the gardens that surrounded the outer walls of quite possibly the most upscale high-rise apartment building on the planet, diamonds dripped from gold trees like icicles, jingling like silver sleigh bells.

Next came the Temple of Meda, Goddess of Technology. The skyscraper was a single gigantic clock tower, accented with exposed gold and bronze gears that made delightful clinks as they moved. Mechanical sculptures of all kinds, including a set of moving metal statues in a fountain, decorated the front lawn.

The fifth temple belonged to Meda's sister Maya, the Goddess of Healing. Big red climbing roses grew up the sparkling walls. The skyscraper look like a fairy castle in a romantic fairytale forest.

The Temple of Zarion, God of Faith and Lord of the Pilgrims, was the sixth one along the Promenade. Tall, dark, and dramatic, it looked like a gothic monastery. Hymns poured out of the open windows, the beautiful, eerie voices raised in song.

Finally, we came to the Temple of Aleris, God of Nature. His skyscraper was a building of opposing elements and reminded me a lot of Storm Castle and the Elemental Plains it sat upon, where all the elements were represented. Fire lanterns lined the path to the enormous front double doors. Koi fish swam peacefully through gentle streams with wooden bridge arches. Wind chimes sang silver songs, and pinwheels hung from the trees. These weren't simple children's pinwheels, however; they were elaborate magical constructions, woven by a master elemental. And magic light glistened over it all, soft and sparkling. Every blade of grass, every leaf, every petal was perfect. Nothing was wilted or yellowed or broken. Everything existed in perfect harmony.

My phone buzzed in my pocket. I pulled it out to find a message from Nero. *Are you safe?*

He must have heard about the explosion in Purgatory.

I'm fine, I wrote back

Where are you?

Where are you? I asked.

On a mission.

Same, I typed out.

Where are you? Nero asked again.

Snickering, I wrote back, *Where are you?*

There was a pause. Then a block of text popped up on my screen. *I will find out what mayhem you are up to, Pandora.*

If text messages could glower, his would have. Honestly, I was kind of shocked my phone hadn't exploded yet.

I speedily typed out, *Don't get your feathers in a twist, General.*

I was about to tuck my phone back into my sweatshirt when it buzzed again. I looked at the screen and found a message from Harker this time.

Stop flirting with Nero, Leda. It's distracting him.

I'm not flirting, I told him.

Keeping secrets from an angel is just daring them to hunt you down, replied Harker. *It's foreplay. You might as well toss your panties at him.*

It's not my fault angels are so weird, I texted back.

There was another pause, during which the two angels were probably bitching about me, then another message from Harker popped up. *What are you up to?*

I tucked away my phone. I didn't tell Harker what I was doing either because he was such a by-the-books, goody-two-shoes angel, and he would report what I was doing back to Nero. And what would be the fun in that? He and Nero had been friends for decades, though their friendship had experienced its share of bumps.

A rush of homesickness washed over me, except it wasn't homesickness for a place. It was for Nero. You know how they say home is where the heart is? Well, my heart was with him. I missed him so much.

My phone buzzed again. I glanced at it.

As though he were here, reading my thoughts, Nero's text read, *I miss you. I want to see you again.*

Smiling, I teased him, *You just saw me.*

No, I didn't. Not really.

How he could sink that much innuendo into a plain text message was a mystery. Or was it just my own wanton mind that was reading into things? We'd reached the Legion office, so I put away my phone before I got distracted.

The Chicago office of the Legion of Angels sat at the end of the Promenade of the Gods, right after the last temple. The building shone like a sleek sheet of blue glass, reflecting the beautiful blue summer sky, along with a few scattered puffy white wisps of clouds.

The inside was as grandiose as a palace. Like in the New York office, murals of gods, angels, supernaturals, and mortals were painted on the walls and ceilings, enacting scenes out of Earth's history. That was a common theme in Legion buildings. In addition to the collage of the Earth's past, the walls showed battles that had been fought here and the angels who'd led this territory over the years.

"Your father looks so much more personable in his painting," I commented.

I pointed at a beautifully painted Colonel Fireswift, awash with soft lighting and heavenly glows. His golden hair fell to his shoulders in soft waves. He wore a white and gold battle tunic and gold boots. And he held a glowing gold sword high in the air as he stared down a huge flying monster. Gold, gold, and more gold. I was sensing a recurring theme here.

Jace looked at the portrait. "The painter took some artistic license."

That was the understatement of the century. For as

long as I'd known him, Colonel Fireswift had worn his hair trimmed to exactly one inch long.

"When they add my portrait to the wall, I'm going to ask them to paint me with a crimson battle gown on." I smirked at Jace. "And a tiara."

"Only angels are added to the wall, and I'm ahead right now."

"Don't get complacent," I warned him.

"I learned long ago not to underestimate you," he admitted. "You fight dirty."

"You bet I do."

We'd stopped in front of a thick dark brown door. Patterns of gemstones had been engraved into the wood. It looked like the ancient cover of an important book, one that had been handmade with no expense spared. Colonel Fireswift's name was the focal point of the sparkling jewel arrangement.

Jace knocked on the door.

"Enter," Colonel Fireswift's deep voice called out.

We stepped inside. The angel's office was as grandiose as the door. The entire ceiling was a mirror, making the room seem larger, as though it went on forever up into the heavens. The walls were covered in subdued, tastefully opulent white marble with accents of gold. There were paintings perfectly framed inside recessed coves in the marble walls, each one the picture of an angel who looked a lot like Jace and his father. It was the history of their family, generations of angels dedicated to serving the gods as soldiers in the Legion of Angels.

Colonel Fireswift sat at his desk, a massive piece of furniture carved from a single tree. I wondered how they'd gotten it through the door. With magic no doubt.

The angel was wearing the black leather uniform of the

Legion. Like always, he looked ready for battle. The leather fit snugly to his wide frame, making him look even stronger, like someone who could punch right through your ribcage, shattering everything in his way. Wrecking ball. That's the word that came to mind whenever I thought of Colonel Fireswift, both in body and in disposition. When his bright royal-blue eyes fell on me, arrogance shone in them. Like he knew he was better than I was.

I considered my options. I needed to convince him to let me join Jace's mission so I could be there to save my sisters. The Legion would prioritize capturing the deserter over saving hostages. I knew better than to appeal to Colonel Fireswift's humanity or compassion; he had neither. Though Jace and his father looked very much alike, Jace was different. Much to the Colonel's chagrin, Jace possessed both humanity and compassion. After all, he'd agreed to help me by bringing me to his father and speaking up for me.

Colonel Fireswift looked me over, from head to toe. "So," he said, clearly unimpressed. "You want to join the hunt for the Deserter." He said it like deserter with a capital D.

I looked at Jace. Surprise flashed across his face, followed by reluctant acceptance. It must have been frustrating that his father always found out about everything.

Then Jace's face went blank. It had all happened so quickly that human eyes would not have picked up the subtle shift in his emotions. Colonel Fireswift, however, did see it, and he was clearly not pleased with his son's momentary lapse in professionalism. Dear gods, Jace had shown human emotion. What a crime.

I couldn't let Colonel Fireswift's inhumanity bother me, so I just kept smiling. "That's right."

Colonel Fireswift arched a single pale brow, which blended into his tanned skin. "Your sisters were among those taken."

Nothing got past him. Except the importance of compassion and other pesky human emotions.

"Yes," I said.

His jaw was as hard and unyielding as iron. "And now you want me to do you a favor by allowing you to go after them."

What an asshole.

"I'm asking you to allow me to do my job to protect innocent lives," I said. "There are still twenty-six people missing from towns all across the Frontier. And Davenport is still out there."

Colonel Fireswift ground his teeth at the mention of the deserter. The fact that Davenport was still at large really grated on him, as though he took it personally. I wondered how long he'd been trying to capture Davenport—and how long he'd been failing miserably at it.

"I fought Davenport at the Doorway to Dusk," I continued.

Colonel Fireswift seemed to think that over for a bit. Finally, he said, "And you survived?" He wasn't impressed, but he did sound a little surprised.

"I'm a survivor."

He said nothing. My continued survival must have annoyed him nearly as much as Davenport's.

"We can get him," I said. "I'd be an asset on this mission."

"An asset to Jace's mission," he said, his eyes reflective. "To his career. To his capture of Balin Davenport, the Deserter."

Yep, because let's focus on what was important:

crushing threats to Colonel Fireswift's ego and advancing his son's career. Not on protecting the human race.

"You and Jace have been neck-in-neck since the beginning of this race," said Colonel Fireswift.

"It's not a race."

He ignored me. "But this game has gone on far enough. You have never been, nor will you ever be, equal to my son. He comes from a distinguished line of angels. You come off the dirty streets of the Frontier. You never stood a chance. You must finally see that now. The middle levels of the Legion are designed to set the future angels apart from those who will never be. Those who never had a chance."

I didn't interrupt him. He looked like he was enjoying himself immensely. In fact, I'd never seen him so ecstatic as he was right now.

The angel cleared his throat, as though he'd realized he'd gotten carried away in the moment. "Jace is in command of the mission. Not you," he finished, his eyes harder, more professional now.

"Of course."

"He gives the orders. And you follow them. As it should be." He gave his hand a dismissive flick, waving us off. "Now get out of my sight before I change my mind."

Jace and I left the angel's office, closing the door behind us. We were halfway down the hall before Jace finally spoke.

"He agreed," he said quietly, as though he still couldn't believe it.

I smiled. "What did I tell you? Nothing to worry about."

Jace shot me a hard look. "That was too easy. What did you do?"

I waited until a group of soldiers had passed us by, and we were alone. Then I stopped, dropping my voice. "Your father really wants to see you beat me."

"I know. Not a day goes by that he doesn't tell me I'm a disgrace to the family, that this shouldn't even be a competition."

"Because I am the dirt beneath your angelic feet."

Jace gave me an apologetic look.

I laughed. "Your father is his own worst enemy. He is so intent on seeing you 'win' over me, that he can't see beyond it."

Comprehension flashed across his face. "You compelled him."

I pinched my thumb and index finger together, so close they were nearly touching. "Just a little."

"Your magic shouldn't have worked on an angel. Not at your level," he said, shocked.

"My Siren's Song was just a tiny nudge to make him go where he wanted to go anyway. His ego did the rest."

"He underestimates you." Admiration shone in Jace's eyes.

I shrugged. "That's the dirty fighting your father abhors, that which he sees as an affront to the proper and dignified fighting the Legion teaches. If you don't know how to fight dirty, it's hard to defend against it."

"I wish I had your devious mind."

"It's never too late to learn. We are immortal after all, so we have all the time in the world to get our hands dirty."

He laughed.

Then, suddenly, he stopped mid-laugh. The pressure in the air had changed, like all the magic in the area was suspended, frozen in time. Nero came around the corner.

The angel's eyes were locked on me, unblinking, intense. My heart let out a nervous, ecstatic thump. He'd promised he would find me and he had. What would happen next?

Two Legion soldiers trailed him: Harker and Jace's sister Kendra Fireswift. With her long golden hair, eyelashes that kissed her cheekbones, and full rosy lips, Kendra had the face of an angel—and the ego to go along with it. She wasn't an angel yet, though. From the metal pin of a flower on her jacket, I saw she'd leveled up since last we'd met, so it wouldn't be long before she realized her angelic destiny.

When Kendra saw me, her nose, so perfect that sculptors would have killed to immortalize it, turned up. She was her father's daughter through and through. She had the same hard, unwavering personality and the same sense of absolute superiority.

We all stopped in the hall and stared at one another.

Harker was the first to break the heavy silence. "A bit brash, aren't you, dragging Leda off into dark corners?" he said to Jace.

"Actually, she dragged me off."

Nero's jaw cracked, echoing off the silence that had taken hold in the hallway, freezing everything.

"I mean she wanted to talk to me about my mission," Jace said quickly.

Nero gave Jace a look that promised he could kill him where he stood without lifting a finger. Harker had gotten it into Nero's head that Jace had a thing for me, which was ridiculous. But angels weren't always rational. Or reasonable, for that matter.

Kendra looked torn between disgust and anger. She wasn't my biggest fan, and she certainly didn't want to believe her brother was pining for me.

Harker was the only one who was completely at ease. In fact, he looked amused by the situation, especially at Jace's discomfort. Jace had gone a bit pale, but he was making a valiant effort not to look too intimidated by Nero. He bowed before the angels, as though he'd just remembered procedure. Immediately, some of the color returned to his cheeks; he took comfort in the routine.

"Pandora, you could learn some respect from your friend." Harker's eyes were laughing at all of us.

But I was looking at Nero. *You can't kill him*, I thought loudly. *He's my friend.*

I was not telepathic, but Nero was. I knew he'd heard me from the slight tug on his lip, a tug that said, *oh, yes I can.*

"I need to speak to you in private," he said aloud.

He turned and walked to the nearest room. I followed him. I was about to shut the door when I felt Nero's magic brush past me, pulling the door closed.

He watched me closely, drinking in my expressions, my mood. "What happened, Leda? What's wrong?"

And then the dam gates broke. I told him about the attack in Purgatory, about how my sisters were taken, and our journey to the Doorway to Dusk.

I'd only been teasing him before by holding back information. Inciting him a little. And, ok, yes, flirting with him. But now that he was here, I didn't want to play games. I needed him. I needed to confide in him, to spill my soul to him. He would understand. I knew he would.

So I told him everything, no matter how much it hurt. I admitted to interrogating the werewolf and the fire elemental. *Interrogating*—that was just a euphemism for torture. I'd killed one man, and I'd nearly killed the other.

If Calli hadn't shot the fire elemental, my magic might have done him in anyway.

"What the hell is wrong with me?" I finished.

"Nothing is wrong with you. It's the price we at the Legion pay to ensure that the world is safe. We sacrifice our lives, our identity, our family, everything—so others can live in peace. But we find a new family: the Legion."

I hardly heard his last words. I was trying not to think about it, about what I'd done, especially not the feeling of the power flowing through me, the high I'd felt while I'd been in the middle of the interrogation. And the low afterwards when I realized what I'd done. Honestly, I wasn't sure which one was worse.

Nero set his hands on my arms. "You did nothing wrong, Leda. You did what any of us would do to save those we love."

There was emotion in his voice, conviction. Like he would have done all that and much more to save me. I could feel his magic wrapping around me like a warm blanket, trying to comfort me.

"I don't want to be calm, Nero," I said, shrugging off the comfort of his magic. "I want to stay sharp and save my sisters, to end this before more families are torn apart. Before more innocents are hurt."

"I wish I could help, but I have an emergency of my own. The Magitech wall in the south is weakening. If it collapses, monsters will flood through the gates and swarm our cities."

"How is the wall weakening? I didn't think that was possible."

Magitech walls were supposed to be unbreakable.

"Neither did I," he said. "But I suppose if you hit a

magic barrier with enough opposing magic over the centuries, it eventually begins to break down."

"When do you have to go?" I asked him.

"I was on my way out now. I came here to gather the last of my team to repair the wall—and fight the monsters if necessary."

"Who is coming?"

"Harker, Major Fireswift, Major Singh, and Basanti, among others."

Wow, those were some heavy hitters.

"If things had been different, I would have come," I told him.

"And I would have wanted you by my side," he said. "But you needed a break. You were supposed to be on vacation." There was a hint of rebuke in his voice—and a lot of frustration.

"Life doesn't throw me breaks or vacations, only obstacles. I have to save my sisters."

"I'll come back and help you when the wall is repaired. In the meantime, be strong and remember to practice your telekinetic resistance. Get Jace Fireswift to hit you with psychic attacks."

"You mean, nudge me in the ass with magic like you do?"

"No, Pandora. Only I get to do that," he said seriously. "And I will kill anyone else who does."

I laughed. "I was just kidding."

"But I was not."

I could see in his eyes that he was dead serious.

"Killing my friends is not the best way to endear yourself to m—"

He swallowed my words—and my breath—with a kiss. Magic, hot and insistent, rolled down my body, melting into my skin. He was drowning me in his magic. I opened up, lapping up his magic greedily, wanting more. I craved the sweet nectar of his magic, a force as powerful as the gods' Nectar.

"Leda." Nero's voice dipped lower, reverberating against the sensitive skin of my throat. "I'm already late."

A strangled, incomprehensible sound broke my lips. I couldn't even think straight, let alone speak.

He stroked his hand down my face. "Oh, Leda. If only we had more time."

"Make time." I was proud of myself that the words had come out. And that I'd sounded so firm, so commanding.

He chuckled. "Not now, love. I have no intention of rushing it." His hand traced my side slowly, so torturously close to my breasts. "Indeed I will torture you many times over before the night is through." His mouth brushed against my neck.

"Is that a threat or a promise, angel?" I choked out, my voice a tormented, inhuman growl. I resisted the urge to throw him against the wall and give into the agonizing hunger that was consuming me, that was threatening to burst out with every deafening throb of my pulse.

"Each gift of magic comes with new powers. Magic we use in battle to kill monsters and defeat our foes."

Where was he going with this? And why wasn't he touching me?

"But that is only one side," he said. "Each magic gift, each power, opens up new ways to make love."

Like the water elemental magic in the pool at Storm Castle, I remembered. The memory was like a phantom, fiery kiss, a wicked twist of pleasure uncurling inside of me.

He held my chin between his fingers and whispered

hotly against my face, "When I return, I will give you a lengthy demonstration."

"Lengthy?" My legs shook.

"Oh, yes. I expect it to last hours."

I hiked up my skirt, hooked my fingers under the band of my panties, and tossed them to the ground at his feet.

His eyes looked at the lacy red panties, then slid across my body. "You're tempting me."

"You've proven amenable in the past," I said without a shred of shame.

A breeze kissed my skin. Soft and hot, it ran along the inside of my thigh with excruciating slowness. A soft moan broke free of my lips. Gods, I had to have him and it had to be now.

"What is that?" I gasped.

"A taste of what's to come." Quick, silken, his magic slipped inside of me, drowning me in pleasure.

"What is to come?" I whimpered. "Death by magic?"

Chuckling, his chest brushed against mine, and my nipples were on fire. My back arched, my legs spread, and I dug my nails into his skin, pulling him in closer.

"Oh, Pandora, you can't even begin to comprehend how much I want you," he whispered into my ear, his breath melting against my skin.

"Don't be too sure about that," I said, my voice croaking.

Nero's lips brushed softly against mine. "I can hardly wait to have you again," he whispered into my mouth.

Then, like a splash of icy water, he pulled away. "But it will have to wait," he said with a wicked smile. "Back to work."

CHAPTER 11

SAVAGE CIVILIZATION

*N*ero and I left the room and went back to the hallway. He faced the others with a perfectly composed, perfectly professional face. I wished I could have said the same, but truth be told, I was rather distracted with thoughts of his promise. But it was a good distraction. That constant tight knot in my stomach, wound up with worry over my sisters, had loosened a bit, and the memories of me interrogating the mercenaries were no longer playing in a constant loop inside my head.

I realized that's why Nero had so thoroughly seduced me. He'd taken me away from my worries and freed my mind from its prison of guilt. Granted, I was still fired up as hell to free my sisters and see the bastards who'd taken them face justice, but I was calmer now, even serene. The rage had fizzled out. Only calm, clear-headed determination remained.

"So, are you ready to go?" Harker asked Nero.

His eyes twinkled as he looked from me to Nero. He knew what we'd been doing. And from the looks of it, so did everyone else. Well, let them know. I wasn't ashamed.

145

Frowning, Kendra looked at me like she didn't know what all the fuss was about. Jace, on the other hand, appeared totally uncomfortable, the most awkward I'd ever seen him. It was as though he didn't know what to do with his hands; he eventually opted for linking them behind his back. He'd diverted his gaze away from me and Nero.

It was then that I realized Nero had a second purpose to what he'd done. Two purposes, so like an angel. By covering me in his magic, he was demonstrating to everyone here that I was his. The message was obviously directed mainly at Jace.

"Let's move out." Nero motioned for Harker and Kendra to follow him, then pivoted around and walked down the hall.

Dozens of soldiers had gathered to catch a glimpse of the two visiting angels, but as soon as Nero's procession started moving, everyone made space for them, folding back to the sides of the hallway.

I looked at Jace. "Let's go."

We walked down the hall to considerably less fanfare, though I did manage to pick up a few jealous stares from the female soldiers. I wondered how many of them would happily push me off a building to have a shot at Nero.

We met up with Jace's team in the armory. The team of four, none of whom I'd seen before, was far smaller than the one he'd had at the Doorway to Dusk. I wondered how many soldiers Nero had taken from Colonel Fireswift's territory for his mission in the south. Nero's position as Nyx's second gave him the authority to do so, a fact which must have had his rival Colonel Fireswift in a rage.

The muscle of Jace's team consisted of two big guys with arms as thick as thighs and thighs as thick as tree trunks. The third soldier was a tall and slender man. There was an energy about him, a nimble bounce. An agility. I'd seen that look in street fighters. I knew the soldier would be fast and deadly with the knife on his belt. If I came across this team at night in a dark alley, I would be more concerned about him than about the two big bodybuilders.

The fourth member of Jace's team was a female soldier. She was very petite, even tiny. And she had a haircut that I could only describe as 'cute'—burgundy-red hair with a jagged cut toward her jaw, parted high on the left side of her head and swept back from her face with a silver clip.

The female soldier's cuteness evaporated the moment she saw me. Her face fell into a scowl. Her three male comrades were just as displeased to see me. Clearly, Jace's team had heard of me, and the stories had been far from complimentary.

"Does your father use me as a shining example of how *not* to be a Legion soldier?" I asked Jace.

"He doesn't need to. Your reputation speaks for itself. You're notorious," Jace said, amused.

I found myself unamused. So apparently my stellar reputation had preceded me to Chicago's Legion office. *And* I was notorious. Great.

Jace introduced me to the team. "Colonel Fireswift has assigned Lieutenant Pierce to me for this mission."

The soldiers shot me looks of disgust, tempered with contempt. I hadn't felt this unwelcome since high school. Here I was an unwanted outsider, a rogue, an intruder.

But I refused to let that get to me. I put on a big smile and said, "Lovely to meet you all."

They looked at me like I was waving around a dead chicken in my hand. Well, I guess we wouldn't be bonding over marshmallows and campfire songs.

As Jace began outlining the mission to his soldiers, I pulled out my phone and messaged Calli and Bella.

Jace stopped. "What are you doing?"

"I'm talking to my family to coordinate our attack plans," I told him.

"I hope you're referring to coordinating an attack on the dessert buffet."

I gave him a flat look.

"Your foster mother and sister are civilians. This is Legion business, and they have no part in it," he declared.

"This is about family," I said, fire burning in my eyes. "The mercenaries took my sisters, so my family is very much a part of this. Front and center."

My four biggest fans in the room muttered a few disgusted comments. I pretended not to hear them.

"What's done is done," I told Jace. "Calli and Bella are already a part of this, courtesy of Legion Regulation 136.5."

"Compelling support from civilian citizens in a time of emergency," he quoted the subtitle.

Shit, he knew that one. What were the chances? The Legion rulebook was a thick tome, a regular chihuahua killer. It was so enormous, so long-winded, that only the most sadistic members in the Legion of Angels had memorized every line. Nero had insisted that I read it, his reasoning being that you had to know the rules in order to break them. So I'd slaved through it line by line until I could quote it by heart. Jace, the son of an angel, had probably picked up the book for a bit of light reading.

"Regulation 136.5 no longer applies here," Jace told me. "You're not stuck in an emergency without Legion support readily available. We have a team of Legion soldiers and resources. And, most importantly, I am in charge of this mission."

His soldiers were perfectly still, but I could see the vicious pleasure gleaming in their eyes. I totally loved them all already.

Until now, I'd gotten pretty far by cherry-picking regulation lines, but that wasn't working with Jace. He was really motivated to become an angel, and knowing every rule by heart was just another tick on the aspiring angel checklist. He'd decided we were in a competition to see who became an angel first, and maybe we were.

Well, if this was a competition, then so be it. I could use an added kick to make me advance up the hierarchy, to get the magic I needed to save Zane. Jace was a worthy challenger. He was hard-working, well-trained, and motivated. He'd pulled ahead of me in the race, so I couldn't afford to slack off.

"Your family needs to stay out of our way. And out of Legion business," he declared.

He was certainly saying all the right things, everything the Legion told him he was supposed to say. Jace lived and breathed the Legion of Angels. For a Legion brat, the offspring of an angel, these rules gave meaning and purpose to their lives. They took comfort in knowing these boundaries were there. Rather than a noose to hang themselves on, they saw the Legion rules as a safety net that would catch them if they fell.

I knew I shouldn't have been mad at Jace for doing his job, but some part of me was upset he was sticking to rules that put the Legion's wishes over saving innocent lives. I tried to swallow that side of myself, that angry voice screaming to get out and tear down the artificial order, to topple those ivory towers and split the marble-paved roads of this savage civilization.

I shook myself free of those thoughts. What was all that? What was that burning need to destroy and rebuild the world in my own image? It certainly wasn't me. Or at least it was not who I wanted to be. The stress must have been getting to me. I was just frustrated that I couldn't do more to save my sisters because there were all these barriers to work around and rules tying me up.

I pushed those destructive thoughts from my head and swallowed my frustration. Working with Jace, using the Legion's resources, was still my best bet to save my sisters. I tuned back into the conversation.

"There's a snowstorm raging all across the Field of Tears," Jace was saying.

That's what the monsters' magic had done to the world. It had thrown the weather so completely out of whack that we regularly had impossibilities like snow in summer and hurricanes in the desert.

"As soon as the storm clears, we'll head out across the Field of Tears to Crow's Crown," Jace continued.

He instructed his team to load up the truck so we'd be ready to drive out as soon as the storm on the plains died down, then he dismissed them.

What's your status? I texted Bella as the four soldiers went off in a very orderly way.

Calli is looking at guns, Bella replied.

That would take awhile. Calli shopped for guns like other women shopped for lingerie.

I've restocked on potion ingredients, Bella added. *I've added more things that blow up. Just for you.*

What the hell was that supposed to mean? On the other hand, well, I did like things that went boom.

Get some of those fireworks ones like you bought me for my birthday, I told her.

Magic Cocktails.

Yep, those are the ones. They're great, I typed back.

How long did it take you to go through them all?

About five minutes.

Silence.

See it this way, Bella. I've never taken out that many monsters so quickly. I just tossed the Magic Cocktails and then all the beasties blew up. It was rather epic.

The silence stretched on.

Bella?

I'm buying enough ingredients to make another ten Magic Cocktails, she wrote back. *That brings us up to twenty altogether.*

Will that be enough?

Of course, she replied. *No one could possibly need more than that.*

Pause.

Bella?

Stand by, she wrote back.

I tapped my fingers against my phone.

Calli reminded me of who we're talking about, Bella added. *So we got enough supplies for me to make you thirty Magic Cocktails. That's the most I can carry.*

I'll try not to blow up any of us, I promised.

I've got a potion for that.

A cure for being blown up?

Yes, it's still in the early stages. Right now, it can regrow as much as a hand.

Well, let's hope we won't need it, I typed. *The team is on standby right now. We have to wait until the snowstorm over the Field of Tears clears. I'll let you know when we head out.*

151

Tucking my phone into my hoodie's pocket, I looked at Jace. We were alone in the room.

"I told you your family cannot be a part of this mission," he said calmly, confident in the cloak of his authority.

"But that doesn't mean they can't go to Crow's Crown and try to free the kidnapped victims themselves."

"I could declare Crow's Crown off limits to civilians."

"But you won't," I told him. "Because despite what you tell your father, you actually don't aspire to be an asshole."

He watched me in silence, mulling over my words. Finally, he said, "You should be careful, Leda. Mixing your personal and professional lives could get us all killed."

"My family was tracking criminals across the plains of monsters long before you joined the Legion, Jace. The plains are a rough and dirty place, not orderly, not civilized. My family and I are right at home there. Just as your father proclaims, as your soldiers all believe, I am fundamentally a savage at my core."

Jace winced at the statement, of the accusatory tone in my voice and the fire burning in my eyes. Even as outrage gripped me, I tried to calm myself, to remember that Jace was my friend and that he was just trying to do his job. He was living in conflict between two sides: personal friendships and professional aspirations. It must have been really hard for him to find a balance.

"My family won't get in the way," I said, softening my tone. I set my hand on his shoulder. "We are a powerful force together, united, in sync. We might just make the difference between success and failure in this mission."

"They are compromising your priorities. If it's a choice between saving your sisters and catching the deserter, which one would you choose?"

Then, looking like he knew the answer all too well, Jace left the room—and left me with those thoughts.

The thing was, he was completely right. I'd choose saving my sisters over capturing Davenport in a heartbeat. I didn't even need to think about it. Did that make me a bad soldier? Probably. But I would think of a way to do both, to rescue my sisters *and* capture the deserter. I would make it work. Somehow.

With those thoughts buzzing around in my head, I headed for the gym. I needed to clear my mind, to take solace in my training, to work so hard that I didn't have enough energy left to worry.

In the gym, I went to the panel on the wall and skimmed through the training modes until I found the telekinetic challenges. Through it all, through all the conspiracies and my personal soap operas, I had to prepare for the next level, to train my telekinetic resistance so that I might gain the gods' gift of Psychic's Spell. Some elusive *something* was standing in my way, blocking my ability to access this branch of magic. I didn't know what it was, but I was determined to power through it. As Nero had said earlier, if you hit a wall hard enough for long enough, eventually your persistence would win out and you'd break through. He'd been talking about monsters, but that strategy worked pretty well with most things.

As I selected the obstacle course from the illustrated menu, I wondered if it was just all in my head. Was it only my own mind standing in my way? Or had I reached the end of the line, the end of my magical potential? Had it been arrogant of me to think that I would just simply rise to the top? Most Legion soldiers never became angels. Not by a long shot.

But even if I might be doomed to fail, I had to try. I

was not a quitter, especially not after I'd come so far. I hit the button for Telekinetic Course 004, and the machines hummed to life, building up the challenges before my eyes.

My first challenge involved crossing a passageway of spelled telekinetic swords. The path was tight, leaving little room to maneuver around the belligerent swords. I lifted my own sword to parry the strikes, each clash of the blades exploding with telekinetic magic that tore down my arms, rumbling to my core. The surges of psychic energy upset my balance, my equilibrium. I stumbled sideways, twisting my ankle as I hit the wall. Gritting my teeth, I pushed forward and endured, fighting through the swords to the very end.

The next obstacle followed immediately, allowing no respite. The walls of the labyrinth moved, constantly shifting, making it damn near impossible to navigate. As I was trying to find some pattern in the seeming chaos, a wall slammed into me, as though the labyrinth had grown impatient with me to move faster through the challenges. It must have been programmed by an angel.

The walls began moving faster. They were twirling and spinning all around me. I ran, sliding and diving between them, trying to make my way through the course. I avoided a wall, only to have another slam into me. It felt like being hit with a hammer of telekinetic magic. As I shook the pain from my body, another wall closed behind me. I was trapped.

Moving in and out, the walls slammed into me from all sides with fists of thunder. I felt like I was being beaten down by an angry street mob. The barrage was relentless, the force of the telekinetic punches knocking me down.

My knees hit the floor. A wall loomed high above me, suspended in the air. Then it bellyflopped to the ground. I jumped out of the way, my body creaking in protest as I pushed it faster, narrowly avoiding the spinning walls. Black splotches danced in front of my eyes in a dizzying kaleidoscope.

I was lost. Even after months of training, this branch of magic was confounding, my resistance to it nonexistent. But thankfully I was quick. All that training with angels had paid off. I spotted an opening in the dancing wall parade, and I took it, slipping through. I could see the end of the course, the exit from my misery. I sprinted toward it.

I burst out of the course, dodging its final farewell kiss. Then I stood there and stared back at the moving, shifting obstacles. Catching my breath, I brushed my hand across my bruised skin. My body looked like a truck had driven over me—then backed up and rolled over me again for good measure. When something with telekinetic magic hit me, it really hurt, more so than any other branch of magic I'd faced so far. It was pure torture.

Get moving, Pandora. If you're still standing, you can do it all again, Nero's voice said in my head.

I chuckled, wondering if it was really his voice, if he was really still close enough to speak into my mind. Probably not. He must have been long gone by now. My mind was just conjuring what I needed to keep going. Harsh as Nero was in training, there was something remarkably comforting about hearing his voice chastise me for slacking off.

You're right, I told Nero. It didn't matter if it was really him.

Taking a deep, calming breath, I lowered into my knees and got ready to tackle the obstacle course again.

A crack of magic exploded in my face.

"Leda Pierce," said a deep voice.

The blinding splotches of light slowly faded from my vision, and then I saw him: the Lord of the Legion of Angels, one of the seven ruling gods of heaven. He was also known as the God of War and the God of Earth's Army. And he was standing right in front of me.

CHAPTER 12

MAGIC AND COUNTER MAGIC

"*R*onan," I said in surprise.

His dark obsidian eyes watched me closely. The last time I'd seen him, they'd been green. Gods seemed to change their features like they were jewelry. The black color matched his dark armor better.

"Thank you for the fashion advice."

Oops. I wasn't watching my thoughts. That was a bare necessity when conversing with gods.

"Why are you here?" I asked.

"Curiosity. Telekinesis is giving you trouble."

"How do you know?"

He shrugged. "The gods are keeping a close eye on you."

Great. I felt like I was under a microscope. Despite what the Pilgrims would have us all believe, I knew the gods were not all-knowing and all-seeing, but they did have eyes and ears everywhere. The question was how often they were watching. I hoped they had better things to do than to keep me under constant observation, but it wouldn't take 24/7 surveillance to realize I'd been having trouble with Psychic's Spell. I'd been working on it for months, after all, and I didn't feel any closer to cracking it.

"And also, Nyx told me," Ronan added.

The First Angel had been watching me since I'd joined the Legion. She thought she could make an angel out of me, and my inability to advance further had thrown a monkey wrench into her well-laid plans.

"Let's see what you've got," Ronan said.

Before I could react, he hit me with a psychic blast that threw me clear across the gym. Even as I was falling, he followed up with a crushing telekinetic weight that smashed into me from above, slamming me into the floor. I felt two bones break in my ribcage, and black stars spun in front of my eyes.

The next thing I knew, I was on the floor. Ronan was crouched beside me, healing my wounds.

"You didn't last long," he commented, helping me to my feet.

Still seeing stars, I snapped back, "You're a god. The fight wasn't a fair one."

"You've jumped into more than your fair share of unfair fights. That never seemed to stop you."

"That's different. You didn't give me time to develop a strategy."

His dark brows arched. "And what kind of strategy could you possibly devise that would work against a god?"

"I'd think of something. Like throwing sand in your eyes. Even gods have to see to fight. In fact, the better your senses, the more sensitive you are."

Ronan laughed. Then he stepped back, lowering fluidly into a fighting pose. "Enough advance warning for you?"

I looked around the gym, searching for anything that

might help me against a god. I came up short. My options were limited. And I was seriously underpowered.

So when he attacked, I just did my best to not fall on my ass this time. Rather than countering his telekinetic punches, I danced away, evading.

"Running away isn't a viable strategy. I expected more from you," he chided me.

He moved fast, his fists a blur. Too fast to follow. Too fast to avoid. He slipped past my defenses and pounded my head with a psychic punch, his fist powered with an extra dose of magic. I blacked out.

When I came to, Ronan was staring down at me. "I told you running away isn't a viable strategy. I'm faster than you. My magic is faster than yours. If I were a hostile enemy, you would already be dead."

"Then it's a good thing you're the kind and cuddly God of War."

He laughed again. "You need to commit to the fight," he said as I stood. "You're distracted."

"I have a lot on my mind."

I told him about my experience interrogating the two mercenaries today—and the high I'd felt from the power I held over them. Even as I prattled on, confessing my sins, I wondered why I was opening up to Ronan. He couldn't possibly understand.

But he surprised me by saying, "Nyx struggled with the same thing."

"Really?"

Nyx always seemed to know exactly what she was doing, like she was totally committed to every decision. She never wavered, and she never lost control.

"Nyx wasn't always like that," Ronan told me, picking up on my thoughts again. "She was raised by her mother's family, humans. She only later came to train with the gods. It was a big change for her."

That certainly explained Nyx's more human qualities. She had a sort of duality—so human one moment, and the next, so inhuman, so like the gods.

"How did Nyx get past the indecision?" I asked Ronan.

"You have to believe in what you're doing, that it's for the best."

"Even when what I know is right contradicts what the Legion wants?"

"This is about your sisters," he said.

"Yes, but it's not only about them. My duty to save lives, especially my sisters' lives, will always outweigh catching the bad guy. I can catch him later. I can't bring someone back to life once they're dead, though."

I knew I should have phrased this more carefully, especially when speaking to the Lord of the Legion himself. But Ronan seemed like the sort of person who appreciated candor.

"You certainly have a way of cutting straight to the core of the issue," he stated, his face impassive.

"My way is not the Legion's way, though," I said. "We're supposed to expect casualties, to eliminate threats by any means necessary. We're told that collateral damage is unavoidable—even preferable to the damage a villain will continue to do if he remains free."

"And what do you think?" Ronan asked me.

Dangerous grounds lay ahead. Ronan might seem approachable. Sometimes, he even seemed almost human. But I couldn't ever forget that he was a god, and gods were not the same as humans. They weren't even the same as angels.

"Perhaps the Legion is right about that, that saving

lives at the expense of capturing a criminal allows that criminal to do more damage for longer," I allowed. "But I can't just sacrifice innocents. Because where is the line? When does the coldness of a Legion soldier doing their duty cross the line into indifference for human lives? Or worse yet, devilish delight at ending lives?"

"You're worried about your power lust."

"How do you not get caught up in the magic of the moment? How do you not answer its seductive call when it's flowing through you, burning like wildfire, screaming to be unleashed?" I asked desperately. "And you just want more and more. Everything else falls away and you become the monster."

That was the way I had felt when I'd interrogated the mercenary. At the same time as I longed to feel that power burning through me, I never wanted to feel that way again.

"The answer is: you learn to control your power," he said. "You've gained so much magic so fast. It's not surprising that it's overwhelming you. Control. It's all about maintaining control."

"You make it sound so easy," I said drily.

"It's not."

Something about the way he said it, about the look in his eyes, made me wonder if he was speaking about himself too. Did even gods struggle with not getting caught up in all their power? Had I caught a rare peek into the soul of the impervious God of War?

"The magic consumes some people," I said bluntly. "They change. They begin to see humans as nothing, as beasts who exist solely for their amusement. That's what happened with Balin Davenport, the Deserter. I've read his report. He certainly has a colorful portfolio of accomplishments since leaving the Legion. He's a cruel and twisted man. Did the Legion's training cause him to be like that? Did his time here turn him into a monster?"

Ronan was quiet for a few heavy moments. "You aren't making your life easy by asking these questions," he finally said.

"I've been accused of a lot of things, but never of making my life easy," I replied. "Or anyone else's life for that matter."

"Keep asking those hard questions, Leda. Just not too loudly," Ronan added. "I've lost too many angels to this cruelty of which you spoke, this hardness that makes them arrogant, makes them believe that they can challenge the gods' authority and hurt anyone they wish to. The angels are the protectors of humanity, the champions. They are given powers mere mortals do not possess so that they can protect the Earth and the humans who live there. Don't make the same mistakes those fallen angels did."

"I'm no angel," I stated.

"Not yet perhaps, but Nyx is convinced you will be."

"And you? What do you think?" I asked him.

"Time will tell." He lowered into a fighting stance once more. He was giving me a warning before he attacked.

It didn't help much. We went for another round of training. Or more like ass kicking.

I kept my distance from him, giving myself time to evade his magic blasts and psychic-powered fists. I even got in a punch. But when my fist slammed into his hard stomach, it only seemed to amuse him, not hurt him. I realized too late that he had drawn me into a trap.

Lightning fast, he snatched hold of my wrist, locking it inside his hand. Then he hit me point-blank with a tele-kinetic blast. It sent me flying across the room. This time I managed to catch myself on the training ropes hanging from the ceiling. He blasted me again, and I fell out of the ropes. I hit the ground with a thump that echoed through the room—and through my body.

"You still have zero telekinetic resistance," he said.

I rubbed my aching head. "Tell me something I don't know."

"Do you usually go out so easily?"

I sighed. "Pretty much."

"How long have Nero and Harker been training you for Psychic's Spell?"

"Months."

"And your telekinetic resistance is not improving?"

"Not really." I tried to get up, but it hurt too much.

"Are you done napping?"

"Come a bit closer and you'll find out," I said, sarcasm biting my tongue.

"You're very bold with the gods," he commented. It was a statement, not a judgment.

"Nero isn't here to make me behave myself."

He actually looked amused. "Just don't forget to be afraid of me. Of all of us."

"Oh, I am afraid," I assured him. "Scared out of my wits actually. But I'll be damned if I let fear freeze me. That does no one any good."

"You are very wise. The other gods don't recognize that. Well, perhaps Valora does. The others underestimate you. They think you are a fragile human," Ronan said. "But humanity is stronger than they think. And you aren't really human, are you? You never were."

I grabbed at his words, latching on to them. "What do you think I am?"

"I don't know," he declared, looking at me closely. "A magical mystery. A conundrum."

"Perhaps that's why I can never gain the power of telekinesis."

"Oh, you can gain it, I'm sure. You just have to go about it differently."

I perked up. "So there's a better way than the usual torture-with-magic-until-you-are-immune-to-it method?"

He laughed. "Oh, no. There's no way around that, I'm afraid."

I sighed. Of course there wasn't.

"Someone with high magical potential often has particular strengths or weaknesses depending on the origin of his or her magic. That's what we call your magical ancestry," he told me. "Take your friend Drake, for example. He has shifters in his family history, so he's strong. And he is predisposed to pick up that type of magic easily. Or consider your friend Ivy. She is good at calming people. That's because her mother was a telepath, a ghost. And Ivy is obviously empathic. It's the same branch of magic. That's how our soldiers can possess hints of some kinds of magic before they reach the corresponding levels in the Legion."

That didn't explain my magic, though. My single pre-Legion magic was my vampire-mesmerizing hair, and I'd never heard of any supernatural with that power.

"When the gods came to Earth, we gave humanity gifts of magic," Ronan continued. "Seven gods, seven gifts. My specialty is telekinesis, so that was my gift to humanity. I turned a few select humans into telekinetics. Humans with psychic power are my children, the progeny of my magical gift to humanity."

"I am obviously not one of your 'children'."

"No, your magic lies elsewhere on the spectrum. Or more specifically, as I suspect, on the opposite end of the spectrum. And that's your problem."

"What do you mean?"

"Just as we all have strengths, we also have weaknesses," he explained. "Your kind of magic—your ancestry magic—might be canceling out the telekinetic power you are trying to gain."

"So what can I do?"

"There's a potion that blocks magic."

I nodded. I'd taken such a potion during Nero's trials. It had stripped the magic from both of us, making us human for a time.

"You don't need to take the complete magic blocker," he told me. "There are potions selectively crafted to block out only one kind of magic, or several kinds, or even all magic except for one. Blocking out your major talents allows room for the minor ones to grow."

Ronan pulled a vial of potion out of his jacket, holding it out to me. "This will silence all your magic—except the power of telekinesis. Your psychic potential is buried deep down inside of you, suffocated by all your other magic. The potion will allow it to grow so you can build up your telekinetic resistance. It will prime your magic. And in time, if you train hard enough, the Nectar will do the rest."

I considered the vial of sparkling silver-blue liquid. Drinking the potion would make me mostly human again. It would make me weak. Ronan wouldn't just crush me in a fight; he would annihilate me.

His dark brows lifted. "Scared?"

I grabbed the vial. "Don't bet on it."

I popped the cap and gulped down the potion. A hint of chocolate chased the taste of peppermint across my tongue. The potion slid down my throat like a frozen river, like a breath of winter. My pulse slowed, my blood chilling. I shivered. I felt as though death had just kissed my shoulder.

The familiar fear took root inside of me, that same unwelcome feeling I'd had before Nero's trials. Except it was so much worse now. This time, my magic had abandoned me all at once, vanishing between one moment and the next. Instinctively, I reached for my magic, grabbing, panicking, but it was gone. Just gone. I could feel only the imprint of its departed warmth, the hollow echo of my magic torturing me, mocking me with its absolute absence.

But there was something hiding in the magic void, a weak pulse blinking in the distance. It was a tiny spark of magic that I'd never felt before. I reached for it, pulling with savage desperation to have it, to hold it. It was weak and undeveloped, but it was magic.

Ronan hit me with a telekinetic blast. I pulled the weak flicker of my magic around me like a blanket, a thin layer of protection against the cold. His spell hit the blanket and fizzled out. I blinked in surprise. The little spark of magic pulsed in appreciation, growing a bit stronger.

This was the whisper, the hint, the precursor to Psychic's Spell. After all these months, I could finally feel it. It was in there after all. It had just been too weak for me to find, buried as it was under all that other magic. Ronan was right. It had been hidden, blocked off from me.

But no longer.

Ronan punched me with his psychic magic again, his attack harder this time. My little spark of magic ate it up and grew a little stronger. It was only a weak trickle of magic, but at least it was magic. And it was all I had right now. I grabbed that magic by the horns, determined to make it mine.

Ronan swung a punch at me. I deflected his strike,

magic twitching on my skin, an intermittent buzz like a downed Magitech power line. The spark ignited when it hit Ronan, dazing him for a moment. I took advantage of the brief lapse in his attacks and swung a kick under his legs. He hit the floor.

He bounced back to his feet immediately, a hint of shock marring his perfect composure. "You never fail to surprise, Pandora. You used telekinetic magic before you drank the Nectar of Psychic's Spell."

"What does that mean?"

"It means that I was right. Your other magic was blocking your psychic power. Your strongest powers lie on the opposite side of the spectrum from telekinesis," he said. "But it also means something more. You possess innate magic, magic from your ancestry—not just magic you gained from the gods' gifts. Your telekinetic magic isn't the only thing suppressed inside of you. There's more magic, and whatever that magic is, it's just waiting to be unleashed. The question is what you will become when it is finally unlocked. There's a bite to your magic, an eagerness, an explosiveness. It is not content to fade quietly into the crowd. Good luck, Leda Pierce. You're going to need it."

Then he was gone, just like that, like he'd never been here at all.

CHAPTER 13

*M*y training session with the God of War had been productive. For the first time, I'd tasted a hint of psychic power. Though the fight itself had felt like running through water with chains of weights dangling from every limb. I could never go back to being human again.

I stretched out my body. Now that the potion had worn off, I was fast again, spry, agile. My muscles felt warm, buzzing in appreciation of the good workout they'd received. My magic muscles felt the same way. I'd frozen a god with my telekinetic magic, if only for a second. I took a moment to stand there and let that sink in. Maybe I wasn't a hopeless case for Psychic's Spell after all.

Hope hardened into determination. I *would* get this. I didn't care how many telekinetic training sessions I had to endure.

I left the gym and walked through the dark halls back to the room I'd been assigned for the night. A quick check on my phone told me that the snowstorm was still raging over the Field of Tears. I didn't have an update from Jace either. He was probably asleep like every other sane person was at this hour.

I didn't regret staying up. The training session had been a real breakthrough. Thanks to Ronan's potion, I'd finally made it past that wall blocking me. I'd never have guessed it was my own magic that was standing in my way, blocking me from developing my telekinetic powers.

But the training session had also left me with more questions than before. What was I? That question was even stronger in my mind now. Did Ronan know something about me? And what about my magic ancestry? Was he holding back information?

The gods had so many secrets. They weren't on the same plane of existence as the rest of us. They didn't think like we did; they considered themselves above us. And they delighted in playing games, even a god like Ronan. He might have been our ally, but he was still a god. A god didn't do anything out of chance, or for the sake of mere curiosity. Everything had a reason. Everything was calculated.

The same went for Ronan's lover Nyx. I liked the First Angel, but she was a demigod, a born angel, the daughter of a god. I had a sinking feeling that Ronan had only told me about Nyx's past—about her prior turmoil of dealing with the very same moral conundrums that were tearing me apart—so that I saw her and him as more human. So that I saw them as people I could trust, people I could confide in.

But I couldn't. Not totally. I had to tread cautiously. Gods, I hated that I needed to be so paranoid, that I couldn't just trust people anymore. When had life grown so complicated?

It's always been complicated, my rational side told me.

I'd had to read into things, even back before I'd joined the Legion, back before I'd played war with angels and gods. As a bounty hunter, I'd tried to get into people's heads, to see things from their perspective. I needed to figure out how they ticked, how they thought, in order to predict their movements. If I could determine where and when they'd be, I could catch them.

Were things really so different now? Was I any more cynical than I'd been back then?

I made it to my room. You know those hotel rooms that aren't bad but aren't anything special either? That's what this room was. The Legion only brought out the red carpet, hot tubs, and canopy beds for angels.

I headed into the connected bathroom and took a two-minute shower to wash off the sweat—and to clear my head before bed. All these mind games were as exhausting as having my ass handed to me by the God of War.

After drying off, I fell into bed. The mattress was surprisingly soft and comfortable considering the hard, cruel angel in charge of this office.

I drifted lazily into a pleasant dream about a sunny summer beach and lots of chocolate mint ice cream. My dream was short-lived, however, hijacked by an untimely visit from the God of Heaven's Army.

Faris stood out like a sore thumb against the tropical gold and turquoise backdrop. His hair was glossy black and shoulder-length today, like ripples of liquid ink. Dressed in a set of black and silver armor, he looked like the lord of the castle. A feathered layer spread across his shoulders from the top of his cloak, sliding down his back like a black waterfall. I couldn't tell if it was a cloak or his wings.

He moved toward me, emanating menace with every breath that he took. "Why did Ronan visit you in Chicago?

What are you two scheming?" he demanded, foregoing all pleasantries. He sure didn't waste any time cutting to the chase.

"Ronan was just training me."

"Why has he taken such a particular interest in you?"

I was tired of his questions. Not to mention just plain tired period. Faris's foul mood was disturbing my much-needed sleep.

"I don't know. Why are *you* interested in me?" I deflected.

He made a derisive noise. "You flatter yourself. You are insignificant."

"Obviously not. You came here to talk to me," I said, smirking.

He caught me in the iron jaws of his magic, his grip as hard as his voice was silky. "Is Ronan training you to fight the gods?"

His magic was cracking me like a nut. It felt nothing like the pleasant buzz of an angel's aura, the power they used to make you want to fight for them. What Faris was doing hurt, and it hurt bad. This was the hard, cruel side of Siren's Song. It was not persuasion through pleasant means, through using people's desires to direct them where you wanted them to go. No, this was crushing someone's will under the heel of your boot.

"Is Ronan building an army to fight me?" Faris snapped, his magic squeezing down on me.

"No. He wants more angels for the Legion."

"To threaten the gods."

His magic was suffocating me. It was getting hard to breathe.

"To fight the monsters and other threats that besiege the Earth," I choked out.

Faris gave his hand a dismissive flick. The invisible claw around my throat that had been slowly squeezing the life out of me roughly jerked away. I coughed, sucking in air.

"I don't believe you," Faris declared, watching me with an expression of utter distaste.

"I don't care if you believe me," I snapped at him. "It's the truth. And my self-worth is not dependent on your approval."

His nostrils flared, my defiance enraging his pride. He knocked me back with a telekinetic blast. It hurt, but not as much as it would have before my training session with Ronan. I really was improving.

Or maybe it hurt less because this was all a dream, and there was only so much he could do to me without actually being here. Could a god kill you in your sleep? I didn't care to ponder the question further. I doubted I would like where it led.

Faris caught me in his magic again. "What is Ronan planning?"

Like a war hammer, his will crashed against mine, trying to crush my mind. My head felt like it was splitting apart in a hundred places at once, but I refused to scream. Faris would enjoy that too much.

"Ronan is not planning anything," I said. "He is just trying to build up the Legion of Angels to fight the demons."

"And why does he think you can help with that?"

"I don't know. Maybe because I am *in* the Legion of Angels." I managed to summon enough strength to roll my eyes.

Faris's magic hit me harder, his phantom fingers tightening around my neck. I could hardly breathe.

"Your impudence does not amuse me," he said in a low snarl.

"Well, your temper tantrum sure amuses me," I snapped back.

Faris threw me aside, and I hit a nearby palm tree like a rag doll.

I stood up, my head hurting more than my body. Because this was a dream and his attack was a mental magic one, I realized. My head was pounding so hard I thought it might explode. I gritted my teeth, holding in the pain.

Faris folded his hands together. "Let's try this again," he said with a coldness that sent chills down my spine. "What are you to Ronan?"

"A tool," I replied honestly. "Nothing more. Just as we all are to the gods."

Faris was watching me closely, probably dissecting every expression on my face. "Indeed."

As he approached me, I couldn't help but wince in anticipation of his next attack. His eyes sparkled with vicious delight. Apparently, my fear amused him.

He stroked his hand down my face, grabbing my chin roughly between his fingers. "But what is this tool's purpose?"

"Ronan thinks I can be an angel."

I watched Faris for his reaction, and as expected, he did not seem surprised. Yes, he wanted me to be an angel as well. He wanted me to advance up the Legion so that I could find my brother Zane, a telepath, and then Faris would use Zane's magic for himself.

But I didn't say any of this. I hardly dared to think it, keeping those thoughts in a secret, hidden place in my mind, locking them away where the God of Heaven's Army would never find them. I didn't want him to realize that I was on to him.

Back when I'd first joined the Legion, Faris had pushed Harker to give me Nectar that would have made me a second-level angel. If I'd drunk it, I would have gained all the gods' gifts up to the power of telepathy, which would have allowed me to use my connection to my brother to find him.

Well, assuming I'd survived the Nectar. Consuming all that magic in a single sip would have killed me soon afterwards. It might have even killed me before I'd gained the power I needed to find Zane, and then I would be yet another causality, just more collateral damage in Faris's immortal quest for power.

Since then, Harker had defected from Faris's side, joining Nyx and Ronan. That might have been what Faris suspected, that Ronan was countering his power plays. I didn't completely trust Ronan and Nyx, but I trusted them a hell of a lot more than I trusted Faris. For starters, they hadn't tried to poison me.

I wasn't going to expose my friend Harker's defection. Nor would I tell Faris about my other friend Stash, the demigod who was being trained by Ronan and Nyx. A troubling thought came to me. Was Ronan only countering Faris and trying to build a Legion army to protect the Earth, or was the God of War actually making a power play himself?

I plugged those thoughts. I had to believe in Ronan and Nyx, in Nero's trust of them, because otherwise I'd have to decide that I could never trust a single soul. If I could put my faith in anyone in this dangerous, cold world of angels and gods I was now a part of, it was Nero.

I would keep these secrets, not for Ronan or even for

Nyx, but for my brother Zane and my friend Stash, for Harker and for Nero, and for myself. And also to piss off Faris.

"You're hiding something. You will tell me what it is," declared Faris.

The anger over what Faris had done helped fuel my resistance, but it was really my love for those I cared about that powered my resolve and allowed me to resist the god who was trying to break me.

His magic hit my mind again, pushing harder. I held on.

He frowned. "Stop fighting me. Tell me your secrets."

"You don't want to know."

"I do," he said, his magic tightening its grip.

I could barely see from the excruciating pain. "Ok." I swallowed hard. "But don't come crying to me if you don't like it."

"I am a god. If I don't like what you have to say, I won't cry. I will kill you."

I cringed. "You see, that's not really convincing me to tell you anything."

Faris gave me a hard look. "You're stalling. There's really no point. Pigheadedness will get you only so far."

"I don't know. Pigheadedness has gotten me pretty far in life. Though I prefer to think of it as strong-minded resolve."

"I grow bored of your games. Spill your secrets, or I'll crack your mind open and drink them from the shattered remains of your tangled thoughts."

Yum, delicious imagery.

"I don't have all day, child. Give me a reason not to destroy your mind."

He was bluffing. He would hurt me, sure, but he

wouldn't break me beyond repair. He still wanted to use me. I was his best bet for finding Zane, so he wouldn't discard me just yet. He didn't seem to realize that if I became an angel and found Zane, I would do everything in my power to protect my brother from him.

"You won't even be able to think ever again. You'll be a vegetable."

I could feel the boundaries of my mind splitting against the strain of his attack. I kept telling myself that he wouldn't shatter my mind, but with each passing moment, it was getting harder to hold on to that conviction. Pain rattled my mind, plucking the stitching that held it together. I could see the way out, the path that promised an end to the pain. The answer was right before me, as clear as day.

I only had to tell Faris what he wanted to know, and the pain would stop.

"Ok, I'll tell you what you want to know." Catching my breath, I met his unyielding eyes. "Those boots don't match at all with your belt."

Faris blinked.

"And the hilt of your sword is clashing horribly with your amulet," I added.

Outrage flashed in his eyes. "How dare you!"

"How dare *me*? No, how dare *you* come into my dreams uninvited and attack me for no reason."

"My reasons are none of your concern."

"Right. Because you torturing me has nothing to do with me," I said, my voice thick with sarcasm.

"What will Ronan do with you when you become an angel?"

I shrugged. "Use me on the front line to fight demons, I suppose. I'm far too much of a troublemaker to put me in command of anyone. I'm much more useful as an expend-able battering ram."

"You're not wrong about that. You are trouble." Faris was frowning. "You're either the best liar I've ever met, or you're just a clueless pawn."

"Or maybe there's really nothing going on."

"We'll see."

I shook, jolting upright in my bed, heaving in deep breaths. Faris would be watching me. And the closer I got to finding Zane, the more his gaze would be turned my way. I would have to be careful.

My bedroom door shook. Someone was banging on it like the building was on fire. That's what had woken me up, freeing me from Faris's interrogation. I slid off the bed and walked to the door. I found Jace on the other side, dressed and armed.

"The storm has cleared. We're heading out." His gaze flickered to the tank top and boy shorts I'd worn to bed. Then, likely thinking of Nero, his eyes hastily met mine. "Get dressed."

I yawned. "What time is it?"

"Five in the morning."

Of course it was. Danger never hit at high noon. It always came knocking in the middle of the night. Because, as I'd told Nero, the universe just didn't give me a break.

CHAPTER 14

MAGIC ORIGINS

*I*t was still dark outside when Jace, his team, and I boarded the train out of Chicago, loaded down with enough gear for twice our numbers. On our way to the station, I'd texted Calli and Bella, but they'd told me that they had already left on the earlier train and would meet me on the Frontier. I wondered if they'd slept at all. Probably not. I hadn't slept either. Having a god invade your dreams wasn't exactly the most restful experience.

The train would bring us as far as the Frontier town of Abyss. From there, we'd drive a Legion truck out onto the Field of Tears, the wilderness that lay beyond the town wall.

"Purgatory. Infernal. Abyss. These Frontier towns have such posh names," commented the female soldier.

"What did you expect?" said Bodybuilder One. "These backwater lands are hardly more civilized than the plains of monsters."

"You could say the same about the pedigree of citizens they produce," added Bodybuilder Two.

They all looked at me.

"You know, Frontier towns have the highest crime rate in the world," said the nimble knife-wielder.

I'd already heard all of this before. More times than I could count, in fact. They weren't wrong. Of course there was a lot of crime in poor areas. When people were desperate, survival took a front seat to propriety. People like these soldiers—privileged citizens who'd never had to worry about when their next meal would come, about whether they would have somewhere safe and dry to sleep that night—could not possibly understand. Sometimes you had to live it to get it.

I tuned out their hateful comments. They were just trying to annoy me, to get a reaction out of me, but I wasn't playing along. I was too tired for that kind of nonsense. And, besides, nothing I could say would change their opinion if they were hellbent on hating me.

Here and now, surrounded by these unwilling allies, I'd never felt so alone. I couldn't help but feel homesick for New York. Things were different there. I knew the Legion soldiers there. Some of them didn't like me or my methods, of course, but they didn't try to provoke me or to mock me. Colonel Fireswift must have been telling tales about me to feed all this hate.

I got up and walked to the empty train carriage next door, in search of a few moments of peaceful rest. I was just dozing off when something tugged at the edges of my senses. I jerked awake to find a god standing over me.

Zarion, God of Faith and Lord of the Pilgrims, was dressed in long robes. His robes bore some resemblance to the humble clothes worn by the Pilgrims, the preachers of the faith, often referred to as the 'voice of the gods'. This god's robes were not plain and humble, however; they shimmered green and blue, as though gemstones had been crushed into the fabric. His sandals were gold, his hair paler than mine, and his nose proud.

"Why did Faris visit you last night?" Zarion demanded.

Zarion and Faris were brothers. To say they didn't get along would have been a major understatement. I had the feeling the only thing keeping the two gods from engaging in open warfare was their fear of Valora, the Queen Goddess who led the gods' Council.

"Did you make a deal with Faris?" Zarion continued. "Are you helping him conspire against me?"

My head hurt, and it wasn't only from the lack of sleep. "Why would I do that?"

"Faris voted in Nero's favor after the trials," Zarion pointed out. "Clearly, you are in league with him."

Oh, yes. *Clearly*. Because there could be no other reason for Faris to visit me. Like, for instance, trying to crack my mind open and steal all my secrets.

"I demand answers," Zarion said, unimpressed by my silence. "I am Zarion, the God of Faith, Lord of the Pilgrims, and I will be treated with the respect owed to me."

I grimaced, my sleep once again disturbed by a paranoid god. The gods and their games were getting ridiculous. Zarion was here because of Faris, who had visited me because of Ronan. I wanted to shout at Zarion.

Instead, I just said, "No disrespect intended, my lord." I even bowed.

Zarion appeared even more incredulous, as though I'd insulted him. But I wasn't mocking him. For once, I was behaving myself.

"This isn't over, Leda Pierce. I will be watching you."

Then Zarion vanished in a huff, his voice continuing to echo in the empty carriage long after he was gone.

"Join the club," I grumbled to the dead space where he'd stood a moment ago.

The gods were watching me closely, just as Ronan had said. Fantastic. That would make it harder to find Zane and the Guardians. It would make it harder to work in secret with Nyx and Ronan and to keep Stash's demigod status a secret.

Stash was Zarion's son, and the god didn't have a clue. A family reunion would not go well. Zarion had already tried to murder Stash in his mother's womb, and the god thought he'd succeeded.

I pushed thoughts of Stash out of my head. All the gods were telepathic. Life would be a lot easier without all these secrets—and all these gods.

I stood up, now completely awake. My latest godly encounter had left my mind agitated. I couldn't possibly sleep now. So I walked back to the train carriage where I'd left Jace and his soldiers. He was alone now.

"Where are your minions?" I asked him.

"Preparing for the mission. As you should have been doing. Instead of sleeping." His lower lip twitched.

"I wasn't sleeping."

"I could hear you snoring."

"What you heard was me *training*."

"It sounded like a bulldozer was rattling the train carriage."

I shrugged. "It was strenuous training."

A smile flashed across his lips.

"Much better," I told him.

He gave me a quizzical look.

"All that frowning will give you wrinkles."

"I'm under a lot of pressure, Leda."

"From yourself or from your father?"

"Both. I have to live up to my potential."

"Why? Living up to your potential is *so* overrated. Slacking off is way more fun."

Laughter broke through his facade. "You don't follow that philosophy yourself."

"Perhaps not," I admitted. "Can I ask you something?"

"That depends. Will it get me into trouble?"

"No," I chuckled. "It's about magic."

"Fire away."

"What do you know about magic and counter magic?"

Surprise lit up his face. "How do you know about that?"

"What's the matter? I know I'm just a thug, but even I know some things."

Jace frowned. "You shouldn't listen to my father's soldiers."

"They're your soldiers too, Jace. You could have stopped them."

"It's complicated," he said.

"Life is complicated."

"If I'd stepped in, you would have looked weak, like someone in need of protection. And then they would have become even more vicious."

"Vicious to me or to you, my knight in shining armor?" I smirked at him.

Jace just stopped, as though he didn't know what to say. "I see. So your plan for winning our little competition is to have General Windstriker murder me in a fit of jealous fury."

"Nah," I laughed. "That wouldn't be fair. I fight my own battles."

"Then why didn't you fight your own battle by standing up to my team? You've never had a problem standing up for yourself before."

"Some battles just aren't worth it. Even if you win, you still lose, you know?"

Jace looked at me for a long time. Finally, he said, "You've really grown up in the last year, you know."

I gave my eyebrows a mischievous wiggle. "Well, not completely. I'm still not above throwing dirt in your face."

"I'm starting to realize beating you won't be as easy as I'd thought," Jace said solemnly.

"As I told you, Firestorm, I fight dirty. This was *never* going to be easy."

Jace nodded, looking reflective.

"Magic and counter magic," I reminded him.

"Right," he said. "When the gods came to Earth, they brought magic. They created seven casts of supernaturals: vampires, witches, sirens, elementals, shifters, psychics, and fairies. And they created the Legion of Angels, the protectors of Earth, soldiers they bestowed with these powers and more. The best would become angels."

Jace spoke the words with reverence—and with hope. His greatest wish was to one day become an angel.

"When supernaturals interbreed with humans, their children are usually born with diluted magic. After a few generations, there's only a hint of magic left. They have the potential but not the magic."

"Like Drake. He's always been strong and fast thanks to his magical ancestry."

Jace nodded. "These sort of people, those with magical

potential, make great candidates to join the Legion of Angels. They're more likely to survive the gods' Nectar than normal humans are."

And the Legion brats made the best candidates of them all. 'Legion brat' was a term for a person with an angel parent. Rather than an insult, the term was one of high esteem. The brats had claimed the expression as their own, embracing their angelic origins and their magic ancestry.

"Every supernatural group on Earth has a patron god, a deity who was the origin of their magic," said Jace. "For example, Ronan created the telekinetics, and Meda made the witches. As a rule, magic doesn't typically mix well with other magic. A shifter can't also be a witch. A vampire can't also be an elemental. If you have magic, you have only one kind of magic."

"Unless you're a Legion soldier," I said.

"Our magic works differently. We drink Nectar to absorb the magic into us."

Or we died. Drinking Nectar was not something to be taken lightly. You trained and trained, and if you were good enough, you built up enough resistance to survive the next sip of Nectar and gain the gods' next gift.

"Think of a Legion soldier as a blank slate, a canvas of magical potential," Jace said. "A candidate must be balanced, not have too much or too little potential in any one magical field. That's why you can't so easily take a witch or vampire and turn them into a Legion soldier. Every so often, one of them survives, but their mortality rate at the initiation is even worse than a mundane human with no magical ancestry. You need people with mixed magic ancestry and lots of magical potential."

In other words, the children of angels.

"This is where we get to magic and counter magic. And

to how the Legion breeds angels," Jace told me. "The Legion breeds angels for two qualities: magic balance and magic potential. To create a child with the highest magic potential, you would need to breed two angels together, but those pairings rarely work out."

I nodded. My friend Nerissa had explained it to me. Like their personalities, angels' magic was sharp, dominating, and unrelenting. So while a dual angel pairing had magic potential to spare, it was severely lacking on the magic balance component. The magic of two angels didn't blend well; it clashed. It was like one nonstop explosion of poison and egos. So when the Legion wanted to breed an angel, they paired them with lower level Legion soldiers, someone whose magic was more amenable.

The only exception I knew of was Nero, whose parents were both angels—but that pairing had only worked because his mother had very light magic and his father had a lot of dark magic for an angel. Their magic had obviously found a balance between light and dark.

"The Legion's breeding methods work, but some angel families have refined them," Jace told me. "Mine, for instance. We've taken the process further."

I wasn't surprised. Colonel Fireswift was precisely the kind of angel who would have optimized every possible thing.

"How do you do it?" I asked him.

"Magic is a spectrum."

Jace drew the magic spectrum on a sheet of paper, eight gifts around a color wheel. It included not only the gods' seven gifts of magic, but also an eighth, that of telepathy. Telepathy was a special gift, one granted only to angels. The telepaths of Earth didn't have the gods to thank for their magic; they'd received it from another source, presumably from the original immortals who ruled the realms before the gods and demons. Some of their magic had made it to Earth.

"Over the centuries, my family has bred us so that each generation has more magic potential than the previous ones. Our ultimate goal is to create children whose magic potential covers the entire spectrum."

"How do you accomplish that?" I asked.

"An angel takes a mate with a specific set of abilities we want to boost in their offspring. These abilities have to be powerful enough not to fade beneath all the magic of an angel, but not so strong that they cancel out the abilities on the opposing end of the spectrum."

"How's that working out?"

"Slowly," he said. "We have managed to boost our magic potential beyond that of any other family, but we are still working on the magic balance. A few weaknesses remain."

I glanced at the magic color wheel he'd drawn. "Which ones?"

His eyes hardened. "Nice try, but I'm not giving anything away."

"You've already given everything away in your lecture about opposing magic," I told him. "All I have to do is think about what your strongest abilities are and use that to determine your weaknesses."

He clenched his jaw.

"Luckily for you, I don't fight dirty." I grinned at him.

"Oh, no. Never," he said drily.

"Come to think of it, I haven't noticed any weaknesses in you or your father," I said.

"My father doesn't stand for any weakness; he annihilates them. And what weaknesses he hasn't yet been able to destroy in breeding, he destroys in training. He trained me and my sister from birth, and he didn't hold back. The fact that we were children was no excuse. He bombarded both of us especially hard with our magical weaknesses to build our resistance early on. That's how he made up for any shortcomings in our magic heritage."

"Nice."

Jace shrugged as though it didn't bother him at all. "Some magic powers still come more easily to us than others. My father is determined to neutralize those weaknesses in breeding. He's made it his mission in life to create the perfect angel, the perfect soldier. For the sake of our family's legacy."

"I didn't realize the Legion would allow an angel any choice in choosing a spouse."

"The Legion doesn't tell you there is choice, but there's always a choice as long as you're breeding for magic and not for something as fanciful as love."

I snorted. "Yeah, because who needs love and happiness when you have duty and power?"

Jace kept talking, so caught up in his explanation that he'd failed to recognize my sarcasm. "There are often multiple spouse choices to choose from within a range of magical compatibility. When that's the case, the Legion allows an angel to pick. The Legion doesn't object to old families of magic producing more angels, especially ones with more power across the entire magic spectrum. After all, those angels would be very valuable assets to the Legion."

As he explained all of this, I couldn't help but wonder what my and Nero's chances were. Were we compatible? Would the Legion approve of us as a match? As soon as the thought fluttered through my head, I felt guilty for even pondering it. Whatever the answer was, it didn't matter. I had to save Zane. That was my purpose in the Legion, my reason for being here. Making magical matches to produce more angels and ensure the Legion's future was definitely not part of the plan.

CHAPTER 15

FIELD OF TEARS

*A*byss, a town along the Frontier in Colonel Fireswift's territory, was bigger than my hometown of Purgatory, but there was a similar feel to it. Frankly, it really did feel like an abyss. A fog hung over the town, and the dull street lamps did nothing to alleviate the darkness. The dreary street corridors were lined with boxy blocks of buildings about six or seven stories high. Standing there felt like being stuck in a dark valley after the sun had fallen behind the mountains.

An old, broken-down monorail hung overhead. It looked like it hadn't been used in decades. Layers upon layers of graffiti were painted over the carriages, the tracks, and the elevated stations—the painted timeline of the town's history.

Like in Purgatory, the bars were full. They were the preferred place for people to drown their sorrows and forget their problems. Music spilled out of the open doorways, an open invitation to all who passed by. An old piano played an upbeat tune that was in stark contrast to the dreary street scene.

The people on the streets did, in fact, look depressed. There was a slouch to the way they walked, like the weight of the world and all its monsters weighed down on their shoulders, crushing them into the ground, into nothingness. Their heads were bent over, their gazes on the ground. It was all very different from the happy music, cheers, and singing emanating from the bars.

It was like when they stepped into those bars, the people transformed completely. They each became someone new. Someone with hope. Someone with dreams that still lived on. Someone the hard, cruel world hadn't completely destroyed.

We drove under the gates, passing beyond the wall onto the haunted lands of monsters.

A few hours later, we stood upon a cracked, dry patch on the Field of Tears, looking across the dusty red earth at the stone fortress. With its four towers, high walls, and drawbridge, Hardwicke's stronghold looked like a bona fide castle rather than the shady digs of an infamous slaver. Word on the street was Balin Davenport had passed through Abyss and headed out onto the Field of Tears. So chances were good he was here now. If all went well, I would free my sisters and the last of the prisoners, and Jace would capture the Legion deserter.

"Security is tight," said Bodybuilder One.

"Especially for a rogue band," added Bodybuilder Two. "They have too many guards patrolling the walls, and they are all heavily armed. We are outmanned and outgunned."

Because Colonel Fireswift had only sent a small team. Sure, Nero had appropriated Jace's old team, but there were more than enough Legion soldiers in the Chicago office. Colonel Fireswift must have figured Jace's victory would look that much better if he took the castle with only six soldiers rather than sixty. That was exactly the sort of thing he would do.

Nimble Knife laughed. "But we have the great Leda Pierce, Pandora, bringer of chaos and destruction."

Jace's soldiers laughed and pretended to shiver in their boots.

I covered my annoyance with a smirk. "It's no wonder you need me if all you're good for is running your mouths and shivering in fear of the stronghold you've already decided you cannot possibly take."

"There are too many guards, and a Magitech barrier surrounds the whole castle. We cannot take it with the resources we have," the petite soldier said, shaking her head.

"No, you just don't know how to use the resources you do have. Or maybe you're just scared."

"How dare you call us cowards," hissed Bodybuilder One.

"A Legion soldier is worth a dozen common thugs," said Bodybuilder Two.

Nimble Knife nodded. "At least."

"But Hardwicke has too many guards," Petite Soldier concluded. "Many more than expected. His forces have gathered here from his other fortresses."

"They are expecting us," Jace concluded. "The numbers are not in our favor." He said it like it hurt to admit it.

"In life, the numbers are rarely in your favor, and luck doesn't just fall into your lap. You need to make your own luck. I'd say it's high time we turned the numbers in our favor," I finished as Calli and Bella parked their car next to our truck.

Jace's hard eyes panned from them to me. "What are

they doing here? I've made my position on this very clear. Your family is not to get involved."

"You've all already given up and decided taking Hardwicke's base is impossible. So what's the harm in trying things my way?" I asked him.

"The harm is to our dignity, to the propriety of the Legion. Your way is *dirty*," Petite Soldier said, pursing her lips in disgust.

"Since we're talking about propriety, let me take this moment to remind you that I outrank you," I snapped back, my gaze dropping to the small metallic insignia of a musical note on her chest, the symbol for Siren's Song, the Legion's third level. "So I'm going to invite you to shut your mouth before you embarrass yourself any further."

Her face turned as red as her hair, but she didn't insult me. In fact, she didn't say anything at all. Finally.

I turned back to Jace. "Let me and my family show you —show the Legion—just how effective these 'dirty' ways can be. What do you have to lose?"

I could see the battle raging inside his eyes. On the one hand, allowing civilians to take part in this mission was a major no-no, but on the other, he really, *really* wanted to catch the deserter. The fortress's defenses were much better than expected. If he played this by the books, at best his mission would fail; at worst, we would all die.

"Very well. You may proceed," he finally agreed. He looked at Bella and Calli. "The Legion takes no responsibility for any maladies that may befall you, including injury, disfigurement, or death."

It was the standard Legion disclaimer, and the words rolled off his tongue like he'd been practicing them since he could talk.

"Are all Legion soldiers so charming?" Bella asked me.

"Why don't you ask your boyfriend?"

Bella blushed. "He's not my boyfriend."

I grinned at her.

"Girls, must I remind you that we have a castle to storm?" When Calli was on the job, she was all business and no nonsense.

Bella and Calli were already dressed in the standard wilderness outfit: tank tops, shorts, and boots. They looked the part. My wardrobe, on the other hand, would need some work.

I peeled off my jacket, stripping down to my tank top and shorts. Without any insignia, it wasn't immediately obvious that I was wearing part of a Legion uniform. I swooped down and grabbed two fistfuls of dirt, tossing it all over my clothes. Then I grabbed the bottom of my shirt and tore it. The fabric ripped halfway up my abdomen. I ran my fingers through my ponytail. A few messy strands tumbled out of my hairband. Almost there. And now for the finishing touch. I pulled out my knife.

"What's that for?" Bodybuilder One asked, watching me closely.

"I'm going to make a few blood stains. For verisimilitude."

Bodybuilder One looked at Bodybuilder Two. "The crazy girl is going to cut herself."

"Oh, I'm not cutting myself," I told him, smiling. "And no one will know the difference."

I grabbed hold of his thick arm. His muscles bulged as he pushed against me, trying to free himself. Holding him steady, I slashed my blade across his arm. I wiped my hand over his cut, then smeared streaks of his blood all over my clothes and skin.

"You're completely out of your mind," Bodybuilder One said, stumbling away from me.

"Please heal Mr. Panic Pants before he bursts any more arteries," I said to Bella.

Even as Bella dabbed a potion over his skin, he continued to glare at me.

Nimble Knife laughed. "Actually, I think she's growing on me."

I winked at him.

The other soldiers just gaped at me in shock.

"This is so crude," Petite Soldier commented in a low voice.

I shrugged. "Sometimes to get the job done, you have to get your hands a little dirty. Didn't your angel leader teach you that?"

Her jaw dropped. I'd apparently rendered her speechless.

I wiped the last of the blood on my shorts, then turned to Jace. "How do I look?"

"Like you wrestled a troll in a mud pit, ran across a live minefield, and then rubbed yourself against some barbed wire to top it all off."

"Perfect."

Calli tossed me a hood. "Ready?"

I lifted it over my head, casting my face in shadow. "Yes. Just don't do it too hard this time," I said. "I have sensitive skin."

Calli snorted. "I'll get you some moisturizer for that."

Then she slapped a pair of handcuffs on my wrists. She moved to one side of me, Bella to the other. It was like that, sandwiched between my sister and my foster mother, that I set down the broken brick path that led to the castle gates.

CHAPTER 16

THE MEDIEVAL MAGITECH CASTLE

*A*s we approached the castle, I looked up at the high stone walls. I counted over twenty guards standing on those walls, all of them armed with guns or bows. The guard on the north tower had a machine gun. The east tower guard stood behind a catapult that hurled magic balls.

And that wasn't the worst part. The whole wall was glowing gold-green, a cheaper, dirtier, less pure flavor of Magitech than the one protecting the walls that separated humanity from the plains of monsters. Hardwicke's wall was likely not strong enough to survive a herd of charging monsters, but it was more than powerful enough to kill a human, or even a Legion soldier.

Two guards stood in front of the closed drawbridge, each one dressed in a suit of shiny armor. Wow, these fellows sure took their medieval fantasies seriously. The guards didn't shoot us on the spot as we approached, which meant they weren't really as clever as they thought they were.

"What business do you have here?" demanded the guard in the silver armor as we stopped in front of them.

"We're bounty hunters," Calli said. "You put out a bounty on this girl."

The red-armored guard took a long, good look at me. He even had the nerve to reach under my hood and touch my hair. I snarled, snapping my teeth at him. He retracted his hand in alarm. I shot him a gleefully savage look.

"Don't get too close to her. She's been out here so long that she's gone a bit crazy," Bella warned the guards.

She'd put on a different voice, one that was rougher than her usual sophisticated accent. It was the voice of the Frontier. She handed the guards the wanted poster of me that she'd made while I was smearing dirt and blood all over myself.

They were paying more attention to her than to the poster. Bella smiled, but I could see the annoyance in her eyes. She'd put a lot of effort into forging that poster. She was proud of it, and these guards were only interested in gawking at her.

"Are you going to let us in already?" Calli said, tapping her foot impatiently. "We're on a tight schedule."

Silver Guard blinked, stammering, "Yes, of course, I wouldn't want to be in the way of your tight schedule." As he spoke the word *tight*, he stared right at Bella's ass. What an idiot.

I rolled my eyes at Bella from behind the guard's back. She swallowed a snort.

Calli grabbed me roughly by the cuffs, tugging me toward the door. As the guards turned to watch me struggle wildly against Calli's hold, Bella plugged a tiny device into a power outlet in the stone wall.

I was still wondering why they'd need a power outlet outside the gates—vacuuming the drawbridge?—when Red Guard hit a button. The magic on the wall faded out, the drawbridge extended, and we walked through the gates.

"You two need to stop goofing off," Calli whispered to us as we entered the castle. "Honestly, I expected more dignity out of a Legion soldier."

"What can I say? You should try to have fun in whatever you do."

"She is the black sheep of the Legion, after all," Bella reminded Calli.

I nodded in agreement.

"That would explain why she's so fond of black feathers." Bella was referring to Nero's beautiful dark feathers.

I looked at Calli. "Why do I always get the lecture anyway? Bella is goofing off just as much as I am, and she's a witch. Even more than the Legion, the witches live and breathe dignity, from their tight corsets to those adorable little boots and cute belts."

We passed into the courtyard between the towers. Armed guards moved about in every direction.

"It looks like they're preparing for war," Bella commented.

Dread sank heavy in my stomach, and I couldn't shake the foreboding cloud hanging over my head. We had to find the prisoners and get the hell out of here. But where could Hardwicke be keeping them?

Inside, I decided, somewhere they could be secured. I scanned the castle towers, trying to locate the prison from the window placement. Surely, Hardwicke couldn't be so cliche as to keep them in the dungeon.

On the other hand, I thought as a group of soldiers in

heavy armor clanked past us, this place was one enormous medieval fantasy park.

We passed from the courtyard into the building. A guard moved forward, stopping us in our path. Tall, wide, and muscular, he would have given Jace's bodybuilder twins a run for their money. The guard also had the benefit of a heavy suit of armor, which made him look even larger. Shiny and gold, the armor made him look like the quintessential commander of the castle guard, which was probably exactly what he was.

He wore a monstrous two-handed sword on his back. This was the sort of fellow who'd hit hard, cutting people apart with the blade, breaking noses and bones with the pommel. In a fight, I'd have to take him out before he had a chance to tear through my team.

"What are you doing here?" The guard addressed Calli, picking her out as the one in charge.

"We've come to collect on this bounty," she replied, roughly tugging me forward.

The Commander's brows drew together. He wasn't buying our story. He sensed something was off.

He paced in front of us, blocking us with his huge, armored body. "Where did you get the girl?" He shot me a critical look. "And what is it that she's wanted for?" He took a closer look at me. "She seems familiar."

"She should look familiar since her face is gracing wanted posters from New York to Los Angeles," Calli countered.

Folding her hands together behind her back, Bella dropped a tiny device on the floor. As Calli continued to argue with the Commander, stealing his attention, the device discreetly rolled across the floor, climbed up the wall, and plugged itself into a power outlet.

A man came down a spiral staircase and walked up to the Commander. He was wearing an expensive suit, the sort you often found on the bankers and businessmen of New York. It was a suit that screamed you had something to prove. No one who was comfortable in his position would feel the need to wear a suit like that all the way out here. He wasn't just showing off that he could survive out here beyond the veil of civilization; he was demonstrating that his expensive wardrobe could survive the wilderness too.

I assessed him. He was somewhere in his early forties. His head was shaved completely bald, a style he'd chosen to hide his receding hairline. Dark, intelligent eyes shone out brightly, assessing me and my family. From the looks of him, he wasn't a fighter. He didn't even carry a knife. Not that he needed to. The big Commander beside him was a human weapon.

"What's going on here?" the man asked.

"These bounty hunters brought in this girl, Hardwicke," the Commander explained.

So this was the infamous slave trader Hardwicke. I'd expected more hair grease—and more hair.

"I don't like the look of her," the Commander added, still glaring at me.

His eyes critical, Hardwicke stopped in front of me and flipped down my hood to reveal my face. Recognition flashed in his eyes. The game was up. He knew who I was. Honestly, I was surprised this charade had lasted as long as it did

"That is a Legion soldier," Hardwicke told the commander of his guards. "You've allowed a Legion soldier inside my castle. And not just any Legion soldier. Pandora, the bringer of chaos, who leaves devastation in her wake wherever she goes."

I smiled. "Aww, you've heard of me."

I twisted my wrists, snapping out of the handcuffs. I went straight for the big Commander. Calli headed off the group of guards who'd turned and run at us following Hardwicke's declaration. Bella hit a button on her phone. A series of booms went off throughout the castle, set off by the devices she'd placed. The castle's power went out, including the Magitech barrier that surrounded the whole place. That would give Jace's team one fewer obstacle to worry about.

The Commander swung his sword at me. Daylight streamed in through the majestic windows high above, sparkling off the massive blade. I dodged and rolled, grabbing two swords from a pair of guards on the ground who'd fallen victim to Bella's sleeping potion. I brought the swords up to meet the Commander's next attack. He blinked in surprise when my arms didn't collapse under the weight of the impact. I guess it had never happened to him before.

"Don't feel bad. Everyone underestimates me," I said, disarming him.

His sword clanked against the stone floor. His hazel eyes flickered to his fallen weapon.

"I wouldn't. You'll never make it. I'm faster than you," I warned him.

He made a run for it anyway. Shaking my head, I went to cut him off from his sword. Even as I stood in front of it, he kept running full-speed at me. The crazy bastard was going to ram me. He'd obviously never fought a member of the Legion before. We got punched, kicked, and rammed each and every day of our lives. He couldn't phase me.

When we were just inches away from an imminent collision, he surprised me by pivoting to the side and launching an enormous fireball at my head. There wasn't enough space for me to dodge, so I hastily cast a shield of ice in front of me. It went up just in time. If I'd been a moment slower, he'd have set my hair on fire.

Muscles and elemental magic didn't generally come hand in hand. I was still coming to terms with the unexpected realization that the huge tank of a man was also a fire elemental, when he hurled an even bigger fireball at me. I countered fire with ice, freezing his flames around him like a steel cage.

He punched through his prison, his fists shattering the ice. His hands locked around my arms, and he threw me at the nearest wall. My body pounding from the impact, I rose to my feet and faced him once more.

"Where are you keeping the prisoners?" I demanded.

"You will find out when you join them." He'd recovered his sword from the ground and set the blade on fire.

"You're not very cooperative," I muttered, dodging the burning streaks of his sword as he swung it continuously at me.

"How many Legion soldiers are with you?"

"Oh, at least a thousand."

"You're lying."

The Commander grinned savagely, withstanding my punch. He grabbed hold of my ponytail and tried to set my hair on fire. The flames didn't take, thanks to the elemental immunity I'd worked so hard to build up. Shock flashed across his face and he paused. I took advantage of his surprise and slammed my fist hard against the side of his head. He went down.

I looked for my next target. Across the room, Bella was

fighting a witch in a duel of powders and potions. Why were all these different supernaturals working together like they were part of a team, as though they were fighting for a common cause? I'd had more than my share of firsthand experience with bickering supernaturals. They didn't even get along with their own kind, let alone with other supernatural groups. What had brought all these people here together?

Bella knocked out the other witch with some sparkling purple dream powder. But as she caught her breath, a guard snuck up on her from behind. I ran forward, tackling him to the ground before he could grab her. The guard kicked me off. Magic exploded, fur burying flesh, and he transformed into a giant tiger. A shifter.

A snarl curling back his lips, he lowered into his haunches and prepared to pounce. Then, suddenly, he froze. A low whine broke his mouth, and he toppled over. Bella looked down at the sleeping beast, a sparkly blue powder glistening on her fingertips.

"Bad kitty," she reprimanded him.

I burst into laughter.

"What?" Bella demanded.

"You've turned into such a badass," I told her.

She frowned at me.

"It's not a bad thing, you know. Even prim and proper witches are allowed to kick ass now and again. I bet Harker thinks it's sexy."

She sighed. "You're incorrigible, Leda. You know that, right?"

I blew my sister a kiss. "I love you too."

The soft clink of metal drew my attention. I turned to see Hardwicke surrounded by a dozen armored guards. They shielded him from all sides as they fled.

"They are going to secure the prisoners," I said to Bella. "Or kill them on their way out."

I had to get to Hardwicke before that happened. The only problem was the horde of armored guards standing between us and him.

CHAPTER 17

A flicker of movement caught my eye. I glanced up at the ceiling. Davenport the deserter ran up the vertical wall like it was nothing. Balancing on a stone ledge, he shot me a wink, then he slipped through the window. Damn it. He was getting away.

I couldn't afford to worry about the deserter right now. I couldn't have gotten to him if I'd tried. But if I hurried, I could get to the prisoners.

Gunfire and magic sounded from the front gates. Jace and his soldiers were now inside the castle, but it would take them too long to fight their way here. We didn't have time to wait for them to help us cut through the guards covering Hardwicke's escape. We had to get to the prisoners now, before there weren't any prisoners left to save.

More guards poured out of the courtyard into the building, surrounding us.

"We are completely outnumbered," Bella said.

"The women of Pandora's Box know a thing or two about having the odds stacked against us," Calli declared.

Then she pulled out her crossbow, shooting at the wave

of guards sweeping toward us. The bolts, spelled with some of Bella's potions, exploded. Guards toppled over, clearing a path for us. We sprinted through the opening before it closed. The guards were too busy with the aftermath of Calli's explosions—and the arrival of Jace's soldiers—to follow.

The long hallway led us to another tower in the castle. There we found a room that held a small metal cage. Sallow-faced teenagers filled it, their bodies pressed against the bars. The kids were crammed in so tightly that I couldn't even tell how many of them were in there. I didn't see my sisters.

Frustration, fear, and outrage flashed hot inside of me, but I couldn't focus on the prisoners just yet. I had to worry about Hardwicke's guards first. They stood in our path, each one in a fighting stance. They'd been waiting for us.

As they unleashed their magic on us, I came to one unsettling realization: it wasn't just many kinds of super-naturals working together here; it was people who each possessed many different kinds of magic. Were there so many more Legion deserters than we'd thought?

I broke through their ranks, leaving Calli and Bella to deal with the remaining guards. I had to get to Hardwicke. I cast a wall of air magic right in front of his nose. He slammed against it and bounced back, falling hard on his bottom.

"Where are my sisters?" I demanded as he jumped to his feet, dusting off his suit.

He shot me a derisive glance. "Get lost."

I strode forward slowly, each step pulsing with rage. He thought he could kidnap *my* sisters and sell them into slavery?

"Give me the key to the cages," I ground out.

Something akin to panic flashed across Hardwicke's face, and then he attacked me so fast I barely had time to react. He was very strong, certainly not what I'd expected from his fancy suit and shiny watch. He moved with the speed and strength of a vampire, casting a continuous storm of elemental spells at me. He followed that up with a potent telekinetic blast. Before my breakthrough training session with Ronan, the spell would have broken a few ribs; as it was, it only knocked the wind out of me.

Hardwicke continued his attack, his magic more varied and powerful than any of his guards' spells. He grabbed me and bit down hard on my neck. Pain exploded from the bite. His fangs dug in deep, tearing my flesh. Blood poured down my back.

I knocked him away from me. This had gone on long enough. Anger burning my blood, I went on the offensive.

"I will drain your delicious blood to the last drop," he taunted me. "But not before I find your sisters, wherever they're hiding in my cages. I will drain them first. You will watch me suck the life out of them."

Fury crashed inside of me, like waves against a rocky cliff. Hardwicke's arrogant smirk faded. He stared in shock at my hair. Shock gave way to wonder as my ponytail began to glow. He froze, his eyes wide, mesmerized. I grabbed my handcuffs and secured him to an iron ring on the blood-stained brick wall. It didn't take much imagination to picture what went on in this prison. My pulse racing, my breaths heavy, I lifted my sword in the air.

Bella and Calli came up behind me.

"Leda, your hair," Bella said quietly.

I drew in a few long, calming breaths. "Just a

moment." I took a final deep breath, and the glow faded from my hair.

I snatched the keys from Hardwicke's belt and tossed them to Calli. She went to the cage, opening the lock. The prisoners walked out on shaky legs. There were ten. No, this couldn't be all of them. There were supposed to be twenty-six, not ten. Where were all the other missing teenagers? Where were Gin and Tessa?

Fear and anger exploding like fireworks inside of me, I marched up to Hardwicke. Without delay, without formalities, I slammed the hard hammer of my siren magic against his mind.

"Where are the other prisoners you took? Where are Gin and Tessa?" My voice was a horrible, deep growl, stomping down with the force of a falling boulder.

Hardwicke gasped in fright.

Dissatisfied with his answer, I locked him inside my magic and squeezed down, trying to force the truth out of him. I was using the style of siren magic that Faris had used on me—forcing, not encouraging; brute force, not finesse. My magic was an iron cage, my rage a fire burning through Hardwicke. The rush of power was like nothing I'd ever felt before. This was how you crushed minds.

"Your sisters were taken separately. They were put aside," Hardwicke said in a dull, emotionless voice.

"Why?" I demanded.

"We are building an army, and we need your sisters."

"Who is 'we'?"

"My allies and I. We call ourselves the Pioneers. We're revolutionaries, freedom fighters. We're creating a new order outside the gods and demons. The revolution is coming."

To anarchists, the revolution was always coming. Over

the centuries, many extremists had tried—and failed—to revolt against the gods. But there was something different about these Pioneers. And that something was their magic.

"Are you deserters from the Legion of Angels?" I asked.

"No, only Davenport has ever been a soldier. We have a few supernatural allies, but most of us are people of the Earth."

In other words, mortals, mundane humans with no magic.

"And yet here you are, wielding magic like a soldier in the gods' army," I said.

There was something all-too-familiar about this. It reminded me too strongly of the incident with Stash's army a few months ago, when supernaturals had suddenly gained more powers, taking on all the abilities of Legion soldiers.

Except Stash's army had been freed and they were all back to normal. Not to mention, Hardwicke wasn't crazy like Stash's people had been. Well, at least not crazy as in feral. He could communicate beyond primitive grunts and growls.

"How did your people get their magic?" I asked him.

He pressed his lips together, resisting the pull of my compulsion.

"How did your people get their magic?" I repeated, clamping down my magic on his mind.

His mouth trembled. He was shaking against his hand-cuffs like a fish on a hook. The words finally exploded out of his hard lips. "We took a potion that gave us all this magic."

"All at once?"

"Yes."

I looked at Bella.

"That shouldn't be possible," she told me. "There is no magic bullet. The only potion I know of that can bestow humans with supernatural powers is Nectar. And it doesn't give anyone all those powers at once."

In fact, we took Nectar bit by bit, one dose at a time, usually over the course of years. Nectar, the food of the gods, was pure poison. It killed people who didn't have enough magic potential to absorb it. Legion soldiers had to train hard to increase our chances of survival. This mystery potion Hardwicke claimed existed sounded too good to be true.

"I want to see this potion," I said to Hardwicke.

"We don't have any of it here."

A convenient lie or simply good security? In either case, it was a big, fat dead end.

"What do the Pioneers want with my sisters?" I asked him.

"Your sisters are special. We need their unique magic."

Just like the elemental I'd questioned had told me. What the hell was up with my sisters' magic? They'd never shown signs of having any.

"Where are they?"

He shook his head. "I don't know."

And he was even telling the truth. There wasn't anything left of his mind to fight me.

"Who has them?"

"I don't know."

As soon as the words left his mouth, Calli raised her gun and shot him in the head. He didn't die immediately, his powers keeping him alive. So she just kept shooting until he stopped moving.

I spun around to face her. "Why did you kill my prisoner? *Again.* I was getting somewhere with him."

"He knew nothing more, and he was a threat," she said calmly.

"A threat to whom? He was cuffed to the wall."

She didn't respond.

"This is about Tessa and Gin, isn't it? About their magic? You know what they're all talking about. You know why my sisters are being hunted."

"Not here. Not now."

I glanced back and watched Jace's team enter the prison room. No one followed them in, so they must have neutralized all of Hardwicke's forces.

"Have you seen the deserter?" Jace asked.

"He got away."

Jace frowned at me.

"There was a whole army between him and me, and he was already escaping out of the window."

His mouth narrowing into a hard, tight line, Jace glanced at the dead man chained to the wall. "Who is that?"

"Hardwicke, the former leader of this castle."

The little vein in Jace's temple bulged with irritation. It looked ready to pop. "Damn it, Leda. I needed him. The Interrogators could have gotten something out of him."

"I'm sorry. There was nothing I could do."

"You could have *not* shot him in the head six times. He was chained up. He wasn't going anywhere."

"He had the strength of a vampire and the magic of an elemental. He was about to break free of his chains. And he had a fireball in his hands."

It was a big fat lie, but I didn't waver in my conviction. As long as I'd been the one to fire the shots and I claimed it was in self defense, the Legion couldn't do much. Sure,

Colonel Fireswift could threaten me, but he wouldn't kill me.

But if Jace found out that it had been Calli who'd shot Hardwicke, he'd be forced to report that back to his father. Colonel Fireswift would then throw her to the Interrogators until they found out why she'd done it. Calli didn't shoot people on a whim. She'd done it because she was scared—scared for Tessa and Gin, for what would happen to them if anyone found out about their mysterious magic. I wished she'd at least tell me what was going on.

"I interrogated him," I told Jace. "He is part of an organization called the Pioneers."

"The Pioneers." He repeated the word like it was tainted.

"You've heard of them?"

"Yes. They've been around for years, hiding in the shadows. Their goal is to overthrow the gods and rule the world. So far, it's been nothing but big talk and treacherous promises. They haven't actually acted until now. What's changed?"

"They've figured out how to bottle magic that a mortal can drink, creating a potion with all the benefits of Nectar, and with none of the risk of instant death."

"That is not possible," Jace stated.

"Are you so sure about that? You fought Hardwicke's guards. You saw for yourself that it *is* possible."

He clenched his jaw. "It should not be possible."

"What is and what should be are two entirely different things. If things were as they should be, monsters wouldn't roam the Earth, and I'd be a millionaire."

He shook his head at me. "You're taking this situation too lightly."

"Right now, Jace, I'm exhausted, not to mention scared out of my mind that something's happened to my sisters."

His eyes panned across the room. "They're not here?"

"They're not here. And they're not the only prisoners still at large."

"I'm sorry. We'll get them back, Leda," he said, so low that his soldiers couldn't hear.

"Thank you," I whispered back.

"Load the kidnap victims and the Pioneers into the truck," he said, louder this time.

His soldiers had already gathered the prisoners together and put the surviving guards in chains. I didn't like them much, but I couldn't deny that they were efficient.

As soon as Jace and his team left the room, I turned to confront Calli—but she was already gone.

———

IT WASN'T until we were back on the train to Chicago that I got a chance to speak to my foster mother. Bella and I found Calli ordering a strong cup of coffee in the onboard restaurant.

"We need to talk," I told her. "Follow me."

I led her and Bella to an abandoned train car. I put up some anti-spy Magitech, then turned to face Calli.

"Time to fess up. You're going to tell us what the hell is going on with our little sisters."

Calli sighed. "It's a long story."

I waited for her to say more, but she didn't. The train rumbled and shook over the tracks, filling the heavy silence.

"Gin and Tessa were taken for their magic," I prompted her.

Calli's face was grim.

"You never told us that Tessa and Gin had magic." I looked at Bella. "Did you know?"

"No."

"Calli, what's going on?" I demanded. "What are Tessa's and Gin's powers? What is making people hunt them?"

"I don't know what their powers are," she said. "But this isn't the first time they've been hunted for their magic. Many years ago when the girls were very young, hardly older than toddlers, the warlords of the wild magic lands, beyond civilization's borders, went to war over them."

CHAPTER 18

CALLI'S STORY

"It was fourteen years ago," Calli began her story. "I had a job that brought me to the Sea of Sin, a vast savannah where monsters roam and the world's most vicious warlords call home. I'd been tasked to recover a magical treasure at the so-called Paragon Temple, an old gold mine abandoned centuries ago. I got the treasure out, but while leaving the ruins, I was besieged by monsters and forced to flee."

Growing up, Calli had told us many tales of the wilderness back from her younger days. They always started a lot like this: with a job that went horribly wrong.

"The monsters drove me to the edge of the savannah," she continued. "To escape them, I ran into a jungle. The beasts did not follow me. I knew that meant whatever lived in the trees was far worse than the monsters, but I had little choice. So I traveled through the jungle, looking for another path out, hoping to evade the monsters and find a way around them to my truck.

"While wandering through the jungle, I soon realized I was not alone. The infamous human warlord Hellfire had claimed this place as his own. I hid from his patrols, taking cover up in the trees. The soldiers were hunting someone. Two escaped prisoners, I overheard. I assumed they were prisoners taken during Hellfire's battle with the Rogue King, another warlord in those parts. Apparently, the Rogue King took issue with Hellfire's territorial claim to the jungle.

"I knew I had to get out of there quickly, before I was caught in the crossfire of this battle of the warlords. As soon as the patrols passed, I hurried off, and not a moment too soon. As I fled, I heard the clamor of the two war bands clashing—bullets and blades, magic and machines. I ran away from the battle as fast as my legs would carry me. And that's when I found them, two girls no older than four years old, curled up under a gum tree."

"Gin and Tessa," I said.

Calli nodded. "They looked so small, so scared. They were holding to each other tightly, afraid to let go. When they saw I didn't belong to a warlord's band, I managed to coax them out of hiding. They told me they'd escaped Hellfire's camp."

"Gin and Tessa were the escaped prisoners Hellfire's patrols had spoken of, the ones the soldiers were hunting," Bella said quietly.

"Hellfire's soldiers weren't the only ones hunting them," Calli told us. "The Rogue King had started a war with Hellfire over them. These two little girls had been out there in the jungle for months, fighting to stay free every second since their escape. They had killed beasts for food. They had killed soldiers to survive. Two young innocents, no longer innocent."

"How awful." Bella's voice shook.

The thought of these two little girls—my sisters—

having to go through all that made me sick to my stomach. "You never figured out what their magic is?" I asked Calli.

"I grabbed their hands, and we ran out of that jungle as fast as we could go. I never saw their magic," she replied. "The warlords had spent months hunting them—and fighting each other—over Tessa and Gin, so I knew their magic had to be very rare and powerful. The girls didn't want to talk about their magic or what had happened in the jungle. They shuddered whenever I asked, so I stopped asking. They spoke in hushed whispers of terrible black beasts in the jungle, so vicious that even the warlords' bands shunned them.

"From those short tales, I gathered that they each possessed a different kind of magic. They'd met in a warlord's laboratory, the atrocities they'd lived through creating an unbreakable bond between them, a bond stronger than blood."

"In all these years, they've never spoken of their magic," I said.

Guilt flashed across Calli's face. "They were four years old, and they were fighting for their lives in a monster-infested jungle. They were far too young to have lived through all that. Those warlords had stolen their childhood from them. On our way across the plains, they fell asleep in the truck. As they slept, looking so sweet, so innocent, I swore I would find a way to give them a normal life, the life they deserved. So when we got home, I carried their sleeping bodies to Zane."

My brother Zane was Calli's first adopted child. He'd been with her longer than any of us.

"I asked Zane to use his magic to block the girls' memories of their early life, to block their suffering so they could live normal lives," she said. "They were so young, and memories fade easily at that age."

Bella took Calli's hand and squeezed it. "I would have done the same thing. The two of them had seen too much." Her voice caught in her throat. "They'd killed too much. They never would have grown up to be the sweet, happy girls they are now, girls full of hope, innocence, and fun. You gave them a chance at a bright life, not one tainted by blood and fear."

Calli looked at me. "You don't agree with Bella."

"You meant well, Calli, but secrets have a knack for not staying buried. And now the secrets of your past have come back to haunt us. The Pioneers have found out about Gin and Tessa, and now they are hunting them down too. What else are you hiding from us?" I asked her. "What else do you know? Did you know about Bella's origin as well?"

"No, I didn't know, but now, looking back, I'm not surprised that she's special. He had a way of leading me to special children."

"He?"

"Never mind."

"The time for secrets between us is over," I told her.

"We're family. From now on, only the truth," agreed Bella.

"Ok," said Calli. "A long time ago, I had a friend. Every so often, he sent jobs my way. He was the one who sent me to the orphanage where I found you, Bella. And because he warned me not to take a job, I was home when Zane's mother stopped by and begged me to take him in. He hooked me up with the treasure-hunting gig that led me to Tessa and Gin. I don't know how, but he always manipulated things so that I found my children. One of his jobs led me to you, Leda, on the streets of Purgatory."

I mulled that over.

"I've always known my children are all special, but I didn't know how," Calli said. "Zane a telepath. Bella the granddaughter of the Dark Lord of Witchcraft. Tessa and Gin so special that people were going to war over them back when they were only four years old."

"And me?" I asked her.

"I don't know, but you are special too. I've witnessed your potential firsthand, kid. Even when you were a child, I knew there was something special inside of you, just waiting to happen. The Legion has been good for you. You're finally realizing your potential."

I chuckled. "That was hard for you to admit, wasn't it?"

Before going independent, Calli had worked for the League, the largest bounty hunter organization on Earth. The free spirits of the League weren't overly fond of the Legion of Angels and their black-and-white world order.

"It's not just about the Legion, Leda. I was afraid to let any of my children go. Because, as you know, danger befalls special people in this world. Trouble follows them. Evil is drawn to them. Monsters seek them out—of both the beastly and human variety," she said. "Each of you has a great destiny, but great is a far cry from good. You are each meant for something special, something that will change the world. Something you might not survive."

"Aren't you being a tad melodramatic?"

"No. I was afraid for you when you joined the Legion, Leda. And then it turned out that my fears were realized, that someone had manipulated you into joining."

"It all started with Zane's abduction," said Bella. "That was the beginning of the journey for each of us. For Zane. For you, Leda. For me. And for Gin and Tessa. It all snowballed from there."

"Ever since I took you all in, I've wanted nothing more than to keep you safe. I swore to protect you in every way I could. And yet when Zane was taken, the hard, cold truth reared its ugly head: I am powerless to protect any of you. I can only watch as each of you is taken from me, one by one. As you're each thrown into mortal danger. And now Gin and Tessa are gone too."

Tears fell down Calli's cheeks. She'd always been our mountain—so strong, so unmoving. It hurt to see her like this.

"Calli…" I choked up on the teardrops of my bleeding soul.

Bella added her tears to mine.

"Ok, enough of that now." Calli wiped our tears away. "Legion soldiers are supposed to be tough, right?"

"Well, I guess I'm just a rebel."

I wrapped one arm around Bella, the other around Calli, and drew them into a deep hug. Hugs had a magic unlike any other; potions healed the body, but it was hugs that had the power to heal the soul.

Finally, I pulled away, clearing my tight throat. "We will get Gin and Tessa back," I promised, the conviction ringing in my voice as surely as in my heart. "We'll find Zane too. And I'm not going anywhere. Honestly, Calli, I'm surprised at you. You should know better. You should know that I'm far too stubborn to die."

Calli brushed her own tears away. "That's true."

Calming my emotions, I rubbed my red eyes. "And I never seek out trouble," I added with a smirk.

Bella snorted.

"You've always told yourself that," Calli chuckled.

"No, I always said it for *your* benefit," I told her. "But

219

since we're all being honest now, I should rephrase: I only seek out trouble when absolutely necessary."

"Which is why you're dating an angel," Bella said with a sweet smile.

"Actually, I only did that to freak out Mom."

We both laughed.

"Ok, you comedians." Calli's eyes twinkled. "In all honesty, Leda, I've come to recognize that your angel gets you into less trouble than you get him into."

I blinked. "Did Nero just get Calli's stamp of approval?" I asked Bella.

"As close to it as he can get," my sister replied.

"Great. I'll have to tell him Calli loves him too. We can invite him to dinner after we rescue Gin and Tessa."

"Just how did the Pioneers find out their magic was special?" Bella asked Calli.

"Hardwicke," Calli said darkly. "I recognized him. He was there, fourteen years ago. Back then, he was a member of Hellfire's war band that hunted Tessa and Gin through the jungle."

CHAPTER 19

CROSSFIRE

I thought about Calli's story the rest of the ride back to Chicago. My sisters had magic, something powerful enough that warlords had gone to war over it. Their magic was unlike anything this world had ever seen, Hardwicke had said. What did that even mean?

Back at the Legion building in Chicago, I found Jace in his sister's office, sitting at her desk. He'd told me earlier that he was using it while she was away. His hair was disheveled, his eyes unsettled, constantly flickering from one point in the room to another. I'd never seen him look so stressed.

"Any news on Davenport?"

"No." He bit out the word.

Jace thought it was my fault that Davenport had gotten away, but I hadn't been lying when I'd told him there was no way I could have made it to the deserter. There had been too many soldiers. Even if my path had been clear, I'd never had made it all the way up the walls to him before he slipped away. He was too fast, and I couldn't fly. I wondered how he'd gotten way up there so fast.

"We'll find him," I told Jace.

He rose to his feet. "I spoke to some of our Pioneer prisoners."

There was no doubt as to what he meant by 'spoke'. After all, he was the son of a Legion Interrogator.

"The deserter has disappeared without a trace," Jace continued. "We can't track him, and no one knows where he was going."

"You're not going after him," I realized.

"No." He didn't look happy. He'd been tracking Davenport for months. Catching the deserter was important to him—and to Colonel Fireswift, who hated traitors even more than he hated me.

"The First Angel has decided that we have bigger fish to fry," Jace said. "The Interrogators will question our prisoners to find out where the rest of the kidnapped teenagers are being held. Then we will free them."

"But not before you destroy the Pioneers for daring to defy the gods."

Save the prisoners and punish a whole ban of traitors all at once? Nyx was nothing if not efficient.

"That's how things are done, Leda. All threats to the gods' order must be obliterated. If criminals get away with defying the gods, then others see that. They will think the Legion is weak. More criminals will rise, swarms of them, too many to control. A plague of crime will consume the Earth. More innocent people will get hurt. I know your sisters are important to you, but they are just two people. Many more will suffer if we don't put everything into stopping the Pioneers' rebellion."

He had a point. Centuries ago, when the world fell to the monsters, many people had turned on one another. Back then, it had been every man for himself. Crime rose as gangsters competed in the scramble to the top, battling one another to fill the power vacuum. That continued until the gods stepped in and brought back order. So as viciously merciless as the Legion could be, they were looking out for the greater good. Sometimes the greater good meant not making any single person important; it meant making the collective of people important.

I was all for serving the greater good—most of the time. But Gin and Tessa were not random numbers in a casualties-of-war spreadsheet. These were my sisters we were talking about. They were important to me. *Very* important. The Legion could make the Pioneers their priority, but I was making Tessa and Gin mine.

The thing was, if the Legion found out about my sisters' magic, they would suddenly make them a priority too. That just wasn't the sort of priority we wanted. If their magic was really so unique, the Legion would turn them over to the gods, who would use my sisters for their own purposes. People had gone to war over their magic; their powers surely weren't something as innocuous as making the world's best pizza.

In that way, Jace's indifference toward my sisters was reassuring—because that meant the Legion didn't know about their magic. As long as there were other kidnapped people still missing, my sisters blended into the crowd. They didn't stand out as special. The Legion was more focused on people like the missing daughter of an angel. She was just a few months shy of her twenty-second birth-day, when she could join the Legion and claim her magical legacy.

Jace met my gaze, his eyes hard. "I know that look."

"What look?"

"That look of calculation in your eyes."

"Oh?"

"It's the same look you got just before you went off alone to rescue General Windstriker on the Black Plains during our first mission. It's the look you get when you're about to take matters into your own hands."

I snorted. "That's my default look. I *always* take matters into my own hands."

"For once, let the Legion Interrogators do their job instead of going off your own reckless adventure," he said, his voice almost pleading.

"Now what would be the fun in that?" I countered with a smirk.

"I'm serious, Leda."

"Of course you are."

A heavy sigh rocked his chest. "If you get yourself into trouble, I can't protect you from my father's wrath. I've already covered for you enough as it is."

"What do you mean by 'covered for you'?"

"My father wasn't happy to learn that Hardwicke is dead. He would have been a valuable source of information."

And that's why Calli had killed him, so the Legion wouldn't find out about Gin and Tessa—or how the Earth's criminal underworld was going to war over their magic.

"I told him Hardwicke was killed in the crossfire," Jace continued. "Because if he knew it was you, he would find a way to punish you."

I didn't doubt that. That's why I'd said that I'd shot Hardwicke, to protect Calli from the Legion's wrath. And now Jace was covering for me.

"You didn't have to do that," I told him.

A smile twisted his lips. "Sure I did. If my father killed

you, he'd ruin our competition. And I want to see the look on your face when I get my wings first."

"Keep on smiling, Fireswift. You'll need these happy memories to make it through the day when I win."

"Oh, really? From where I'm standing, I've already won."

"Then you must be standing on your head, doofus."

"Watch your mouth, *Lieutenant*," he snapped, but a hint of amusement tainted his sharp rebuttal.

I drew my mouth into a smile. I could tell from his shaking shoulders, Jace was trying really hard not to laugh.

"Have you ever considered that I'm just letting you think you're winning?" I asked. "Then, at the last moment, I'll jump out ahead, leaving you in the dust."

"There's little time left for your miraculous save, Pandora."

True. He had just two levels to go before he became an angel, and I still had three. Plus, right now I had more important things to worry about than leveling up my magic. Like saving my sisters.

And I wasn't doing very well on that task either. I still had no idea where Gin and Tessa were being held. I'd broken Hardwicke's mind, and he hadn't been lying when he'd said he didn't know where they were. Maybe some of his soldiers would know. Maybe they'd overheard something during a prisoner transfer. That was an awful lot of maybes.

"Your mind is somewhere else," Jace said seriously.

"Yes, sorry. As fun as this competition between us is, I have a lot on my mind right now."

"Understandable. You should give your mind a break and try to get some sleep while you still can."

He had a point. I hadn't slept much last night. And who knew when we'd have to head out again.

"I'll let you know as soon as I know anything," he promised, setting his hand on my arm.

I forced a cheerful smile; lately, it had been hard to keep my spirits up. "Thanks," I said, then I left the office.

But I didn't go to my room. My mind was too busy, buzzing with worries. Sleep would be impossible. I hurried down the hall, my body as restless as my mind. There was only one remedy for that.

I went to the training hall, hoping to tire myself out. I found Meda and Maya waiting for me there instead. Though the sister goddesses were dressed in identical green satin dresses, their accessories differed. Meda had embellished her dress with a gold belt; potion vials dangled from it like tree ornaments. She wore a slender dagger at her waist as well. Silver strands of gemstones hung from her sister Maya's belt. And they were both wearing gold headbands set with emeralds.

"You have quite a problem," Meda said.

Her tone was very relaxed, very casual, but I knew there was magic beneath those innocent, sweet facades. The two sisters were powerful and dangerous goddesses.

"You should ask your sister Bella to look at the potion the Pioneers take to gain their powers," Maya said.

And then, before I could respond, the goddesses were gone. Talk about cryptic. I couldn't decide if they thought they were helping out, or if they were just being purposefully vague. But on the plus side, they hadn't tried to kill me. I was going to call that one step up from my most recent heavenly visits.

I browsed through the training programs on the panel

and selected one called the Wall of Woe. Now that was a great name.

As soon as I activated the training program, a telekinetic barrier slid out of the floor, swallowing me in a glowing blue bubble. I poked it with my finger, and it nipped back with a hiss. It seemed like I was supposed to break through the barrier by neutralizing the telekinetic energy.

Someone stepped into the gym, but I couldn't make out the face through the blurry barrier.

"You're not sleeping," Jace's voice spoke over the hum and hiss.

"My mind is too busy to sleep." Thinking back on what Meda and Maya had said, I decided to go out on a limb. "Have your people looked at the Pioneers' blood?"

"Why do you ask?"

"Hardwicke told me the Pioneers supernatural powers come from a potion."

"Before he attacked you and you had to shoot him." Jace was not buying my story.

"Yeah, well, you know me. I talk to people in battle all the time."

"I know. But they don't always talk back. Especially not to volunteer important information."

"He didn't exactly volunteer it willingly."

"Oh?"

"I might have crushed his mind like a nut and squeezed his secrets out of him," I admitted.

Jace was quiet. With the blurry blue bubble blocking my view, I couldn't gauge his reaction very well. I couldn't even see his face.

"Jace?"

"You crushed his mind," he said slowly. "While fighting him."

Actually, while fighting him, I'd mesmerized him with my hair. And as he stood there frozen, I'd cuffed him to the wall.

But all I said was, "You're not the only one who can multitask magic, hotshot."

"Have your abilities been evaluated yet?"

"Evaluated?"

"Scored. Not everyone possesses all magical abilities equally. We all have our strengths and weaknesses."

"Magic and counter magic."

He nodded. "Eventually, the Legion evaluates all of us who survive long enough. It's how they decide where to put us, where we'll be the most useful. People with powerful witchcraft magic go to the Legion research laboratories and hospital departments. Elementals with earth and metal magic become the Legion's blacksmiths. And people with exceptional siren magic become Interrogators."

"I think I recall a few memos about testing on my schedule," I said. "But I've missed all my appointments so far. I've been a little busy stopping psychopaths to play lab rat."

"If my father finds out about your siren magic, he'll make you an Interrogator."

I didn't want to be an Interrogator. "I don't think I have the right temperament for the job."

"He won't give you a choice."

"Then it's a good thing you're good at keeping my secrets."

He fell silent again.

"Jace?"

"I'm still here."

"So what did you find in the Pioneers' blood?" I asked him.

"Nothing. No traces of magical substances. In fact, their blood was completely human. It was devoid of magic."

The Wall of Woe zapped me. I gave it the evil eye. It shifted from dark cerulean to a blue so light that it was nearly transparent. I could finally see Jace. The haze of the bubble made his face glow; there was an unnatural glossy sheen to it, like all his features had been partially blurred out.

"That's impossible," I told Jace. "Hardwicke's guards all possessed supernatural powers. Some of them could wield more than one supernatural power."

"Including Hardwicke?"

"Yes, he pretty much had them all. So how can your lab's test claim they possess no magic? There should be traces of the magic potion in their blood." Unless… "Idiots," I muttered.

"I hope you're not talking about me."

"No, not you. Your father's Interrogators. They mucked this all up brilliantly."

"How?"

"What's the first thing Legion Interrogators do before they begin questioning a supernatural?"

"As a rule, they administer a magic-blocking potion to neutralize their powers."

"And that's why the labs didn't find any magic in the Pioneers' bodies."

"The Interrogators' potion obliterated any traces of it," Jace realized.

"Right. In their attempt to make the prisoners not a threat, the Interrogators made them useless. That means if we want to analyze the Pioneers' potion, we need to capture a fresh new prisoner. If only we knew where they're all hiding."

"The organization's cells are independent. None of the common soldiers know anything about the other cells. Otherwise, we would have taken them out years ago."

"How about you give me a go at finding the Pioneers?" I said.

"You?"

"Before joining the illustrious Legion of Angels, I used to be a bounty hunter, remember? I'm good at tracking people."

I'd been doing it for a decade, ever since Calli had started bringing me on jobs.

"I doubt my father would agree to that," he said.

"Because you need to get all the credit."

"Yeah, sometimes I wonder if this is more about putting you down than about pushing me up."

I wouldn't have been surprised. Colonel Fireswift considered it blasphemy that a dirty street rat like me could make it into the Legion of Angels, let alone had any shot of becoming an angel before his son.

"What your father doesn't know won't hurt him," I said.

He looked at me like my hair was on fire—or more like I'd tried to set *his* hair on fire.

"What do you know about the Legion deserter?" I asked. "Most specifically, how was his magic evaluated?"

"The Legion's tests determined that witchcraft is Davenport's strongest power by a long shot. He must be descended from witches."

"Don't you think that's a bit too much of a coincidence?"

"What do you mean?" he asked, his eyes lighting up with excitement. He was hoping to nab the deserter as part of this after all.

"Davenport was working with the Pioneers. What if he's the one who designed the Pioneers' magic potion? You said his specialty is Witch's Cauldron," I pointed out.

Jace's face fell in disappointment, as though he'd expected that I had something better. Apparently, my wild theory had fallen far from the mark.

"No one, not even a former major in the Legion of Angels, is so good that he could create a potion to bestow magic upon mundane humans," he stated. "You simply cannot give people the power of the Legion without the consequences. Nectar and Venom are the only potions with the power to bestow magic. What you're saying isn't just crazy talk; it's heresy."

"Then how do you explain the Pioneers' powers?" I shot back.

"I can't," he said, chewing on his lower lip. This affront to the rules of the world as he knew them was bothering him.

It was bothering me too. There were so many questions, so many things that just didn't add up. And the deeper I dug, the more I found myself buried in uncertainty.

The Wall of Woe zapped me again, irritated that I'd been ignoring it. I swore at it under my breath.

"It's on a timer, you know. It's going to crush you if you don't break through," Jace told me.

"Lovely. The Legion's training program designers sure don't half-ass it."

I made a fist and punched the Wall of Woe. It punched back, slamming me against the other side of the barrier. I made two fists this time and punched harder. Even as the barrier pushed against me, shooting jolts of magic up my arms that ricocheted to every part of my body, I stood my ground and bore the pain, hitting it harder and faster like it was one enormous punching bag. The barrier groaned, a hairline crack in the telekinetic energy forming. I aimed my next punch at the crack, smashing it again and again. The opening swelled to the width of my shoulders. Then the bubble popped, dissolving like a piece of burnt tissue paper.

The unnatural glow faded. I froze as soon as I saw Jace's face. He looked worse than a person-of-interest did after the Legion's Interrogators were through with them. My eyes dropped, snagging on the split and bloody remnants of his leather vest.

"What the hell happened to you?" I gasped.

"I was training with my father."

His father had punished him—except the sadistic angel had called it 'training'. To Colonel Fireswift, training and torture were one and the same.

"He did this because Hardwicke is dead." Anger shook my words.

Jace said nothing, but he didn't have to. I knew I was right.

"How could a father do this to his son?" I said in disgust.

"He is an angel."

"I'm getting tired of that excuse."

"You don't understand. You dance with angels, you are an angel's lover, but you still don't understand them."

"We all justify the angels' actions by saying, 'that's just how angels are'. But that's no excuse. It would be like if a vampire killed someone and people said, 'oh, oops, he couldn't help it. It's simply in his nature.' " I frowned. "Well, I'm calling bullshit. We can all help it. We can all choose to be something other than a monster. I understand angels make tough and ugly choices, like torturing enemies to save innocent lives. But there is a line, a line we must not cross. That line is family. Every time your father lifts his hand to 'teach you a lesson', he crosses that line. This isn't training. It's brutality. And it's not ok."

With that said, I stormed out of the gym, my outrage propelling me toward Colonel Fireswift's office. I pushed the door open and barged into the room without ceremony.

I gave the angel a long, hard glare and declared, "What you're doing to your son is not ok."

Annoyance flickered across Colonel Fireswift's face, before coldness swallowed his aggravation. "You forget your place as a soldier in the Legion of Angels."

"You forget yours as a father. You can't torture your own children."

"It's not torture. It's training."

"Have you been hurting people for so long that you can no longer tell the difference?"

"How dare you challenge centuries of Legion tradition." His voice was a whisper of menace.

"I will challenge anything I know to be wrong."

He stared at me in utter disbelief, as though he'd forgotten that he'd told himself I wasn't worth an emotional response. "I don't like you."

I let out a dry laugh. "I'd never have guessed."

"You are mouthy, rude, and you think the rules don't apply to you. You get too personally involved with people. You need to maintain distance so your judgment isn't clouded."

"Please tell me more about my best qualities."

"I don't like you," he repeated. "And you don't like me. You think I'm cruel and vicious."

"You said it, not me."

"I am an angel." His words rang with pride. "For us, the ends justify the means. How often have you found yourself in the same situation?" His brows lifted knowingly.

I opened my mouth to challenge the accusation, but no words came. Instead, memories flashed through my head—interrogating the werewolf and the fire elemental, cracking Hardwicke's mind in my desperation to save my sisters.

"My civilized methods are preferable to your uncontrolled, dirty tactics," Colonel Fireswift stated calmly.

I pulled my mind out of the pit of guilt and turmoil that I'd dug myself into. "I throw rocks and sticks at my opponent to catch them off guard. I engage in unorthodox fighting. You torture and kill your subordinates. And your family."

"If you survive long enough, you will come to understand."

I huffed in disgust. But before I could think of a more articulate response, distressed shouts echoed down the hallway, spilling into the open doorway of Colonel Fireswift's office.

Legion soldiers were professional, well-trained, and had near-perfect control over their emotions. They didn't typically shout out in alarm. Which meant something was wrong. Very wrong.

I rushed out of the room. Colonel Fireswift was right beside me. As we came around the corner into the open atrium, I stared in shock at Harker. His uniform was torn to shreds, his face blackened by dirt and ash. Burns and blood covered his arms. A dozen other soldiers stood behind him. The best of them were in no better shape than Harker. The worst of them were so broken that they had to be carried in by their comrades.

Colonel Fireswift came to a stop in front of Harker. "What happened?"

"The failing wall in Memphis was a trap. We lost people." His face was haunted, his voice grim. "An angel is dead."

As the gravity, the finality of his words sank in, I looked around frantically, my pulse racing.

I grabbed Harker by the shoulders and demanded, "Where's Nero?" I shook him harder, screaming, "Where the hell is Nero?!"

CHAPTER 20

DEATH OF AN ANGEL

*H*arker's tired eyes met mine. "Nero stayed behind to clean up the mess. He'll be fine." He spoke the words with confidence, but he looked worried, even as he turned toward Colonel Fireswift. "Colonel Battleborn is dead."

Three angels had been working on a single mission? The situation must have been even more dire than I'd thought. The way Nero had spoken, it had sounded like the barrier had just been weakened. Were the monsters already really so close to breaking through the wall?

"I need to check on the wounded," Harker said. "Basanti is in the hospital wing."

"Is she ok?" I asked.

His expression was dark. "She's a fighter."

Jace, Colonel Fireswift, and I followed Harker to the infirmary, which was in a state of chaos. Every bed was taken by a soldier, and there were still more injured lying on the floor. The doctors rushed in every direction, completely overtaxed. I couldn't remember ever seeing a Legion hospital so crowded with wounded soldiers.

I spotted Basanti. She was lying unconscious on a bed at the edge of the room, right under a window that looked out on a magnificent blue and pink sunrise. The colorful morning sky seemed to mock us with its beauty.

Harker scanned the room, taking in the devastation. He looked awful. It wasn't the burns or dirt that stained his skin and hair, or the tears in his clothing. It wasn't even the cuts and gashes in his body that refused to heal. It was the haunted expression in his eyes, like he was staring straight at the end of the world.

"What happened?" I asked as a doctor began healing Basanti's wounds.

I was almost afraid to ask. And I was even more afraid of his answer.

"This whole thing was a setup," Harker said. "The Magitech barrier at Memphis wasn't breaking down because of monsters, and it wasn't succumbing to the effects of old age. It was sabotaged from the inside. The saboteurs took down the barrier. They lured us in by creating a threat so horrible, so serious, they knew it would bring in the Legion's best, including multiple angels. This was a trap, designed to deal a major blow to the Legion of Angels. We weren't supposed to survive."

"Did you capture the saboteurs?" Colonel Fireswift asked him.

"No. They killed themselves before we got to them." Harker met Colonel Fireswift's gaze with darkness in his eyes. "They were six of our own. Legion soldiers."

Shock flashed across Colonel Fireswift's face. It was an expression I'd never seen there before. "Deserters? Six at once?"

He looked disgusted, angry, outraged, and worried—all at once. That was another new expression for him. But a moment later, his face hardened with resolve, his cold, cruel shield sliding into place once more.

"No, they weren't deserting," Harker said. "They were committing suicide. The saboteurs never expected to survive this ordeal. They were hoping they'd take us down with them."

Colonel Fireswift's mouth tightened into a hard line. "Fanatics then."

"No—"

Raised voices clamored behind us, drowning out Harker's words. Doctors rushed about frantically, gathering around a convulsing female soldier on one of the beds. Her body rattled and shook, her wounds pulsing blood. Bathed in crimson, I hardly recognized her. It was Major Kendra Fireswift, Jace's sister, Colonel Fireswift's daughter.

And she was dying.

Her face contorted in agony as the life dripped out of her. The doctors rushed around her bed, trying to save her, but nothing they did made a difference. They were losing her.

Colonel Fireswift rushed to his daughter's bed, pushing the doctors aside. He set his hands, aglow with healing magic, on her chest. Desperation crinkled his brow as he poured magic into her. But his angelic healing powers were no match for whatever was killing her.

Jace stood on the other side of her bed. He had no healing magic, but he wasn't idle. His hands were a blur as he mixed potions and cut bandages, trying to stop the bleeding.

Beneath the splashes of crimson, Kendra's face had grown deathly pale. She was screaming so loud that the windows were shattering all around her.

"What happened to her?" I asked Harker in horror.

"She was poisoned," he told me. "The saboteurs used bullets infused with Venom. She was hit. And now the dark magic is destroying her light magic, unraveling her piece by piece, strand by strand."

I stepped forward, determined to help. I didn't know what I was going to do, but I had to do *something*.

Harker caught my arm. "It's no use," he said in a low whisper.

"I can save her," I whispered back. "I can suck the Venom out of her. Just like I did to Basanti."

"It's too late. The poison has spread too far for her to survive. At this point, sucking the Venom from her would only expose your dark magic. There's no hope for her."

I watched Kendra convulsing against her father's hold, her blood splashing him and Jace. Acid rose in my throat.

"How can you be so sure?" I demanded.

"Because I've seen this poison work. I've already watched half of our team die in agony to it. I tried to heal Selena. I watched her die in my arms, unraveling to nothing." There was a haunted look in Harker's eyes. "We very nearly lost Basanti. The Venom bullet only grazed her arm, but if Nero hadn't been so quick to cut away the infected flesh before the poison spread, she would be dead too. Selena and Kendra were some of our best, next in line to become angels. They were both chosen for this mission for their powerful magic. And now they're dead because of it."

"Colonel Battleborn?" I asked.

"He was hit with a Venom bullet as well. He died even faster than Selena."

The more light magic you had, the faster the Venom killed you—and the more it made you suffer as it ripped the shreds of your light magic apart.

"How did Legion soldiers get their hands on Venom?" I demanded.

"I do not know. But the Legion has suffered a mighty blow today," Harker said darkly. "Colonel Battleborn."

Kendra's screams had stopped. She lay motionless on the bed, but even in death, she didn't appear to be at peace.

Harker's face was blank. He was blocking out his emotions before they overwhelmed him. "Selena and Kendra, both rising stars, both so close to becoming angels."

Colonel Fireswift removed his bloody hand from his daughter's forehead. He stepped back from her bed, his eyes aflame with manic energy. I saw the moment that he lost it, the moment his control snapped and his pain consumed him. I just couldn't move fast enough to stop what happened next.

Magic exploded out of the angel. The shock wave cut through the room, toppling everyone in its path. What remained of the glass doors shattered, raining down like tears, the tears the angel himself could not shed.

The Legion had suffered heavy losses today, and we were going to lose a whole lot more people if someone didn't stop Colonel Fireswift now. Harker ran toward him, but his brush with death had taken its toll. He was slower, less coordinated than usual. Colonel Fireswift tossed him aside easily.

The wounded soldiers in the room weren't in any condition to restrain an enraged angel. The doctors were no match for him either. One look at Jace was all it took to realize he would be of no help. He was just standing there in shock, holding his dead sister's hand.

Which left me.

I rushed toward Colonel Fireswift, intercepting him

before he split a hospital bed—and the patient on it—in two. I put myself between the bed and the angel.

"Colonel Fireswift," I snapped sharply.

He didn't even seem to realize I was there. His pain had blinded him.

I'd just been arguing with him, telling him off for being inhuman, and then this happened. He'd lost his daughter. Much as I disliked him, I couldn't feel anything but bad for him right now. His eyes glistened with unshed tears. I could see the agony eating away at him, forcing him into a rage. He actually *could* feel and care. Apparently, he was more human than I'd thought.

The revelation, unfortunately, didn't do me any good. I wasn't strong enough to contain an enraged angel. If only Nyx were here. Or Nero. My heart thumped out a sharp jab of pain.

Colonel Fireswift threw a chair at Harker. I caught the flying piece of furniture and tossed it aside.

"This is your fault," Colonel Fireswift growled at Harker, his voice more beast than man. "She's dead because of your incompetence." His words dripped menace.

Harker was injured. In a fight, he wouldn't stand a chance. Colonel Fireswift would destroy him. The Legion would lose another angel, and I would lose a friend.

Colonel Fireswift swung a punch at Harker. I slid between the angels, catching Colonel Fireswift's fist between my hands and pushing back. Surprised, the angel stumbled back a step.

"Get out of my way," he snarled at me, magic flashing in his eyes.

"No."

He swung a punch at me. I tried to evade, but he was too fast. Pain exploded in my body as his fist crashed into my stomach. I doubled over, coughing up blood. He moved around me to get to Harker, but I mirrored his movements, making myself the shield between the two angels. The look Colonel Fireswift shot me declared loud and clear that he had no qualms about breaking right through me.

The rational part of me knew I was no match for Colonel Fireswift, but the rebel in me refused to listen. Sure, he was faster, stronger, and had buckets more magic than I did. By the rules of this universe, I didn't have a chance in hell of beating him. But I also didn't play by the rules.

As he moved in for his next barrage, I hit him hard with my siren magic, locking it around him. "Hasn't the Legion lost enough today?" I said, my voice as soft as my magic was hard. "We can't afford to lose Harker too."

He slowed but not enough. He was still moving.

"Would the First Angel want you to kill an angel?" I asked him.

He stopped, his breathing slowing. The fog of his rage must have cleared enough for him to recover his mind and realize what he was doing. Disgust washed across his magic —disgust that even for a second, he hadn't been in complete control of himself.

His hands trembling in anger, he glared at me. *How dare you put your unclean magic around me,* he growled in my mind.

My magic isn't dirty. It is the same as yours, Colonel. It comes from the same Nectar as yours.

Your magic is nothing like mine, he replied, disgusted.

Normally, Colonel Fireswift didn't have a problem telling me off in front of everyone, but he wasn't shouting at me now. It wasn't for my benefit; he just didn't want to show weakness in front of his soldiers. He didn't want any of them to know that my magic had frozen him, if only for a moment, just long enough for him to regain control of himself.

I come from a long and prestigious legacy of angels. You came out of some trashcan on the Frontier.

I'd have liked to give him the benefit of the doubt and said it was his pain talking now, but he was always like this. He made it really hard for anyone to feel sorry for him—which, I guess, was completely the point. He thought anyone worthy of sympathy was weak by definition. He didn't get it at all.

I did feel sorry for him and Jace, though. My friend's face was pale, his eyes red. He was trying really hard not to cry right now. As far as I was concerned, he had every right to cry. He'd just lost his sister.

The Legion did not agree. It was expected of Jace and his father to show no emotion. That's what it meant to be a soldier in the Legion of Angels, to be above mortal affairs and human emotions.

"Finish your report, Sunstorm," Colonel Fireswift barked at Harker.

"We managed to get the magic barrier back up, but not before a few hundred monsters poured through the hole."

"The city?"

"Larger parts of Memphis were destroyed by the monsters in the aftermath of the wall's collapse," said Harker. "We hunted down and killed the monsters, but it cost us. Half of our team is dead, killed by monsters or Venom bullets."

"And the traitors?"

"None survived," Harker told him.

"Why did our own soldiers turn on us?" I asked.

"I questioned one of the dying Legion traitors. He told me the Pioneers were pulling their strings."

"The Pioneers?" I gasped.

"So you've heard of them."

"We've exchanged blows," I said darkly. "What in the world would compel six Legion soldiers to help the Pioneers?"

"Leverage," he replied. "The Pioneers abducted the soldiers' loved ones and threatened to kill them if they didn't cooperate."

"Teenagers?"

"Yes."

"Abducted from their homes or vacation spots all across the Frontier?"

His brows arched in surprise. "Yes."

So that's what the Pioneers had been up to when they'd kidnapped all those teenagers. They'd targeted the loved ones of Legion soldiers. To not arouse the Legion's suspicion, they'd taken lots of other teenagers as well and sold them as slaves to rogue vampires. The rest they were keeping as leverage. The question was, what were the Pioneers planning next?

"Only six Legion traitors were involved in this catastrophe," I said, thinking it through. "Only six, and they took down a large part of the wall. If the Pioneers manage to extort enough Legion soldiers, they could take down the whole wall. The barrier that has stood for hundreds of years between civilization and the wild lands would fall, and monsters would flood through the gates. They would kill our people and lay waste to our cities. Centuries ago, we built the walls and pushed the monsters back. There's no guarantee we'll be able to do the same again. This could be the end of humanity."

"The Legion's defenses are only as strong as its weakest link," Jace spoke, emerging from his cocoon of misery.

He had a point. Whether or not the Legion wanted to admit it, its soldiers still had some of our humanity and ties to the mortal world.

Jace pulled out his phone. "I have the names of the kidnapped people who are still missing."

Jace was trying to pull himself together, to push through the pain. Even as his father struggled to stay calm, to not explode again, Jace was really stepping up.

"We need to check which missing teenagers have a connection to a Legion soldier," he said. "We should lock up those soldiers now, just to be safe. We can sort out the guilty later."

Harker nodded. "Agreed."

Jace began reading off the names of the people still missing. He paused when he got to Tessa and Gin, giving me a pointed look. It was the sort of look that reminded me of Colonel Fireswift. He was really channeling his father right now.

"I haven't received any blackmail notes from the Pioneers. They haven't tried to coerce me into doing anything. And if they're stupid enough to try, they've got another thing coming. They've picked the wrong person to manipulate. I'm not betraying the gods or the Legion. No way, no how. I won't help the people who took my sisters. I am going to make them pay for what they've done, for all the lives they've ruined and all the people they've hurt. And they will woe the day they took my sisters," I finished, my voice ringing with emotion. Anger flushed my cheeks, conviction pounded in my pulse.

Harker and Jace exchanged glances, then returned to the list, apparently satisfied by my answer. Because it was all true. I *would* make those bastards pay. After what they'd done, they deserved nothing less.

What I didn't say was that this wasn't just about manipulating Legion soldiers. There was something bigger happening. My sisters' magic was playing into the Pioneers' plans in some other way. But how? What exactly were Gin and Tessa, and why did the Pioneers want them so badly?

CHAPTER 21

PSYCHIC'S SPELL

*T*he night was long and full of heartache—sorrow for those who were gone, fear for those who had not yet returned. The training hall had become my midnight refuge, the sanctuary where I fought insomnia, slowly wearing my body into exhaustion. This was starting to become a habit, and I wasn't sure it was a good one.

It had been nearly a day, and Nero still wasn't back. Had he been killed or captured? The urge to go track him down was overwhelming. I had half a mind to run off after him, even as reason spoke to me, telling me I didn't have a clue where he was. No one did. The last anyone had seen or heard of him, he was chasing the last remaining horde of monsters through the ruins of Memphis.

If only we'd exchanged blood the last time I'd seen him, then I could find him now. Then I wouldn't be so powerless. I really hated being powerless.

I was training old school tonight. No magic and no flashy barriers. Just obstacles that required raw strength, speed, flexibility, and endurance. I'd gone back to basics, back to the very beginning of my Legion days. The whole point was to hurt my body so hard that I couldn't feel anything but the pain in my muscles, not the pain eating away at my heart.

It didn't work as well as I'd hoped. I could almost hear the deep echo of Nero's unwavering voice resounding off the gym walls, shouting at me to get off my ass and keep moving. The memory of him hurt more than my abused muscles.

"Leda Pierce," a voice said as I reached halfway up the wall of spikes.

Surprised, I slipped, cutting my hand on one of the spikes as I tried to catch myself—and failed. I fell off the wall, smacking the ground like a sack of flour.

I glanced up, my eyes meeting those of my unexpected visitor. It was Aleris, the God of Nature, and I'd fallen to the floor right at his feet. That couldn't have been a coincidence.

He looked down at me, a reserved expression on his face. He was dressed in plain beige robes decorated with nature. Flowering vines crisscrossed his chest like a breastplate of armor, and glossy black gauntlets covered his forearms. At first glance, they looked like metal, but they were nothing so common. They were made from thick wooden vines intertwined to form a thin magical armor I bet was as strong as any metal.

"Are you in the habit of falling to your knees before the gods?" he asked me. There was no humor twinkling in his eyes or echoing in his voice. Sarcasm probably wasn't even in his vocabulary.

I rose to my feet. Rather than replying with something snarky, I said, "To what do I owe the pleasure of your visit, Lord Aleris?"

"The other gods are all focused on you right now."

When he spoke with that quiet arrogance of his, his voice was like the wind, soft but projecting far. "They seem worried. I wanted to see what's gotten them so worked up."

I took a long, slow drink from my water bottle, wondering at his bluntness. Why would he admit that the gods were worried? Then again, they had every reason to be unsettled right now. The Legion was crumbling to pieces from the inside, its own soldiers coerced to work against the gods' will.

"There's a lot going on right now in the Legion and in the greater world," I said.

Aleris watched me in reflective silence, not giving away anything more. Of course not. After all, he was a god. He was less confrontational than the other gods, but his goal was the same: for me to tell him everything I knew. Well, it was high time we turned the river of knowledge in the other direction.

"And what do you think?" I asked him.

"I am still undecided about you and your place in everything. One thing is for sure, however: you are at the center of all the chaos. Whenever trouble breaks out, you aren't far away. What I'm still trying to ascertain is whether you are drawn to the chaos, or the chaos to you."

And then he was gone, just like that. Just like a god.

I was still looking at the spot where Aleris had disappeared when Harker entered the gym. Though his injuries had healed, he still looked as bad as I felt. He was haunted by what he'd seen, the sight of the Venom destroying his comrades from the inside. And like me, he was worried about Nero too.

I managed a small smile. "You couldn't sleep either, huh?"

"No."

I snatched two swords from the rack on the wall and tossed one of them to him. We both needed to get our minds off of our worries.

"So, are you going to ask out Bella again?" I asked him, trying to lighten the mood.

Harker parried my strike. "I don't know. The last time I asked her, she said it wasn't a good idea. I have the feeling she doesn't quite trust me." He set his sword on fire and swung it toward me.

I countered by casting a frozen sheet of magic across my blade. Fire clashed with ice. The flames went out, the frosty glass shattered into tiny icicles, and we were both back at square one.

"Of course she doesn't quite trust you. You did try to poison her favorite sister, you know," I pointed out.

"You're not ever going to let that go, are you?"

I smirked at him. "Nope."

I didn't mean it. Harker had made a mistake. He'd thought he was serving the gods, but Faris had just been manipulating him, using his faith to gain the upper ground over the other gods.

"Your past mistakes don't matter," I told him. "What matters is what you're doing now. And what you will do in the future."

He moved quickly, sliding under my defenses. He locked my arm in his grip and pulled hard. Pain blossomed in my shoulder as he popped it out of its socket.

I sidestepped his followup attack, cradling my pulsing, aching arm. "Though maybe you should be less…less like an angel," I said through my teeth. Grimacing, I popped my shoulder back in.

"What do you mean, 'less like an angel'?"

"Angels have an annoying habit of deciding things for people—and for always knowing what's best for them."

I snatched hold of his arm, sinking my magic through it. His hand shifted into a gargantuan tortoise shell that dropped to the ground like an iron ball, taking him down with it. He tried to lift his arm off the floor, but the shell that was his hand did not budge. He shot me an irked look.

"Like feeding Bella your blood," I said. "Especially when she didn't know the consequences."

He pushed against the enormous weight of the shell, his muscles bulging from the strain. "I did that…" He locked his free hand around his trapped wrist and heaved. "… to protect her." His face was turning red. "… to save her."

I swung a punch at his head to end our fight. He was glued to the floor, and he still somehow managed to duck to the side. In a world without magic, that would have been impossible. In a world with magic, it was still cheating.

"You know, the 'I'm just protecting you' excuse is the same failed logic that got Nero into trouble," I warned him.

"I don't get your point. Nero marked you and you threw up a big fuss to make him remove it, but in the end, you are his."

He evaded my next punch as well. The laws of gravity didn't even seem to apply to him. His leg swept out, kicking my feet out from under me. My back smacked the floor.

Harker looked down at me. "You didn't just accept your fate. You embraced it."

I kicked back up to my feet. "See, that's the angel

talking again. Yes, I'm his, but he's mine too. Angels and gods think so one-dimensionally. The road to heaven is paved in one-way streets. But for a relationship to work— to *really* work—it needs to go both ways."

Harker was silent for a moment, as though considering the idea. "There might be something in that," he finally said.

I grinned at him. "Don't be shy to tell me I'm right, Harker. After all, I managed to glue you to the floor."

He gave his arms a hard heave. The shell launched off the floor, his arms following in a smooth arc. He held the shell over his head for a moment—just to show that he could—then he slammed it down like a hammer. My spell broken, the shell cracked into a thousand tiny pieces, then dissolved to smoke.

I just gaped at him.

"As much as you'd like to make yourself out to be a badass, independent, take-no-shit rebel, you're one of us, Pandora."

"One of what?"

"An angel. Not in name but in nature. You make decisions for your family, for your subordinates, and even for your superiors. You couldn't be more of an angel if you had wings." Harker's smile widened as mine faded. "You marked Nero. I can sense it on him—your magic, your scent, your unique magical perfume. It is the mark of an angel, faint but unfading. That is the first mark from a non-angel that I've come across. How did you do that?"

I shrugged. "I don't know. Perhaps love is more powerful than magic," I added with a mischievous wink.

Harker laughed. "Who would have guessed that you're such a romantic."

"Yeah, you know me. All flowers, sunshine, and lacy petticoats."

He snorted.

I gave him a sly look. "But we're not here to discuss my love life. We're here to discuss yours."

"I was under the impression that you thought I wasn't good enough for your sister."

"No one is good enough for my sister," I told him. "But she likes you. I can see it in her eyes when she talks about you. I can feel it when you're around her. And, besides, you did a very brave thing."

Actually, he'd done two very brave things. One, he was playing double agent, spying on Faris and reporting back to Ronan and Nyx on how the God of Heaven's Army was plotting against the other gods. And two, he was protecting the secret of Bella's origin. But I didn't elaborate. There could have been gods watching.

"And you care about her."

Harker said nothing.

"It's not a mortal failing in an angel to care about another person," I told him.

A dark look crossed Harker's face. "Nowadays, Leda, it just might be. The Pioneers exploited our weaknesses, our human connections. Legion soldiers betrayed us in order to protect the ones they loved. None of us can afford to have weaknesses, especially not angels."

"We'll get the Pioneers, Harker. They won't use our people again."

Determination gleamed in his eyes. "Yes, we'll get the Pioneers. And the next threat. And the next one after that. We will always get them in the end. But what about the people we put at risk in the meantime? What about the people we lose?"

I put my hand on his shoulder. "Stop," I said gently. "You'll drive yourself crazy thinking like this. You can't isolate yourself from the world."

"That's how the Legion wants us to be: isolated, alone, no weaknesses in our armor."

"And that's no way to live. Life isn't clean. It isn't perfect and orderly and always on schedule. It's not spotless swords and sterile sheets. It's unordered lists and dirty laundry. Life is messy and chaotic and, best of all, unpredictable. Our weaknesses, the people we love, our imperfections, not knowing what's going to happen every second of every day—that's what makes it all worth living. The Legion believes those soldiers' loved ones were their weakness. But that's not true at all. Our enemy is arrogance, the blind assertion that we have no weaknesses, that we are completely apart and cut off from 'lesser' humans. Instead of this blind belief that we are infallible, instead of the Legion ignoring that we have connections, they should be protecting those we care about. Because it's not magic that will win this war and save humanity. It is compassion."

Harker blinked. "Good speech."

"Thank you."

"What they say about opposites attracting has to be true. You must drive Nero insane with all the 'unordered lists and dirty laundry'."

"Often, yes," I laughed.

We didn't say another word about Nero. We were both worried about him and trying hard not to think about it.

Harker cleared his throat. "Enough slacking off. Show me what you've got."

But before I could plan my attack, he thrust his hands in front of his chest. Telekinetic magic exploded out of his fists. It hit me like an invisible wrecking ball. I caught myself as I began to slip, planting my feet on the ground.

"You've been practicing," Harker declared when the psychic storm had finally dissipated.

"I have too many sleepless nights of training to thank for that. Plus an unexpected visit from the Lord of the Legion."

"Ronan visited you?"

"Yes. He gave me some tips. And a potion."

The door to the gym swung open. I turned eagerly toward it, fully expecting to find Nero standing there. My hope fizzled out when I found Colonel Fireswift instead. Jace walked in behind him.

Colonel Fireswift's face was cold and expressionless again. Whatever brief emotional outburst he'd had, it was over. The vicious, calculating angel had returned, and he had me caught in his crosshairs.

"Come with me, Pierce," he said. "I'm promoting you and Jace."

I didn't harbor any hope that Colonel Fireswift had decided I wasn't such a dirty street rat after all.

"The anarchists are bleeding the Legion dry," he said, his eyes burning with cold fire. "They are trying to cut off our power, to weaken us by killing our angels and future angels." He frowned at me. "I don't like you, but you're ready for the next level." His gaze shifted to Jace. "The Legion needs you both to step up."

Jace nodded, his face set with determination.

"I know you're ready, so don't you dare die." Colonel Fireswift's voice was as hard as diamonds. "I forbid it. To die is treason."

It was so ridiculous to say such a thing—that my death would be an act of treason—but I got what he meant. We were fighting for something big, something beyond our own personal needs. The Legion could be cruel, but we were all that stood between the monsters and the end of humanity. As we'd just seen, even the great Magitech wall could fail the people of Earth. The Legion, however, could not afford to fail them.

Colonel Fireswift led the way to the grand hall. The room was packed. Every Legion soldier in the Chicago office must have been standing here, and yet the hall was as quiet as a tomb. No one spoke; they hardly moved. A promotion ceremony at the Legion of Angels was typically characterized by tuxedos and ballgowns, but no one was dressed up today. They were all in uniform, all standing in perfect lines with nearly identical expressions on their faces. It felt more like a funeral than a promotion.

My gaze shifted from the black silk banners hanging on the walls, to the vases of white roses on the tables. It *was* a funeral. A funeral for everyone we'd just lost.

Stepping onto a raised platform at the center of the room, Colonel Fireswift began the ceremony. "Traitors have besieged the Legion of Angels. They have defiled our halls, turned their backs on their immortal duty, and killed our comrades. But from the ashes, we will rise stronger than ever before."

Jace and I stood beside him, the only candidates at this unexpected promotion ceremony. Jace was in uniform, but I was still wearing my sweaty workout suit. No one seemed to care.

Colonel Fireswift recited the usual Legion lines. "We bear witness here today as two of our own challenge themselves once more to take their next step in life, to strengthen themselves and the Legion in preparation for the days to come."

"For the days to come," repeated the audience.

"Leda Pierce, step forward."

Colonel Fireswift's voice was gruff. He wasn't nice, but this sure beat his usual disposition. He didn't make any derisive comments this time. Today, he was all business. This ceremony wasn't about personal feelings. It was about refilling the void in the Legion's upper ranks.

I faced him.

"Sip now of the gods' Nectar," he said.

He was hiding his pain well, but it was still in there. I actually did feel sorry for him. I couldn't shake the memory of the agony in his eyes when he'd lost his daughter. It haunted me, the sight of that strong and hard angel breaking down, losing himself to his anguish.

"Consume the magic of their sixth gift. Let it fill you, making you strong for the days to come."

"For the days to come," everyone repeated once more.

He set the goblet in my hands. I lifted it to my mouth and drank, not thinking, just doing. I had to trust that I was prepared enough. Much as Colonel Fireswift hated me, he was not trying to weed me out this time. His dislike of me was less important to him right now than his need to see the Legion survive this—and his desire to crush the bigger threat, the Pioneers who'd dealt such a heavy blow to us this day.

The Nectar poured down my throat like a burning river, igniting my magic and awakening my senses. I felt alive again, invigorated. It was as though a weight had lifted from my chest, evaporating my worries. I knew it was just the high of the Nectar, but I didn't care. I hadn't realized until now just how long I'd been holding my breath, or how long I'd been buried beneath the burden of things I couldn't control.

My whole body was buzzing with magic, but I tried to keep my steps steady and straight as I moved aside for Jace. Colonel Fireswift went through the lines again with him, but I hardly saw the two of them. I didn't hear them at all.

An explosion of applause snapped me out of my daze. I glanced to my side to find Jace standing beside me. The audience was clapping in celebration of our survival.

"The Legion is counting on you both—on *all* our soldiers, to step up," Colonel Fireswift declared, his voice filling the room. "You must all train harder than ever before. This isn't just about your individual survival. It's about the survival of the Legion. It's about the future of the Earth."

His speech continued, but I didn't hear another word because Nero had just stepped into the room.

His clothes were torn and bloody, but even so, he was the most beautiful thing I'd ever seen. My heart raced. Rather than not breathing, I was breathing too fast now. I was just so happy to see him, so completely overjoyed that he was alive.

I rushed forward, crossing the room in a few mere steps. I didn't care about the whispers from the soldiers in the audience. I stopped right in front of him. Thoughts were buzzing around inside my head, unordered and chaotic. There was so much to tell him, and how did I choose to open? By tripping over my own tongue.

"You're covered in blood."

"It's not my own," he replied, a tormented look in his eyes.

Nero had seen a lot of horror in our world, but this experience had been so horrific, it had rocked his composure. I didn't know what else to say to him. Words could not express my sorrow for what he'd been through—or my relief at seeing him again.

"I was so worried I'd lost you," I whispered.

He reached out, his hand softly caressing my cheek.

That did it. I collided with Nero, our bodies crashing together as I kissed him. Into that kiss, I poured my anguish, my relief, my love—everything that had been bottled up since I'd learned what had happened in Memphis.

He kissed me back, and everything else faded away. It was just Nero. At this moment in time, nothing else in the world mattered.

CHAPTER 22

*W*hen that whirlwind of a kiss stopped, we were standing in a bedroom. Draped in silk and satin, it was a room worthy of an emperor—or an angel. The suite's highlight was the canopy bed, a triumph of carpentry large enough to comfortably fit four people. Its four wooden posts were as thick as tree trunks and embellished with etchings of scantily-clad angels. Luxurious gold curtains were drawn up over the sides. A footstool with matching gold fabric sat under the windows.

"You shouldn't be thinking about the furniture, Pandora," Nero chided me softly.

He zipped down the front of his torn leather vest, revealing smooth, soft skin over a hard, sculpted chest. He peeled the torn garment off of his body and tossed it to the floor. Diffused light filtered inside through the gauzy curtains that rippled across the windows, basking his skin in a soft glow.

I just stood there, mesmerized by his stunning perfection.

Nero lifted his hand to me, his fingertips a soft whisper

as he traced the sensitive spot on my neck. He circled tightly around me, his caress dipping between my shoulder blades to follow the curvature of my spine. His fingers closed on the clasp of my sport top and paused. A soft gasp broke my lips as the bundle of fabric fell to my feet.

He faced me, his gaze drinking me in from tip to tip. His green eyes lit up with gold and silver sparks, devouring me with the ferocity of a starving man. "Gorgeous." The word kissed his lips like a lover's caress.

The room smelled of vanilla and orange blossoms. The curtains around the bed were rippling in the wind, though the window was closed. It was like magic.

"It *is* magic," Nero told me.

The magic breeze kissed my skin. It whispered down my arms, cresting my breasts.

"What are you doing to me?" I gasped, his magic touch igniting the fire in my blood.

"Magic is very versatile. It can be used to make war…"

Warmth poured down my bare back like a river of fire, sparking a symphony of sensations.

"…or to make love." His voice dipped lower.

He besieged my body with elemental magic, and I didn't even try to fight it. I spread open the gates of my magic, inviting him in.

"Next time, you go off risking your life…you're taking me with you," I said, my breaths short and stuttered.

"You can come with me whenever you like."

Heat trickled over my hips, down my thighs, kissing my curves. A desperate ache was building between my legs. I bit my lip, holding back a moan.

"Don't ever hold back anything from me," Nero said, his voice rough with lust.

I met his gaze and saw my own desire reflected in the

embers of his eyes. An intense, relentless desperation took hold of me. I grabbed him, my fingernails digging deep into his back.

A ruthless, sensual growl rumbled deep in his throat, a promise of dark and sinful fantasies. His hands locking around my hips, he tugged me roughly against him, and my breasts slammed against the hard wall of his chest.

He met my eyes for a moment, and he declared seriously, "I love you." Then his mouth closed over mine, ravaging the inside with such savage, insatiable need that it left me breathless.

His mouth dipped to my neck, teasing my throbbing vein between his incisors. Every flick of his tongue, every nibble of his teeth, fueled my desire, feeding me and making me hungrier all at once.

I heard the sharp, satisfying pop of his fangs breaking the surface, the burst of pain trailed immediately by a deep, aching desire. My lips found his neck. Too impatient to tease, my fangs penetrated his skin. His blood spilled into my mouth. Hot, spicy, smooth, and as sweet as honey, it slid down my throat, setting my tastebuds on fire. He tasted like Nectar, the food of the gods, a little drop of heaven.

We drank deeply from each other, our hunger fueled by our passion and fear, by our relief at seeing each other again. I gave all of myself and took all of him in return. His blood burned through my body like a wildfire, consuming me. Ripping apart and rebuilding, burning down and building up—every draw of his mouth sent a shock wave of pleasure crashing and cascading through me.

A soft, desperate moan parted my lips. "Nero."

He tugged the shorts off my hips and my panties along with them.

"If I'd known magic could be this much fun, I'd have trained mine even harder," I said.

He chuckled. "I'll remind you of your words the next time we train together."

"I don't think that would be appro—"

His magic crashed over me, drowning me in aching bliss. Desperate for more, I slid my siren magic over him, projecting my desire onto him. Making what was mine— everything I felt—his.

He froze.

I paused, cautiously meeting his eyes. Had I broken some unspoken angel rule?

"Are you all right?"

"No one has ever dared project their magic onto me."

I held my breath.

"You should dare more often." He grabbed me by the hips and threw me down onto the bed.

I looked up at him and saw he was now as naked as I was. His huge, hard body loomed over me, those gorgeous wings spread wide, a stunning canvas of black, green, and blue. The sight of them made me feel so small.

He grabbed me roughly, flipping me over. As my hands and knees hit the mattress, his hand traced my inner thighs, spreading them. A single finger dipped inside of me, tracing, teasing. Heat surged between my legs, consuming me in a whirlwind of fierce sexual longing. A second finger slipped in. A third. Oh gods, more. I arched my back and tilted my hips back, opening myself up to him. His hand stroked harder, faster, drowning me in hot, slick pleasure.

Then, suddenly, he pulled away. I growled out a complaint. A gasped moan swallowed my protest as he thrust hard into me.

"Show me what's inside of you, Leda," he said, his breath burning against my neck. "Share everything you feel."

I cried out as he took me harder, completing me body and soul. Pleasure pooled between my legs, blossoming, swelling. I shook, tense, balanced on the precipice of release.

"Please," I moaned. "Oh, gods, Nero, please."

His restraint shattered, unleashing the untamed primal force that lurked beneath the angel armor. I ground myself against him, meeting his rough strokes with desperate fervor. My legs were quivering, a blind searing heat pulsing through me, building and twisting back on itself. I dug my fingers into the sheets, shuddering as my body contracted, exploding in a wave of pure ecstasy.

"Oh, I missed you so much," I sobbed out, the after-shocks rocking me.

I poured out my magic. I shared my feelings, my emotions, my desire—I opened up everything to him, bared myself. It was just me, unfiltered and unshielded. He'd seen me without my clothes, but he'd never truly seen me naked, stripped of everything. I showed him every secret, every dark corner of my mind and soul, giving him all that I had. That was the power of Siren's Song. There was nothing better than this, nothing more intimate.

He showed me how wrong I was when his magic hit me like a high-speed train. He'd opened up a window into his soul, just for me and no one else. I experienced the full force of everything that he was, the endless labyrinth of delightful complexity; the torn soul, a firestorm of light and dark, of strength and of fear. And of his love for me, so deep it made me dizzy with desire. I had to have him again.

And he wanted me. I could feel the intense longing in his emotions, in the pulse of his body, in the way that he filled me so deeply. He began to move gently inside me, teasing my soft, sensitive flesh swollen with desire.

His mouth brushed down my neck in soft butterfly kisses. I squirmed impatiently. I didn't want him to be gentle; I wanted him to release the shackles of propriety and take me hard and rough.

He flipped me over. Looking down on me, he set his hand over my heart and declared, "Your soul is so beautiful."

I met his eyes. "So is yours," I said solemnly, without smirk or sass.

He leaned down and kissed my forehead softly. Hot, sweet anticipation swelled inside of me as his hands gently parted my thighs. He gripped my hips and thrust once into me—then he pulled back, his muscles hard and tight as he loomed over me, his eyes alight with dark delight.

"More," I moaned, my fingernails digging into his back in wild, feverish desperation. I arched my back, tilting up my hips.

He slammed me back down on the mattress. His hands locked around my wrists, pinning me to the bed, he plunged deeper into me, each movement forceful and relentless. I cried out, swept up in a blur of pleasure that blinded me to everything but Nero.

The bed shook and groaned under us. Lust, raw and unbridled, burned in his eyes. He was so close. I wanted to see him lose that last shred of control, for that final thread to snap.

Blind, savage desire rocking my body, I moved with him, synching to his rhythm. Nero's shoulders locked up, his muscles tensing as he gripped me tightly, pulling me up to meet him. His whole body shook, and he groaned deeply into my mouth. Like a storm of fire and lightning, ecstasy crashed through me again and again, devouring me.

When my eyes could focus again, I looked around at the ruins of the bed we lay on. The canopy beams were broken, the bed curtains drooping.

"We destroyed your beautiful designer emperor bed," I said, breathless, my heart still pounding hard in my ears.

"It won't be the last time," Nero said with a self-satis-fied smirk. "Don't worry about it." Yawning lazily, he wrapped his body around mine and held me.

I snorted. "I love you, Nero Windstriker."

"Of course you do," he said with even more smugness, kissing my neck.

I laughed again. Then I closed my eyes and fell asleep in his arms.

———

WHEN I WOKE UP, Nero was still lying beside me. I held him close, stroking my hand across his, so afraid that I was going to wake up at any moment and find this had all been nothing but a Nectar-induced dream. And that Nero was still missing.

I'm here, Nero spoke inside my mind. *This is real.*

If this were a dream, you'd say exactly that.

His lips brushed my shoulder. "I heard about your encounter with the Pioneers. You get into all kinds of trouble without me."

I snatched hold of his hand and kissed his fingertips. "I get into even more trouble with you, angel."

Nero's laugh rumbled against my back.

I turned to look over my shoulder at him. The way he

was looking at me was simply breathtaking. It was the glow in his eyes, the love in them. I could scarcely believe that this was all real. Just a year ago, I'd been living on the Frontier of civilization, hunting escaped convicts. Now I was a soldier of the sixth level in the gods' army and the lover of an angel.

Tears pooled in my eyes, my heart swelling. Nero wiped the tears from my face, watching me closely, silently.

His gaze was so intense, so…world-shattering. Yes, that was the word. He'd changed my whole life.

"Penny for your thoughts?" I said, succumbing to my desperate need to fill the silence, to know what he was thinking.

Nero looked me over, his hand tracing the curvature of my hip. "Your magic is so strong now. With each level that you gain, your magic magnifies. It's intense, like nothing I've ever felt before. It is not a single strand or a single flavor or scent of magic. It's not light or dark. It's a rich, complex blend of both light and dark magic."

"So you want to eat me?" I teased him.

"Each and every moment of every day," he said solemnly, silver and gold swirls glowing inside his emerald eyes.

My heart jumped a beat. "Ronan paid me a visit while you were gone."

The glow faded from his eyes, and they went hard. "Oh?"

"He talked to me about magic and counter magic. It was his potion that helped me build up my telekinetic resistance."

"Be careful with Ronan," Nero cautioned me. "He might be our ally, but he is still a god."

"Oh, I don't trust him *that* much." I paused, then added, "I talked to Jace too."

Nero continued to stroke his hand up and down my arm. "Did you?" He sounded perfectly calm, like a tiger right before it pounced and tore you to shreds.

"Jace told me how his family has been trying for centuries to create offspring of perfectly balanced magical potential. Basically, they want all the magic without any of the counter magic."

He snorted. "They have certainly been *trying*. But sometimes the less you try, the better things turn out."

I wondered if he was thinking about his own parents, who had married for love rather than for duty—and had become the only two angels to ever have a child together.

I glanced back, smiling. "Well, I think you turned out all right."

His brows arched. "*All right*?" he repeated, as though offended.

"Spectacularly then," I amended.

He nodded. "Better."

Then he fell oddly quiet. His hand stroked my side absentmindedly, but his eyes were drifting. His mind was a million miles away.

"Where are you, Nero?" I asked him.

He met my gaze. "It's been a long few days."

I saw the darkness in his eyes, the guilt. His people had died on the Memphis mission. But it wasn't just guilt that I saw in him; it was anger and hunger for revenge against the people who'd engineered the massacre. The Pioneers.

Unfortunately, the Legion Interrogators had gotten nothing useful from the prisoners we'd captured at Hardwicke's fortress. We didn't know who the Pioneers were, where they were, or what their end game was. That had left

Nero with an enemy he longed to strike back against, but as it stood now, he had nothing to strike at but empty air. The Pioneers were nowhere and they were nothing. They were phantoms you couldn't see or hit.

"Gin and Tessa are among the kidnapped people still missing," I said.

My words drew him out of his own mind. "Frankly, I'm surprised Colonel Fireswift promoted you instead of locking you up as a potential traitor."

"Jace wanted to lock me up."

"And what did you say?"

"I told him I wasn't going to turn against the Legion. What I was going to do is hunt down the Pioneers and make them pay for everything they've done."

"You must have been convincing."

"You know, I really was," I said. "It didn't hurt that I put a little magic behind my speech."

"Cheating again, Pandora?"

"Simply using the resources at my disposal," I countered.

"Good," he said, his eyes twinkling with approval. "But grand speeches aside, Leda, you need to be prepared for the possibility that the Pioneers will try to use you. They might dangle your sisters' lives in front of you in exchange for your cooperation."

"The Pioneers won't kill Tessa and Gin. They didn't take my sisters so they could control me. They took them for their magic."

Surprise flashed in Nero's eyes. Apparently, he hadn't realized they had magic either.

"What kind of magic do they possess?" he asked me.

"I don't know. All we do know is that their magic is not of this world."

He frowned. "That is vague."

"I know. 'Not of this world' could mean any number of things," I said. "But I think it means *literally* not-of-this-world. As in, magic we do not have on Earth, something from some other realm in the magical cosmos." I paused. "We should ask Damiel."

Nero looked at me as though I'd suggested that we march off into the depths of hell and challenge a demon to a duel.

"Damiel has traveled," I continued. "He's been around a lot. He has seen things none of us have, especially during his many years in hiding. He traveled to other worlds."

"I don't question his knowledge but rather his intentions," said Nero. "Are you sure you want to trust him with the information about your sisters being special?"

"Haven't we been through all of this already? Damiel is not our enemy. What he did—his time in hiding, staging his death before your eyes—was for you."

"Damiel might not be our enemy, but he is an angel," Nero said. "He has a habit of using sensitive information against people. You don't know what he will do with this knowledge, but you can be sure that he will do *something*. Information is a weapon, and my father wields it far too well."

"We have to trust some people," I told him. "And hasn't Damiel earned our trust?"

"You know better than to trust an angel, Leda."

"You are an angel, and I trust you."

"I love you. I would move heaven and earth for you, so our interests are aligned."

I felt the sincerity ringing in his words, the passion and conviction resonating in his voice. Even his skin seemed to glow a bit brighter as he spoke. The raw, brutal romanticism of it all was almost enough to bring me to tears.

"Then we need to make sure Damiel believes his interests are aligned with ours too," I said. "And we'll start with what it is that he wants most of all from us."

Nero nodded in approval. "*Now* you're thinking like an angel."

CHAPTER 23

WEB OF MAGIC

*D*amiel's interests and ours were aligned as far as he needed us to help him find his wife Cadence. Locating her had been his mission, his purpose in life, since the two angels had been separated two centuries ago.

And he knew Nero and I were his best bet. Damiel's magic alone was not strong enough to track Cadence. Even his bond to her couldn't break through to the Guardians' realm, but Nero had a bond to her as well. Born in blood, strengthened by magic, the bond of mother and son was a powerful one. Since becoming an archangel, Nero's magic had only grown. If I became an angel, together these intersecting bonds that linked us all together would work in unison, the magic of each feeding off the others, building and culminating. Then we might just be powerful enough to break through the Guardians' magic barrier to find Cadence and Zane.

If Damiel wanted us to help him, he'd have to behave himself, and he knew it. We could trust him—at least as much as we could trust any angel.

So the next day, we went to meet with the legendary Damiel Dragonsire. Nero had asked him to come to Chicago, but he hadn't said why. To do so would have been a violation of the angel code of conduct, subsection 'Power Plays'.

Breaking that code completely, I'd invited Bella and Calli to the meeting, and Harker too. I didn't question Harker's loyalty, not after all he'd done for Bella. He was already keeping the secret of her origin; I knew he'd keep Tessa's and Gin's secrets as well.

Besides, we would need all the help we could get if we were going to keep my little sisters safe—both from the Pioneers and from the Legion of Angels itself. The Legion was not above turning people into weapons. In fact, it did exactly that each and every day.

We met with Damiel in an apartment building in the city. The angel was staying in the penthouse suite, of course. The elevator doors slid apart, and we stepped into a very extravagant, very modern open living room decked out in marble and gold. Floor-to-ceiling windows with a gorgeous panorama view of the whole city lay beyond the massive leather sofa. At least twenty people could have sat there and still had elbow room to spare.

"Subtle," I commented.

Damiel came out into the kitchen, smiling. He was wearing a t-shirt and a pair of artfully torn jeans. His hair was slightly disheveled in a stylish, purposeful manner. It made him look casual, approachable, like someone you could trust.

"I'm glad it pleases you," he said with a bow.

He continued to smile, waiting, his eyes twinkling with private delight. I had the sinking suspicion that he knew exactly what we were going to say. Maybe he did. He was telepathic after all. I'd been blocking my thoughts, but I wasn't sure if Bella and Calli could do the same. Zane had always been too polite to read our thoughts without permission, but most angels possessed no such moral scruples.

"I'm sure you've heard of the recent tragedy that has befallen the Legion in Memphis," I said.

"Yes. The Pioneers have been restless lately, their random acts of terror growing bolder each week. I told Nyx she should have had me hunt them down months ago." Damiel looked at me, his bright blue eyes reflective. "Your sisters are among the Pioneer's prisoners who are still missing."

He really did know everything that was going on at the Legion. I suppose it wasn't surprising considering he used to be the head of the Interrogators.

"You think this has something to do with your sisters' special magic," Damiel continued. "You think the Pioneers took them for the same reason the warlords hunted them all those years ago, when your foster mother Callista found them."

Calli folded her arms across her chest, giving Damiel the sort of look that, when I was younger, had prompted me to make myself scarce. Except Damiel was a several-hundred-year-old angel. He didn't scare easily. He just countered her look with an amused one of his own.

"You're reading our minds." Calli didn't look happy about it.

Damiel continued to smile. "Not this time. I've been watching the supernatural underworld for some time. I have focused especially on looking for sources of powerful magic."

To help him in his quest to find Cadence.

"I first heard whispers of two very special girls many years ago, when the warlords of the Jaded Jungle were fighting over them," said Damiel.

"What do you know of their powers?" I asked him.

"That they are supposed to be unlike anything in this world."

"So we've heard. But what does that mean?"

"Your sisters come from other realms."

Just like I'd thought.

"What kind of magic do they possess?" I asked.

He shook his head. "The rumors weren't that specific. After the warlords lost them, no one ever heard another thing about them. They just disappeared, as though they'd never existed. No one could find your sisters. Until now."

"Could you identify their magic if you saw it?"

He gave me a smug look.

Of course he could identify their magic. Sorry I'd ever doubted his supreme archangel majesty.

"Can you help us find my sisters?" I asked.

"Perhaps. Tracking is tricky magic, you see. There are so many people on Earth, so many streams of magic. It's all very busy, very crowded."

"But it's not a problem for a *legendary* Tracker like you."

Damiel chuckled. "Nero told you about that, did he?"

Nero had told me that Damiel was the best Tracker there was. He was the best Tracker and the best Interrogator. He could hunt down anyone the Legion wanted to find and extract any information out of them.

That's how he'd managed to stay hidden for so long. It's how he'd staged his apparent death and covered his tracks. He'd put on a very convincing show, right in front of Nero's eyes. Sooner or later, all archangels developed special powers above and beyond the Legion's usual magic spectrum. Damiel's unique combination of magic, his skills as a Tracker and an Interrogator, had allowed him to maintain the charade that he was dead for centuries.

"Nero is always so eager to boast about his old man," he said with a warm smile.

Nero gave him a flat look. "Yes, all the time. To anyone and everyone who will listen." His tone was as dry as sandpaper.

I almost laughed.

Damiel did laugh, and it was a good-natured one at that. He patted Nero hard on the back, then looked at me. "I can help you find your sisters. I can't promise it won't hurt, however."

"Whatever it takes," I said to him. "I don't bruise easily."

Damiel laughed again, and this time it was me that he slapped on the back. Maybe I'd spoken too soon because his friendly slap had bruised me down to the bone.

"Leda," Damiel said, motioning for me to give him my hand.

I did. Then Damiel looked at Nero, holding out his other hand. Nero set his hand in his father's.

"Now you two link hands," Damiel instructed us.

The moment we all linked, a shock of power surged through me, up and down my arms, like I'd just grabbed a lightning bolt. As the magic burned through me, crumbling my defenses to ash, my heart raced so hard that I thought it might explode. Blotches danced in front of my eyes. My vision was going dark. Blackness swallowed me.

Hold on, Leda, Nero said in my mind, his voice a tether in the darkness. *It will get better.*

The pain will go away? I asked hopefully.

No, the pain never goes away. You just get used to it.

I choked out a laugh.

Lying to you won't make it hurt less, Nero said sensibly.

That's one of the things I loved about Nero. I could always count on him not to bullshit me.

Like you would tolerate anyone bullshitting you.

I laughed again. Gods, I loved him. And he was right. I was getting used to the pain. The pounding, excruciating, mind-splitting agony was dulling into a distant but persistent thump. My vision was improving too. I could see Nero now. We stood side-by-side, two bright spots inside a sea of blackness.

"Excellent," Damiel's voice penetrated the darkness. "Now if you two lovebirds are finished playing footsie beneath the abyss, let's get started." He faded into sight, a third bright spot in the deep black sea. "I'm using my blood connection to Nero, who is connected to you, Leda, through your bond. And you are connected to Calli and Bella and to your little sisters. You're the focal point, Leda, the prism through which all our magic connects."

So that's why it hurt so much. The magic of two archangels was tearing through me like a river of raging rapids.

"A web of magic is stronger than a single strand," Damiel said. "We will use it to locate your sisters. Your link to your sisters will boost my and Nero's telepathic range."

It was the same trick Nero and I planned to use to find my brother and his mother once I had gained the power of Ghost's Whisper.

"Your brother and Cadence are no longer on Earth," Damiel said, picking up on my thoughts. "It requires a lot more magic to breach dimensions and cross worlds. Your sisters are, however, on Earth."

"Yes. I can feel them," I said excitedly, a familiar feeling washing over me. I could sense Gin and Tessa. They felt so close, like I could reach out and touch them.

"Keep calm," Damiel told me. "Don't pull too hard on your connection to them. Too much tension will make the strands of the link snap."

I glanced down and realized I was tugging hard on two interwoven strands, two ribbons glowing with magic. One was gold-red. The other was silver-blue. When I touched the braided ribbons of magic, I felt feedback, a hum, a musical note against my skin. Somehow, I could feel that the gold-red one was Gin and the silver-blue one was Tessa. I followed the ribbons with my mind.

Scenes flashed past almost faster than I could process them. I saw mercenaries taking Gin and Tessa in Purgatory, grabbing them along with the other teenagers. Later, in a dark room, a cloaked mercenary handed my sisters over to a Pioneer leader. I dove into the mind of the Pioneer, fast-forwarding in time to a large, underground room. Flames licked the hearths of twelve fireplaces. The red light flickered and sizzled, casting shadows across the backs of the twelve men who'd convened there, one standing in front of each fireplace.

"Hardwicke's mercenaries have taken another forty prisoners from towns along the Frontier," said one of the men. Like all the others, his face was shrouded in darkness.

"Have you sent our demands to the Legion soldiers?" asked another.

"Yes. They will cooperate to save their precious loved ones."

Laughter spilled out of the darkness where another man stood. "The Legion is not as impervious as it makes itself out to be."

"I say we strike now."

"The Legion is weak, ready to be toppled," agreed another.

The laughing man laughed once more. "The Legion is tearing itself apart from the inside. And thanks to our potion, we can create an army to finish the job. We can take back the Earth from those foreign invaders who call themselves gods."

As the Pioneers spoke, I relayed everything back to Nero and Damiel.

"Which Legion soldiers have been compromised?" Nero asked me.

"I don't want to condemn them to death because they have held on to a piece of their humanity."

"I will restrain them, not kill them, if possible," Nero promised.

I realized it was the best I was going to get. Nero's first duty was to protect the Legion of Angels from threats both internal and external. If the Legion fell, so would the Earth. We were the shield that stood between humanity and the monsters.

So as the Pioneers discussed the Legion soldiers they'd blackmailed, I repeated their names to Nero.

The light in the dark room shifted, throwing off the shadows. For the first time, I could make out a face in the crowd. I recognized one of the Pioneer leaders. It was the district lord I'd seen dining at the Silver Platter in Purgatory as his starving servant, chained to the column, looked on.

I walked past the circle of Pioneers, straining my eyes to see their faces. I saw more district lords from Purgatory —all of them, in fact. And the remaining Pioneer leaders consisted solely of district lords from other towns across the Frontier.

The realization hit me with the force of a high-speed train. The Pioneers *were* the district lords. One by one, they were taking over the poor, neglected towns of the Frontier, and they were doing this all right under our noses as they plotted to destroy the Legion of Angels.

CHAPTER 24

*W*e rode in the back of a Legion truck headed for Purgatory. All roads seemed to lead me back there.

The truck's wheels rumbled over the bumpy road. The hum of the engine filled the dead silence hanging heavy in the air. Nero sat across from me. His face was serious, devoid of emotion. It was his game face. In preparation for the coming battle, he was putting his mind in the right place to be cold, calculating, and merciless—the perfect angelic trifecta.

Beside me, Bella's hands lay folded together in her lap, as steady as her pulse was erratic. She was scared for Gin and Tessa. We all were. Our little sisters were being held by a group of psychopaths who'd unleashed monsters on a city of thousands of people, just to swing a punch at the Legion.

"They'll be all right," I told Bella, reaching over to squeeze her hand.

She squeezed back.

I looked out the window at the dark curtain of clouds

overhead. Fat snowflakes began to drop to the ground like goose down. It was the height of summer, but out here near the plains of monsters, the weather was always so variable, so unpredictable.

"It's snowing," I commented.

The truck's windshield wipers were swiping back and forth, trying to clear the snow, but it was coming down too fast now. They couldn't keep up with the buckets of fluffy white powder. Visibility was so low that I could hardly see past our truck.

The out-of-season weather almost felt like an omen that things were about to change big time. I hoped that didn't mean the Pioneers would gain the upper ground. As harsh as the Legion could be, they were nothing compared to the anarchy and cruelty I'd witnessed from the district lords. If they rose to power and took over, the whole world would deteriorate into an unending gangster shootout.

The truck came to a stop, and everyone hopped out, our glossy black leather contrasting starkly with the whirling white snowstorm. There were nine of us: in addition to me, our team consisted of Bella and Calli, Nero and Harker, as well as Basanti, Alec, Soren, and Drake.

"Any news?" Basanti asked Nero.

"Not yet."

We waited for the signal that the attacks were about to begin. In towns all across the Frontier, the Legion was running coordinated strikes on the district lords. Now that we knew they were the force behind the Pioneers, we were taking them all out. I couldn't help but feel a sense of deep satisfaction at their impending demise, even as I came to terms with what that actually meant for me. I was going into a battle in which I would likely have to kill people.

Killing people was not like killing monsters, no matter how evil they were.

"Get into position," Nero told Harker. "It's about to start."

Harker ran off toward the entrance that led into the tunnel system connecting the castles of Purgatory's district lords. Basanti, Alec, Soren, and Drake followed him. A few minutes later, an explosion lit up the stormy, snowy sky. Burning chunks of the gold and ivory gate flew in every direction. Gunfire roared, blades clashed, and magic sizzled. Harker's team had engaged the enemy soldiers.

But they were just the distraction. Nero, Bella, Calli, and I ran down Twilight Alley, the gathering point of the town's young delinquents. I'd spent a great deal of time there in my days as a homeless orphan.

I ran in front, leading the way down an unnamed narrow passageway. This was where I'd hidden from the street gangs, groups of big and mean kids who preyed on the weak and solitary, stealing our food and anything else of value that we had. Once, while hiding here, I'd seen a district lord and his posse go through a thick door, the kind that looked like the entrance to a safe or a bomb shelter. The tunnel beyond the door was a secret passage to the district lord's castle—and, more importantly, to the tunnels that connected all the district lords' castles together.

"You ready?" Nero asked me as we stopped in front of the solid metal door.

I nodded and took his hand, gathering my new telekinetic magic into a point. I could feel Nero directing my magic, channeling it into his own. A blast of our combined power slammed into the door, crushing it inside its psychic fist. Calli stood beside us, ready to shoot any enemies lying in wait.

The tunnel was empty. Harker's team of heavy hitters must have drawn all the Pioneers' fighters to the main entrance. So far, everything was going exactly to plan. We entered the tunnel, moving toward the central underground interchange. The district lords might have been working together to overthrow the Legion, but they still didn't trust one another. They had to be keeping the prisoners in a neutral location, and based on the blueprints, my best guess was the underground level below this one. Was that too obvious to be true? Perhaps, but in my years as a bounty hunter, I'd found that people weren't as clever at hiding as they thought they were.

We met no one all the way down the tunnel, but that all changed when we reached the intersection before the staircase. Gunfire drummed over panicked shouts as the Pioneer fighters scrambled to block Harker's team from advancing further into the tunnels.

"There must be at least fifty of them!" a Pioneer shouted.

"And they've got three angels!"

Harker and his team of four soldiers must have been putting on a really spectacular show. I heard Basanti's manic cackle echo down the tunnel, magnified with magic to sound like a whole pack of hyenas. The Pioneers listened, looking positively ill. Their potion might have given them all the same powers as we had, but there was no magic pill for willpower or courage. In fact, they'd completely skipped the willpower step in lieu of a quick fix.

"We can still sneak past them to get to the stairs," I said, watching the Pioneers. "They have their backs turned to us."

The red light over the staircase flashed on, pulsing

repeatedly. A pack of large guard dogs bolted up the stairs. From the looks of them, they'd once been large dogs, but they now resembled werewolves in beast form.

Yet there was something wrong with their bodies. They weren't fully proportional, like some of their parts didn't belong with the others. They looked like they'd been pasted together from several different animals of several different sizes and species. They were a mismatch of various fur colors, yellow and silver, brown and black—a rushed blend, a discordant melody of lines and colors.

The beasts smelled like blood and rusty metal and wet fur—and a strange subtly-sweet smell that felt familiar. I couldn't quite place it, but I was sure I'd smelled it before.

I spotted a laboratory past the pack of wolves, pointing it out to Bella. She nodded, and we ran toward the glass room as Nero and Calli covered us from enemy soldiers.

"See if you can find a sample of the potion," I told Bella. Nyx had instructed us to obtain the potion for testing. If we could find a sample, we could figure out how the Pioneers had accomplished the impossible.

As Bella looked through the lab, I stood guard beside her. Nero and Calli had each moved to one of the two lab entrances.

But a guard dog got past them by making an entrance of its own. The beast jumped straight through a glass wall, battering it with its hard, boar-like tusks. As the glass shattered, I went to intercept the monster.

I swung my sword, flames flaring to life across the blade. I killed the beast in a single stroke of fire and metal, but there was already another one springing through the hole in the glass wall. It opened its mouth and breathed fire. Shit, the guard dogs could do magic too.

I countered the stream of fire with a swing of my now-icy sword. The flames sizzled out into wafts of steam. Unconcerned, the beast just spat another fireball at me. I'd been researching the monsters of Earth, and I hadn't read about a single one like these dogs.

And that's when I realized the Pioneers had given them the potion too. It hadn't just made them big and ugly monster amalgamations; it had given them magic. From the looks of the dogs, the potion hadn't fully taken to them like it had with the humans. It seemed the Pioneers hadn't yet figured out the canine formula of their potion.

Speaking of the potion…

"How's it coming?" I asked Bella.

"I've got a sample."

"Good. Then let's get you the hell out of here so you and Nerissa can analyze it."

The guard dog spat a wad of goo. I cut to the side, but a few green drops sprinkled across my uniform, burning holes right through the leather. Great. Not only did the beasts spit fire; they also spat toxic acid. A siege wasn't complete without toxic-acid-spitting beasts.

I froze, watching in shock as the speckles of splattered green spit peeled off the floor, moving as though controlled via telekinesis. They floated into the air, suspended like a hundred buoys bobbing in the air. Crap.

The spit shot straight at Bella. I jumped into its path, casting a psychic shield to counter the forward thrust of the toxic spit bubbles. I was too slow. One of the green bubbles hit the vial in Bella's hand, shattering it. At least the acid hadn't gotten on her skin. Who knew what that would have done to her.

Frowning, I faced the juiced-up monster. It snarled at me, showing off fangs coated in toxic saliva.

"Now you're just asking for it, Wolfie," I growled at it.

I grabbed the bobbing bubbles of poison spit with my mind and shot them at the beast, setting them all on fire for good measure. The punch of my toxic telekinetic spell pushed the beast out of the lab. It landed in the tunnel with a thump, then exploded next to a group of Pioneer soldiers, showering them in monster blood.

I looked at Bella, who'd already taken another few vials of potion. "According to the lab notes, the potion dies quickly outside either the special cooler or a living body," she explained as she loaded them into a transport cooler.

We left the lab. The Pioneer forces were streaming in from every direction, flooding the corridors. I saw Harker's team surrounded by enemies. Calli's jacket was ripped open, her undershirt saturated with her own blood, but she refused to leave. She just stood there, bleeding out as she continued to shoot at the Pioneers.

"You have to go," I told her. "Nerissa and the other doctors just arrived. They're waiting outside. They'll heal you."

"I'm fine."

"No, you're not fine. You're bleeding out everywhere. Don't be stubborn."

She snorted. "You can't lecture me about stubbornness."

"Sure I can." I waved Drake over. "The same way I can knock you upside the head so my friend Drake can carry you to safety."

Her mouth hardened.

"Gin and Tessa wouldn't want you to die to save them," I told her. "They want to see you again."

Resignation shone in her eyes. I'd hit the right note.

"Ok," she said, looking at Drake, sizing him up. "Try not to drop me."

"I wouldn't dare drop Leda's beautiful mother."

Calli glanced at me. "I like him."

"I thought you would," I replied as Drake lifted her carefully into his arms. "Don't worry. I'll get Gin and Tessa out of here."

Drake carried Calli through the tunnel that led to the back entrance. It was still empty, which was more than I could say for this hall. The Pioneer guards seemed to multiply by the minute. I found Harker and ran over to him.

"You need to get Bella out of here, so she can bring the Pioneers' potion back to our lab," I told him.

Harker looked across the battle scene, his face conflicted. He didn't want to abandon his soldiers, but he also wanted to keep Bella safe.

"We need to analyze the potion. Nyx's orders," I reminded him.

That sealed the deal. Harker led Bella down the tunnel, away from the fight. I went over to Nero. I didn't even need to say anything.

"We'll hold off the guards so you can find your sisters and the other prisoners," Nero told me.

Thank you.

There are likely more Pioneers guarding the prisoners. Be careful, he replied.

I'm always careful.

He made a noise that bore a suspicious resemblance to a snort. *Go before I change my mind, Pandora.*

I made my way toward the staircase, using my sword to cut through the last remaining guard dog. I paused on the top step, looking across the battleground. There were so many more enemy soldiers than we'd expected. The Pioneers' organization was enormous, their supporters plentiful. Were there really so many people willing to take up arms against the gods?

As I ran down the stairs, I could hear Nero calling in more Legion soldiers to fight the Pioneers. They could have just left now that they had the potion, but Nero wanted to give me the chance to save my sisters. Who knew what the Pioneers would do with Tessa and Gin. Based on everything I'd seen and heard of them, I just knew I couldn't let them have my sisters.

At the bottom of the stairs, the hallway was clear, but I could hear voices shouting up ahead. I locked on to that sound and sprinted all-out down the hall, bursting into a prison block. The Pioneers were waiting for me.

I didn't stop moving. I dashed past the first two guards, flinging them aside with a psychic blast. The remaining four guards closed around me from all sides. Their movements were so slow, so human. I knocked them out easily. Either their potion had worn out, or they'd not yet taken it.

I stepped over the Pioneers strewn across the cobbled ground and hit the green button on the wall. All the cells swung open, and the prisoners shoved and pushed to get out, as though they were afraid that the doors would close again if they didn't move now. I scanned the crowd of dirt-stained teenagers. My sisters were not among them. Of course they weren't. Because that would have been too easy. Hardwicke had said they'd been set apart for their magic. Where were they?

I picked out the only prisoner who didn't appear to be on the verge of a nervous breakdown. She must have been the daughter of an angel.

"Get everyone out of here," I told her. "Follow the

hallway to the end. General Windstriker is there. He'll help you all out."

She nodded and guided the others toward the door. I ran deeper into the prison, passing empty cells and the occasional laboratory table. Ahead, an eerie blue glow pulsed against the walls like a flickering flame. Somehow, I was completely positive that beacon would lead me to my sisters.

The light was so close now. Everything was blue. I ran into the next chamber—then skidded to a stop. A translucent blue veil of magic blocked my path. It was cloudy, foggy, like looking through a pool of water, but beyond the glowing ripple, I could just make out Tessa and Gin. Two guards held to my sisters, who kicked and pushed against them, trying to get to me. I moved toward the veil.

"It's about time," a voice said from behind, surprising me. "Doesn't the Legion teach its soldiers punctuality anymore? I've been waiting here for you for so long that my foot fell asleep."

I spun around to face the familiar voice. It was Balin Davenport, the deserter. I'd been so focused on my sisters beyond the veil of magic that I hadn't even seen him lurking in the shadows of the room. Moving as quick as lightning, he knocked me aside with a combined punch of magic and muscle. I slammed against the wall. Damn, he hit hard. I jumped up, but I wasn't fast enough. The deserter now stood in front of the veil, barring my path to my sisters.

"Move." My voice was a low growl. "Or I'll move you."

He laughed.

I swung a psychic punch at him. He caught my fist and threw me to the ground. I kicked back up to my feet, preparing to strike again.

He yawned. "I've grown bored of your stubbornness, Leda Pierce."

In a flash of magic, wings sprouted out of his back. They were a brilliant, iridescent mixture of blue and green, bearing a striking resemblance to a peacock's feathers.

"You're not supposed to have wings," I said, frowning.

According to Jace, Davenport had been one level shy of becoming an angel when he'd deserted the Legion.

His smile was vicious. "A lot can change in a few hundred years."

And then I felt it. His magic wasn't light; it was dark.

"You're a dark angel."

The veil rippled faster, and dozens of Dark Force soldiers spilled out of it, surrounding me. The Pioneers weren't the end of this. This went much deeper. It was a scheme born in hell.

"Please spare me the inner monologue," said the dark angel.

He flicked his wrist, and the soldiers of hell unleashed their magic on me. From all sides, over and over again, they blasted me. It felt like being hit with a thousand hammers all at once. It hurt to stand. It hurt to breathe. Each draw of breath was pure agony, like alcohol burning in my lungs. Clenching my teeth, I stood there, doing my best to endure the pain.

"You're tougher than you look," the dark angel commented when the magic barrage finally stopped. "Just like she said."

"She?" My lips barely moved. My voice was a weak croak.

The dark angel ignored my question. He waved at his soldiers. "Well, what are you waiting for? Hit her again. And don't stop until she's down."

Blasts of dark magic bombarded me from every direction. I tried to run out of their path, but I was too slow. I tried to resist, but my body was giving out. Fireworks of pain pounded at my head, dragging me into the abyss. And then everything went black.

CHAPTER 25

THE ARENA

*I*t was the smell that woke me up—the sweet, almost too-ripe scent. It was that brief, overwhelmingly sweet moment just before fruit became rotten. My stomach rumbled. I was starving. How long had I been out? How long had it been since I'd eaten? My lips were dry and cracked, my parched tongue as rough as sandpaper.

I forced my eyes open, squinting under the blinding lights. It took my vision several seconds to adjust. The first thing I saw was sand. Lots and lots of sand. It was bright yellow, the color of a banana. I lay on my side, my cheek pressed against sand as soft as velvet. That's what I was smelling, what smelled so good: the sand. I wanted to eat it all. Fantasizing about eating sand? I must have finally lost my mind.

It all came rushing back to me. The attack on the Pioneers. Tessa and Gin behind the magic veil. The Deserter, now a dark angel of hell. He had my sisters. And he had me. He'd told me that he'd been waiting for me.

He'd known I would come. Was this a trap? And why? What was it about me and my sisters that he wanted?

"You can't possibly imagine how exhausting it is to listen to your thoughts," the deserter said in a bored voice.

I pushed off the ground with my hands, rising to my feet. There he stood, his wings out, proud as a peacock.

He didn't have to show his wings. Angels and dark angels could hide them; they could make them disappear completely. They brought them out when they wanted to make an impression—in this case, to intimidate me. Well, I wasn't playing along.

I gave the dark angel's wings a casual, dismissive look and declared, "I've seen bigger."

The dark angel's hard black eyes glowed like two smoldering lumps of coal. His lips drew back into a vicious smile. "Your smart mouth won't help you here."

Wherever *here* was. I looked around. I saw that the yellow sand did not cover a beach, and the bright lights weren't from the tropical sun. Instead, I was trapped in a deep pit. It looked like a fighting arena, the kind where desperate supernaturals battled one another to earn enough cash to buy their next meal—or to feed their addictions. They fought, bled, and died all for the entertainment of the voyeuristic, bloodthirsty masses.

Back when I'd been a kid living on the streets of Purgatory, I'd seen a few of these tournaments, but I'd never fought in any of them. My lack of magic had saved me from that fate—that plus my quickness at avoiding the big scary underlings of the district lords who went out child-snatching on the streets. A few of us street kids would risk coming to the fights to steal money and food from the drunk spectators. None of us fought in the pits if we had a choice.

If a district lord found a kid with even a smidgeon of magic, they'd forced him or her into the fighting pit. The district lords would pit their prized child fighters against those of other district lords. There was no shortage of sick people who got a thrill out of watching little children fight —and sometimes kill—one another.

Fights would often break out amongst the spectators. Some people only came to the fights to get their blood pumping, to fight their neighbors, or watch their neighbors fight. The fighting in the stands drew even more people to the arena. It was a vicious cycle, a fantasy world outside reality, where you could succumb to your savage nature and behave in ways you normally could not under the gods' strict order.

And the spectators could do all of this in perfect safety. The worst that ever happened to them was a broken lip or a bloody nose. They didn't die like the fighters down in the pit. I'd always found it hard to believe that people would pay good money for a punch to the face, but, as Calli liked to say, intelligence wasn't for everyone.

I looked at the deserter. "What am I doing here, Davenport?"

"That's Soulslayer. Colonel Soulslayer."

Right. Because he was a dark angel now, a soldier in hell's army. He'd cast off his old name, right along with his soul.

"Soulslayer, huh?" I said. "Cute name. Did you pick it out all by yourself?"

He just glared at me, clearly unimpressed with my commentary.

"So how did you end up as a lapdog of hell?"

"How did you end up as a lapdog of heaven?" he shot

back with a cruel smile. "Oh, that's right. Your brother, a ghost, was abducted."

He knew too much.

"And you know nothing at all," he retorted.

He must have read my thoughts again. Damn it. I was too weak right now. My hollow stomach roared in agreement. I needed to eat something to boost my magic back up again.

The dark angel's smile turned more vicious. A moment later, a beep screeched out from the surround speakers. A side door slid open, ushering a monster into the arena. Huge, black, and covered in scales, it looked like a dinosaur.

No, its dimensions were too elegant, too smooth. It wasn't a dinosaur, I realized as it spread its translucent, black-purple wings. It was a dragon.

Its long dark tongue flickered out, lightning-fast. Green eyes the color of toxic acid locked onto me, and flames that matched those vicious eyes danced across its teeth. They were sharp and pointed, meant for tearing its prey apart. Violently.

I just stood there and gaped at it.

The dark angel let out a short laugh. "That's more like it."

Apparently, my shocked silence was highly amusing. I forced my dropped jaw closed. "I've never fought a dragon before," I said, nonchalant.

The dragon stomped forward loudly. Under its feet, the sand popped up and down like popcorn. The beast was charging right at me. It sure didn't waste time making friends.

I rolled out of its path, narrowly avoiding being trampled by a twenty-ton dragon. Then I jumped up, only to drop my body to the ground to avoid the gush of green flames that poured out of its mouth. I hopped back up and ran away, looking for a safe spot, a place to gather my thoughts and figure out what on Earth I could possibly do against a dragon.

Soulslayer, who was somehow now sitting up in the stands, protected behind a cage of Magitech much like the walls that kept out the monsters on Earth, grabbed me with his magic and pulled me into the dragon's path. The dragon slashed me before I could get away. My arm bleeding, the leather of my jacket peeling away, I jumped onto the dragon's back and ran up to its neck. If I stayed behind it, it couldn't get to me.

Soulslayer's magic blasted me off the dragon, and I fell to the ground with a thump. Pain exploded across my left side as several bones snapped. My breathing labored and heavy, my side bleeding and broken, I got up and threw an irked look at the dark angel up in the stands.

"Fight or die," he said coolly.

Like that was even a choice. Somehow, I didn't think the dragon was eager to open up a peaceful dialogue with me. It seemed too intent on tearing me to shreds.

I avoided the dragon's swinging tail and jumped up to its back. Putting all my strength into it, powering through the agony in my ribs and the black spots dancing in front of my eyes, I broke a spike off the beast's back. The dragon roared. I jumped down, spike in hand, and stabbed it through the dragon's foot. The monster staggered, tripping over its own weight.

I didn't have long before it came at me again, angrier than ever before. I ran for the side door the dragon had come through, trying to force it open.

But Soulslayer's magic clamped down on my body. He

tossed me at the thrashing dragon. I was nearly crushed under the beast's feet as it tried to free itself from the spike. I rolled out of the way.

"I said fight, not run away," the dark angel barked.

I glared up at him. "Well, it's not really a fair fight, is it? Not with you interfering."

"Life is not a fair fight."

The dark angel followed up that pearl of wisdom by opening another door. A second dragon entered the pit, just as the first dragon freed itself. Both beasts turned their burning green eyes on me.

———

THIS ALL STARTED with a single dragon, but believe it or not, it only went downhill from there. Each battle was harder than the previous one. Each foe tougher and less willing to forego a chance at killing me. The dark angel must have emptied the kennels of hell to unleash these monstrosities on me.

Over the next couple of days, I fought battle after battle against monsters I hadn't even known existed. At least I thought they were days. They could have been hours or minutes or weeks for all I knew. Starving, bleeding, and sleep-deprived, I'd lost all sense of time. I knew only two things: the fights, the slaying of monsters intent on slaying me; and the time in between when I slept as my body struggled to heal the burns, cuts, and broken bones the monsters had inflicted on me.

With each passing battle, my magic grew weaker. The respites felt shorter, and the fights were definitely longer. I was going into new battles with lingering injuries from the previous ones, wounds my body no longer had the magic to heal.

I was famished. That strange yellow sand was looking better and better. In my dazed hunger, I could hear it calling out to me. I had to remind myself more than once that it wasn't a good idea to eat sand, especially not strange glowing magic sand that talked to me.

I was growing weaker, my optimism fading. I was in desperate need of a shot of cheer. The only good part about the fights was at least they kept my mind off the eerie sand telling me to eat it. How was that for a silver lining?

I stood at the center of the arena, my arm bleeding from the birds who'd spent the better part of an hour diving at me. Their beaks cut like knives. I swung my bloody sword, felling the last bloody bird in the bloody flock. This fight had cost me a lot. Crimson drops dripped from my body. As it sprinkled across the sand, the yellow grains hissed and steamed in response. Weird.

A whole flock of birds, dozens of them, lay on the arena ground like a black carpet. They were like very large crows, each the size of a cat. And together they'd been absolutely deadly—pecking, diving, evading, swooping, scratching. It was really hard to take out a killer bird swarm when you couldn't fly.

I glared up at the stands, where I knew the dark angel was lurking. "Why am I here?" I demanded for at least the hundredth time.

Soulslayer didn't answer, just like so many times before. All he ever said was, 'fight or die'.

I flicked the last dead bird off my lightning blade. The sword popped and sizzled out, dissipating. Then I collapsed to the ground, exhausted.

The ring of the bell chimed once more. It was a sound I'd come to hate and fear. The next battle was about to start. My rest denied, I pulled my tired body off the ground, preparing myself to face my next foe. It swooped out of the open door —a big black bird, larger than all of the others put together. It was the emperor of all birds. And it was breathing fire.

I tried to create another sword out of lightning, but my magic didn't come. The bird landed with a thump and stomped toward me, shooting a miasma of fireballs and other elemental magic out of its mouth.

I shook out my hands. Sometimes when one branch of magic was dry, there was still some juice left in the others. I drew on my telekinetic magic. I could still feel some of the Nectar in me from the gods' last gift. I swept my psychic spell over the dead birds. They lifted off the ground, hovering for a moment in the air. Then I shot them all at the big bird, blinding it behind a mass of black feathers.

Big Bird fireballed, froze, zapped, and blew them out of the air. I came around, snatching up four dead birds still glowing with Big Bird's spells. One was burning, one was solid ice, one sizzled with lightning, and one was trapped inside a whirling mini tornado. I smashed the four birds together, combining the lingering spells on them to set off a clashing elemental explosion under Big Bird's ass.

The bird shot up and collided with the Magitech barrier. As the bird swayed, dazed from the impact, I searched the arena for something—anything—to help me in this fight against the jumbo bird. I didn't see anything but the dead crows. The elemental spells had faded from their bodies, so they were of no use to me anymore.

I looked down at the sand. It had begun to glow. As I continued to stare at it, I realized why it felt so familiar. The sand was laced with Venom, the demons' equivalent to

Nectar. Just as Nectar, the food of the gods, bestowed Legion soldiers with light magic abilities, Venom bestowed the dark magic ability counterparts to the demons' Dark Force.

I'd had Venom before. Someone had laced my Nectar with it when I'd gained the power of Siren's Song. When I'd drained the Venom out of Basanti, more Venom had gotten into my body, merging with my magic. The Venom in the sand was singing to me now because I was weak—because my body was in desperate need of healing and food.

I glanced up at the stands. The dark angel was watching me closely. From the look on his face, he'd realized that I'd figured it out. I swooped up a handful of sand. He leaned forward, looking almost eager.

He wanted me to consume the Venom. But why? Did he want to turn me into a soldier of the Dark Force?

No, it was something more. This was all too staged, too planned. He must have known I possessed light and dark magic, that unlike others, I could consume both Nectar and Venom.

I sniffed the sand in my hands. It smelled good, like chocolate cake with cherries and ice cream on top, like the end of all my suffering. But Soulslayer wanted me to take it, the person who was holding my sisters hostage. The person who had trapped me here and was having me battle in this arena like a lab rat. His intentions were not benevolent.

Concentrated dark magic—poison—that's what Venom was. But there was also light magic nearby. I could feel it. Where was it? I searched the arena, honing in on the Magitech barrier. This place had not been built solely for me. It was a lot older than that.

It was for training, I realized. Training for the Dark Force. The barrier was sizzling with concentrated light magic. With Nectar. Just as Venom was poisonous to Legion soldiers, Nectar was poisonous to soldiers of the Dark Force. It was meant to hurt when they banged against the Nectar-infused barrier, a punishment for failing in training. And maybe it had another purpose: to build up their resistance to light magic. That would be the angel way, to kill two birds with one stone. And the dark angels were no different.

Allowing the yellow sand to pour out between my fingers, I walked up to the barrier and thrust my hands through the Magitech field to grab the bars. I gripped them tightly, even as the magic pulsed through me, trying to overload my body, to knock me out. And it hurt like hell. But then again, every fiber of my body already hurt so what was a little more pain? I began to bend the bars, the tubes the magic field was running through.

Soulslayer jumped to his feet. "What are you doing?" he demanded.

I just held on, gritting my teeth, bearing the pain. I broke a magic tube off from the net. I tossed that charged tube to the ground, igniting it against the sand beneath the bird monster's feet. Light and dark magic clashed, and opposites ignited to create a mega explosion. The bird blew up.

I peeled my burnt and blistered hands off the bars and stumbled to the center of the fighting arena, stepping over a burning pile of bird goo. Then, planting a big smile on my face despite the pain, I swept my stiff body into a deep, smooth bow.

"You cheated." Soulslayer sounded offended. "I want to see your magic at work, not your cheap tricks."

"Let her do it her way," a female voice echoed through the arena, seeming to come from every direction at once. "I want to see this."

Before I could speculate about that voice, the bell chimed once again, and the next monster entered the arena.

———

I WAS JERKED RUDELY awake by a dark angel. He hadn't been gentle about it either. My body screamed beneath his magic's hard grip. My vision blurred, my head spun, and I almost passed out again.

"Wake up," Soulslayer snapped, then released me. "It's time for dinner."

I shot him a skeptical look. He hadn't fed me since bringing me here. Maybe he wanted to poison me for some new fun. I wouldn't put it past the sadistic dark angel. After all, once he'd broken some of my bones right before a fight. Sometimes, he used potions to block parts of my magic like Ronan had. Except Ronan had done it to help me, and Soulslayer was doing it to torture me.

I'd come to realize that the dark angel was trying to get a reading on my magic, both light and dark. He dropped me in situations that tested my powers. That's why I was in the arena. Maybe poison was the new test, the latest experiment to see how I'd handle it—how my magic would handle it.

"I don't need food to poison you," Soulslayer said.

I'd given up on hiding my thoughts long ago. I didn't have the energy left to do it. Most of the time, I was just thinking about enacting my revenge on the sadistic dark angel who was torturing me. He was free to read those thoughts all he wanted.

I decided I would eat. I needed my strength a lot more than I needed to piss him off. Besides, the biggest poisons were Nectar and Venom, and I'd already survived both.

"The food isn't poisoned. In fact, it's just what you need to survive the next fight," said Soulslayer.

The fateful bell rang again, and the gates opened. Someone was pushed into the arena. A human. A bleeding human. That was the meal Soulslayer was offering me. I should have known it wouldn't be that easy.

The door slammed shut, trapping the man in the arena. He was meant to tempt me. Like a shark smelling blood, my senses were heightened, my body alert. My body was screaming at me to drink from this poor person, to drain his blood to heal my wounds and feed my starving body.

But I was immortal. It took a lot more than an empty stomach to kill me. As painful as they were, I wouldn't die from my injuries either. They just made me weak. I couldn't feast on this innocent person just to alleviate my discomfort.

The man met my eyes, his own widening. He spun around, banging desperately on the door. He was completely terrified. It must have been all the blood splashed over me. I'm sure my hungry eyes weren't helping either; I could feel them burning silver.

I put my hands up in the air. "I'm not going to hurt you."

The man continued to claw at the door. He was scratching so hard that his fingernails were bleeding. The sharp tang of fresh blood only made it harder to resist the hunger.

You're stronger than this, I told myself, swallowing hard. The burn in my eyes faded.

When it became clear I wasn't going to tear the man's throat open with my fangs and feast on his blood, Soulslayer frowned in agitation. He waved his hand, and the door slid open once more. The human bolted for the opening, but he didn't make it far. A gigantic white furry bear-man beast charged out, meeting him halfway. Before I could blink, the monster grabbed the man and swallowed him whole. I stared at it in shocked outrage.

"You should have drunk from him when you had the chance," Soulslayer chided me. "Now, it's too late. Your stubbornness didn't save him from death. All you did was deny yourself relief from the hunger."

Smacking its lips, the monster lumbered toward me, obviously still hungry. Anger sparked in me as I looked at its furry face, stained crimson with blood. I grabbed one of the legs from the dead big bird. It was as hard as metal. I swung it at the bear-man, slashing across its tummy. I struck again. My rage propelled me, making me forget the pain—anger at the dark angel for doing this, for bringing innocents into this sick game of his. Colonel Fireswift was harmless compared to the darkly vicious Soulslayer.

I drove the metal leg through the beast's heart like a long stake. The monster spluttered, then dropped dead to the ground. Yellow sand swirled, puffing up from the impact of the heavy body.

I glared up at the dark angel. My body pulsing with pain, I swore, "I will kill you."

"Finally, we're getting somewhere," Soulslayer said with satisfaction.

Disgusted, I sat down on the sand. I was so done. I was not playing along anymore. I was tired of these games.

That ominous, hateful beep sounded again. The gates opened, releasing another monster. I kept my butt planted firmly on the ground.

"Get up," Soulslayer commanded.

I didn't move an inch, even as the monster slinked toward me. As sleek and black as a panther—at twice the size—the catlike beast moved slowly, taking its time to assess its prey.

"Get up," Soulslayer said again.

Magic pulsed behind his voice, his siren's song compelling me to obey. I let his magic bounce right off of me. Resisting him didn't hurt half as much as I already did.

Surprise flashed in his eyes, but his smugness quickly returned. "You're bluffing. You won't let yourself die. If you're dead, who will find your brother?"

"No, you're bluffing," I shot back. "You have no problems pushing me to the brink of death, but you won't actually let me die. You're too invested in gauging my magic to kill me."

His smile faded, his bluff called. "You are every bit as repugnant as they say."

"You bet I am." Grinning made my cheekbones feel like they would crack apart, but I did it anyway.

A calculated smile curled Soulslayer's lips. "If you don't play along, I'll just put your sweet little sisters into the arena. I wonder how much I have to hurt them before they scream."

I jumped up, angry tears burning my eyes as I glared at the dark angel. "Before this is over, I will kill you," I promised him again. Then I faced the monster.

CHAPTER 26

DISTINCTLY MEDIEVAL

The next time I woke up, I was not in the fighting arena. I didn't smell the delicious, tempting magic of the yellow sand calling to me, and I wasn't squinting under the glare of the blinding floodlights.

The lighting in this room was diffused. It sparkled softly against the black marble floors and the white marble that covered every wall. A symbol of intersecting circles sat at the center of the floor. It was a symbol I didn't recognize.

The room was both opulent and sterile, like a hospital mixed with a bank. I tried to move, only to discover that I was chained to a wall. A basket of tools lay on a nearby table. It was filled with syringes, scissors, needles, forceps—and some things I didn't even want to imagine what they did. One thing was clear, however: it was a torturer's toolbox.

No, on second thought, this wasn't a bank or a hospital. It was a five-star dungeon.

I might have been able to use some of the tools to free myself, but the basket was just out of reach. My magic was of no help either. It was a weak hum, fizzling in and out

307

intermittently, blinking like a lightbulb that needed to be changed.

Across the room, Gin and Tessa were trapped in twin cells, each of my sisters tied to the wall beyond a glowing magic barrier. Their heads drooped to the side. I called out to them, but they didn't wake up.

I tried to break free of my restraints. The chains, infused with powerful dark magic, burned like acid against my skin as I struggled. They didn't budge at all.

I heard the sharp click of approaching footsteps, then a swoosh as the glass doors to the room slid open and Soulslayer stepped into the bright marble dungeon. Without saying a word to me, he roughly grabbed hold of my arm and stuck a needle in me. He took enough blood to fill a small vial, then brought it to a machine on the desk past the small table of torture tools. I'd seen Nerissa use these machines. They tested the magic in blood.

"Why am I here?"

As expected, he didn't answer my question. Nothing new there.

As he inserted the blood sample into the machine, the glass doors opened once more. This time a woman entered the dungeon. Divinely beautiful, she wore her black, glossy hair long. It flowed past her waist like a curtain of black silk fluttering in the wind. Her eyes sparkled green-blue, the color of blue fir trees. She smelled like freshly-fallen pine needles, burning together with a potpourri of wood and metal, like a sleepy forest after a snowfall.

She wore a black leather uniform adorned with armor pieces that looked as much like jewelry as armor. Metal guards set with gemstones covered her forearms. She wore a matching headband. No, a diadem, a sign of power and sovereignty. There was magic in her gemstones, a potent magic that magnified her own. I could see it in the unearthly glow of the gems, the mesmerizing swirl in their jeweled depths, like an ancient story was playing out inside of them.

Her magic was dark and rich. I'd only ever felt such powerful magic in the presence of a god. She had to be a demon, the gods' dark magic counterparts.

"Progress?" the demon asked Soulslayer.

I recognized that voice. It was the one that had spoken to the dark angel in the arena.

"I've taken a sample of her blood. The machine is analyzing it now," Soulslayer told her.

The beautiful demon came over to me, stopping at the wall I was chained to. "I am Sonja, Demon of the Dark Force, the Dark Lady of War, the Mistress of Telekinesis, and Queen of the Psychics," she introduced herself.

Gods and demons always had so many titles.

But it was the title 'Demon of the Dark Force' that caught my attention most of all. The Dark Force was the demons' version of the Legion of Angels. Sonja was the demon who ruled over the Dark Force. Her equivalent was Ronan, Lord of the Legion of Angels.

"So I'm in hell," I said. "It's cleaner than I expected."

"The old stereotypes of hell are so very wrong. Fiery pits and burning volcanoes. Pillars of fire, sulfur and smoke." Her nose crinkled up. "Nothing but fantastical lies spun by scared humans and encouraged by the reprehensible gods."

"Reprehensible? And what is all of *this*? Kindness?"

I couldn't move my arms because they were bolted to the wall, but I moved my gaze from my chained limbs, to my sisters locked up in their cells.

"This is *progress*." Pride rang in Sonja's voice. It danced off every syllable.

My chains clinked as I pushed against them. "Your kind of progress is distinctly medieval."

"You need to free your mind from these mortal misconceptions. They are so limiting. See things for what they truly are."

"You have me chained to a wall," I said drily. "There's really no room for interpretation here."

"Well, I can't very well have you running away, now can I?"

She said it patiently, like she was speaking to a child. It wasn't even a question. It was a statement of fact, plain and simple. Like one plus one is two. And that she was sick and tired of explaining it, thank-you-very-much.

"Your peacock-winged minion threw monster after monster at me for who knows how long," I said. "You abducted my sisters and me. How am I supposed to see things how you do if you won't even tell me why you took us? And how did you convince the Pioneers, who shun all divine intervention on Earth, to take your potion and do your bidding?"

I was going out on a limb here, guessing the demon had made the potion, but it was the best theory I had.

"Well, of course the Pioneers didn't know they were working for me," said Sonja, amused. "They purchased their superhuman potion from Balin."

The dark angel had been masquerading as a mercenary. The spells in place that kept demons out of Earth had holes in them, areas weak enough for someone with less potent dark magic to get through. That's how dark angels and other Dark Force soldiers made it to Earth.

"The Pioneers' potion seems to defy magical laws," I said, prompting her further.

"Not really." Sonja's laugh was deceptively sweet, a poison thorn hiding beneath a beautiful blossoming rose. "The key ingredient of the potion is my blood."

I just let Sonja keep stroking her own ego. Immortals loved to show how clever they were. Usually, it was annoying, but right now Sonja's ego was filling in the gaps, providing me with much-needed information.

"Just a drop of my blood was needed per vial, mixed with some other ingredients that mask my blood and make the magic die as soon as it leaves a human body or the safety of the magic containers. It is one of Valerian's better ideas."

Valerian, the Dark Lord of Witches, was another demon. He also happened to be Bella's grandfather. So he and Sonja were allies, plotting to use the Pioneers to destroy the Legion. How many other demons were involved? Gods and demons generally formed alliances on a case-by-case basis—allies in one battle, enemies in another.

"But the potion isn't a real magic pill," I realized.

"Oh?" Her eyes twinkled.

"You were controlling them. As long as your blood was inside of them, you held the reins. The magic they used was you channeling your magic through them. There is no miracle magic potion, no new way to make supernatural soldiers without the consequences. The Pioneers never had any magic at all."

"Do you think I'd actually give divine magic to a group like that?" Disgust rolled off her tongue.

Of course she wouldn't. She'd just been using them. In

their desperate quest for power, the Pioneers hadn't even considered the reality that a potion like theirs shouldn't be able to exist. Any witch could have told them that. They didn't know they were drinking demon blood, or who'd really given it to them. They didn't know that they were just Sonja's tools. They only knew that the potion made them powerful —strong enough to rid the world of gods. And then after that, they'd move on to wiping out the demons. They would be the heroes who freed the Earth from its foreign invaders.

The Pioneers were such fools. And I'd been a fool to think that they were the real threat.

I looked at Soulslayer. "You were the shooter on the roof in Purgatory, the one who killed the werewolf mercenaries. You left the final werewolf alive on purpose."

"Of course I did. It wouldn't have taken much magic to make my bullet pierce the pitiful ice spell you'd cast around him."

"But why? Why leave him alive when we would have gone after the prisoners anyway—" The answer hit me like a falling block of bricks. "You wanted us to think something fishy was going on, that this was more than just your everyday kidnapping. To draw me into your trap."

"You're starting to see things as they are," said Sonja. "The hazy cloud of humanity is lifting from your eyes. That which limits you, constrains you, prevents you from reaching your true potential, is falling away."

"And what is my potential? You obviously brought me here for my magic, just like my sisters."

"I want to understand your magic and your sisters' magic, to harness it to strengthen the Dark Force."

"Fourteen years ago, you were the one who told the Rogue King that Hellfire was holding two girls with powerful otherworldly magic."

"Yes."

"When Hellfire attacked, Gin and Tessa escaped into the jungle," I said, talking it through. "You sent in your soldiers. Those were the 'black beasts' my sisters spoke of, monsters even the warlords feared. Dark Force soldiers dressed in black leather, the most fearsome creatures in the whole jungle. You were going to capture my sisters for yourself, but Calli found them first. She brought them home, far away from there. Their memories wiped, their magic masked, there was no trace of them. You couldn't find them."

"Yes, for fourteen years the girls remained hidden, but I knew they would turn up eventually. Their magic was too extraordinary to stay secret." She hit me with a smile as sweet as it was sharp. "But in the end, I found them because of you."

I blinked in confusion.

"Leda, you really do draw far too much attention to yourself. You led me straight to your sisters."

My empty stomach clenched up with guilt. My journey to gain the magic I needed to find Zane had put my sisters at risk. This was all my fault. I should have kept my head lower.

"Don't fret. It was Callista Pierce's failing as much as your own. Gin and Tessa are of ancient breeds. So few of them are left, and those that remain are scattered throughout the realms. In their natural, fully-powered state, they are too powerful to easily capture. But these two sweet girls can't even use their powers. Your foster mother practically gift-wrapped them for me," Sonja said with a smirk. "All I had to do was be patient for them to turn up again."

Patience, the favorite immortal virtue.

"You'd be surprised. Some of my fellow demons are horribly impatient," she said, reading my thoughts. "Every few years, they—*they* meaning usually Ava or Alessandro—try to launch yet another failed attempt at building up an army of supporters here on Earth, soldiers who will supposedly break the Legion and topple the gods."

Like the army the demons had been building last year, right around the time I'd joined the Legion. That grand army hadn't made it very far.

Sonja made a derisive noise. "If it were that easy, we would have done it centuries ago. I've told them time and time again, we need to play the long game."

Since stepping into the dungeon, Sonja had talked a lot, but she hadn't really given much away, and I didn't think that was an accident. I still had no idea what my sisters' powers were. All I knew about the magic was it was rare. Sonja wanted to give their powers to the soldiers of her Dark Force—and, I was guessing, to the demons as well. Then the demons would possess powers the gods did not. Sonja believed that would give them the upper hand in this immortal war.

"Enough chitchat. Let's begin." Sonja waved over Soulslayer. "Give her the first dose."

The dark angel grabbed my arm, his grip ironclad, unrelenting, cruel. He pricked me with a needle, injecting me with something.

It was Venom. I felt it immediately—the burn in my veins, like a firestorm consuming me, burning me alive. The tidal wave of magic crashed and rocked inside of me, pulling me under. My vision grew splotchy, clouded. I saw only fire.

"What the hell are you doing?" I demanded.

"Your sisters have rare and powerful magic, but you,

my dear, are something else altogether," said Sonja. "You are one of a kind. The first. The only."

As the demon and the dark angel closed in on me, I hardly felt the pricks of their needles. The tiny jabs were nothing compared to the inferno blazing inside of me.

"First what?!" I shouted. "Only what?!"

I had to keep them talking. And I had to stay conscious. The Venom was making my head fuzzy, groggy. The fire of dark magic was burning through what was left of my energy.

"Amazing." Sonja's voice snapped me awake.

I blinked and saw the demon sitting at the desk, looking at my blood through a microscope.

"The Venom is balancing against the Nectar inside of her," she told Soulslayer. "They are becoming one, inter-locked, cohesive. It's remarkable."

I could feel the battle of light and dark magic in my blood. They were fighting, clashing, but slowly, they began to reach an equilibrium, a harmony of opposing magics.

"I saw that in the previous samples after the arena battles. Her light and dark magic worked together. She used both sides of the magic spectrum in unison," said Sonja. "But seeing the Venom and Nectar work inside her body, at the core, as they merge, as they become part of her, is something else altogether. It's simply amazing."

Perhaps it was amazing on paper. In reality, as the Venom and Nectar tried to negotiate a balance inside of me, it burned like a wildfire through my body, drowning me in agony.

"After another dose of Venom, her dark magic will be up to the same level as her light magic."

"And then?" I asked. It hurt to speak.

Sonja turned to look at me. "Then we will push you

higher, alternating Venom and Nectar." Her sparkling eyes, alight with delight, turned to the microscope again. She obviously couldn't wait to see the results of her experiments. She really was the epitome of the mad scientist.

"Your plan won't work," I told her. "You can't level up my magic with Nectar and Venom alone. It requires training."

"We will train you if necessary," she replied with a dismissive flick of her hand. "As I said, I am patient. We will do this for years if need be."

I coughed, choking on the Venom's magic.

"But I don't think it will take so long," she said.

The river of fire raging inside of me was splitting me apart.

"You overestimate me," I said.

Sonja laughed. "You don't know what you are, do you?"

I didn't ask her. I didn't want to give her the satisfaction of withholding information I so desperately wanted to know.

"The gods are too detached from reality to see anything right in front of their eyes," Sonja continued. "Which is why they missed your friend Stash, the demigod. They don't know Damiel Dragonsire survived his execution either. They don't realize Cadence Lightbringer is alive, being held by the Guardians. They miss everything."

How did Sonja know so much?

"We are not on Earth, but we are watching. Always watching," Sonja told me. "Nyx must have figured it out. She always had an uncanny ability to cut through the bullshit."

Soulslayer tensed at the mention of the First Angel of the Legion.

Sonja glanced at him. "Ronan won't survive the war to come. Nyx will join us."

They obviously didn't know the First Angel at all. She would never roll over. She wouldn't cooperate, and neither would I. They would just have to kill me.

"You *will* cooperate. You will train and embrace the magic and survive." Sonja's smile was savage. "Because, otherwise, your sisters will pay the price. And you will never rescue your brother."

"He is safe," I stated in defiance.

A shrill laugh broke past her lips. "If you truly believe that, you are even more naive than I'd thought. Your brother is in the greatest danger of you all. You will soon come to wish that either we or the gods had taken him instead of the Guardians."

I frowned at her. "I don't trust you."

"Good," Sonja said, nodding. "That's the first truly intelligent thing I've heard come out of your mouth."

My chains disappeared in a whiff of smoke, and I dropped off the wall. Soulslayer caught me by the shoulders. He dragged me across the room like I weighed nothing. I didn't resist. My limbs were limp, my body shaking. I couldn't have lifted a cup of water if I'd tried, let alone a sword.

My vision blurred. My sisters' cells faded out, dripping into darkness.

"She needs some time for the Venom to settle before we can push more magic into her," Sonja's voice echoed in my ears.

Soft footsteps sounded her and Soulslayer's departure. They left me alone to the firestorm of opposing magics trying to balance, to merge, inside of me. I was shaking so hard that my teeth rattled in my mouth. I clenched my jaw, just trying to stay conscious.

Time melted and twisted. I wasn't sure how long my mind drifted in that half-conscious state between dreamland and reality.

"Leda?"

I tried to pull my head out of the magical storm raging inside of me.

"Leda?" Tessa called out to me again from the abyss.

The sound of her voice was like a tether. I held on to it and pulled myself back into consciousness.

I blinked, clearing my vision. The demon and the dark angel were gone. Tessa stood in the cell across from me, looking at me from behind the glowing magic barrier. Gin's cell was empty.

I tried to go to Tessa, but my body didn't cooperate. I was chained to a wall again.

"Where's Gin?" I asked her. My voice was as broken as the rest of my body.

"Gin is gone," Tessa said, her face gloomy. "They took her."

They must have done that while I'd been drowning under the magic of Venom, because I hadn't noticed it at all.

"I will get you both out of here," I promised Tessa.

The glass doors to the dungeon slid open with a whisper. Four soldiers marched in. One of them carried Gin. As the soldiers drew closer, as I got a better look at my sister, my heart locked up. Pain paralyzed me. But as the soldiers set Gin's lifeless body on a table in the middle of the room, the floodgates of my agony tore open, and I screamed out. My sister was dead.

CHAPTER 27

IMMORTAL MORTALITY

*A*s the soldiers left, a soft voice cut through my agony. "Gin isn't really dead," Tessa said. "She will rise again."

Hope stuttered in my chest. When I could breathe again, I asked, "How?"

"Gin is a Phoenix, an immortal with the power to be reborn," Tessa explained. "She can't be killed, no matter how hard she's hit. Well, at least if there is a way to kill her, the dark angel hasn't found it yet."

Relief rushed through my body, even as anger pooled up deep inside of me. Soulslayer had hurt my sisters.

"He put you in the battle arena," I said quietly.

"Yes."

Soulslayer had told me he wouldn't make them fight if I did, but I wasn't surprised that he'd broken that promise. He was a sadistic beast.

"Sonja unlocked our memories to unlock our magic." Tessa's tone was dark. She sounded more mature, like she'd grown up a lot since the festival in Purgatory. Her chirpy girlishness was gone.

I looked away from Gin's lifeless body. It hurt to see her like that.

"And your magic?" I asked Tessa.

"I'm a djinn."

"Like a genie?"

"Not quite. Djinn are part of the same branch of magic as genies, our wish-granting brethren, but djinn have inter-dimensional jumping powers. On a smaller scale, we can teleport short distances. We can also reach into the interdimensional ether and summon creatures from other realms."

"I've never come across magic like yours or Gin's."

"Gin and I came from other worlds, just like the gods and demons."

So Damiel had been right.

"What are the constraints of your interdimensional magic?" I asked Tessa.

"In theory, it ignores all protection wards and barrier spells."

The demons could use Tessa's power to enter the Earth, to bypass the gods' wards and bring in their armies with them. They could use it to teleport monsters beyond the wall into human cities. The results would be catastrophic, and the demons would certainly be more than willing to step in and save the Earth—at the cost of humanity's absolute allegiance.

And Gin's magic was just as dangerous in the wrong hands. Even gods and demons could be killed, but a phoenix was always reborn. I imagined armies of constantly reviving soldiers, ones who could jump around the battlefield and jump between realms. The perfect army.

"Can you use your magic to get us and Gin out of here?" I asked Tessa.

"Hellfire captured me when I was very young. I never

learned to make interdimensional jumps, only the small ones."

"Can you get out of your cell?"

Tessa held up her hands, showing me the pair of matching metallic cuffs locked around her wrists. Green magic slid over the cuffs like a layer of fog, lighting up the runes engraved into the metal.

"No, Soulslayer put these on me to block my jumping magic," she said, frowning at the beautiful cuffs. "They have settings to block different levels of jumps. The lower the setting, the further I can jump. Whenever I'm in my cell, he sets them to block all jumps, but sometimes he tones them down in the battle arena. The first time he put me and Gin in there, I realized the bracelets weren't blocking my short-range jumps. I thought I'd gotten lucky, that the dark angel had forgotten to set them properly."

"The angels don't forget things. Soulslayer did it for a reason."

"I was using my short-range jumps to evade a beast when my magic suddenly stopped working. If not for Gin, the beast would have killed me then. In the next battle, my magic was working again. Sometimes on, sometimes off, always unpredictable."

"He was toying with you," I said, my anger simmering beneath the surface.

"Yes."

I formed two fists and pulled against my chains. The metal groaned.

"He killed Gin over and over again, in so many different and grotesque ways." Tessa's face paled. She looked liked she'd be ill. "He wanted to see if she would still come back to life."

"How many times did Soulslayer's arena kill Gin?"

"Fifty. Maybe more."

Acid churned and rose in my empty stomach, but I had to keep my wits about me. So I swallowed my disgust and struggled to clear my mind.

"I tried to save her, but I wasn't always fast enough to jump away. And the bracelets were blocking my magic half the time." Tessa's shoulders slumped, her words heavy with guilt.

"It's not your fault," I told her.

A tear slid down her cheek.

"Look at me, Tessa."

She wiped her eyes with the backs of her hands and met my gaze.

"You did everything you could," I said. "This isn't your fault. It's Soulslayer's."

"When the dark angel captured you, he was so busy torturing you that he left me and Gin alone for a while. We heard your screams." Her voice shook. "Sometimes he came here to taunt us with your pain. He enjoyed hurting you, Leda."

"Forget about that now. The past is in the past. This ends now. We're getting out of here."

"How?" She sounded desperate.

"I will think of something. I promise. I'm going to get you out of here. And I'm going to make Soulslayer pay for hurting you and Gin," I added.

"Don't worry about us, Leda. We'll be fine. We've endured much more." Her eyes hardened with determination.

I didn't ask Tessa about what had happened all those years ago when she and Gin had been held by the warlords —or about their months in the jungle.

"They pitted us against monsters and soldiers," Tessa

said, guessing where my mind was. "We did what we had to do to survive."

They'd done what they had to do to survive—at such a young age. Seeing the look in Tessa's eyes, I understood why Calli had asked Zane to wipe their memories. She must have seen that same look back then. Children deserved a chance at a normal childhood, a chance at innocence. They shouldn't have to kill in order to survive.

On the table, Gin woke up screaming in agony as flames erupted all across her body, bathing her in fire.

Tessa looked away. "It hurts every time she is reborn in fire."

The flames slowly died down, then they went out. Gin lay on the table, shaking. Her clothes were ashes all around her. The soldiers hadn't bothered to chain her up. She looked so weak that she couldn't move.

The glass doors parted, and Soulslayer glided into the room as smooth as honey. He grabbed Gin off the table, casually threw her over his shoulder, then dropped her into her cell. The magic barrier went up. Gin was still spasming, her naked body shaking on the floor. The dark angel didn't even throw her some clothes or a blanket.

"Stop," I growled.

He turned to look at me.

"This isn't the end," I said in a low snarl.

He just watched me, a bored expression on his face.

"For what you've done to my sisters, I will tear you apart piece by piece, watching you die in agony as your resolve crumbles and your soul shatters into a million pieces."

He clicked his tongue. "Temper, temper."

I heaved against my chains. The links snapped. As I worked on freeing my legs, the dark angel calmly walked over to me and hit a button on the wall. A Magitech barrier slid over my body, encasing it like a translucent cocoon. It held me so tightly that I could feel the magic singeing my eyebrows. Soulslayer considered me, his face arrogant.

I pushed out with my magic, punching it against the Magitech barrier. Cracks formed. I hit it again. The cracks multiplied, ripping the threads of magic apart. The barrier shattered.

"Sonja will be so pleased," Soulslayer said with a dark smile.

The marble wall I was pinned to zapped me with a massive jolt of magic. The shock tore across my back, shooting down my legs, sending my body into convulsions. My chains popped open, and I dropped to the ground in a heap. The whole room was spinning. I couldn't see straight, couldn't focus. And I couldn't pull myself off the floor.

Get up! I mentally shouted at my battered body.

Soulslayer grabbed me by the neck and slammed me hard against the wall. New chains flew out of the holes in the marble, locking me down. The dark angel tore off the remaining sleeve of my jacket and threw the rag of tattered leather onto the floor. Then he grabbed a syringe and injected a potion into me. I tried to move and found myself unable to even twitch. He'd completely paralyzed me.

As I dangled there limply on the wall, frozen, Soulslayer pulled out his phone and began to type. I must have been really delirious because the first thought that flashed through my head was: *I wonder how the phone reception is in hell.*

Black spots danced before my eyes. Through those splotches of darkness, I could vaguely make out the silky stride of Sonja stepping into the dungeon. She and Soul-slayer were talking, but my ears were so clogged that I couldn't hear anything but muffled noises. Sonja lifted a syringe from the side table and moved toward me. She was going to draw yet another blood sample.

I couldn't move a single muscle, but I collected my telekinetic magic into a point and punched out with it, flicking the syringe to the ground. Sonja picked up another one and tried again. I flicked that one away too. This time, I heard the syringe clink against the marble floor. My ears had finally cleared.

"Must I remind you that I am the Mistress of Telekinesis?"

Her magic caught the next syringe I flicked away. I countered with light magic, wrestling for control over the tool. Demons were weak against light magic, but after all these weeks or days or however long it had been, I didn't have much strength left in me.

"Now, that's quite enough of this nonsense," Sonja said.

She tightened her telekinetic grip on me, wrapping it around my whole body. Her hold was so tight that I couldn't push against the magic with my own. My magic winked out, and a moment later the needle pierced my arm. Sonja took a sample of my blood, and looked at it under her magic microscope.

"Your magic has blended beautifully," she said. "Dark and light are complementing each other nicely. You are everything I'd hoped for. Such a perfect blend." She looked up from the machine and asked, "You never had any magic before you joined the Legion?"

Not really. All I'd had was my weird hair that mesmerized vampires—and my hair was only growing more bizarre the more magic I gained.

"Curious," she commented.

There was no point in devoting my overspent magic into blocking my thoughts right now. Sonja already seemed to know everything I knew and then some.

The demon smiled. "True."

"Then why don't we stop playing games, and you just tell me what you want from me? Why do you want to grow my magic? Is this about finding my brother?"

"Your brother is certainly intriguing, but no, this isn't about him. This is about the future of the Dark Force. That future is your magic—and making more soldiers like you."

Tessa and Gin possessed powers that even the gods and demons did not. So of course Sonja wanted to find a way to give their magic to her soldiers. But I didn't have any rare powers. All of my abilities were the standard Legion of Angels powers.

"You're thinking about this all wrong," Sonja told me. "This isn't about your abilities, Leda. It's about the *nature* of those abilities, the source of your power. It's about your balance of dark and light magic, your ability to absorb Venom and Nectar and to access the entire magical spectrum."

"So you're going to bottle my magic, just like you did yours. And then you're going to give it to your soldiers," I guessed.

"No, I'm not going to bottle your magic. I'm going to breed it." Her eyes were glowing like turquoises. "I'm going to breed you to create the ultimate super soldiers, soldiers with the power to use and resist spells across the entire dark and light spectrum."

"That will take centuries."

She shrugged. "You're immortal, and I'm willing to wait."

Nero's mother Cadence was an angel, and it had taken the Guardians centuries to equalize her light and dark magic. I wasn't willing to spend my life in a cage. And I sure as hell didn't want to be part of a demon's breeding program.

"Don't be so melodramatic," Sonja told me. "After all, it's nothing different than what the Legion already does to its angels. They decide who the angels will marry."

I glared at her, daring her to try to breed me like some race horse.

"So you thought you'd become an angel, save your brother, and then live happily ever after with your angel lover Nero Windstriker? Life isn't that simple." Her laugh was too delicate to have come from a demon. "Oh, I see." She met my defiant glare. "You didn't think that far ahead, did you?"

I had to admit to myself that I really hadn't. Well, sure, the thought of my and Nero's future had crossed my mind, but I'd always pushed those thoughts away. I'd always told myself it was because I didn't have time to think about such things.

Sonja gave me a pitying look. "You are young. You might not have thought decades ahead, but I can assure you that Nero Windstriker has. He knows the day may come when the Legion finds you're compatible with someone else and marries you to that soldier."

"That's none of your business," I snapped.

But looking back, the signs were there. Nero was glad I was moving up the Legion, but he often seemed troubled by my progress—almost helpless. He'd told me I was going up the ranks so fast. Was it *too* fast for him? Did he fear my becoming an angel because he knew it would tear us apart?

Sonja was right. Nero must have thought about this future at least once or twice, a future he believed to be inevitable. It must have hurt him, but he still always helped me. He pushed me to grow my magic, even if that meant it would ultimately drive us apart. He really loved me.

The thought of not being with Nero hurt. That's why I'd never dared to consider our future. I was scared. Scared that the Legion would drive us apart. Scared that I'd lose my nerve and stop pushing myself to level up my magic, just so we could stay together.

"So this is the point where you promise Nero and I can be together if I just help you." My throat was tight, my eyes hot.

Sonja's laughter danced off the cold marble walls. "No. I don't make promises I can't keep. Your magic is too valuable to risk on an imperfect mating."

"There's more to being with someone than magic, you know."

"Oh?"

"Yes," I said, her amusement sparking my defiance. "Like love."

Sonja snorted. "Love is such a trite stereotype. It's an illusion, a moment of misguided insanity that leads you to do very stupid things. And those stupid things tend to have disastrous consequences. Your conception was the rare exception to the rule, a magical fluke."

All at once, I forgot myself, that I was tied to a dungeon wall being experimented on by the Demon of the Dark Force. "What am I?" I asked eagerly, latching on to her words. "Am I from another world like my sisters?"

Sonja met my eyes, her arrogance fading away. "No,

you're not from another world. You're not from any world as you know it."

"I don't understand."

Sonja sighed. "Of course you don't, child. There has never been another like you, an immortal soul born mortal with the powers of light and dark."

"I wasn't born with magic. I had none before my first sip of Nectar ignited it."

"You could not use your magic, but you were born with it all, every power the Legion can give you," she told me. "Your light and dark magic sides—equally powerful— were canceling each other out, neutralizing each other so that you could use neither. That's why you believed yourself to possess no magic."

My mind struggled to process her words, to make sense of them. Light and dark in equal amounts, the opposite sides of the magical spectrum cancelling each other out. It wasn't all that different from what Ronan had talked about.

"Your light magic side comes from your father and your dark side from your mother," Sonja continued. "It is divine magic."

"Divine? So that means…"

"You are both god and demon. Your father is a god and your mother a demon."

CHAPTER 28

LIGHT AND DARK

I covered my shock with sarcasm. "Please don't tell me this is where you admit to being my mother," I told Sonja, rolling my eyes.

The demon laughed. "No."

I expelled a deep breath of relief. The Demon of the Dark Force wasn't very motherly. She was not cruel for cruelty's sake like Soulslayer, but she also didn't care how many people were used and misused along the path to her achieving her goal. Sonja firmly believed that her way was the only way, the only path, that it was best for everyone.

"Unlike your mother, I am not foolish enough to have an affair with a god."

"Who is my mother?" I asked her. "And who is my father?"

"Your father was a mistake, a misguided affair. And your mother is the naive fool who fell for his charms."

"Which god? Which demon?"

Sonja's lips pursed up in disgust, and she returned her attention to her work.

"At least tell me if they are still alive," I said.

"Yes."

The gladness I felt wasn't born out of a desperate wish to meet the mother and father I'd been missing all my life, and I harbored no delusions that my parents and I could be one big happy family.

No, I knew no such fantasy was possible. I had my real family, not in blood but in spirit: Calli, Bella, Zane, Gin, and Tessa. That was the family of my heart. I had no use for the cold, careless embrace of the gods and demons.

That spark of excitement was the curiosity burning in me. I just had to know who my parents were. I had to know where I'd come from.

"You have your parents to thank for your glowing hair," Sonja said, absently touching the end of my braid.

"How so?"

"Your hair is a manifestation of their special powers."

"What does that even mean? Glowing hair is not a magical specialty."

Sonja pulled out a notepad and began quickly jotting down notes. She did not, however, answer my question.

I glanced at the complex patterns of symbols she'd drawn on the paper. "What happened to my parents? What brought them together? And what pushed them apart? Do they know I'm alive? How did I end up on Earth?"

Sonja looked up from her work, frowning. "Enough questions."

She closed her notebook and picked up a syringe filled with dark sparkling fluid the color of amethysts. The demon grabbed my arm and injected the Venom into it. The dark magic surged inside of me, a flash of fire in my blood.

"This is Shifter's Shadow," Sonja's voice echoed beyond the flames.

As the Venom burned through me, everything shifted inside my body. The two sides of my magic wanted to be one, to exist in total harmony. It was no easy battle, however, for two opposing magics to find balance.

I felt lightheaded, drowsy. A slow rock, like that of a boat bobbing on the ocean waves, drew me under, and when I opened my eyes, I wasn't in hell anymore. I was on the open sea.

I SAT in a boat on a sea of beautiful turquoise water. Golden tropical sands sparkled across a nearby island. The sun shone down on me, warming my skin and bringing a smile to my face. It was comfortable and safe out here, so far away from all the conflict, the pain, the constant battles. It was a life without magic and all its baggage, a life without monsters and the immortal war between gods and demons. It was, quite simply, peaceful.

I stretched out my legs in the boat, wiggling my naked toes. They brushed against someone's leg. I glanced at my brother Zane. He sat opposite me in the boat, facing me. He wore a light cotton shirt and beach shorts, and in his hand, he held a fishing pole dipped in the sea.

"We've been out here for hours, Zane," I said. "Let's give it a rest. The fish aren't biting today."

"Patience," he replied with perfect serenity. "I'm about to catch one."

"You can't possibly know..." I stopped, my daze darting to his twinging fishing line. "How did you know?"

Zane got a firmer grip on the pole. "Magic," he said with a wink.

I snorted. "There's no such thing as magic."

The memory of a battle flashed through my mind. I saw myself lifting a flaming sword in the air to fight a gargantuan monster. It was a daydream, nothing more. I shook my head, clearing the fantasy from my wandering thoughts.

Zane had already reeled in the fish and dropped it into the bucket. His line was in the water again. I must have dozed off.

"It's a big one," Zane said as the line began to twitch again. He was straining to hold the pole steady. "A little help here, Leda."

"Why do you need my help when you have *magic*?" I smirked at him.

I got another flash, this time of an angel, his dark wings extended, magic crackling off of his skin, igniting the air around him. I cleared my head again, but the image of the angel lingered for a few seconds, an image burned into my mind.

I helped Zane hold the pole steady. I could feel something fighting and thrashing on the other end, resisting with everything that it had. Zane reeled it in. He dropped a second fish into the pan. It was even bigger than the first one.

It bounced against the bottom of the bucket, and I caught another flash of the angel. He was sliding the sleeve off my shoulder, kissing my skin. Heat flushed my body.

As the image faded from my mind, I saw Zane staring at me strangely.

"What?" I said guiltily.

"Nothing." He was grinning from ear to ear.

I blushed, unable to shake the feeling that my brother could read minds—and that he'd just caught me red-handed fantasizing about a sexy angel.

"Do you believe in angels?" I blurted out.

"Do you?" Zane countered.

I was still considering my response when Zane's line began to swing about wildly. Whatever he'd caught this time, it was enormous. I reached over to help him, but as my hands closed around the pole, a torrent of images crashed through my head. I saw myself fighting monsters, sparring with angels, battling the forces of hell. Magic shot across the battlefield like fireworks.

The images streamed by faster. I saw cities rise and fall and immortals being born. I watched gods and demons clash. Lifetimes of memories flashed by in the blink of an eye.

Then I was ejected from the memory stream. My mind spun, trying to make sense of what I'd just seen.

"You've tapped into the memories of the Guardians," Zane told me.

The name 'Guardians' sparked something in me, and I recalled the Black City, where I'd first experienced the memories of the Guardians in dreams and visions. And then I remembered who I was. What I was.

I looked around at the boat, the beach, and the water. "This isn't real." I suffered a moment of profound loss, though I'd not lost a thing. You couldn't lose a paradise that you'd never had.

"No," Zane said. "It's not."

"And you're not really here with me."

"No."

"What was all of that? How can I see the memories of the Guardians?" I asked him.

"The Guardians got their powers from the original immortals, who possessed balanced light and dark magic. Just like you, Leda. For some reason, your balanced magic allows you to see into the collective pool of memories of light and dark magic. You sit at the peak, Leda, at the crossroads between light and dark," Zane added. "You can dip your toes into both pools and see all the magical strokes that created the picture that is today."

"But how do I do that?"

"Patience." He held up the fishing pole with one hand and indicated the pail of fish with the other.

"My favorite virtue," I said drily.

Zane chuckled. "With a bit of practice, you'll get it. You always do."

"Is that what the Guardians told you?"

I couldn't help but think back to what Sonja had said about the Guardians. She'd told me they were more dangerous than anyone else and that Zane was in great danger. But could I really trust the demon? Sonja certainly hadn't done anything to inspire confidence.

"The gods and demons split from the original immortals. And in doing so, they split magic. They created this black-and-white, light-and-dark reality," Zane said. "The Guardians have a prophecy about a divine savior who will be born human, with equal light and dark magic. She will grow her magic one ability at a time, and someday she will upset the balance of power."

"And they think that's me."

"Yes. And so does Sonja. She wants to control you as that instrument of change, the end of the immortal war. She thinks your magic will help her overthrow the gods and lead the demons—and especially her—to great power and supremacy."

That was pretty much in line with what Sonja had said. The demon wasn't really hiding anything.

"The Guardians have a different interpretation of the prophecy than Sonja does," Zane said. "They believe you will change the balance of magic back to the middle, back to mixed magic of light and dark origins. They believe the savior is a god killer and demon slayer."

That's me, making lots of friends throughout heaven and hell. Chances were good that if the gods and demons had shared the Guardians' belief, I'd already be dead.

"What do you think?" I asked Zane.

"One prophecy, a thousand possible interpretations. I think we'll just have to wait and see."

"Patience," I sighed. It always came back to that.

"Exactly."

"I don't want to be a part of some prophecy."

"Because you hate being the center of attention," Zane teased, a twinkle in his eyes.

"I don't try to be the center of attention. Drama just finds me."

"Like a magnet."

"If I punch you in a dream, does it still hurt in the real world?"

Laughing, Zane drew me into a hug. "Just hold out a little longer, Leda," he whispered into my ear. "Help is on the way."

Then he shoved me over the side of the boat. I hit the icy water and jerked awake.

———

I woke up chained to the dungeon wall. My body felt as limp as an overcooked noodle. I tried to move my toes, but

I couldn't feel them. I shifted my eyes to look around the room. Sonja was watching me closely, a syringe of dark purple Venom in her hand. My mouth watered, reacting to the poison's overly sweet scent.

My mind was less amenable than my body. When Sonja tried to inject me with the Venom, I knocked the syringe away with a flick of my magic.

"You will give up fighting me eventually," the demon responded to my defiance.

I pushed against my chains. Sonja grabbed the gun from her hip holster and shot me in the leg with a dose of Venom. I felt the familiar fire of the immortal poison, the pain as it clashed with the Nectar already inside of me. I wondered why Venom hurt and Nectar felt so good. If I had sipped Venom first, would it have been the other way around?

"Stop fighting," Sonja snapped. "Give up on this foolish hope. No one is coming for you. Neither your friends nor your angel lover can come here. Only a true master of dark magic can open the gateway to hell. It takes at least a dark angel. Not even the lower soldiers of the Dark Force can do it. An angel of the light hasn't got a chance, not even one like your lover, who fancies himself a little dark." Sonja's expression was downright haughty.

I wasn't sure if my talk with Zane had been him speaking to me, or if it was simply my tortured, desperate mind playing tricks on me by showing me what I wanted to see. Maybe help was coming, but I couldn't depend on it. I had to get myself and my sisters out, not stand idly by and wait to be rescued. There had to be a gate or something that led out of hell.

But first things first. Before we could leave, I had to get out of these chains. The task was a tad impossible as long as Sonja was watching me, but she'd leave as soon as she was done noting my initial response to the Venom. As much as she loved to wax eloquent about how patient she was, she didn't like to stand around and twiddle her thumbs.

I tested my chains, but I was bolted to the wall pretty securely. I didn't have the strength to break through the restraints. My body had gone too long without food.

But I'd had food, I realized. Venom was the immortal food of the demons, and Sonja had given it to me twice. That was pure magic, pure energy for my system. I just needed to access it. If I could just push past the heavy, overloaded feeling of my body trying to cope with the new magic, I might be able to do it.

"Fascinating. The Venom is actually activating the dormant dark magic inside of you, igniting it," Sonja commented as I felt my light and dark magic reach an equilibrium. "I think you can handle something a little more potent."

I was still wondering what could possibly be more potent than Venom when Sonja turned around with a syringe in her hand. Inside, two sparkling substances—onyx and white—swirled around each other, as though they were alive. Venom and Nectar. And as the demon moved toward me with that syringe, I realized she was going to inject both into me at once.

I tried to push out of my restraints, but they didn't budge no matter what I did.

"Fairy's Touch. Light and dark, together." The elated look on Sonja's face sent me into a panic.

"It won't work," I told her, trying to calm my staggered breaths. "It's too much magic at once."

Sonja didn't even seem to hear me. "I will be the first to

see the full spectrum of magic merge into a living body all at once, in complete harmony."

"It won't work, you psycho! You're going to kill me!" I shouted.

Sonja paused, considering me.

"And if I'm dead, that's the end of your experiment to create the perfect army."

The needle tip was against my arm. "That's a risk I'm willing to take."

Well, it wasn't a risk I was willing to take just because a crazy demon thought she'd roll the dice with my life. I had too much to live for.

I pushed out with my telekinetic magic, knocking Sonja back. She tripped over the table of tools, and they rained to the ground. The syringe flew across the room. Recovering her balance, Sonja caught the syringe inside a bubble of her psychic magic, lifting it higher. It floated in the air beside her as she approached me, looking considerably less elated and way more pissed off than she had a moment ago.

An explosion rocked the building. Beyond the glass doors, gunfire thundered. The walls of the dungeon groaned, and the ground shook with the force of an earthquake. Sonja paused. The syringe froze midair too.

"It sounds like the gates of hell aren't as impenetrable as you thought," I commented.

"It's just one of the other demons annoying me like they always do," Sonja said with a dismissive flick of her hand.

"Then why do you look so worried?"

Her lips tight, Sonja hurried out of the dungeon, drawing her sword as she ran. The milky-white sliding doors to the lab swooshed shut behind her.

A familiar twinge tugged on my senses. It was Nero. He was here.

Still groggy from the Venom, I forced myself to concentrate and calm my nerves. I focused my magic into a sharp, telekinetic point. It shot out from my body, breaking through the chains. They crumbled and rained to the floor in tiny metal slivers.

I slid down the wall, landing in a crouch. One leg gave out under me, and my knee slammed against the hard, unforgiving floor. I rose slowly, cursing the idiot who'd thought it was clever to cover the floors of a torture chamber with glossy, slippery marble. I stumbled, staggering in my steps as I moved toward my sisters' cells.

But Tessa and Gin weren't there. Soulslayer must have taken them away for testing while I'd been busy blacking out. I had to find them and get them out of here, but as I took off running toward the sliding doors, the walls around me exploded.

CHAPTER 29

EMPRESS OF HEAVEN AND HELL

*S*treaks of red and orange light flickered before my eyes. I blinked, trying to clear my blurred vision. As the world slowly faded back into focus, I realized those streaks of light were flames dancing in the air. They fell so slowly, they almost seemed suspended in the air.

I reached out to touch them, and my fingers brushed up against a transparent layer, like an invisible shell. I'd surrounded my body with a telekinetic magic barrier to protect myself from the falling roof. It had been an automatic defense, something driven by instinct rather than conscious thought.

The nearby flames and particles of debris from the explosion were caught in the barrier, floating within that defensive invisible shell like a school of fish. My skin glowed, my elemental magic resisting the extreme heat.

Outside my safety bubble, things didn't look good. Fires raged, and the walls were crumbling. My telekinetic barrier was all that was holding up the roof. If it went down, so would the roof. All that marble and gold and stone would collapse on top of me. That was, if the fires didn't burn me alive first.

Leda.

I couldn't see Nero, but I could feel he was so close. I drew on our connection, on the magic that linked us together. Just knowing he was there gave me the resolve to bear the pain of my failing magic.

I coughed. The smoke was slowly suffocating me. Something stung my arm. I slapped it. When I looked down, I saw it was not a bug; it was a clump of burning ash that had burnt me. It had made it through a small hole in my barrier. I forced the hole closed.

A flicker of movement drew my eyes across the room. Soulslayer. The dark angel was stuck in the room too. He was also holding up the swirling storm of fire and debris. We were two bright points in the darkness, like two stars in space, masses swirling around each of us.

"Where are my sisters?" I demanded.

"Trapped back there." He indicated the collapsed corridor behind him.

"We have to get them out."

He scoffed at my words. "Why would I risk myself for two girls?"

"Because you can't let those two girls die. You are hell-bent on using their magic."

"That's not worth my life."

It was like talking to a wall. "Would Sonja agree?" I asked him.

"I'm a dark angel," he said proudly. "We are priceless. Do you have any idea how much work and magic goes into creating one of us? Sonja would not have me risk my life to save two little girls, no matter how curious their magic might be. Especially not now, at a time of crisis, when we are under attack. And when you, her prized pet, is trying to escape."

I changed tactics. "So you've given up. The Legion is attacking, and you're running away scared. You've admitted defeat, that you're no match for the Legion. You're letting two unique magic users slip between your fingers."

Soulslayer frowned at me. "Sonja told me of your silver tongue, of your siren's song. It won't work. You won't trick me into risking my life to save those brats."

"I guess that's the difference between the Dark Force and the Legion. The Dark Force is nothing but a bunch of *cowards*. Just like you. That's the real reason you left the Legion. You couldn't cut it."

The dark angel's eyes narrowed. "You aren't worth all this trouble," he hissed viciously. "If you weren't Sonja's prize, I'd kill you where you stand."

"Help me save my sisters. You can kill me later." I was working my magic around him, trying to get into his head.

He shook himself, brushing off my magic attack. "I don't have to kill you." A dark smile curled his lips. "You are weak."

His words just echoed what I was thinking myself. My magic was cracking under the strain. I'd put everything I had into holding back the debris, and it wasn't even close to enough. That was why my siren magic hadn't worked on him. I didn't have enough magic to spare.

"Your magic will fail," he said. "I need only stand here and watch the building kill you. How will you die? Will the fire burn you? Will the smoke suffocate you? Will the rocks crush you?"

His eyes shone with vicious delight as he contemplated the possible causes of my impending death, just as he'd enjoyed torturing me in the arena.

And now he was trying to kill my sisters too. Gin would survive, just to be killed again and again. And Soulslayer would revel in it all.

He was sick.

Rage flashed through my body, burning hotter than the fire in the room. No, I wouldn't let that psychopath win. I refused to give him the satisfaction of dancing over our graves. Tiny fireflies of magic ignited around my shield.

The dark angel considered me with a bored expression. "Try not to burn yourself, sweetheart."

The flames around me burned hotter, funneling into a pillar of fire that hit the dark angel's barrier like a battering ram. The nearly-transparent shield shook. I caught debris in my psychic net and slingshot the pieces at him. Chunks of stone streaked across the room like bullets. They popped against his barrier, then went out.

"Rage will only get you so far. You're weak," Soulslayer sneered, but his jaw was tight with concentration.

I didn't stop hitting him with magic. Pieces of debris came at him from all corners of the room, adding to my bombardment.

The dark angel fought back. Burning debris shot at me like a school of fish, flowing as one continuous river. Streamers of rock and metal crashed against my shield. Most of them sizzled out, but a few broke through small holes in my defenses, slashing my skin. I hardly even felt the pain. At this moment, I knew only the fight: my defenses and my attack.

I formed a few debris streams of my own. My streams and his collided in a clash of fire and stone as we each tried to make it past the other's defenses. Fire burned my skin. I slapped out the flames on my body and kept fighting.

The ceiling groaned. Heavy chunks of rock crashed

down on us, each flicker against my magic shield like a punch to the head. The back wall split open, revealing Gin and Tessa. I extended my barrier around their huddled bodies, protecting them from the fire and debris.

Once the shield was secure around them, I took a closer look at them. They were dirty and covered in scratches, but they didn't appear seriously wounded. And at least Gin had some clothes on now. Tessa was still wearing the magic-jamming bracelets that prevented her from teleporting.

Soulslayer charged at me, pushing me out of his way as he bolted for the exit. The force of his magic collapsed the area around me and my sisters. The psychopath was leaving us all here to die to save his skin.

I jumped out, shouting, "You coward!"

I drew in the power currents sizzling from the walls, weaving them into a magic whip. I swung my lightning lasso and latched it around the dark angel's ankle. I yanked him back across the room.

"What the hell is the matter with you?" I held him trapped inside my band of lightning, enduring the pain of his magical backlash as he struggled to free himself.

In a flash of magic, his wings shot out. They flapped hard and fast. He was trying to leverage his wing strength to overpower me and break free. My pulse pounding in my ears, I gripped tightly to my whip. I wasn't letting him get away like that, not after all that he'd done to us.

I pulled him around, and his back slammed into my chest. I locked my arms around him. His wings were now trapped, unable to move. I had his arms pinned to his sides.

He pushed against me with all his strength. He was bigger and stronger than I was, and anger was a poor substitute for food. My grip was slipping. He was going to break free.

I hit his mind with my siren magic. It was a punch as hard as any telekinetic strike. I might have been no match for him physically, but he was no match for my mind.

I pushed him into his own mind, trapping him there. Even as his body went still, his mind banged against mine, thrashing to break my hold over him. Blood poured out of my nose and my head rang, but I held on, refusing to budge. Soulslayer wouldn't be getting out. He had tortured my sisters; he was fully prepared to kill each and every one of us. And if he got free, he would torture and kill a whole lot more people.

No, he wouldn't. I wouldn't allow it. He wouldn't be hurting anyone ever again.

I slammed my mind against his, crushing his will under the weight of mine. His mind stopped fighting. It was mine. He was mine. I'd broken a dark angel. Adrenaline surged inside of me at the realization of my power. I wasn't weak anymore. I could do anything. I could control anyone. Humans, supernaturals, angels…gods?

I laughed at the delightfully crazy idea. Imagine me barging into the gods' council and making them all behave themselves. Then I'd go to hell and do the same to the demons. This immortal war would be over once and for all, the realms finally united under a single glorious banner. *My* banner.

I laughed again, even as a little voice inside of me whispered quietly. What was it saying?

Leda, Vanquisher of the Corrupt. Empress of Heaven and Hell and all the Realms? it said.

Yes, I replied defensively.

And why not? I'd bled for this Earth. I'd sacrificed to

keep its people safe. The humans were too busy fighting one another to rule themselves. And the gods and demons didn't understand mortals; they didn't know what was best for them. But I did. I'd been mortal. I had the light and dark magic of gods and demons. I was the perfect choice to rule over them all.

The gods and demons each believe the same, said the voice. *As do the Pioneers.*

That's different, I scoffed.

No, it's not. The gods, demons, and Pioneers see themselves as champions of peace and freedom—as long as your freedom doesn't challenge their authority. We all know what happens when someone doesn't fit into their world order.

They were labelled as corrupt, as unclean, as tainted. Just as the gods had done to Nero's father.

Nero. The thought of him quelled the euphoria of madness burning inside of me. I began to remember where I was—and what I'd been contemplating.

The thrill of crushing Soulslayer's mind had gone straight to my head. I'd lost my mind. I'd succumbed to the fantasy that I could take on the gods and demons too. In that moment of madness, I'd truly believed that I could control them all and rule over not only heaven and hell, but over all the realms. I didn't have enough power to pull that off. And even if I could do it, I certainly shouldn't do it.

My siren's song hadn't just seduced Soulslayer's mind; it had seduced mine too. I'd been so caught up in the thrill of having that much control over someone so powerful—bolstered by the knowledge that I could make him do anything I wanted—that I'd gone crazy with power lust. I'd lost myself.

I pulled back from the sweet temptation of my magic,

the layer that I'd wrapped around Soulslayer's mind. I wasn't this person, and I didn't ever want to be.

I released my hold on the dark angel and stepped back. He didn't run. His legs just gave out, and he fell to the floor. A few seconds passed, but he didn't get up. I went to him, flipping over his heavy body. I felt his pulse, but there was none. He was dead.

"How could this be?" I gasped in shock.

"You really are everything I'd hoped you to be," Sonja said.

I whirled around to find the demon standing there. It was not quite a smile on her face. It was more like a sense of elation, of things realized. It was all her hopes and fears bundled into one tidy package.

Sonja was standing too close to Gin and Tessa. I rose slowly to put myself between my sisters and the demon. Magic flashed, blinding me. When my vision cleared, the demon was gone. Tessa and Gin were still there.

I stared down at the dead dark angel. How was he dead? Had I killed him?

I took a closer look at his body. His neck was broken. After I'd crushed his mind, high on the power, I'd gone further. I'd crushed his body too. And I'd had him so under my spell that he hadn't even fought me.

Angels were nearly indestructible, and yet I'd broken him. I looked down at my shaking, bloody hands, the hands of a monster. I'd lost all control over my magic. Worse yet, when I was caught up in the moment, I didn't even want to control it.

My sisters approached me.

"Stay away," I said, backing up. "I don't want to hurt you."

"We know you would never hurt us, Leda," Gin told me.

"You came to save us. And now we're all going to get out of here," added Tessa.

I just stared at the dead dark angel, frozen, Sonja's words looping over and over again inside my head.

There has never been another like you.

Forget the beasts on the plains. I was the true monster created in this unending war between heaven and hell.

"Leda!" Gin shouted, shaking me.

There was a creak from above, and the ceiling came crashing down. That snapped me out of my mind's prison. I pumped more magic into the telekinetic barrier to hold off the chunks of stone. It was withstanding the barrage of the collapsing columns—for now.

I spotted a doorway lit up with flames—and beyond that, part of the building was still intact. "Let's get out of here," I told my sisters.

As soon as we began to move, the debris and flames floating around us grew heavy. Seams split open across my barrier. I stopped. We couldn't make it through the debris field. I wasn't strong enough to adjust the barrier to handle the shifting streams of debris and fire as we walked. We were stuck.

I saw Nero past the doorway of fire. My heart skipped in relief—and alarm. Nero was battling a dark angel. Magic flashed between them—streaks of fire and lightning, of wind and ice. Chunks of marble burst out of the ground and broke off the walls. The two angels shot the polished stones between them.

Nero avoided one of the dark angel's rocks, but a second one grazed his arm, the sharp, broken edges cutting his skin and drawing blood. Nero didn't stop. He just kept fighting, as though he weren't injured at all, a look of fierce, unrelenting determination etched into his face. A vicious gleam shone in his green eyes. His leather clothes shone with blood, and most of it wasn't even his own.

Damiel was fighting two dark angels at once. They were bombarding him with everything they had. Damiel managed to evade most of it, but not all. The pieces that got through didn't seem to bother him. Deflecting and reflecting, he shot most of the dark angels' spells and debris back at them.

Calli and Bella were there too, battling the soldiers of the Dark Force. Bella brewed and threw potions. She conjured smoke and curses, explosions and pepper mist. And all the while, Calli stood back-to-back with her, shooting the soldiers. When she ran out of bullets, she pulled out a bow and shot arrows coated in Bella's potions.

It all played out in silence. I couldn't hear anything anymore. I was so busy putting all my magic into my shield that my senses were shutting down. My legs felt like lead. I could hardly stand.

Something brushed against my arm. I glanced to the side. Tessa was tapping my shoulder. She was speaking to me, but I couldn't hear a word. I had to read her lips to decipher what she was saying.

Your ears, Leda.

I lifted my fingers to my ears, and they came back coated in blood. No wonder I couldn't hear.

Fire and debris swirled and spun around me, repelled by my psychic spell. Close to me, the pieces moved slowly, but further out they were whirling around fast, crashing and clashing in explosions of fire and stone.

Nero and the others stood at the doorway to the

dungeon, watching us from across the pool of swirling debris. The Dark Force soldiers had fled.

I felt a phantom nudge. It repeated. The third time it brushed against me, I realized it was Nero. It smelled like him. As though a sound could smell like something, but somehow it did. I opened up my mind.

Come to me, Leda, nice and slow, Nero's voice spoke inside my head.

Panic froze me as I looked across the burning, churning debris field. The columns holding up the room had already shattered. Only my magic was preventing the whole roof from collapsing on us.

The pieces of the stone columns swirled around inside the wreckage. As soon as I moved, the debris would change course. I couldn't adjust my psychic shield fast enough to keep up with it. The barrage would tear my shield apart, and if it collapsed, so would the room.

Of course, it would all collapse soon anyway. I couldn't hold it up much longer. We were all going to die. I'd defeated the dark angel, but I hadn't won.

Nero's voice cut through my panic. *I will help you hold up the ceiling.* His voice was calm, reassuring. *I won't let it fall on you. I promise. Just start walking to me.*

Swallowing the fear bubbling inside of me, I grabbed my sisters' hands and began to walk toward the doorway of fire. The marble and concrete chunks shifted, but Nero's magic was right there to hold them back, even as my own strength faded.

Behind him, the Dark Force had regrouped, their numbers swelling to strike back hard. Calli, Bella, and Damiel went to hold them off, but there were too many enemy soldiers. They wouldn't be able to hold them off for long.

Don't worry about them. Focus on coming to me, Nero told me.

I continued to walk slowly, holding tightly to my sisters' hands. The debris grew wilder, restless. Nero's magic knocked the pieces of broken rock aside.

Keep walking.

My hearing came back all at once. I heard the crash and smash of debris like rocks on a rooftop, the hiss of fire, the rattle and shake of my barrier. It was a storm of sensory overload. I heard every pebble trying to cut us, every boulder trying to crush us, every wisp of ash trying to suffocate us—like death taunting us from just beyond the veil.

After what felt like an eternity in hell, we finally made it to Nero. He parted the curtain of fire to allow us to escape the dungeon. The flames snapped back in place behind us.

Nero drew me into an embrace. He was here. He'd come all the way to hell for me.

"Don't you ever do that again," he hissed harshly into my ear.

"Go to hell?"

"Yes."

"It wasn't by choice, you know," I said.

He squeezed me tightly to him, but it didn't hurt. In fact, I wished I could just collapse into his embrace. I knew he would catch me. He always caught me.

But I couldn't do that. I had an image to maintain, after all.

"I'm never letting you out of my sight again," he said.

"That might prove difficult given our line of work."

"I'm not joking, Pandora."

He kissed me. It was a rough and desperate kiss—one

loaded with his fear of my life, his powerlessness, his turmoil, his annoyance at me for running off and getting captured, and his relief at having me back again.

He pulled back and faced the collapsing room. The debris in the dungeon dropped all at once to the ground. Nero's magic held back the avalanche of marble and concrete. Everything crashed together in wild directions, reforming into thick columns of melded material to hold up the new ceiling that had formed. It was just in time too because if the dungeon had collapsed, our room would have been next.

I just stood there and gaped, shocked at the scale of power he'd used.

Damiel had built a barricade to block off the Dark Force soldiers. He walked over to us, looked at Nero's columns and ceiling with a critical eye, and declared, "They're not straight."

Nero folded his arms across his chest and gave his father a cool look. "Feel free to do it yourself next time, old man."

Damiel smiled. "I wouldn't dream of denying you the opportunity to practice. You obviously need it."

Nero just glared at him.

"You're contemplating leaving him here in hell," I said.

"The thought had crossed my mind."

"You can't do that," I told him.

"And why is that?"

"First of all, he's your father."

Nero snorted.

"And he's injured," I added.

Nero gave his father's minor wounds a cursory glance. "He'll heal."

Damiel's blue eyes twinkled.

"And he came all the way here to help you rescue me," I said to Nero. "Leaving him behind wouldn't be honorable."

Nero's mouth hardened.

Damiel chuckled. "She's got you there."

"Thank you for coming." I turned toward Calli and Bella. "But how did you get here?"

"I did some research in the forbidden dark magic books Damiel got for me," Bella explained.

Damiel looked as modest as an angel.

"I found a spell that can create a passage to hell," Bella continued. "It was very complicated, but finally I managed to make it work." She actually did look modest.

"A passage that is closing soon." Damiel pointed out the subtle, near-invisible flicker in the air. It was only a few feet from me, and I hadn't even noticed it. "Let's get out of here."

Calli picked up Gin. Nero picked up me.

When I protested, he leveled a hard, commanding stare at me. "Have you seen what you look like?"

"No, actually. I haven't had the chance to look in a mirror recently."

I glanced down at my body. The battle arena hadn't been kind to it—and my battle with the dark angel had only made things worse. Gashes, deep holes, and cuts marred my skin. Parts of my flesh were missing—burned, torn off, or both. There was blood everywhere. Most of my clothes were missing too. My tattered shorts had once been full-length pants, my jacket was gone, and my tank top was hardly more than a sports bra now. I didn't even have shoes on anymore.

"I look like a zombie," I said glumly.

"No, you're far too pretty to be a zombie," Nero stated.

There was nothing romantic about the matter-of-fact way he said it, but it still made my heart melt. I leaned my head against his shoulder, just happy to let someone else worry about how we were getting out of here for once.

Damiel lifted Tessa into his arms. A few weeks ago, she'd have blushed and gushed like a silly, angel-obsessed schoolgirl. Now, she simply thanked him for coming. Remembering her past, living through the torture Soulslayer had inflicted on her and Gin, had made her grow up fast. I just hoped the experience hadn't destroyed who they were.

And what about me? When I'd battled Soulslayer, a monster had come out, taking me over. Had I changed too? Or was I just starting to become who I'd always truly been deep down inside of me?

For me and my sisters, our origins had come knocking, ripping away the bandages that concealed the past, exposing what we truly were. As we escaped hell, I wondered how things could ever be the same.

CHAPTER 30

IMMORTAL DESTINY

J stood on the balcony of the apartment I shared with Nero, a great suite which sat atop the sparkling white obelisk that held the Legion's east coast headquarters. It was the perfect angel residence. The view over New York was simply breath-catching, but I didn't have much breath left in me to spare. I was still catching it from our dash through hell. That had been two days ago, and even though I'd slept every moment since then, I was still tired.

Bella stood next to me. She was dressed in one of her school outfits: a high-collared, cream-colored blouse with a black opal brooch at the collar; and a pencil skirt with a cute ruffle along one side. Her ankle-high brown leather boots matched the belt around her waist. Her nails were brushed with pale pink polish, her strawberry-blonde hair braided and pinned to her head, milk-maid style. A leather handbag hung from her shoulder, large enough to hold a few spell books.

"Calli visited while you were sleeping," Bella said. "She's feeling guilty. She tried so hard to protect Tessa and

Gin from the pain of their past. She had Zane wipe their memories to give them a fresh chance at life, but she only made it worse. She says she left Gin and Tessa helpless, without the memories of their magic or how to use it to protect themselves. I'm not sure Calli will ever forgive herself."

"Parents often make horrible mistakes while having the best of intentions."

I looked back to find Damiel standing in the open doorway between the living room and balcony. "Aren't you supposed to be hiding your face?"

Magic rippled over Damiel's masculine body, shifting it into something else entirely—something decidedly more feminine. A tall and sexy supermodel now stood before me wearing a black bandage dress and silver stilettos. Her glossy dark hair shimmered in the sunlight like black diamonds.

"Better?" the model said in a sultry voice.

It was a good disguise, a seamless magical spell of shifting magic. Even knowing I was looking at Damiel, I could only see through his spell if I concentrated really hard—and concentrating that hard gave me a spectacular splitting headache.

I didn't know how many people knew Damiel was still alive, but I doubted the knowledge extended far beyond the First Angel. He was Nyx's secret weapon, someone she used to take care of all the unspeakable things even the Legion couldn't admit to doing.

That was assuming Damiel continued to help Nyx once he got what he wanted, which was to save his wife Cadence. Angels were a bit self-serving like that. And Damiel had been waiting to save his wife for two hundred years. Nero didn't completely trust his father, but I had a feeling Damiel would pull through in the end. He was a better person than either of them could admit.

A small smile twisted Damiel's lips. "How many times must we remind you, Leda? We aren't people. We're angels."

He was reading my mind again, but I didn't tell him off. I just chuckled. This time, I'd let him listen in.

Since our return from hell, I'd been keeping my mind carefully closed. I didn't want to confront what I'd learned about my origin. I was having trouble coming to terms with it all myself. I needed to process it. Maybe it would get easier with time.

The other reason I was keeping my thoughts under lock was I didn't want anyone to know what had happened in that dungeon—that I'd crushed the dark angel's mind and body. And that in my power high, I'd dreamt of ruling supreme over all the known realms.

Bella smiled at me. "It's good to see you laugh. You've been so serious since we returned from… Returned home."

She didn't say 'hell'. Clearly, it was tough for Bella too. After all, she'd only recently learned that she was a demon's granddaughter.

If only she'd known what I was, the daughter of a demon and a god. I was a magical anomaly, a monster. When I closed my eyes, I saw the dark angel's mind cracking under the force of my power. I heard his screams. I saw his head hitting the ground and the lifeless look on his face as he lay there dead.

My wounds were healed on the outside, but inside I was broken.

Bella hadn't asked what I was, though she must have realized that I'd found out. She was giving me time to be ready. I wondered if I ever would be.

"I'm going to find Calli's friend," I said, changing the subject. "The one who led her to all of us," I kept talking. Everything would be fine if I could just keep talking. "I have to know why he wanted Calli to take us in."

"You'll find him," said Bella. "You always do."

Nero stepped onto the balcony. He stopped as soon as he saw Damiel in the body of a woman. A hint of surprise flashed across his face, but it was soon swallowed up by hard, cold composure.

"That's not funny," he told his father.

Damiel smiled demurely. "Your lady asked me to put on a disguise."

Nero opened his mouth, but before he could speak, a knock on our apartment door drew him back inside. Damiel summoned a tube of lipstick out of thin air and began applying it to his mouth.

"You've got some on your teeth," Bella told him helpfully.

Damiel's teeth squeaked as he wiped away the excess lipstick with his index finger. "It's not as easy as it looks."

"Being a woman?"

Damiel pulled out a mirror and tried in vain to wipe off the wayward lipstick. "I should have just shifted into a tiger," he grumbled.

Nero and Harker stepped onto the balcony. Harker saw Damiel—and he just froze.

"It's Damiel," Nero told him.

Harker blinked. "It looks just like her." His eyes panned across Damiel's disguise. "Right down to the—"

Nero elbowed him in the ribs.

Harker lifted his gaze and glanced over at Bella and me. "Eyes."

Damiel giggled. It was a distinctly non-angel sound,

contrasting starkly with his previous assertion that he was an angel, not a person. He certainly was making an effort to stay in character.

"Who is Damiel supposed to be?" I asked Nero and Harker. They obviously knew her.

"Sergeant Jordan. She was our trainer back when Nero and I first joined the Legion." Harker added with a smirk, "Nero had a huge crush on her."

Nero's face was unreadable, but I was pretty sure that right now he was fighting the urge to murder his best friend. He watched me for my reaction.

But I didn't even feel jealous. Maybe this ghost from the past didn't bother me, or maybe I was just still too numb from everything that had happened recently.

My gaze flickered from Nero to Harker, finally settling on Damiel. "She has nice eyes."

Harker coughed, swallowing an emerging laugh. Nero's face remained impassive.

"How is it you can so perfectly replicate a woman from nearly two hundred years ago?" I asked Damiel. "You weren't even around here back then."

"I might have been in hiding, but I always kept an eye turned toward Nero."

Nero didn't look impressed. The silence stretched on. I could practically picture the tumbleweed blowing across the balcony.

"Leda," Harker said, finally breaking the silence. "This is for you." He handed me a leather-bound folder. The gold Legion of Angels monogram on the cover made it look very exclusive.

"What's this?" I asked.

"Your registration packet for the Crystal Falls Training. It commences next week."

Already? I'd lost so much time in hell. The Crystal Falls Training was upon me, a long and intense magic workshop for level six and level seven Legion soldiers. I wasn't sure I was ready to dive back into training just yet.

Nero walked around behind me. He set his hands on my shoulders and gave them a supportive squeeze.

"One of the level seven soldiers from this training will become an angel to fill the void left by Colonel Battleborn's death," Damiel said lightly, as though we were discussing tea parties and cupcakes, not angels and death.

The Crystal Falls Training was supposed to be one of the hardest the Legion had, and it would be even tougher for me. I was a new level six, and I'd be training alongside hardened soldiers who'd been at level seven for years—soldiers who would do anything to become an angel. If they wanted to succeed and gain their wings, they couldn't afford to lose to anyone, especially us level sixes.

"Nerissa told me tales I wish I could forget, stories about soldiers poisoning and sabotaging the competition." I looked at Nero for confirmation that it wasn't true.

"Don't eat anything another candidate offers you," he said.

"And always sleep with a knife under your pillow," added Harker.

Laughter burst from my lips. "You two aren't any help at all."

Damiel stretched out his arms, yawning loudly. "Well, children, I'd best be going. The First Angel's prisoners won't torture themselves, you know."

The completely casual way that he said it made me hope he was joking, but I wasn't counting on it.

Damiel transformed from the brunette model into the sunset-haired angel Leila Starborn. Then he jumped over the handrail and flew off across the city on gorgeous white and gold wings.

After he was gone, Bella turned to me and said, "I have to get back to the university now."

Harker stepped forward. "I'll walk you out."

Their light chatter trailed them as they left our apartment and entered the stairwell. The last thing I heard was Bella diplomatically rejecting his latest attempt to ask her out. Something about that made me laugh. After everything we'd all just lived through, I guess it just felt good to see a sign that some things were back to normal.

We stepped back inside, Nero watching me every step of the way, just as he'd been doing since our return from hell. As promised, he'd never let me out of his sight. He'd never been further away than the next room, close enough to storm in and grab me if a portal to hell spontaneously opened up under my feet. Gods, I loved him.

"You know you can't come to the Crystal Falls Training with me," I told him.

"Says who?"

"I'd imagine says Colonel Dragonblood, the angel in charge of the training."

"I outrank him."

"So?"

His voice dipped lower. "So he can't tell me what to do."

"You make it sound so simple."

"It is as simple as this: if Colonel Dragonblood has a problem with my presence, he can take it up with me."

"But the rules—"

"Since when have you cared about the rules, Pandora?"

Fair point.

"I love you," he declared solemnly. "And I'm not ever letting you go."

His hand curled around my neck, drawing me in closer. He swooped his mouth over mine, capturing my breath. Hard and hungry, his tongue thrust between my lips, ravaging the inside, drowning me in his magic. He was pouring all of his emotions—all of himself—into that kiss. I'd never experienced anything like it before.

"I should have been there for you." His lips brushed against mine. "I should have kept the deserter from taking you."

"It's not your fault. I ran into that."

His hold on me tightened, like he was afraid to let me go. "I could have saved you from that suffering."

I'd told him and the others about how Soulslayer had tortured me in the arena and hurt my sisters, but I'd stopped there. I hadn't told them what I was. I hadn't told them how I'd killed the dark angel by crushing his mind. And I hadn't told them the worst of it all: that a part of me had fed off of that rush of power. That part scared me most of all.

But I had to share it all with someone. The weight of this secret was crushing me.

"We have to talk about what happened in hell," I said.

He waited for me to continue.

"I told you what happened with the dark angel, how he tortured me and my sisters," I kept talking, not pausing to breathe. I had to get this all out before I lost my nerve. "Soulslayer tortured us at the bidding of Sonja, the Demon of the Dark Force."

Nero's face was hard. Something cracked loudly, and I jumped in surprise. I looked down. One of our barstools had shattered in his hand.

"But I didn't tell you everything Sonja did to me."

Nero took my face in his hands, his touch so gentle. It was hard to believe that these were the same hands that had just pulverized our barstool.

He dipped his forehead to mine. "You don't have to tell me anything."

But I had to tell him. I couldn't keep this secret to myself. It was eating away at me.

"She injected me with Venom. Twice. She was bringing my dark magic up to the same level as my light magic. If you hadn't come when you did, she was going to inject me with a dual dose of Nectar and Venom."

His touch was soft, but I could hear the angry beat of his pounding pulse.

"She would have kept going until she made me an angel with both light and dark magic."

Which was blasphemy according to both the gods and demons.

"I am not surprised," Nero said. "She obviously found out about your ability to absorb Nectar and Venom, and she wanted to use it for herself—to figure out how you work and how she could exploit that special power."

"See, the thing is, Nero, she didn't need to figure out anything," I told him. "She already knew how I can use both light and dark magic. She told me where I came from, and then I saw for myself firsthand. I am a monster."

"Leda—"

"I killed the dark angel." My heart hammered in my chest. The icy fingers of fear gripped me, bringing me back to that dungeon—and everything that had happened there. "I didn't just break Soulslayer's mind, I destroyed it, shattering it into a million pieces. I got so caught up in my own magic, so blind with power lust, that I broke his neck without even realizing it."

"He tortured you," Nero said.

But I wasn't looking for excuses to assuage my guilt. "A part of me enjoyed breaking him." Tears poured down my cheeks. "Did you hear me, Nero? I'm sick, just as sick as the dark angel who relished in torturing me and my sisters. I am a monster."

"No."

"Do you know what I was feeling as I crushed Soulslayer's mind? It wasn't guilt, or even something as innocent as relief that his reign of terror was over. It was *excitement*. I was so enamored of my grand and mighty magic, which had brought a dark angel to his knees, that I started to wonder what else I could do. How high could I go? I fantasized about taking on the gods and demons. Once I crushed their minds, I would rule supreme over all the realms. From their ashes, I would build my empire."

"You were lost in the moment," Nero said. "It happens to everyone, especially to those who've gained so much magic so fast."

"I can't control it, Nero." I wiped my tears away. If only I could wipe away the stain on my soul. "And it's getting worse. One day, I really will lose my mind, and then the monster within will take over, a cruel fiend who destroys everything that stands in my way."

"That's not you."

"It *is* me. That's what I'm telling you, Nero. When the monster takes over, I want to challenge the gods. I want to destroy every single one of them to make way for my reign and embrace my so-called immortal destiny. You have to put me down," I sobbed. "It's what the Legion does to monsters and threats to humanity and heaven. I am all of the above."

"No," he said, his voice harsh and angry. He caught me by the shoulders. "Look at me, Leda."

I swallowed back my sobs and met his eyes

"I'm not going to kill you. *No one* is going to kill you."

"Soulslayer—"

"Had it coming," he growled. "After what he did to you and your sisters, he didn't deserve to die quietly. If you hadn't killed him, I would have. I guarantee it would have hurt him a hell of a lot more than what you did—and that I would have enjoyed it a hell of a lot more than you did."

Gold fire burned in his eyes. He was not exaggerating.

"I am more of a monster than you'll ever be," Nero told me. "You are kind and caring. And you have a frustrating habit of throwing yourself into danger to save the people that you care about. Is that the profile of a monster?"

"But you don't know—"

His hands stroked down my cheeks. "I know."

"No, I mean you don't know what I am."

"I don't care what you are, Leda. I only care *who* you are."

His words were so romantic, so sweet, that it hurt. Here he was professing his love, and he didn't even know the full truth of it. I had to tell him.

"I don't even know how I destroyed the dark angel's mind when his power is so much stronger than mine," I said quietly. "If my magic grows, if this power grows, could I do more? Could I really destroy a deity? While I was chained up in the demon's dungeon, Zane came to me in a dream. He said the Guardians call me a god killer and demon slayer. If the gods and demons find out, they will kill me."

"No one is killing you. I won't let them." He folded his arms around me, wrapping me in his hard embrace.

He was offering himself as a shield against anything and everything that might hurt me. I would have been a fool not to accept. But, still, he had to know what he was getting into.

"My mother is a demon." I watched his face for his response. "And my father is a god."

"I had considered the possibility."

It wasn't the response I'd expected after dropping that bomb on him.

"And it doesn't bother you?" I asked. "The gods and demons would call me a disease, a scourge of unnatural, unholy magic."

"Of course it doesn't bother me." He shot me an offended look.

My heart skipped a beat. "That's how I can absorb both light and dark magic, both Nectar and Venom."

Nero was just listening. And I couldn't stop talking.

"Sonja wouldn't tell me who my mother and father are, but I'm going to find out."

"That way lies danger, Leda."

I sighed. "I just have to know. And I have a plan."

"Don't tell me you're going to march into heaven and hell, demanding answers."

He knew me all too well.

"Pretty much." A hard, determined smile stretched my mouth. "After all, we are long overdue for a family reunion."

AUTHOR'S NOTE

If you want to be notified when I have a new release, head on over to my website to sign up for my mailing list at http://www.ellasummers.com/newsletter. Your e-mail address will never be shared, and you can unsubscribe at any time.

If you enjoyed *Psychic's Spell*, I'd really appreciate if you could spread the word. One of the best ways of doing that is by leaving a review wherever you purchased this book. Thank you for your invaluable support!

Fairy's Touch, the seventh book in the *Legion of Angels* series, is now available.

ABOUT THE AUTHOR

Ella Summers has been writing stories for as long as she could read; she's been coming up with tall tales even longer than that. One of her early year masterpieces was a story about a pigtailed princess and her dragon sidekick. Nowadays, she still writes fantasy. She likes books with lots of action, adventure, and romance. When she is not busy writing or spending time with her two young children, she makes the world safe by fighting robots.

Ella is the *USA Today*, *Wall Street Journal*, and International Bestselling Author of the paranormal and fantasy series *Legion of Angels*, *Immortal Legacy*, *Dragon Born*, and *Sorcery & Science*.

www.ellasummers.com